The Order of Brigid's Cross

The Wild Hunt

(Book One)

by

Terri Reid

D1714037

Come cuddle close in daddy's coat
Beside the fire so bright,
And hear about the fairy folk
That wander in the night.

Robert Montgomery Bird

THE ORDER OF BRIGID'S CROSS – THE WILD
HUNT (Book One)

by

Terri Reid

Copyright © 2015 by Terri Reid

iii

The author would like to thank all those who have contributed to the creation of this book: Richard Reid, Sarah Powers, Virginia Onines, Denise Carpenter, Juliette Wilson, Jennifer Bates, Lori Langham and the amazing Hillary Gadd.

Prologue

The air was cold and damp and smelled of mold and rotting garbage with an underlying hint of urine. Despite that, Detective Sean O'Reilly had always liked the feeling of the Grant Park Underground Garage. It was like an ancient castle, solid and unyielding. A place like what he was sure his Irish ancestors had inhabited, although the family joke was that they'd have been in the kitchens doing the grunt work rather than in the throne room being served.

There were only a few cars down at the lowest level when he got off work, usually no earlier than nine o'clock. Most of the daytime residents of downtown Chicago had already been home for several hours and were watching their favorite televisions shows. But Sean stayed late, knowing his cat, Tiny, would understand. He'd complain, loudly, Sean smiled as he thought about it, but he'd understand.

The rubberized soles of his shoes didn't echo on the concrete garage floor, but Sean thought they ought to. Echo off the floor and bounce off the walls, like a scene from an old film noire movie, everything dark shadows and ominous sounds.

1

Sean liked being down in the bowels of the city. He thought it was an appropriate place for a cop to park. Kind of like his own personal Bat Cave.

Walking down the center of the garage, he passed from one section to the next. The thick concrete walls and faded black numbers on the floor were the only things that distinguished one area from another. But as he moved farther away from the staircase and into the farthest reaches of the garage, he began to notice vapor hovering above the garage floor, like a thin, barely perceptible mist that was moving towards him from the far end of the garage. *Must have something to do with all this moisture,* he thought absently.

The concrete wall in the next section was surrounded by a dark puddle. The dark liquid pooled around the side he could see and looked like it continued to the other side. He glanced up to the low ceiling to see signs of leakage. *Must have been a pretty heavy rain,* he thought, *to reach all the way down here.*

He started to bypass it when the scent caught his attention. The copper taste in his mouth turned his stomach. It wasn't a puddle of rain water. It was blood.

His mind immediately flashed back to the images of the victims, eight of them, who had been massacred on the streets of Chicago in the past few weeks. What little remained of the victims had to be

2

identified by either dental records or, in two even more disturbing cases, DNA. This guy was an animal, and the sooner they caught him and tossed him in some dark, lonely place for the rest of his life the better, as far as Sean was concerned.

Pulling out his radio, he swore softly when he realized there was no signal this far down in the garage. Now he had to make a choice: turn around and get backup or continue on and finally get a chance to catch the bastard. The choice was easy.

Sean slapped the radio back into its holster and pulled out his gun. He was going to catch the killer.

He slipped past the wall, and his stomach turned as he spied the remains of the latest victim. There was a sparkling gold, high heel shoe in the middle of puddle. The victim had been a woman. He looked at the disemboweled remains. There was nothing he could do for her now, but her blood was still putting off steam in the cold spring air. So she hadn't been dead for long. And Sean knew that meant the killer couldn't be too far away.

At the edge of the puddle was another, smaller, mark on the ground. He hurried over to examine what looked like a partial footprint saved in blood. The track, diminishing in size as it moved away from the crime scene, led farther into the garage. He flicked off the safety of his gun. He was going hunting.

3

He noiselessly jogged in the direction the killer's path led. Moving through each new section, he stayed close to the few remaining vehicles for cover, listening for any noise that might convey the killer's whereabouts.

Finally, as he moved to the last section, he heard the slow, shuffling footsteps of the killer. *He must have been wounded,* Sean thought, *to be moving so slowly.* He crouched low, his gun drawn, and darted alongside a panel van parked in the far corner of the garage. He inched his way alongside and peered through the driver's window into the shadowed section ahead. He saw a shadow. The guy was a freaking hulk!

That's okay, the bigger they are, the harder they fall.

He sprinted forward. "Police! Freeze!" he shouted, his voice echoing throughout the garage.

Then he saw it, and his blood ran cold. There it was. The creature from his nightmares. The bear-like monster with long claws and fanged teeth had haunted his dreams since he'd seen it in a forest in Ireland when he was a boy. The scars the beast had inflicted on his arm started to burn and, for a moment, he was twelve again and terrified he was going to die.

The creature turned and looked at him, blood, still fresh, dripping from its teeth. The victim's blood. That was all it took to bring him back to reality. Tonight an innocent woman had been killed by this creature, and others had died the same way. This wasn't Ireland, and this wasn't some damn enchanted forest. This was Chicago. This was his city. And he wasn't going to let some oversized beast get away with murder.

"Hey, Magilla, I'm not twelve anymore," Sean growled through gritted teeth. "I said it once, and I'm only going to say it one more time. Police! Freeze!"

The creature started to lunge, and Sean lifted his gun and shot it in the heart. The impact knocked it back a few feet, but it regained its footing and came at him again.

Sean shot again, and again, and again. He emptied the entire magazine into the beast, but it only slowed it down. He was out of ammunition, so he pulled out his taser. He set it at the highest possible setting, aimed and shot. The probes attached themselves to the creature's chest, and Sean shot 50,000 volts of electricity into its body.

The creature roared, grabbed the lines and ripped them from his chest, pulling the taser out of Sean's hands. The gun clattered uselessly to the ground.

Sean reached back and pulled out the final weapon in his arsenal, his wooden nightstick. He moved into a hand-to-hand combat position, his stick in his right hand, and faced the creature. He knew he needed to stay away from its poisonous talons; he'd already seen what those could do. He prayed he could find some spot of weakness before he became victim number nine.

The beast approached him slowly, its black tongue darting in and out along its elongated jawline, its yellow, reptilian eyes never blinking, staring coldly into Sean's soul. He remembered those eyes. He remembered the last time he faced the beast clearly now. He remembered thinking he was going to die.

He lifted his right arm up and waited. He needed it to be close enough to get around it and attack it from the rear. It moved closer. Sean feinted to the left and dashed to the right, but the creature quickly mirrored his movement. He tried moving to the left, but the creature moved just as fast, blocking him and forcing him past the section wall and towards the corner of the garage.

Sean knew the only way out was through the beast. And he knew he was out of options. He screamed at the top of his lungs and ran towards the creature, his right arm and nightstick raised defensively. The creature bellowed back and raised its arm, talons clicking into place, to attack.

A glimmer of light. Sean heard the soft sound of air being pushed, and the beast suddenly froze in

6

its tracks. Coldblooded eyes widened in shock and the creature bobbled forward. Sean jumped back and watched as, instead of moving, only the monster's head tottered forward, leaving the stump of its neck exposed as it fell with a crash to the ground. The skull split in half, green ooze spilling out, but a moment later, both the creature and its remains crumbled to dust.

Sean looked up from the dust on the cement floor and saw her. Once again she was wiping the green ooze from the blade of her broadsword. But, she was no longer the little girl who had saved him in Ireland. She was a woman. A tall, strikingly beautiful woman.

"You," he stuttered.

"Aye, and here you are trying to fight off a Heldeofol with naught but a stick again," she said, shaking her head. "Did you learn nothing from your last experience?"

"Aren't you a hallucination?" he asked.

She smiled brightly at him. "Aye, Sean the Brave, I'm only a dream."

And then she disappeared.

Chapter One

The basketball thumped rhythmically against the cracked concrete that had once been a smooth playing court. The stripes of black paint outlining the boundaries had long since worn off leaving only a gray shadow and an occasional chip of darker paint left in its place. Weeds had grown through the crumbled pavement, and litter was strewn everywhere. But the neighborhood teams had learned to maneuver around them so the ball wouldn't take a bad bounce when they were working their way forward for a lay-up.

Once bright orange, the thick, metal, support poles and baskets were now rusted with shards of peeling paint, and where the white fabric of the basket webbing had hung, now only a few dirty strands of thread blew in the wind.

On the border of the basketball court, the tall, chain-link fence had been broken and lay on its side next to empty liquor bottles, beer cans and used needles. It was a harsh contrast to the few pieces of playground equipment left in the nearby play yard.

But even decrepit and nearly obliterated, this place was still magical; it was a place where a boy from the inner city of Chicago could pretend he was Michael Jordan or Derrick Rose. He could dash down the court on a lay-up and then jump into the air with a slam dunk. His worn Salvation Army gym shoes could turn into the latest high-end athletic footwear, giving him the ability to float in the air towards the goal. His skinny arms could be ripped with muscles and tattoos. And he could even hear the crowds at the United Center scream his name. "Jamal. Jamal. Jamal."

"Jamal! You stop your daydreaming and get up to the apartment, now!" his grandmother screamed from the fourth floor apartment window. "What are you thinking, child? Making me wait on you?"

"Yes, ma'am," he answered, as the crowds were silenced and the magic slipped away into the shadows. Tucking the old basketball under his arm, Jamal made his way across the courtyard to the lobby of the housing project where he resided.

"Hey, Jamal," Devonte stepped out from the shadows underneath the metal and concrete staircase, pulling his long shirt down over the front of his pants.

Jamal could hear the girlish giggles from the corner and bit back a smile. Yeah, Devonte was at it again. He already had two baby mamas, but it sounded like he was working on number three. But at twelve, nearly thirteen years old, Jamal couldn't let Devonte know he was close to grinning in embarrassment. He had to be cool.

"Hey, Devonte," he replied, walking towards the stairs.

9

"You think 'bout what I ask you?"

Jamal shrugged. "Yeah, but I can't. My grandma, she won't let me join no gang," he said.

Devonte grabbed Jamal's shirt and yanked him close. "Who you think gonna watch out for you when you Grandma is gone?" he snarled. Then he nodded slowly, released Jamal's shirt and smiled. A smile that reminded Jamal of the alligator he'd seen at the zoo. "And how you gonna protect your grandma if you ain't one of the boys? We boys, we take care of our peoples. Don't wanna see your grandma get sliced."

Jamal wasn't stupid, he knew how things worked. He'd been chosen and he didn't have a choice. If he didn't join Devonte's gang, his grandmother would be marked and there was nothing he could do to protect her. "Whatcha want me to do, Devonte?" he asked, his voice showing no emotion.

"Hey, homie, you're putting too much on it," Devonte said. "No big deal. You just show up tonight in the park. We havin' a thrown down."

"I ain't got no hammer," Jamal said.

Devonte nodded again, reached behind and pulled a pistol out of the back waistband of his low riders. "I got you covered, man," he said. "You meet us at the park at nine and we show you what it means to be a homie, you got me?"

Jamal took the gun and stuffed it under his shirt and nodded. "Yeah, man, I got you."

He turned away and hurried up the steps, taking them two at a time. He knew he was going to get in trouble. His grandmother didn't like when he was late for dinner. When he finally pushed through the apartment door, his grandmother was standing in the middle of the room, her hands on her hips, waiting for him.

"Boy! What took you so long?" she demanded. "Don't tell me you stopped to talk to one of those worthless pieces of humanity that hang out in the lobby."

"Grandma, you know I have to be nice to them," he said, backing towards his bedroom. "It would cause us a lot of trouble if I acted like I thought I was all that."

"Well, you are all that compared to them," she insisted. "You go to school, you get good grades, and you go to church. What do they do? They get their food stamps and their welfare checks, they sell their drugs, they fight their wars, and they have sex like cats in heat."

"Grandma, we living on their turf right now," he said. "And if we want to be safe, we got to play by their rules."

"This is God's turf," she argued. "We ain't got to play by nobody's rules but God."

11

"Well, I ain't quite ready to meet God yet," he said. "And I ain't ready for you to meet God either. So, for now, we just play their game. Okay?"

Her hands slipped from her hips and she stared at him. "Boy, you ain't gone and done something stupid have you?" she asked, her voice trembling slightly. "You ain't joined up with them and their gang?"

He stopped and really looked at the woman before him, the woman who had been more mother than grandmother throughout his whole life. The woman who had cared for him, taught him, lectured him, and held him when the world was too hard and his fears too great. He looked at her coarse gray hair, frizzy and uncontrollable, sticking out of the sides of her head. Her skin was lined, and there were age spots on her cheeks. Her frame was bent and she walked slower now. She would be no match for a young, tough, gang member. He had seen what they had done to other old women, and he couldn't have that happen to his grandmother.

"Grandma, I ain't done nothing that would disrespect you," he said honestly.

She searched his eyes for a moment, not satisfied with his answer, but he returned her gaze with a steady one of his own. "Fine then," she finally said. "You go get washed up. Supper's done. I'll put it on the table."

He hurried to his room, pulled the gun out of his waistband, stuck it underneath the mattress of his bed and then ran to the bathroom to wash up. In just a few minutes he was seated across from his grandmother with his head bowed, waiting for grace to be said. He felt his grandmother's hand in his and he suddenly realized how thin and fragile she had become.

"Father, we thank thee for our daily bread," the old woman's voice shook, but she spoke with conviction and familiarity. "We thank thee for our safety in this frightening world. We ask for a blessing on this food. We ask for thy continued guidance and grace. We ask for thy watchful eye on Jamal. In Jesus name. Amen."

"Amen," he repeated and gently squeezed her hand before letting it go. Even if something happened to him, even if he died, now that he was a member, the gang would look out for his grandmother. He could be grateful for that.

With trembling hands, she carefully spooned the macaroni and cheese onto his plate while he took a piece of bread from the plastic bag and spread margarine across it.

After helping herself to some food, she paused, her fork in mid-air, and looked at him. "You need to stay in tonight," she said.

"Ain't nothing gonna happen tonight," he said.

"I just got a whisper," she said. "And you know my whispers, they ain't never wrong."

His stomach twisted into a knot and he struggled for a moment to keep his voice calm. She spoke the truth. Her whispers had never been wrong. Her whispers had warned her the night her daughter, Jamal's mother, had been killed. Her whispers had kept them safe all these years in the projects. He didn't know how she did it or who she was connected to, but he couldn't deny the power of her whispers.

"I'll stay in Grandma," he said. "I'll just go in my room and do my homework."

She smiled and nodded. "You're a good boy, Jamal," she said.

I sure hope your whispers are wrong tonight, he thought, *'cause I don't have a choice this time.*

Chapter Two

At 8:40, Jamal opened his bedroom window, leaned out and looked around. The street light behind the apartment shone on the collection of garbage containers and refuse scattered on the ground below. He studied the fire escape that hung outside the living room window. It was about three feet away from him, and if he used the ledge just below his window, he could climb over to it. Problem was, would Grandma see him climbing down? If that old fire escape made a lot of noise, she would go to the window for sure. He pulled himself back in and walked over to his closet. Sliding open the wood laminate door, he bent over, picked up his baseball bat and went back to the window.

Leaning out as far as he could, he pushed the top of the bat against the ironwork of the fire escape. Nothing happened. He tried it again, this time pushing the bat with all his might. The escape jiggled and screeched against the motion. He pulled himself back inside just as the living room window slid open and his grandmother poked her head out. "Who's out there?" she called, her voice shrill in the night air.

Sighing, he quietly slid his window closed and bolted it securely. Sitting on the edge of his bed, he wondered how he was going to slip out of the house without her knowledge. He looked at the red digital numbers on his alarm clock. 8:45. Even if he ran he was going to be late. With a sigh, he pulled the gun out from beneath his mattress, stuck it back into his waistband and pulled his shirt over the bump. Grabbing his jacket, he held it behind his back and went to his bedroom door.

Clasping his doorknob, he slowly twisted it, noiselessly sliding the latch from the faceplate, and then peered around the door to the living room. Had she gone into her bedroom? Could he sneak out without her seeing?

The answer to both questions was no. His grandmother was in her favorite chair watching a program on the Christian channel and slowly nodding off. But as soon as he stepped into the living room, she'd know.

"Hey, Grandma," he called to her. "I'm pretty tired. I think I'm going to call it a night."

She turned from the television to him, and grasping both arms of her chair, she pushed herself into a standing position. "You going to bed already?" she asked, worry creasing her already wrinkled brow. "You sick or something?"

He shook his head quickly. "No," he said. "I have a big test tomorrow, and I thought I'd get up early and study for it."

"That's a good idea," she agreed, nodding approvingly. She started to lower herself into her

16

chair when her breath caught and she started to cough.

"Grandma, you okay?" he asked, dropping his jacket and hurrying to her side.

She nodded, but the coughing continued. He could see she was having trouble breathing. She'd had these spells before, but it seemed to him that they were getting more frequent and more severe. He panicked when he noticed that her coloring around her mouth was getting grayish, a sign the doctor had told him meant she wasn't getting enough oxygen. "Where's your medicine?" he demanded, more frightened than he'd ever been in his life.

She weakly raised her arm and pointed to the cabinet over the stove. Rushing over, he pulled the dark bottle off the shelf and yanked the silverware drawer out, picking up a spoon. Running back to her, he opened the bottle and poured some of the dark brown elixir on the spoon.

"Okay, Grandma, you gotta hold still, just for a second."

She tried to muffle the coughing, but her body still shook with small spasms. Holding her chin like the doctor had shown him, he steadied her mouth and poured the spoonful down. Then he put the spoon down and held her frail body in his arms. "It's okay," he whispered. "You just have to take those deep breaths the doctor showed you."

17

He felt her tremble in his arms, and he held her tighter. Finally, she drew in a deep breath and the coughing stopped. Slowly lowering her back into the chair, he settled her down and then stepped back to get a good look at her. The greyish coloring seemed to be receding and her breathing was steady. "You okay?"

She nodded and smiled, although tear tracks still stained her cheeks. "I'm better," she wheezed. "Don't know what I woulda done if you hadn't been here."

He thought about the window, and his stomach knotted. But he looked at her and smiled. "Guess those whispers of yours are watching over you," he said. "Why don't you go to bed? I'll roll the television in there, and you can watch it until you fall asleep."

"Now, boy, I don't cotton with those people what got TVs in every room of their house," she said. "Ain't natural to have those boxes speaking to you wherever you go."

He put his arm around her and helped her from her chair. "Well, I think we can do it this one time. Just so you can watch your show and rest," he suggested. "That okay?"

She stepped forward and was surprised she had to lean on him. "I suppose for one night it ain't going to do no harm," she agreed.

He walked her to her room. "Do you need any help?" he asked.

"At the point I need you to help me get ready for bed, that's just about when you can pack me up and send me to an old folks' home," she said, grabbing on to the edge of her dresser for support. "You just give me a few minutes to wash up, and I'll call you when I'm ready for the television."

Backing out of her room, he nodded. "Yeah, you just call me when you're ready."

He walked over to the television cart and rolled it away from the wall. Unplugging the old television, he wondered if there would ever be a time when they had a new, thin screen that could be mounted on the wall. He shrugged. It didn't really make a difference since they couldn't afford cable.

He pushed the cart across the old, shag carpeting and stopped outside her bedroom, then perched on the arm of a chair until she called. Glancing over, he saw that it was already nine o'clock. Well, there was nothing he could do about it. Besides, he thought, a throw down should last at least an hour. I'll be there. I'll just be the reinforcements.

"Jamal," his grandmother's voice came from behind the door. "I'm ready now."

He opened her door and pushed the television in so it sat alongside her bed. Then he bent and plugged it in. "This a good place for it?" he asked.

She nodded as she aimed the remote at the television and it turned on. "Works just fine," she said.

He looked at her. Lying against the pillows, her face seemed so little and delicate. "I love you, Grandma," he said, leaning over and giving her a kiss on her cheek.

She hugged him. "I love you too, Jamal," she said with a soft smile. "Goodnight."

"Goodnight Grandma."

Chapter Three

The streets were deserted as Jamal jogged towards the park. He figured people were either hiding inside or actually at the park by now. A throw down in this neighborhood usually meant semi-automatic guns with stray bullets that could easily pierce a door, window or even a wall. Usually, when the word spread, people took to an interior room in their home. Even though the park was two miles away, the fight often spread to the surrounding area where no one was safe. Jamal was glad his grandma's room had no windows. Because gun fire was so common, she would probably just sleep through the noise, and if there were any sirens, they would be far enough away she wouldn't be disturbed.

He was about a block away from the park, and he could see the cars and vans pulled up onto the grass, forming a circle around the middle of the park. Suddenly, an explosion of gunshots rent the air and echoed down the street. Screams followed, but they were drowned out by an even more explosive round of gunfire.

He stepped into an overhang of a closed grocery store and pulled the gun from beneath his jacket. He held it in both hands, feeling the cold metal against his palms. It felt heavier than he had imagined. He had never fired a gun before. He didn't even know if it was loaded. But, he had to trust Devonte. He had no choice.

With the gun palmed in his hand and the sleeve of his jacket hiding it, he slipped out onto the sidewalk again and slowly made his way towards the park, using the backdrop of the boarded up stores for protection. Sliding along the front of each store, he would pause and peer up the gangway between buildings to make sure no one else was hiding there, waiting for an easy kill of an unsuspecting member of their rival gang. The going was slow, but he wasn't about to take any chances.

Finally, he reached the corner of the block. He hid behind a newsstand, locked and closed up for the night, and took a few deep breaths, trying to calm his pounding heart. The gun war hadn't slowed, and there were no sirens in the distance indicated cops coming. "You got no choice, Jamal. You got to do this," he whispered to himself. "You gotta go now."

He started to run out to the street when the ground rolled beneath his feet, and he was thrown backwards to the curb, his gun skidding across the asphalt. He scrambled after his gun but stayed down low. The ground rumbled again, and Jamal could hear a thundering sound in the distance. *What the hell?*

He glanced up, but the sky was clear and the moon was full. Except… He watched a gray cloud race across the sky, dark and rolling, moving in his direction. He crawled backwards, his eyes still on the sky, his hands scraping against concrete, as he moved as quickly as he could. Finally, he hit against something solid and he forced himself to look away from the sky and over his shoulder for a moment. He was up against the smooth metal surface of the newsstand. He should be safe here.

Then he looked up again, and his heart jumped to his throat as the rotating cloud covered the moon and angled its descent towards earth. "It's a tornado," he cried, struggling to his feet. "I gotta get inside."

He jumped up and dashed back to the first vacant storefront. The former plate glass door was now boarded up with various-sized pieces of plywood that crossed over each other in several layers. The large, showcase windows had also been boarded over, and gangs from the area had spray painted them with ugly, black marks.

Jamal reached out and yanked on the metal pull bar on the door, hoping to snap the lock and get in. The door jiggled slightly as Jamal desperately fought against the lock, but the metal held, and the door stayed closed.

Suddenly, the wind increased, and trash cans and cardboard flew down the street in front of him. The wailing sound of wind rushing through the buildings reminded him of a video he had seen on the news when a hurricane had hit the east coast. This tornado was coming fast and hard. Desperate, he threw his shoulder against the door, cracking one of the pieces of plywood. He ran against it again, and it split in the middle. Prying his fingers into the crack, he pulled on the wood, trying to increase the six-inch gap, but the wood was too thick.

He dashed away from the door and out of the overhang, frantically looking up and down the street for anything he could use to pry off the plywood. All of a sudden, the wind seemed to change direction. Instead of between the buildings it was howling down the street, creating a wind tunnel down the sidewalk. Jamal's body was shoved by the gust, and he rammed his head on the brick façade. Then, the wind twisted and came from the other direction, bringing with it an assortment of debris relentlessly pelting his body. Aluminum cans, newspapers, paper cups, pebbles and garbage hit his back, pounded his body, and smacked against his arms as he protected his head from the onslaught.

Struggling against the wind, he stumbled back towards the door and the slight shelter the overhang provided. The wind hit again, nearly lifting him off his feet. He pushed forward against the gust, trying to reach the door, his heart pounding as the wind pulled him back towards the street. For a moment, he was paralyzed, the force of the wind equaling the power of his limbs. He dug deep and forced himself to push harder. Finally, he slapped his body against the brick façade and like a rock climber, dug his fingertips into the gaps between the bricks for grip, trying to find a solid hold. Inch by painful inch, he fought to move closer to the doorway, fingertips scraped and bruised as he pulled himself forward, fighting the drag of the maelstrom.

Finally, he reached the boarded door, shoved his hands back into the small gap in the plywood and held on for dear life. The wind screamed against the building, almost sounding human, and his body was shoved sideways. Squeezing his fingers tighter, he held on as his legs were lifted off the ground and pulled. Shoving his hand farther in for more grip, he felt the jagged plywood slice through his hands, but he still held tight. "Oh, Lord, please help me hold on," he cried.

Suddenly there was quiet. His body smashed against the door, ripping his hands out of the gap and cutting them deeply. His stomach turned when he looked down and saw the damage; skin, muscles and tendons had been severed to the bone. The pain was immense. He breathed in, ready to scream, but the sound died in his mouth when he saw a movement out of the side of his eye. He reached for the gun that was no longer there.

Jamal faced the street to meet his enemy, but what he saw was not what he expected. The cloud, the tornado was at street level now. But it wasn't a cloud, it was an army, and they were walking out of the cloud. There were at least a hundred of them marching towards the park. The leader was tall—over ten feet. His body was thick, and on his head he wore the skull of some kind of giant deer. The antlers extended for yards in either direction. He was riding on a giant, gray horse that breathed steam through its wide nostrils while its sharp, stone hooves destroyed the asphalt beneath it.

Other creatures followed, some riding and some on foot. They were tall and thin, just like their leader, and their clothes looked like ragged shrouds. Moss and tree bark hung on the sharpened angles of their bodies. Their limbs, long and sinewy, reminded Jamal of willow tree limbs. But instead of soft leaves and tender branches, these limbs ended with twisted hands and fingers. Elongated and spindly, their hands dragged against the ground as they walked, and their sharp fingernails kindled sparks on the pavement.

They were monsters, monster soldiers, he realized as he noticed the weapons they bore. Nothing like the weapons of today, but Jamal knew they would be deadly. Both sword and bow, cast in bronzed metal, glimmered softly against the streetlights.

Then he heard the shrill howl and his blood ran cold. Peering between the soldiers and the horses, Jamal could see wolf-like creatures prowling, snapping at each other with their overlong canines dripping with pus-like drool. Their eyes glowed red in the dark night, and their claws clattered against the pavement.

26

Then their scent hit him, and he nearly vomited. Death. They smelled like death. He had smelled it before, finding a dead cat back behind the projects, its body almost too far gone to recognize what it was. But that was a smell you never forgot, and it was heavy in the air around him.

Jamal bit his lip until it bled. He sat in horrified silence as the legion marched past him and into the park. He prayed they wouldn't look his way. He prayed he would be safe. Then he heard the screams. Horrified human screams. The soldiers had found their prey.

Wrapping his arms around his legs, he bent his head forward and wept like a child.

Chapter Four

Detective Sean O'Reilly's stomach twisted as it did every time he walked past the doors that opened into the lobby of the emergency room of Cook County Hospital. He stepped onto the tiled floor and heard the noises that were unique to a hospital. Soft-soled shoes against linoleum, the murmur of the intercom, the quiet, anguished sobs of family members and the constant beeping of monitoring equipment. Those sounds reminded him of the worst hours of his life.

It had been years since he had carried his sister, Officer Mary O'Reilly, into the hospital with a gunshot to her gut. Years since he and the rest of his family sat in the waiting room, crying and praying that she would not die. Years since he discovered she had thrown herself between him and a bullet with his name on it.

She was fine now, he reminded himself, more than fine. She was on her honeymoon in Scotland with a guy who worshipped the ground she walked on, and he'd better keep it that way. Sean smiled slightly. *Yeah, things were good with Mary.*

He shook off those thoughts as he watched Detective Adrian Williams approach him. Adrian was a behemoth, six feet five inches of solid muscle. He walked like a bodybuilder, Sean thought, with a grin.

His damn arms were so muscular he couldn't rest them at his side, so he looked like he was always carrying some invisible beach ball. Well, a beach ball that weighed 300 pounds.

"Hey, Skinny," Sean greeted his friend. "How are things in the 'hood?"

Adrian had worked in the Gang Enforcement Division of the Chicago Police Department for about six months. Before that, he worked with Sean in the Special Crimes Unit. He'd been Sean's rookie detective and was a quick learner and devoted law-enforcement officer. Sean had beamed like a proud daddy when Adrian had received his promotion.

"Hey, Irish, nice to see you up and sober," he teased back.

Sean glanced at his watch. "Well, it's only midnight," he replied. "The real drinking doesn't start until two or three."

Adrian nodded, but the joking disappeared from his voice. "Yeah, well, after what I've seen tonight I just might join you."

Noting the change in his friend's demeanor, Sean's smile dropped, and he lowered his voice. "So, what went down?"

"Worse throw down I've ever seen," Adrian said, wiping his hand over his eyes. "O'Reilly, you won't believe the crime photos. The bodies were hacked to pieces."

"Hacked?" Sean asked. "Like knives?"

"Uh, uh, had to be bigger than that," Adrian said. "There were heads laying a couple yards from the bodies they belonged to, and those heads, man, they were sliced clean off. Arms, torsos...laying everywhere. It was bad. It was like nothing I've ever seen before, and I've seen a lot."

"So, maybe machetes?" Sean asked. "Maybe we got some international throw down going on here?"

"Yeah, could have been a machete," Adrian said, nodding slowly. "But the perps who used them had to have been on roids."

"Or high on something," Sean added. "So have you done any blood work?"

Taking a deep breath, Adrian leaned in a little closer. "Well, if we had arrested someone we would have done blood work. But we've got nothing," he said quietly.

"No perps?"

"We've got nothing but a hundred maybe a hundred and twenty dead bodies," he said. "Two different gangs, almost everyone's a corpse."

"Almost?"

"Yeah, well, that's why I called you in," he said. "We got this kid, looks like a new recruit, who got there a little late. Probably saved his life. He saw it going down, but he's not making any sense. I figured if anyone was an expert on not making any sense, it was you."

"Funny, real funny," Sean said. "Do you think he's covering for himself?"

Adrian shook his head. "I found him huddled against an abandoned building, crying his eyes out," he said. "His hands were ripped to pieces, but he didn't even seem to notice. He was in shock. And when I told him who I was, he about jumped into my arms he was so happy to see me."

"Well, Skinny, you are kinda cute," Sean said.

"Yeah, not that cute," Adrian replied. "This kid is scared, past scared. And whatever he saw, it doesn't sound normal to me."

"Can I talk to him?"

"Yeah, they took care of his hands, but it's his head I'm worried about."

Sean followed Adrian through the security doors of the emergency room and back into one of the triage rooms. Adrian pushed open the door and stepped inside. "Jamal, I want you to meet a friend of mine," he said as Sean entered behind him. "Detective Sean O'Reilly."

"Hey, Jamal," Sean said, coming up alongside the hospital bed. The kid couldn't have been more than twelve. His head was pressed against the pillows like he was trying to hide. His eyes were round and wary as he looked beyond Sean, searching the room.

"The place is secure," Sean reassured him. "We got the hospital on lockdown. Nothing could get this far in."

The boy relaxed visibly. "They was in the cloud," he stammered. "They was in the freaking clouds."

Pulling a chair next to the bed, Sean sat down so Jamal could look at him, face to face. "Why don't we start from the beginning?" he suggested. "That way, I get a whole picture of what happened and we don't miss anything important."

Jamal nodded rapidly. "Yeah, okay," he said.

"You hungry?" Sean asked him, sitting back against his chair, trying to look relaxed.

"I ain't ate since supper," he answered.

Sean smiled at him. "Well, I remember when my brothers and I were your age," he said. "We'd have to eat every hour or so. I bet the cafeteria has something. What would you like?"

The boy glanced quickly around the room and sunk further into his pillow. "I don't care," he whispered.

"Hey, Skinny," Sean said to Adrian, relieved to see the young boy smile at the name. "How about picking up some food for us?"

Adrian nodded, understanding that a calm and relaxed witness was a better witness. He and Sean had played this routine before, each one getting the chance to be the errand boy. "You want me to get you some food?" he asked and the boy retreated further into his pillow.

"Yeah, and don't get us that green crap you eat," Sean replied, sharing a grin and wink with Jamal. "We don't want salads or vegetables. We want a couple of cheeseburgers and some fries. Right, Jamal?"

Leaning forward, the boy nodded. "Um, right," he said.

"And if they've got those cookies, you know those giant chocolate chip ones," Sean added, "We want those, too."

Jamal smile and nodded. "Yeah, that'd be good," he said.

"What do you want to drink?" Sean asked.

"Chocolate milk?" the boy asked hopefully.

"Oh, yeah, good call," he replied with a smile. "Chocolate milk — cold chocolate milk. Perfect."

Sighing loudly, Adrian nodded. "It's going hurt my heart just getting this for you," he said.

"Yeah, but you'll get over it," Sean teased, and Jamal actually giggled.

Once the door had closed behind Adrian, Sean crossed one leg over the other and stretched out in the chair. He looked at the boy, nervously glancing from the door back to Sean. No, he wasn't ready yet. He still had to calm down a little. Sean glanced at his watch. It was twelve-thirty. Well, the only thing he had been planning on doing that night was sleep. He had time to kill. "So, while we're waiting for food, why don't you tell me what sports you like to play?"

Chapter Five

A few hours later, sitting in his car in the parking lot outside the hospital, Sean studied his notes again and shook his head slowly. "What the hell?" he whispered, and then he picked up his phone and dialed. The call went to voice mail, but Sean hung up and dialed again.

"Hello?" a weary voice answered.

"About time you answered your phone," Sean said.

"Bugger it! Do you know what time it is?" came the slightly irate Scottish-accented voice on the line. "This had better be important."

"I know what time it is," Sean replied with a wide smirk on his face. "And if you were back home, it would be about eight o'clock in the morning. What are you doing sleeping the morning away?"

"Piss off," Professor Ian MacDougal muttered. "I'm going back to sleep."

"Ian, something's happened," Sean stated, his voice going from teasing to serious. "And I need your help."

Hearing a long sigh, Sean could picture Ian pulling himself out of bed and moving to the computer station he had across his room. Ian was not only the founder and head of the MacDougal Foundation for Paranormal Research but also a Fellow from the University of Edinburgh working through the University of Chicago and the Chicago Police Department on a study of Criminology and Parapsychology. For the past few months he'd been working in Freeport, Illinois, with Sean's sister, Mary, studying her interaction with ghosts and working with her to solve some of the mysteries that she had encountered.

"Okay, the damn machine is booting," he growled. "What's it you need?"

"Okay, I'm going to describe something to you, and then, maybe, you can help me with where to even start looking," Sean said. "A tall creature, like ten feet tall. Long, sinewy limbs that are so long they drag on the ground with razor-like nails that are so tough that as they are pulled along the asphalt, they spark…"

"Sean, Sean," Ian said. "I told you to stay out of strange bars when you're looking for a date. She turned you down, did she?"

"Not funny, Professor, not funny at all," Sean said. "His clothes are ripped up and thin, like sheets."

"Shrouds perhaps?" Ian suggested and then he was silent for a moment. "Sean, I see that Gillian is online at the moment. Would you mind if I shared your information with her? She's some background in legends and such."

Sean knew that Gillian, Ian's fiancée, was a researcher, and since she was originally from Ireland, perhaps she would have a different perspective on what was going on.

"No problem," Sean said. "The more input the better."

"Okay, I've sent her what you described," he said. "And she wants to know what their faces were like."

"Faces," Sean said, scanning his notes. "Oh, yeah, the head guy has a helmet like a reindeer skull."

Sean could hear Ian typing in the background, pausing and typing again.

"She says it sounds like the Elk King," Ian said.

"The Elf King?" Sean spat. "Listen, I know I said reindeer, but this guy has nothing to do with Santa Claus."

Ian chuckled softly. "No, she said the Elk King," Ian said. "With a 'K.' She says he is the leader of the Wild Hunt."

"The Wild Hunt?" Sean asked slowly, a frisson of trepidation running up his spine.

"Aye, it's the fae version of a fox hunt," Ian said, "except the hunters tend to slay any mortals who happen to be in their path or grab them up and take them down to Tír na nÓg with them."

"Slay as in cut up in pieces?"

"Let me ask."

Once again, Ian paused to type. "She says their main weapons would be broadswords, so I'll say yes, that would be right," Ian replied slowly. "She wants to know why you're asking about this, Sean, and quite frankly, so do I."

"Well, as near as I can see," Sean said, "the South Side of Chicago either had a visit from the Wild Hunt last night or something doing a really good job at imitation."

"What?" Ian asked, incredulous. "But that's impossible."

"When can you be here?" Sean asked.

"Mary and Bradley arrived back last night," he said. "Gillian and I can pack up and leave in the morning. I can be there before noon."

Sean nodded slowly. "Thanks. It's a gruesome scene. You might not want to bring Gillian," Sean said.

"I'll ask her on the drive down," Ian replied. "She might prove more useful than you think."

"Okay, I'll see you then," he said. "I'm going to get home and get a little sleep."

"Um, Sean," Ian inserted before Sean could hang up.

"Yes?"

"Gillian just messaged me that she wants you to do her a favor and place something iron across your doorway after you're in," he said.

"Something iron?"

"Aye, she says she'll explain tomorrow. Just do it."

"Okay, you're the professor," Sean agreed and then hung up the phone. "And you just gave me the creeps."

He looked down at his notes, remembering the pleading look on Jamal's face when they finished the interview. "You believe me, don't you?" the boy had asked.

Sean nodded. "Yeah, I believe you, and I'm going to go call a friend of mine who knows more about this kind of stuff," he had replied. "But Jamal…"

"Yes, Detective O'Reilly."

"Maybe for right now, you shouldn't answer anyone else's questions," Sean had advised. "Just pretend the drugs they gave you kicked in and you're too sleepy. Okay?"

The young man nodded and smiled. 'Yeah, okay, I can do that."

"Good, I'll see you tomorrow," he had promised and hurried to his car to call Ian.

Closing his notebook, Sean put his car into gear, pulled out of the parking spot and headed across town to his apartment near the lake. The streets were nearly deserted and the few vehicles he passed were either Chicago Sanitation trucks or large, rumbling Chicago Transit Authority buses. He flicked on his turn signal and was waiting at the light for the chance to hop onto the expressway when he remembered another obligation.

"Damn, I nearly forgot," he muttered, looking over his shoulder to make sure no one was behind him and then inching over into the through lane before the light changed. Instead of Interstate 90, Sean drove up Harrison Street and turned left into the tunnel that was known as lower Wacker Drive.

Built in the 1920s, the lower level of Wacker Drive had been created to accommodate the delivery trucks using the below-level street to access buildings that stood alongside the Chicago River. The thick concrete pylons had to be strong enough to withstand the heavy downtown traffic above and the low concrete ceilings were created to give trucks just enough room to maneuver in the shadowy recesses of the expensive retail stores and office buildings.

Sean wondered what Mary would see if she were down here. She often got a glimpse of the history of a place. Would she see mobsters dumping a concrete-booted victim into the depths of the Chicago River? Prohibition-dodging socialites sneaking out of vintage limousines with their boot-legged liquor hidden beneath their coats? Dock workers unloading the ships that traveled down the Chicago River? Or drowning victims from the unfortunate Eastland steamship disaster where 844 people died just off the docks of lower Wacker drive?

He shivered as he wondered about the unseen hundreds he probably shared the tunnel with that night. Of course, he reasoned, the current view wasn't much better. The skeleton frames of old boat moorings and docks on the river side of the road lay deserted, except for the scampering of large river rats. The other side of the four-lane road had been a labyrinth of service docks for stores, restaurants and office buildings, but now the concrete slabs and sidewalks had become a community for many of the city's homeless. Large appliance boxes, small lean-tos and even old camping tents created a neighborhood of those who either shunned humanity or had been tossed away by society because they didn't fit the mold.

He spotted the woman he'd been looking for, alone as usual, huddled in a small corner where a concrete wall protected her from the worst of the cold winds. She stood with her wooden staff in her old, gnarled hands, watching her surroundings and her precious grocery cart fervently. That's how he had first met her, fighting off a group of young thugs intent on stealing that cherished cart. Sean pulled his cruiser up to the curb, grabbed a white paper sack from the seat next to him and exited the car. "Top of the morning to you, Hettie," he called, walking towards her.

She smiled at him, exposing her nearly toothless gums, and nodded. "Tis the middle of the night, foolish mortal," she called back. "Are you blind?"

"Oh, but Hettie, me darling, when I see you, I only see sunshine and summer days," he replied.

She snorted rudely, but the smile widened on her wizened face. "For all your charm, you won't be getting under me skirts," she taunted as he drew nearer.

Her tiny body was bent and probably broken in a dozen places. But she proudly wore a long, green ball gown that was too large for her thin frame and a thick wool shawl that Sean had given her that matched the color of the gown. Her nose and her ears had outgrown the rest of her facial features, reminding Sean of the picture of a goblin he'd seen as a child. She held her staff in front of her, partially for protection, he thought, and partially for support.

Sean slapped his hand against the middle of his chest. "Hettie, once again you puncture my heart with your harsh words," he said, handing her the bag and smiling at her soft cackle. "Have I no hope?"

Reaching inside the bag she pulled out the Styrofoam cup filled with tea laced liberally with cream and honey. She eagerly pulled the tab up and drank greedily, her thick tongue darting around her dried lips to gather any stray drops and her small, dark eyes closed in pleasure. "I thank ye, Sean," she whispered, her now opened eyes moist, "for the lovely things you do for me."

Smiling at her, Sean pulled a lighter from his pocket. "I know your answer, but I have to ask," he said. "Will you not come with me so I can find you a safer place to stay?"

She shook her head, pulled a blueberry scone out of the bag and brought it to her nose, taking a deep, appreciative sniff. "I would if I could," she said. "But I must stay here, at me post, until I am needed."

Sighing, he bent down and set a fire to a small pile of firewood she kept contained in an old grill base. "Can you at least let me leave some matches for you?" he asked. "So you can light your fire yourself?"

Shaking her head, she smiled at him. "I can't touch fire," she explained once again. "It's against the rules. But I do so love to be warm. Thank you kindly, Sean O'Reilly."

Standing, he smiled at her and bowed his head in a courtly manner. "Thank you for allowing me to be of service, Hettie."

"You are a good man," she said. "And when you have need of me, you've only to call."

"Thank you," he replied politely. "I will remember that. See you tomorrow, Hettie."

"Have a good morrow," she said and then she looked beyond him towards the river and the night sky. Her eyes seemed to glaze over, her voice deepened, and she spoke softly, "And beware, Sean O'Reilly, there is a dark cast in the sky. Things are changing."

Chapter Six

She'd only screamed once, but somehow that scream created an internal compass in twelve-year-old Sean O'Reilly and he ran steadily, instinctively knowing he was going in the right direction. Not once did he consider turning and running the other way, to get help from someone older and, perhaps, stronger. He knew if he did not help, she would not survive.

The woods were his enemy in his quest. Leaves and branches slapped against his face and arms as he pushed through the dense brush. And when the vegetation did not seem to hold him back, the roots of the trees and the rocks on the ground caught at him, trying to trip him up at every turn. But his young legs were both steady and agile and he ran ahead, avoiding their snares.

The day had started warm, and now sweat trickled down his forehead and bloomed on the front and back of his t-shirt. He wiped his forearm across his face, slick from heat and humidity, and continued on.

Slowing as he neared his destination, he realized he needed to have the element of surprise on his side. Placing his feet carefully one in front of the other, heel first and then slowly lowering the ball of his foot before lifting off again, imitating an Native American he'd seen hunting in a movie, he glided forward to the edge of the grove. He could hear movement, but the foliage in front of him blocked his vision. Reaching forward, he grabbed hold of the curtain of leaves and pushed them aside.

It must be a bear, he immediately thought, as he stared at the back of the huge beast. The hide was shiny in spots, like the fur had worn away, but in other areas tufts of brown, black and silver hair grew thick and long like a lion's mane. It was standing upright, and the thick muscles in its back confirmed its power.

It was only when he had moved past the shelter of the trees and stepped into the clearing that he saw her. She was probably his age, only her build was far more slender and she was taller, several inches taller, than he. Some of her long, red hair, which fell down to her waist, was caught in the branches of a low-hanging tree, and as she twisted and turned, trying to escape, the beast came closer. Sean realized that he only had a moment to act. A moment until the hunter found its prey.

Desperately looking around for a weapon, he finally knelt and picked up a large stone. He could throw it at the beast's head, frightening it away. But he had to throw it at the right angle. Stepping forward quickly, thinking only of the girl and his need to help, his foot came down on a small twig. "SNAP!"

It shouldn't have sounded so loud. It shouldn't have echoed through the forest. It shouldn't have turned all of the attention towards him. But it did.

The beast turned slowly, and the blood in Sean's veins ran cold. He had never seen anything like it. It was a creature that hid in the darkest corners of your nightmares. Its head had the girth of a bull, but a boar-like snout glistened in the middle of it with sharp, sabre teeth protruding from either side of the snout. Its yellow, reptilian eyes zeroed in on Sean, and the boy felt his heart skip a beat. This was no time for cowards, he decided with a shaky breath. Summoning all his strength, Sean whipped the stone through the air, aiming for its eyes.

The stone sailed through the air, and Sean watched it hurtle towards its destination. Time seemed to slow as the rock came closer to the face of the beast. He nearly shouted with relief when the stone proved his aim to be true, but rather than incapacitate the beast, it merely harmlessly bounced off the thick hide and plopped down into the thick, mossy ground. The creature chuckled and stepped towards Sean.

Panicked, he looked around wildly and saw the large tree limb on the ground. He dove, but the creature, surprisingly agile on its feet, did the same. Sean grabbed hold of the limb at the same time the creature, with its talon-like fingernails grabbed hold of Sean's arm.

47

Sean screamed as he felt his flesh being scraped away from the bone. Twisting with his other arm, he swung the branch against the creature's head. Over and over he pounded away as the beast shook him hard enough to make his teeth rattle. But he wasn't going to give up. For a moment Sean thought he might win. The limb was large enough to knock the creature's head to the side with each new blow. Sean felt a strange surge of endorphins, and he gritted his teeth, putting all of his power into the strike.

This time, the creature lost its footing and stumbled sideways. Sean cried with triumph and was ready to strike again when he felt a pinch on his arm. He turned and watched in horror as one of the creature's talons opened and a narrow, translucent, bone-like needle buried itself into his arm. He struggled to pull it away, but the hold was too great. Striking blindly with the tree limb, he watched the creature's bone darken as black liquid ran through its hollow core and flowed into his arm.

"No!" he screamed and tried once again to pull away, but the instant the poison was in his system, he could feel the numbing begin.

"Help," he whispered weakly, as the forest began to blur before his eyes.

He twisted away once again, and this time, the creature opened his grip and released him. He fell backwards, his limbs too heavy to respond.

Everything seemed to be once again moving in slow motion. As he fell, he could see past the creature to the tree that had held the red-haired girl captive. Now, only a few strands of her hair hung on the branches where she had been. Good! He thought with a little satisfaction. At least she got away.

He hit the ground with a thump, leaves and small twigs spewing up around him, and lay at the feet of the beast like a sacrificial offering. Looking up, through his blurred vision, he could see long streams of frothy saliva streaming past the beast's canine teeth and down its throat. It growled in appreciation, and a long black tongue darted from its mouth and wiped the foam away.

Damn, I'm dinner, Sean realized, and immediately felt bad for saying a word his mother would raise her eyebrows over.

Then he thought better of it. I'm going to die. I can say damn all I want to. Damn. Damn. Damn. Damn.

The beast cocked his head and looked down at Sean. It lifted one arm up and stretched its fingers, the razor-sharp claws making a clicking sound as they snapped into place like a multi-tined sickle. Then its reptilian eyes met Sean's. The look was cold, cruel and triumphant, and Sean knew this would be the death blow. He braced himself but didn't close his eyes. There was no way he was going to face death with his eyes closed. He took a deep breath.

The glint of sun on metal blinded him for a moment, and he panicked, not able to see the creature. He heard a swish of movement against air and braced himself for the impact. After a moment, when the glare was gone, he realized the creature's arm was still posed for the kill, but it wasn't moving.

His gaze traveled from the arm to the head. It seemed to be moving, but not with the rest of the body. More like a bobble-head on the top of a toy body. Then suddenly, he realized the head was no longer attached to the rest of the body, but falling towards him. He braced himself once more, this time for the weight of the head crushing him. But as it fell, the head, along with the rest of the body, disintegrated, becoming nothing more than miniscule specks of ash in the air.

"It doesn't look like much once you've wacked its head off," the girl said, wiping green ooze from the blade of her broadsword with a rag.

"What?" Sean murmured, finding it hard to comprehend that he was not going to die.

"Heldeofol," she replied. "Nasty creature. Poisonous. I've never seen anyone daft enough to take it on with just a stick."

Even in his nearly unconscious state, Sean didn't like her attitude. "Saved you," he gasped.

"Oh, aye, you helped," she replied casually. "But don't be looking to get a medal for it. I'd have

50

*been out of the fix on my own in a moment or two.
You really had no reason to bother yourself."*

Sean glared at her.

*"Well, no need to get nasty," she said,
kneeling down next to him.*

*She lifted his arm and tore his shirt away to
expose his wounded arm. "Ah, he got you right
good," she whispered sympathetically. "It's a scar
you'll wear for the rest of your days if I'm not
mistaking."*

*Glancing down, even in his woozy state, he
could see his arm did not look good. The wound was
red and puckered, and blood was oozing around the
edges. Small veins of black poison crisscrossed
underneath his skin and traveled up his arm, nearly
to his shoulder. She ripped a piece of his shirt,
formed a tourniquet and tied it high on his arm.*

*"We can't have the poison get to your heart,"
she explained. "Then you'd be a goner for sure."*

*Pulling a few leaves from a nearby tree, she
put them in her mouth and chewed on them a little
before pulling them out and placing them on the
wound. Sean scrunched up his nose in disgust and
she laughed. "Aye, I know, 'tis disgusting, but it's the
only way to release the healing properties."*

*She sat back on her heels and looked at him.
"Your wound is deep and poison is traveling quickly.*

51

There is a way I can help you, but you must know we will be bound because of it. Do you agree?"

Sean could barely hear her through the pain of his wounds and the lethargy caused by the poison.

Nodding, he took a deep shuddering breath and watched in detached interest as she withdrew a small silver knife from a sheath at her waist. She lifted his hand and drew her blade across the mound of flesh below his thumb and then repeated the same process on her own hand. She placed the knife back in the sheath and placed their hands together, her hand on top so the blood flowed from her body into his.

"Bound," she whispered.

"Bound, bound, bound."

Meow. Meow. Meow.

Sean drifted from his dream to near wakefulness, feeling as though his breathing passages were being crushed; the weight on his chest and neck were almost unbearable. He managed to pry open his eyes and saw the beast upon him. Staring down at him with gleaming emerald eyes, the beast opened its mouth, revealing sharp razor-like teeth. For just a moment, Sean thought he was back in Ireland. Back in the forest behind his grandmother's property. Back to the event his parents had convinced him had just been a run-in with a thorny vine that held hallucinogenic properties. Back to the incident that he had dreamt of ever since.

The beast on his chest cried out in a voice far more diminutive than expected. "Meow."

"Tiny, get the hell off of me," Sean growled, lifting the giant marmalade tomcat off his chest, plopping it onto the mattress next to him and rolling onto his stomach, grabbing his pillow to cover his head. "I'm still sleeping."

Having little to no regard for his human, Tiny, purring with pleasure that he had finally awakened the man, proceeded to knead, his claws out, Sean's back. "Ouch, dammit Tiny, stop it!" Sean yelled into the mattress.

The cat merely purred louder and increased the kneading until Sean sat up in bed. "Tiny," Sean yelled, glancing over at the clock. "It's seven o'clock in the morning. I got in at three. I've only had four hours of sleep. Can't you give me a break?"

The cat lifted up its front paws and threw its body against Sean's chest in an affectionate rub. "I know it's time for breakfast," Sean said, rubbing the sleep out of his eyes. "But, really, you could live on the fat of the land for weeks."

Ignoring Sean's hurtful comments, the cat lovingly threw twenty-five pounds of vibrating hair against the man's chest. Sighing loudly, Sean whipped the covers off his legs and stood up. Clad only in boxers and a t-shirt, he looked at the robe hanging on the back of the bedroom door. "No, if I put my robe on, I'll stay up," he muttered. "One can of cat food and I'm back to bed."

He pulled the door open and strode down the hall into the kitchen, immediately going to the cupboard that held several months' supply of cat food. His refrigerator and cabinets might be empty of human food, but he always made sure there was plenty for Tiny.

Grabbing a can of wild Alaskan Salmon cat food, he suddenly felt his personal early warning system respond and froze.

"Well, I feel a little overdressed," a woman's voice stated.

Sean turned quickly, automatically reaching for a gun that wasn't there. "You!" he exclaimed.

She nodded her head in acknowledgement, flipping her long, red hair behind her shoulders, and slipped onto a bar stool on the other side of the kitchen counter. She was dressed in workout clothes, black capris and a short sleeved shirt. "How are you doing, Sean?"

He stared at the woman who had been in his dreams since he was twelve. A woman who, until a few months ago, he thought was just an unusual, but incredibly hot, figment of his imagination. The same woman who only weeks ago had saved his life by beheading some kind of creature in the bowels of the Grant Park Underground Parking Lot.

"I don't remember if I thanked you," he said.

She shrugged easily. "Doesn't matter," she said, the Irish lilt in her voice even more pronounced. "I don't believe I thanked you when you saved me life so many years ago."

He leaned back against the stove, glanced down at his boxers and blushed. "I—I apologize for my attire," he grimaced, dropping the can, rushing over and pulling out a chef's apron from a drawer. He slipped it on and tied it securely in the back. "Well, I guess this is better than nothing."

She grinned. "You never know," she said. "I might have preferred nothing."

"Yeah, well, not until you at least take me out for dinner," he tossed back.

Tiny jumped up on the counter and knocked his head against Sean's hand. "Yeah, just a minute, Tiny," he said, picking up the can of food again. "You don't have your sword."

She smiled again. "I don't generally take it on social calls," she replied.

"Is this what this is?" he asked. "A social call?"

She nodded. "Aye," she said, "and a warning."

Pulling the top off the can, Sean scooped the contents out of the can into Tiny's dish, and the cat lumbered across the counter to his breakfast.

"I normally don't like cats," she said, running her fingers along Tiny's back, the cat arching in response. "But this one has charm."

"Thanks," Sean replied, but kept his mind on the conversation. "You said something about a warning."

She stood and walked over to the door, lifting the metal trivet he'd hung on a hook and shook her head. "This is aluminum," she said, "not iron. It won't do you any good unless you're planning on placing a hot pan sideways on your door. You need iron. Solid iron."

"It looked like iron."

She looked at him, her green eyes meeting his hazel ones. "As we both know, looks can be deceiving."

"Can I just ask why I need iron?

"Protection."

"From what? Vampires and werewolves?"

"No, that would be garlic and silver bullets," she replied. "Iron is for fae."

"Who the hell are you?" he asked calmly.

She walked over to him and he was reminded again how tall she was, like a nubile Irish goddess. He was six feet four inches tall and she was nearly his height.

"That's not my story to tell," she said. "Not yet."

"Why should I trust you?" he asked.

She shrugged again. "I didn't ask for your trust, although you should realize by now that we both fight for the same side."

She moved to leave, but he reached forward and grabbed her arm, surprised at the relief he felt when her flesh was tangible beneath his hand. "Not so fast," he said. "How did you get into my apartment? Who sent you? Who are you working for?"

She met his eyes, and he saw a glint of humor in them, and also a glint of challenge.

"Ah, well, that's for me to know," she whispered, and then disappeared in front of him.

"And you to find out," her voice echoed in the room.

Chapter Seven

"I know you're in here and I'm going to find you," Sean yelled, ripping through the clothing and pulling it from hangers onto the floor behind him. Finally, all that was facing him was a blank wall. Running his hand through his hair in confusion, he shook his head and muttered, "Well damn. Could it have just been another hallucination?"

Stepping away from his hall closet, he waded through the sports paraphernalia, jackets, shoes and other miscellaneous items that had occupied the space before he had emptied it out. He leaned against the back of the couch and gazed around his apartment. It looked like a small tornado had touched down; closets were emptied, rooms torn apart and furniture upended. Any place that might have hidden an adult had been thoroughly searched. His scrutiny brought him back to the deadbolt on the front door. It was still in place. Still locked from the inside. There was no way she could have…

He ran his hand through his hair again. Nothing in his world made a whole lot of sense anymore. What happened to the good old days when a little good investigatory work told you the good guys from the bad guys? Monsters, demons and Elk Kings were the stuff novels were made of, not something that should be running down the streets of his city.

"I must be losing it," he sighed and pushed himself off his perch.

He picked up his golf bag and studied the clubs for a moment, then glanced at the front door. Hefting one out of the bag, he shook his head. "No, it had to be iron, not an iron," he decided and stuffed it back in with the others.

After the apartment was put back in order, Sean looked at his front door with a gleam of satisfaction in his eyes. A collection of large, heavy, cast-iron skillets were hanging from bungee cords attached to hooks screwed into the wall above his door. "That ought to keep them out," he said, stepping back and admiring his work. "If the iron doesn't work, slapping their heads against a pan sure will."

An hour later Sean was showered, dressed and sitting at his dining room table patched into the District's computer system. Accessing the records file, he started entering the information he received from Jamal during the interview. Shaking his head, he looked at his notes again. "This is nuts," he muttered. "There wasn't a cloud in the sky last night. How could there be tornado-like winds?"

Opening another window, he typed in the web address for the local weather site and accessed their weather history. Last night in Chicago at nine P.M., the wind was calm, the sky was clear, the barometric pressure was holding steady and the temperature was in the mid-fifties. No tornadoes in the vicinity. No high or low pressure systems in the vicinity. What the hell happened?

Glancing over at the television that was on, but muted, he noticed that the news ticker at the bottom of the picture mentioned the park where the attack had occurred. Reaching over, he grabbed the remote and turned on the sound.

"This is Channel 7 news reporter Mimi Garcia at the scene of last night's horrendous gang fight on the city's South Side."

The camera scanned the scene, showing yellow police tape cordoning off a majority of the field beyond a playground. The police were keeping the camera crews far enough away from the scene that nothing grisly or gruesome could be aired.

"Sources on the scene have estimated the death total to be over one hundred, but those same sources have confided that because of the brutality of the murders, it will take the Coroner's Office weeks before they can piece the bodies back together to get a final count. There has been no official comment from the Mayor's office yet this morning. But detractors wonder if the Mayor is even concerned with the death of a hundred gang members."

The scene switched to the front of Cook County Hospital.

"The lone survivor is said to be in good condition at Cook County Hospital."

"What the hell?" Sean growled. Slapping his mug down, he lifted up his cell phone and called the police station. "Yeah, this is O'Reilly," he said. "Can you find out who the hell is spilling their guts to Channel 7 and shut them down? And have someone go to Cook County and make sure the survivor has some security."

Returning to his computer, he paused again when he heard a light knock on the door. "Just a minute," he called, pushing back his chair and walking across the room. He peeked through the spyhole in the door and saw Ian and Gillian standing on the other side.

Professor Ian MacDougall was not your typical professor; he was tall, with blonde hair and blue eyes and the body of an athlete. He was a little younger than Sean, in his early thirties, but his looks and his age often camouflaged his intellectual capabilities. A computer prodigy at a young age, he then turned his questing mind towards researching a topic that had interested him since his own near-death experience at the age of three, paranormal psychology.

His fiancée, Gillian Flanagan, had the creamy skin and the soft scattering of freckles that were characteristic of her Irish background, as was her lively personality and quick wit. Her sparkling brown eyes, auburn hair, impish smile and diminutive height brought to mind the pixies that had been fabled to roam her homeland. But those who knew her realized her petite frame housed an IQ and a personality that transcended her outward appearance. She was always ready for a lively discussion. Whether it was about the best beer to be found in the world, Guinness, or international relations and economics, she always had an opinion and she wasn't afraid to voice it.

"Okay, give me a second," Sean said, unhooking the pans. "I have to de-iron the door."

A few moments later, the pans stacked on the bar stool next to the door, he swung it open and let them enter.

"De-iron the door?" Ian asked. "Is that an American thing I haven't heard of yet?"

Sean angled his head in the direction of the stool. "You told me to put iron over the door to protect myself," he said. "That was the best I could do."

Chuckling, Gillian stepped forward and hefted one of the pans. "Aye, that'll do just fine," she said, turning to Sean. "Would you be expecting a pack of boggarts to be coming this way?"

"Boogers?" Sean asked, scrunching up his face in disgust.

Gillian's grin widened. "No, boggarts, you dunderhead," she replied, pausing for a moment to think. "Um, goblins, I think that's the term you use."

"Oh, goblins," Sean said. "That sounds much better than boogers."

Ian walked past both of them and found Tiny perched on the back of the couch, nearly purring loudly enough to cause the room to vibrate. Absently scratching Tiny's head, he looked around the apartment. "You've done some cleaning I see," he said.

"Well, I had a little search party this morning," Sean explained. "I had a visitor who appeared in my apartment, gave me a little advice and then disappeared before my eyes."

"A ghost?" Ian asked casually, because in his line of work the appearance of spirits had become an everyday occurrence.

Shaking his head, Sean closed his door and hooked one of the pans back over the door. "Not unless ghosts walk around with swords killing monsters in underground parking garages," he replied.

"A monster in the garage?" Gillian asked, walking over and scratching Tiny's oversized belly. "There's a good boy. Do you like a scratched tummy?"

She smiled up at Sean and teased, "Was it one of those white alligators that grow up in the sewer system?"

"No," Sean said. "She had a name for it. Hell devil or something like that."

The smile left her face, she stopped scratching Tiny, and her voice held a serious note when she asked, "Was it Heldeofol?"

"Yeah. Yeah, that was it," Sean said. "Ugliest thing I'd ever seen."

"You saw it?" she asked. "Really got a good look at it?"

"Well, yeah, actually twice in my life," Sean explained. "Once, when I was twelve and our family was in Ireland visiting my grandmother, I was in the woods and heard someone call out. I ran over to see if I could help, and this red-headed girl was fighting off a bear. Well, it looked like a bear from the back."

"But it wasn't a bear," Gillian inserted.

Sean shook his head. "No, it wasn't like anything I'd ever seen," he replied. "I looked around, found a big rock, grabbed it and tossed it at the beast's head. I got its attention. That's when it grabbed me by the arm."

"Did it inject you?" she asked.

"What?" Sean asked, surprised by the question.

"Heldeofols have long claws on the ends of their fingers. Under one claw in each hand they have a hollow, narrow bone pointed on the end, like a needle. Once they've captured their prey, the bone extends from the claw into the victim, puncturing its skin and injecting venom into its system," she explained.

"Where were you when I was twelve?" he asked.

Grinning, she shrugged. "A wee babe in arms, I'd say. But why do you ask?"

"I felt it, the injection, and then I started getting really woozy," he answered. "And I knew I was a goner. And this thing, this Heldeofol, was looming over me; I guess it was waiting for me to take my last breath."

"It does like its food deceased," she agreed.

"But then this girl, this red-head, stepped up and sliced its head from its shoulders," he said. "And as soon as the deed was done…poof… the big bad ugly disintegrated."

"What happened next?" Ian asked.

"It gets a little fuzzy," Sean said, extending his hand and pointing to a thin scar across his palm. "I think she cut my hand and her hand and held them together."

"Blood mingling," she said softly. "Well, no wonder."

Chapter Eight

Sean studied Gillian for a long moment. "That's an unusual response," he said. "Is there something you'd like to share?"

"Aye, there is," she replied decisively. "But first I'd like to hear about the crime you're investigating."

Sean walked over to his computer and opened a new window. "The crime scene photos have been uploaded," he said. "These will tell you more about the scene than I can. But, I have to warn you, they're pretty grisly."

Gillian pulled out the chair in front of the computer and nodded. "I can take it," she said, sliding into the seat. "And it's important that I see them."

Sean glanced over to Ian, who shrugged his shoulders in bewilderment. "Okay," Sean said. "Let's take a look."

After entering the settings for a slide show, all three watched as the horrific scene was displayed before their eyes. Even with his years of police work, Sean's stomach twisted as he viewed the mutilated corpses strewn throughout the park. Many of the dead were headless, their decapitated, sightless heads lying several feet from their bodies as if they were separated with violent force. Pools of blood darkened the background of the photos, with macabre crimson-splattered grass and bushes surrounding the remains.

"Whoever or whatever killed these people, there were a lot of them," Ian said as they neared the end of the photos.

"Why do you say that?" Sean asked.

"Look at the circumference of the crime scene. No one was running," Ian pointed out. "Whatever it was descended quickly and was able to not only catch them all off guard but also deal with them swiftly enough that they didn't have time to retreat."

"But there are easily one hundred bodies here," Sean said, clicking back to the overview photo. "How could anything, even an army, do so much damage so quickly?"

"It would take very sharp implements and an extremely long reach," Ian said.

"Aye," Gillian agreed and she glanced up at Sean. "And the boy who saw this, he said he saw the Elk King?"

"Well, no, not exactly," Sean said. "He described some crazy fantasy creature with tree-like limbs who was wearing a deer skull for a hat. Then I called Ian, and he said it could have been the Elk King."

"And do you believe the young man?" she asked.

Sean shrugged. "As impossible as it seems, yeah, I believe him," Sean said. "He didn't seem to be high, and he was scared to death."

"Where is he now?" Ian asked.

"He's still at the hospital," Sean said. "They're keeping him there under observation for a couple more hours. They'll hold him until I give them the okay."

"So, we have a few hours?" she asked.

"Yeah, why?" Sean asked.

"There's someone I'd like you to meet," she said. "He might help answer your questions. But then again, he might just give you a whole new bunch to worry about. I need a moment of privacy to call and set things up."

"Does this have anything to do with your blood-mingling comment?" Sean asked.

She nodded and a small smile spread across her lips. "You are a clever one, aren't you?" she said. "Aye, it might answer a few questions in that area, too."

"Then I'm all for it," he replied.

Gillian pushed the hanging cast iron pan to the side and slipped out the door to the hallway.

"Do you have any idea what this is about?" Sean asked Ian.

Shaking his head, Ian stared at the closed door for a moment and then turned back to Sean. "Not as much as I want to know," he admitted. "I know she works for the Catholic Church and researches ancient church artifacts. She's done some work at Trinity College in Dublin, and the church approached her for this job in Chicago."

"It sounds a little strange," Sean said. "Why would the church know anything about the Elk King?"

"I have to admit, I'm a little curious myself," Ian replied.

Gillian poked her head back into the apartment. "He can meet with us directly," she said. "He's very eager to meet both of you."

"The plot thickens," Sean whispered to Ian.

"Aye, and into the dragon's lair we go," Ian replied. "Grab your coat, Sean, I'll drive."

"Thanks, but I'd better take my own car," Sean said. "I'll need to head over to Cook County Hospital once we're done."

Chapter Nine

The boarded-up Catholic cathedral sat as a lonely, monolithic reminder of its neighborhood's past. The stone building, more like a castle from a fairy tale than a public building, had been built in the Romanesque style of architecture with thick walls, curving arches and small windows in the narrow towers that stood as sentinels to the several-storied main building. The land around the church was derelict and deserted. As if from an urban version of Sleeping Beauty, the church lay in wait for someone to break the solitary spell.

"Boy, this place has changed. I remember coming here when I was a kid," Sean said after he parked his car next to Ian's in the dilapidated parking lot. "It was for a funeral for one of my dad's friends. He was shot on the job."

"I understand it was closed in the early nineties," Gillian remarked, climbing out of Ian's car. "There weren't enough parishioners to support it."

Shaking his head, Sean looked up to the verdigris-covered copper of the octagonal spire and then let his gaze skim down the side of the building. Enormous sheets of plywood covered what Sean knew had been marvelous stained-glass windows. Other smaller windows as well as all entrances into the church had been also boarded over. "But why this one?" he wondered. "There were so many other smaller churches that could have been closed up. Why did they choose this one?"

Gillian slipped her arm through both Ian's and Sean's arms and led them towards the back of the church. "That's a very good question," she said. "And once we're inside, I hope our explanation will answer it."

"Inside?" Sean asked, stopping in his tracks. "Are you sure it's safe? This place has been vacant for more than twenty years."

"Aye, so we'd hope you'd believe," she said with a telling smile and pulled him forward. "Come on now, we've someone to meet, and we've not time to waste."

The back entrance to the church was surrounded in stonework, slightly lighter in color than the rest of the church façade. It formed a ten-inch wide arch around the solid oak door, which was ornately curved with a Celtic cross on the top and an inner arch in the center, surrounded by an engraved Celtic chain. The door, well over twelve feet tall, was solidly barred from any intruders. Gillian slipped her arms from the men's arms and walked up to the door.

"And how do we get through that?" Sean asked.

Gillian looked over her shoulder at Ian and sighed. "Is he always this impatient?"

Ian nodded. "Aye, and this is him being easy-going."

She chuckled, glanced around quickly, and then pressed the flat of her palm against one of the archwork stones that was positioned at her shoulder height. She lifted her hand quickly away. The stone piece slid forward, exposing a small control box.

"What the hell?" Sean exclaimed softly.

Gillian took hold of the box and angled it up so her eye was in line with a small, square, glass window and pressed a small button on the side.

Sean saw the beam of light glow against the top of her eye and scan to the bottom. "A retinal scanner?" he stammered.

Gillian backed away from the box, tilted it back into its original position and slid it back into place, a sharp click of an internal mechanism confirming its position. Suddenly, the center arch portion of the giant oak door moved back and slid to the side, allowing an entrance to the church that was wide enough to fit them one at a time. "I'll go first," Gillian stated, "but be quick in following. We can't have the door open for too long."

She slipped inside the opening and Sean turned to Ian. "Do you trust her?" he asked.

Nodding his head, Ian turned to Sean. "With my life," he replied solemnly.

"We don't know what's in there."

"Aye, and we won't until we go inside," Ian said, slipping past Sean and entering the church.

"Why the hell do I even bother?" Sean muttered, stepping forward and following Ian.

The door closed behind him with a suction sound like they had been hermetically sealed inside the building, and he glanced back quickly.

"No need to worry, Sean," Gillian grinned. "This is not a web, and I am no spider."

She turned to her right and opened a small, metal panel on the wall. Inside were a number of small breaker switches that she flipped on. The interior of the building was suddenly illuminated, and instead of the dilapidated ruin Sean expected, he was met with an interior that looked much more like a modern research center with white walls, stainless steel accoutrements, tile floors and LED lighting. He slowly looked around his surroundings and shook his head. "Okay, this is getting dammed weird, if you ask me," he said. "And too much like a creepy science fiction movie. What? Are we going to meet the crazy monks now?"

A short, rotund man dressed in black cleric clothing with a white collar stepped out from behind a door ahead of them and smiled. "Well, eccentric perhaps. But crazy? I don't think so," the priest said as he walked towards them.

Sean guessed the man to be in his late fifties or early sixties. His hair had receded to the point of near non-existence, but his blue eyes were clear and intelligent.

"And, sorry to disappoint, but I am merely a priest, not a monk," the priest continued. "Although I've heard that I do bear a striking resemblance to Friar Tuck. Hello, Gillian, my dear, good to have you back."

"Hello, Father Jack," she replied. "Here's the company I phoned you about. This is my fiancé, Professor Ian MacDougal." She turned to Ian and motioned with her head in the priest's direction.

"Oh, sorry, yes," Ian muttered, coming forward with an extended hand. "I apologize. I must say I'm a bit overwhelmed by your facility."

Father Jack took his hand, shook it with a surprisingly strong grasp and chuckled. "Well, as we don't generally have many visitors," he said, "I can't really say if that's a normal reaction, but it is understandable."

He looked past Ian to Sean. "And who is this?"

Sean stepped forward. "I'm Detective Sean O'Reilly of the Chicago Police Department," he replied, not allowing himself to be charmed by the engaging priest.

"Sean O'Reilly," the priest mused for a moment, and then his smiled widened. "You wouldn't perhaps be related to Timothy O'Reilly, would you?"

"Yes, sir, he's my father," Sean said, looking slowly around the hall. "What is this, a mind-meld and you're peeking into my thoughts?"

The chuckle turned into an outright belly laugh, and wiping his eyes after a few moments, the priest leaned against the wall for support. "I'd say you are your father's son," he choked. "Timmy wanted solid proof, evidence, before he'd believe anything."

"I don't see anything wrong with that," Sean replied.

"Well, there's that thing called faith," Father Jack said. "And it can't be seen or touched."

"And it can't solve crimes either," Sean said. "Or be used as evidence in a trial. The judges have a real hard time with police officers saying, 'Trust me. I know he's guilty.'"

Acknowledging the accuracy of his statement, Father Jack nodded. "That's very true," he replied.

"But you see, I'm not in the trial by jury business. I'm in the confession business."

"I've had more than a few men confess when they're looking down the barrel of my gun, Father," Sean replied. "And I'm not just interested in making a collar. I'm looking for truth."

The priest studied Sean for a moment and then nodded his head slowly. "Then you're in the right place, Sean O'Reilly," he said seriously. "And we have need of a man with your talents."

Chapter Ten

Gillian, Sean and Ian followed Father Jack down the narrow hall to the other end of the church building. The hall seemed to be endless. Finally, Father Jack opened a large door. "Welcome to the chapel," he said. "Although, it's nothing like what it used to be."

The room was nearly vacant, the scars of past furnishings still present on the old, wooden floor. The air still held the scent of decades of burning candles and incense, and some of the walls in the small enclaves, where Sean imagined the candles used to be housed, were dark from the years of smoke. The tall, plastered walls that encompassed the room were dingy grey, but Sean could see lighter places where the edges of the pews had protected them from becoming discolored. It was an interesting sight, row after row of lighter, chair-like shapes facing the altar as if a ghostly congregation was waiting for a sermon. Down the middle of the room, the wood floor was shiny and unblemished, probably where the carpeted runner had lain Sean thought.

Turning to the front of the chapel, Sean could see that it was also empty, and except for the raised dais at the front of the room, there was no evidence of it being a former altar.

"What happened to all the stuff?" Sean asked.

"They were sent to churches all over the world," Father Jack said. "The pews went to a church in Lithuania. The statuary went to churches all over the country, except for those donated by prominent families; they were returned to them for their own use."

"So some local hotshot has a Virgin Mary standing in his foyer?" Sean asked.

Biting back a smile, the priest nodded.

"I don't see any problem with that," Ian commented, stepping up next to Sean. "I've got religious artifacts in my home."

"Ian, you live in a freaking castle," Sean said. "You're supposed to have that kind of stuff there, right next to the suits of armor. But it's a little weird to have a saint looking over your shoulder while you're sitting on someone's plastic-covered sofa in the living room."

"I agree that is odd," Ian replied.

Sean nodded with satisfaction. Finally, someone was agreeing with him. "Yes, it is," he said with a pleased nod.

"People actually have sofas covered with plastic?" Ian asked incredulously. "What's the use?"

Sean groaned and Father Jack laughed.

"Well, back to the reason I brought you here," Gillian interrupted, rolling her eyes in frustration. "There are some things you need to see before we talk about the Elk King."

Immediately alert, Father Jack turned to Gillian. "The Elk King?" he asked softly. "Here…in Chicago?"

"Aye, it looks like the Wild Hunt paid a visit to a local park and interrupted a gang fight," she informed him.

The priest closed his eyes and crossed himself, then looked up with sorrow on his face. "How many?"

With a sad shake of her head, she replied. "At least a hundred. They haven't given Sean the full body count yet."

Sean watched the interplay between the priest and the young woman. The grief on the old man's face was too raw, too personal. There was more going on here than mere interest. He decided to push the envelope and see what kind of reaction he'd get.

"They're still piecing bodies together to determine the count," Sean stated baldly, watching the priest's face. "There are body parts scattered all over the park."

Father Jack's face blanched and he swayed slightly. Gillian rushed to his side, sending Sean an angry look as she helped the priest to a chair. "You had no right—" she began.

But Sean wasn't ready to back away yet. "Did you know this could happen? Could you have done something to prevent it?" he demanded.

With a shaky sigh, the priest slowly nodded his head. "Yes," he whispered. "Yes, I knew something like this could happen."

He knew? Sean felt the rage grow inside him. *He knew this was going to happen, and he never called the police?*

Following him over to the chair, Sean was ready to berate him when Gillian stepped between them. "He knew…we both knew… there was always a possibility," she said. "But we didn't really believe this could happen. They had always observed the conditions of the contract."

"A contract?" Ian asked. "What contract would have stopped this kind of massacre?"

Father Jack lifted his head and with a determined nod, met Gillian's eyes. Sean could see the change in his demeanor. The casual, friendly man of the cloth was gone, leaving a more resolute man in his place. "If it's already begun, we can't waste a moment," he said, shaking his head decisively. "You both deserve to hear the truth. Gillian, would you please remove the screens?"

The men watched as Gillian walked to the wall near the entrance and opened yet another metal panel. She flipped a switch, and the soft rumble of mechanized equipment echoed throughout the large room. Around the two-story room, at eight-foot intervals, large, white, thirty-foot screens had been positioned over what Sean knew to be windows that used to house stained-glass. Slowly, the screens were rolling upwards, revealing the windows Sean recognized.

"These are amazing," he said, walking to the center of the room and looking up at the tall, majestic panes.

He turned slowly. Each window was unique, although all had the influence of Celtic drawings he'd seen on his visits to Ireland. All kinds of creatures, from reptiles to mammals, were drawn into the complicated, intricate designs that glowed with color, even without the benefit of sunlight. Snakes, drawn as Celtic knots, intertwined with other snakes within a golden border on one of the windows; in the center was the image of a saint holding a book in his hand. Around him were swirls and lines, all interconnecting and filling in the background.

"I don't think I've ever seen anything like them in any other church I've been to," he added.

Gillian walked back from the panel and joined Ian and Father Jack at the chair. "That's because they are nothing like any other stained-glass windows,"

Gillian said. "These are taken from the Book of Kells."

"The Book of Kells," Ian repeated. "Weren't you working on those at Trinity?"

"I was. Yes," Gillian replied. "The original book, or what we have of the original book, is housed there on display. I was doing some research on the origin of the book."

"Who brought them here?" Ian asked.

"The answer to that question is a little complicated," Father Jack replied. "And before I share it with you, I must have your solemn oath that you will not share this information with anyone else."

Sean turned his attention from the windows back to the priest. "You know I can't make a promise like that if this has anything to do with an ongoing investigation," he said.

"This has nothing to do with your investigation," the priest said. Then he paused and added, "And everything to do with your investigation."

"So, it's a mystery," Sean replied cynically. "Sorry, Father. That might have worked when I was in Catechism, but I need real answers now."

The priest met Sean's eyes, studied them for a moment. "If you wouldn't mind, I'd like a word alone with Gillian," he said.

Sean nodded. "Take your time."

He stood, less shaky now, and together with Gillian walked back to the door, both silent until they had firmly closed the door behind themselves.

After Father Jack and Gillian left the room, Ian joined Sean in the middle of the room, studying the windows. "So, you're the brains here," Sean said softly, glancing over to the closed door. "What's the Book of Kells?"

"I've not done a lot of research into the book," he said. "But I do know that no one knows where it was created, who created it, and why it was created such as it is."

"Well, you've been very helpful," Sean mocked.

Ian chuckled softly. "Aye, but I can tell you some of the figures in the drawings predate Christianity and are powerful, pagan symbols."

"Pagan symbols?" Sean asked, a note of skepticism in his voice. "I don't see any pentacles or ankhs."

Shaking his head, Ian softly groaned. "You are so American," he replied. "I keep forgetting that.

Actually, the snake is a pagan symbol. The legend of St. Patrick running the snakes from Ireland did not refer to reptiles; it referred to pagans being run out by Christianity."

Ian stepped closer to the windows. "This is a very odd combination," he mused. "Very odd indeed. I'd like to see what Gillian found in her research."

"And so you shall," Gillian said from the doorway.

The men turned to see Gillian and Father Jack reentering the room. The priest came up to Sean and took a deep breath. "I've never done this before, but, knowing your father as I did, and knowing a little more about you, I've decided to risk sharing my information with you, without an oath."

"I appreciate that, Father," Sean said. "I can promise that I will be as circumspect as I can with it."

The older man smiled. "Well, as you don't yet know what you're getting into," he said, "don't make any promises you might not be able to keep."

He turned to Ian. "And you, young man," he said.

"I have no problem promising your secrets will be safe with me," Ian said, interrupting the priest. "I've secrets of my own and understand the importance of discretion."

Nodding, the priest smiled at the two men. "Then come with us," he said, "to my living quarters. We'll be more comfortable there as we discuss what we must."

Chapter Eleven

Although the apartment located on the second floor of the church building was dated, it felt warm and welcoming. The walls had been painted the color of wheat just before the harvest. The area rugs were vintage Oriental with colors from nature, from a deep sunset rose to a vibrant forest green. The leather furniture was old and worn enough to resemble the texture and color of tree trunks, and the pictures on the wall were landscapes of nature like birch forests in the fall and a full moon rising over a primordial forest. Gazing around upon entering, Sean felt like he was stepping into a forest and not the typical residence of a man of the cloth.

"I like your apartment," Ian voiced Sean's thoughts as he looked around the room.

Father Jack smiled, but Sean felt there was a secret behind it. "Well, it's comfortable," the priest said. "And it makes many of my associates feel more relaxed."

"I can see why," Ian said, sitting next to Gillian on a large, leather, love seat. "It's reminds me of the forests back home. I can almost smell the scent of the trees."

Turning quickly at Ian's words, Father Jack took a moment to study the young man before he spoke. "That's an interesting observation," he said slowly.

Ian shrugged easily. "It was just a passing thought," he said.

Sean sat on a chair where he could watch the faces of all of the members of their small party. He knew there was an underlying secret shared between Gillian and Father Jack, and the priest's reaction to Ian's simple comment was another piece he needed to add to the puzzle.

"Now that we are up here," Sean said, "why don't we get down to business? What is the information you have for us?"

The priest leaned forward in his chair, placed his elbows on his legs and steepled his hands in front of his face. "First, I need to give you a little background," he said. "How well do you know Irish history?"

"Probably less than I know about American history," Sean said, "which starts and ends with a high school American History course."

"I've studied it a little," Ian said. "But it was not my major field. As I recall, Ireland has a long history of being conquered by many different groups, all wanting the island for themselves."

Nodding his head slowly, the priest gazed around the room, meeting the eyes of each of the members of their party before moving on to the next. "I've a story to tell," he said. "And if you will humor an old man, I promise to answer your questions."

Then he began to speak and Sean soon found himself mesmerized by the words. "Ireland is an old place. Although the earth itself is the same age wherever we travel, there are still some places upon it that seem *older* than others. Sequoia National Forest, Easter Island, Stonehenge, Machu Picchu, and the Egyptian pyramids are just a few of those places scattered throughout the world. And sometimes, nestled within seemingly normal places, there are spots where the ancient world touches the modern one. There are no signs that point out these anomalies, no border crossings or geographical markers, but those who stay in tune with the earth know when they've found such a place. They can feel it in the subtle difference of the air against their skin, in the chills up their spine, and often the instinctive recognition of coming home to a place they've never been before."

Sean recalled the woods beyond his grandmother's home in Ireland and shivered. Yes, he understood exactly what Father Jack was speaking of.

"Perhaps because it is such a place the Tuatha da Danann decided to invade ancient Ireland and call it their new home. No one knows where they came from. The early texts of Ireland only speak of a people who arrived in flying ships," the priest continued.

89

"Flying ships?" Ian interrupted. "As in UFOs?"

Standing, Father Jack walked over to a small bookcase and pulled out an ancient, leather-bound book. "This is the *Lebor gabála Érenn* or *The Book of the Taking of Ireland*," he said, carefully turning to a page that had been saved with an old bookmark. "This is an accounting dated 1150 A.D. The people of Ireland remember their arrival this way, '*In this wise they came, in dark clouds from northern islands of the world. They landed on the mountains of Conmaicne Rein in Connachta, and they brought a darkness over the sun for three days and three nights. Gods were their men of arts and non-gods their husbandmen.*'"

"So the early occupants of Ireland thought these guys were gods," Sean said. "If you had any kind of advanced civilization, I don't think it would be that hard to do that."

"Please, let me continue," the priest requested, and at Sean's nod, he went on. "These tall, red-haired and fair people were able to conquer the *Fir Bolg*, who many say are the ancestors of the leprechaun or were a race of goblins, and the *Fomorians,* another fearsome warrior tribe, and claim the land and the people as their own."

He stopped and studied both Ian and Sean. "Have you no comments about leprechauns?"

90

Sean shrugged, "I'm trying to be open-minded here."

"There are more things in heaven and earth, Horatio, than are dreamt of in your philosophy," Ian responded.

The priest smiled widely. "Ah, Shakespeare," he said. "Very good. Very good indeed. So, I will continue."

"The Tuatha da Danann were different from the earlier conquerors of the island. They were a magical people who charmed the natives of the island and intermarried with them, sharing their red hair and blue eyes with generations of Irish. The royal class of the Danann were teachers of medicine, smithing, communication and druidry, and the lower class were farmers or shepherds," he said. "So advanced were they in their science and medicine that the *Lebor Gabala Erren* tells of Nuadu Airgetlam, the king over the Tuatha da Danann, surviving the injury of having his arm hewn off during battle. This would have been a mortal wound for most people. But even more amazing, the ancient text goes on to state, *"but a silver arm with activity in every finger and every joint was put upon him,"* which replaced his original arm. At that point, he could rule again."

Sean sat forward in his chair. "Wait. What? Are you talking about a functioning prosthetic arm in the twelfth century?"

Father Jack nodded. "That's exactly what I'm talking about," he said.

"That's impossible," Sean replied. "That kind of technology wasn't available then."

"Or perhaps it was and it was lost," Father Jack suggested.

"So what happened to these guys," Sean asked, "if they were so amazing? How could anyone conquer them?"

"Actually, they were nearly invincible. The only thing that seemed to harm them were weapons made of iron," the priest said. "They ruled the people of Ireland for nearly 200 years. Then, ancient texts tell us that the Milesians, invaders from northwest of the Iberian Peninsula, attacked the island. The Milesians defeated the Tuatha da Danann."

"How did that happen?" Ian asked. "They seem like a fairly advanced civilization."

Nodding his head in agreement, the priest turned to Ian. "There are many different versions of what happened next. The most prevalent is that when the Milesians came, the Tuatha da Danann knew that a battle with them would incur a great number of casualties, so they made an agreement with them. If they took their ships out to sea and were able to once again land upon the coast of Ireland within the space of three days, they would share the land," he said. "The Milesians agreed and went out to sea. The

Tuatha da Danaan caused a great storm to occur, so great that they believed their enemies would not be able to land their crafts. But they underestimated them, and so, according to the agreement, they allowed the Milesians to divide the country."

"So who took what?" Ian asked.

"Well, the Milesians were not foolish, and they had heard of the magical powers of the Tuatha da Danaan. So the cunning Milesian truce entailed that the Tuatha da Danann could have all the land under the ground while the Milesians kept all of the land on top of the ground," he replied. "The Tuatha da Danann retreated to underground sites scattered around Ireland that are still renowned today for their mystical qualities, like Brugh na Boinne. These underground sites are said to be portals to Tír na nÓg, the land of eternal youth."

"I've heard of Tír na nÓg," Ian said. "That's the land of the faeries."

The priest nodded again and smiled. "Yes, the Truatha da Danann remained beloved by the people of Ireland, who later revered them as gods," he said. "And as history became legend, they were known as the 'People of the Mounds' or 'People of the Sidhe,' which is the Irish word for mound. Later, that was shortened to Sidhe, and, after many centuries, they were known simply as faery."

Chapter Twelve

"Faeries?" Sean asked dubiously, standing up and facing Father Jack. "This whole thing was about a faery tale? Do you think I'm an idiot?"

"Not an idiot, but a wee bit foolish and strong-minded, yes," a familiar female voice said from behind him.

Sean whirled around. "What the hell?" he whispered.

Just like this morning in his apartment, the tall, red-haired woman stood before him, an older version of the girl in his dreams. She was dressed in a flowing green tunic, blue jeans and tall, brown, leather, high-heeled boots. Her long hair was loose, trailing down her back. "'Tis not hell I've come from," she said softly. "But a place not too far distant."

"Who are you?" he stammered.

Gillian rose and placed her hand on Sean's shoulder, tightening her hold when he involuntarily flinched. "Sean, I'd like you to meet Emrie Murdock. Em to her friends."

Shocked, Sean turned to Gillian. "You know her? But she's not real. She's...I don't know what the hell she is."

"Aye, you do know," Em stated softly. "You just don't want to believe."

"I don't believe in things that are impossible," Sean insisted, shaking his head. "Is this some kind of trick?"

"No, Sean, not a trick. It's never been a trick or a spell or even a hallucination," she said. "When you were poisoned by the Heldeofol the only way to save you was to mingle our blood. We are bound."

"My apartment…," he began. "You disappeared…"

"Well that's a little trick called faery glamour," she admitted with a shrug. "It lets you fade into your surroundings like a chameleon."

"So, you were still there, in my apartment?"

She nodded. "The entire time. It was intriguing to watch you tear your dwelling apart looking for me."

"Yes, but…," then he froze, and a slight red hue appeared on his cheeks. "I, um, I took a shower."

A half-smile formed on her lips, and she met his eyes, her own dancing with mirth. "Yes, you did," she replied evenly. "And a fine, strapping lad you are."

Sean opened his mouth and finally closed it when he realized he had absolutely nothing to say.

Gillian, feeling sorry for Sean, decided to intercede. "I'm sorry. I called Em and asked her to check on you," she admitted. "After what Ian messaged me, I was worried about you."

Looking back and forth between the two women, he shook his head. "You know each other?" he asked.

"Aye," Em replied. "We both belong to the Order."

"The Order?"

Taking a deep breath, Father Jack leaned forward and nodded. "And that will be the next part of our story," he said. "So, Sean, why don't you sit down and let me explain the rest."

In a shocked stupor, Sean slowly sat back down in his seat. "Please, Father, explain so I can assure myself I am not losing my mind."

But as he heard Em's soft chuckle behind him, he wondered if any explanation would help him keep his hold on sanity.

"For the moment I'd like you to suspend your disbelief and take the information I just shared as a possibility," Father Jack said. "Can you do that?"

Sean nodded, still trying to take it all in. But then he glanced over at Ian who was sitting back in his chair. One leg crossed over the other, his chin on his hand, he was studying Gillian, who was still standing next to Em. The usual look of adoration for his fiancée had been replaced by another, more intense gaze. This was a look Sean had seen before when Ian was studying out a problem, when he was intense, calculating, logical, and allowed no room for emotion.

"Ian?" he asked.

Ian turned, but it took a moment for him to stop his thought process and answer. "I don't know, Sean," he finally said. "Gillian, a moment please? In private."

Ian stood, walked over to the door, opened it and stepped outside into the hallway.

Gillian followed him and closed the door securely behind them. Ian stood, facing away from her, looking down the narrow hall.

"Ian, what is it?" she asked.

"I'm a little overwhelmed here. I'm not only trying to accept the information the good father is sharing, but suddenly I'm realizing I'm not sure I know the woman I'm engaged to," he replied, finally turning towards her. "Who are you?"

"Ian, I'm still me. The woman you met in Scotland," Gillian insisted, taking his hand. "I'm still the person you fell in love with. But in the past few months, while you've been here in the States, I've had a whole world open up before me. Things I never considered before, important things, are occurring right before our eyes."

"You could have told me," he said, shaking his head emphatically. "You could have let me know what you were doing."

She took a deep breath and shrugged helplessly. "It wasn't my story to tell," she replied, hoping he would understand. "I took an oath that I wouldn't talk about it. And now, as soon as I was able, I shared. All I ask is that you keep an open mind."

He pulled his hands from hers and strode farther down the hall. "An open mind, that's all you ask?" he questioned harshly. "You ask me to suspend all logical and scientific data and believe in faery tales. That takes more than just an open mind. That requires one to step into the field of impossibility."

Gillian stood where she was and folded her arms over her chest, glaring back at him. "Oh, and there's nothing you've asked me to accept that's beyond believability?" she threw back at him. "Oh, aye darling, I'm just living with a cute little brunette for nearly half a year, but truly, nothing's going on. We're just watching dead people together."

"I never laid a hand on Mary," he shouted back.

"Aye, I know that," she yelled back. "And I know it because I trust you. I trust you with my heart, you oafish, stupid Scot. Do you think I wouldn't know if you'd been lying?"

"Of course you'd know," he shouted back, striding back to her, "because I'm a damned poor liar and I'd never do that to you."

She punched him in the arm. "Aye, and you knew I'd cut your bloody bollocks off if you ever did, and with a dull knife."

He grinned. He couldn't help himself. "You would, yes," he agreed.

"Don't laugh," she said, punching him again. "I'm still angry—you didn't trust me."

Sighing, he pulled her into his arms and laid his head on hers. "You're right. I didn't, and I should have," he said. "It's just that you have this whole other piece of your life that I haven't been part of."

She pushed gently against his chest. "Stop it. I'm not ready to make up," she said. "I'm still mad at you."

Keeping his arms firmly around her, he smiled. "Aye, and you should be," he said.

Giving up, she laid her head against his chest and nodded. "I want you to be part of it," she said, her voice softer. "I want us to be a team. As I was studying the Book of Kells, all I could think about was what you would think when I finally showed you what I'd discovered."

He stepped back, bent down and placed a soft kiss on her lips. "Forgive me, Gillian, darling," he said sincerely. "I've been naught but an oafish, stupid Scot. I'd like to know what you've discovered."

She smiled up at him and nodded. "And wait 'til you see what I've found, Ian Michael MacDougal. I'm going to knock your socks off."

Chapter Thirteen

"Are we all together then?" Father Jack asked when Gillian and Ian came back into the room holding hands.

Ian nodded. "Yes, Father, I'm ready to hear some more."

The priest sat back and took a deep breath. "Well, now that you have a background on the Tuatha da Danaan, let me tell you that the plan to keep the Sidhe underground did not work as well as the Milesians thought it would. They were not only magical, but also clever, and so they kept up with their mischief making. Not really going to war, but causing enough trouble to keep their captors in a state of constant worry. The original residents of the island still revered the Sidhe. They'd leave them gifts and share their stories with their children, not only to show reverence but also to warn their children away from the dangers of interacting with the Sidhe."

"Dangers?" Sean asked.

"Well, the Sidhe lived by the rules spelled out in the truce, but they also knew every loophole," he explained. "For example, the truce forbade the Tuatha da Danaan to capture the inhabitants of Ireland and bring them below ground. However, if a mortal happened to be invited or persuaded into the depths of Tír na nÓg and there partook of a bite of food or a drink of wine, they would be guests, not prisoners. And so they would remain within the depths for the remainder of their lives."

"Wait, I've heard fables about not drinking or eating anything a faerie offers you," Ian said. "Or you will stay in faery forever."

The priest nodded. "And so it is with most fables or legends. There is a truth behind them."

"But I thought these beings, the Sidhe, cared for the inhabitants of Ireland," Sean said. "Why would they capture them?"

"Well, it's our opinion that they cared for the people as long as there was a symbiotic relationship," he said. "The Sidhe needed three things to remain strong. The first was a group of people to worship them and remember them."

"Ah, like the old gods of Asgard who knew they would cease to exist once the people of earth forgot about them," Ian said.

"Exactly," the father replied with a nod in Ian's direction. "And the second was to provide a fresh gene pool for the Sidhe's thinning blood line. They may be immortal beings, but they needed strong, fresh partners in order to produce healthy offspring."

Em snorted, and when Sean glanced at her, she quickly turned away.

"They also needed human emotion," the priest continued.

"Excuse me?" Sean asked, turning back.

"Somehow they receive energy from human emotion," he said. "They feed off our feelings, and the more powerful the feeling, the more energy it gives them. And whether the emotion was terror or pleasure, they didn't care, as long as it was intense. Powerful emotion like that either involved sex or torture, which is why the inhabitants would warn their children away from places the Sidhe were known to visit."

"My grandmother in Ireland used to share stories like these with us when we'd visit," Sean said and then he looked over his shoulder once again. "And she warned us to stay out of the woods."

Smiling at him, Em moved a little closer. "I've never admitted it before, but this is a day of truth-telling," she said to him. "Had you not entered the woods and distracted the beast, I would have been killed. You saved my life, Sean O'Reilly."

The little boy that dwelt inside of him wanted to fist-pump and yell, 'I knew it!' But years of working as a cop and years of relying on a partner overcame the youth, and he nodded. "And you saved mine," he said. "So we're even, I suppose."

Grinning, she shook her head. "Well, no, as I recall I saved your life twice," she said, her mouth splitting into a wider smile. "So, really, you still owe me a boon."

He saw the twinkle in her eye before he reacted to the taunt and he nodded. "Well, let's see what I can do about that," he finally replied. "Now, Father, let's fast forward a little here because I need to get to Cook County Hospital. What's the bottom line?"

Father Jack looked over at Gillian and nodded. "Gillian, why don't you explain what you've learned in the past six months," he said. "That will make the tale go faster."

He turned to Sean. "I'm an Irishman," he said, a note of apology in his voice. "And I can't seem to keep a story short for the life of me."

Gillian sat on the arm of the chair that Ian occupied. She first glanced down at her fiancé and then at Sean. "As you know," she started. "I was researching the Book of Kells, which was supposedly created in about 6 A.D., and I noticed some discrepancies with the pages. The creators were supposed to be scholars, monks who spent all their time creating the illuminations that graced the pages of the books. But there were inconsistencies that I'd never seen in other ancient texts. There were pages that were duplicates of each other. There were sentences with large spaces in them. There were misspellings. It was all quite odd."

She took a deep breath, pressed her lips together for a moment and then began again. "And then I started to concentrate on what most would consider the mistakes," she said. "I began looking closer at the inconsistencies, and I found the Book of Kells actually seemed to have an older book beneath it, a subtext. The drawings and the words were covering or, perhaps more accurately, hiding the older text and drawings."

"Hiding?" Ian asked. "Hiding what?"

"An ancient agreement between the Tuatha da Danaan and the earliest representatives of the church," she said. "An agreement that allowed the Tuatha da Danaan aristocracy, otherwise known as the Seelie Court, full rights above the ground if they agreed to seal the others, the Unseelie Court, below."

"Why would the church want an agreement like that?" Sean asked.

"Because the aristocracy actually had something to share," Gillian explained. "They were the ones who were gifted in medicine and the sciences. They were the architects and the astrologers. And, most importantly, they weren't the soldiers or the creatures of the fae, and they had the power to seal the others up in Tír na nÓg."

"So, what was in the original document?" Ian asked.

"It was the agreement, and it was also a map of Tír na nÓg and the portals between this world and the other," she explained. "If you study the Book of Kells, you can see familiar land masses hidden in the pages. These portals are all over the world, placed there before civilization came and built great cities around them."

"So, there are portals in Chicago?" Sean asked.

"That's why we're here," Father Jack inserted. "Members of our Order have been strategically located throughout the world to guard the portals and to immediately report if there has been a breach in the opening."

"Your Order?" Ian asked.

"The original agreement between the Tuatha da Danaan and the church was called Brigid's Cross," Gillian said. "Saint Brigid was one of the first patron saints of Ireland. Some claim she was a great abbess who did wonderful things for the people of Ireland; although there is also some documentation that she was one of the ruling class of the Tuatha da Danaan, a queen."

"So, soon after the original document was signed, a holy Order was created to ensure the pact was obeyed, by both sides," the priest said. "It was called The Order of Brigid's Cross and has been in existence since the early days of the church in Ireland."

"But why cover up the agreement?" Ian asked. "Why not just hide it away?"

"They tried hiding it away," Gillian said. "It was hidden on a small island in the Inner Hebrides called Iona. But when the monks fled the Viking raids in the eighth century, they had to take it with them. Instead of allowing this agreement to be discovered, which would be a huge setback to a church that had spent centuries trying to quash the belief in faery;, they decided to cover it up."

"And how did they feel when a brilliant researcher was able to see through their cover-up?" Ian asked Gillian.

She smiled. "At first they were a little shocked," she admitted. "And then they brought me into the Order."

"You're a nun?" Sean exclaimed.

Chuckling, Gillian shook her head. "No, the Order of Brigid's Cross is made up of all kinds of different people, from necessity. The risk is too great for the secret to come out."

"What risk?" Sean asked. "People are sophisticated enough to realize that there are all kinds of things out there that we don't understand. My

107

sister, Mary, with her gift to see ghosts has been accepted, for the most part."

Father Jack sat up in his chair and faced Sean. "And what would happen if a terrorist organization somehow found the document and was able to control the power behind the captive Tuatha da Danaan? How would our troops stand against brutal, immortal magic?"

"The Wild Hunt?" Sean whispered. "That's what this is all about. Someone has figured it out."

"We're not sure," Gillian said. "Em's been following up on leads, but they've all led to dead ends."

"Em?" Sean said, turning in his seat. "And how do you fit in to all this? Are you one of the aristocracy that was allowed freedom?"

She murmured an angry word that was not in a language Sean understood, but the tone and inflection made it clear it was not complementary. "What the pact did not do was protect the inhabitants of Ireland from the aristocracy the Church so blithely allowed above ground. So, you had the lusty, immoral Sidhe hunting for virgins to seduce and despoil as part of their sport," she spat. "And then, unfortunately, the Church had to get into the damage control business, with all of the little half-human bastards being born throughout the countryside."

"Damage control?" Ian asked.

"Aye, because once a human has lain with a faerie they have a longing for the faerie that can never be broken," she said. "Like a drug addict and their first high, they crave more. But there isn't more, so they waste away, longing for something they will never obtain."

She shrugged. "The mothers of these children were unfit to raise their children," she said bitterly, "if they even remembered they gave birth to them. The female children were taken into St. Brigid's Orphanage because we could be taught and trained."

"The boys?" Sean asked.

"The boys had too much of their fathers in them," she replied. "They were looked after, as much as possible, but most became mercenaries looking for a good fight to quell the anger in their hearts."

"So what does that make you?" Sean asked.

She met his eyes, and he saw both anger and pain. "A bastard," she said finally. "That's all I am."

Chapter Fourteen

Sean drove down the streets on the outskirts of downtown without really paying attention to the scenery; he had too much on his mind. *Faeries. Really?* He was a grown man. How in the world could he believe in faery? In the Tuatha da Danaan? In Tír na nÓg? In Seelies and Unseelies?

Then his thoughts went back to Em and their first encounter in Ireland, which he had finally come to accept was real. He thought back to the stand-off in the Grant Park underground garage and the creature he faced there as well. And finally, he recalled Jamal's frightened testimony of creatures that seemed to have stepped out from the pages of a book, a book of faery tales.

How could he not at least consider the chance that these things were possible?

Turning into the parking lot of Cook County Hospital, he parked in the area reserved for the police and hurried through the ER doorway to the receptionist. "I'm here to see Jamal Gage, the young man who was brought in last night," Sean said, showing the woman behind the bullet-proof glass his badge.

She turned and typed on her keyboard, watching the monitor in front of her, and then looked back up at Sean. "Sorry, he was released this morning," she said.

"What? He wasn't supposed to be released until I gave the okay," Sean replied. "Who gave the release order?"

She looked back down to the monitor. "Says we got a call from the First District, and they gave us the go ahead."

"Who picked him up?" Sean asked.

She shook her head. "Told us to give him bus fare and send him on his way."

"What?" Sean exclaimed. "You sent a kid who had just survived a major gang fight home on a CTA bus?"

"Hey, I thought it was pretty raw, too," she said, "but you guys get to call the shots."

"Who called it in?" he demanded. "I need a name."

She pushed a few other buttons and shook her head. "We didn't get a name," she said. "Sorry."

He took a deep breath. It didn't do any good to get mad at the receptionist. She was exactly right. She was just following directions. But when he found the idiot who had initiated the instructions, he would get mad. Oh, yeah, he would get good and mad.

"You got an address?" he finally asked.

She wrote it down and handed him a slip of paper with the location of a well-known housing project not too far from his location. "Thanks," he said. "I appreciate it."

"Hey, sure," she replied, and as he turned away, she stopped him. "And Detective?"

He turned. "Yes?"

"Thanks for restoring my faith in the police department," she said with a slight smile. "I pretty much wrote you all off this morning when I sent that little boy on his way."

He nodded. "Yeah, you're welcome."

As he walked out of the hospital, he pulled out his cell phone and called Ian. "You still there with Gillian?" he asked when Ian answered.

"Yeah, what's up?"

"Is there any reason I should be suspicious when the kid from last night is released without authorization and pretty much set up to be taken out?" he asked.

He heard Ian relating the information to the group.

"Sean, this is Father Jack," the priest's voice boomed through the phone. "You need to be very careful. The Order has been around for a long time, and we have people located throughout the city in various positions of power. But just as in everything in this world, there is always opposition. There are those who would have the contract voided and the Unseelies released. Not just fae, but mortals with the idea of using their powers for gain. The other side has more money, more power and they don't follow the same rules we follow. The fae are amoral. But the humans who work with them are evil. There is no right or wrong. There is only what's best for them."

Sean nodded. "Okay, so I should be suspicious."

"No," Father Jack replied. "You should be paranoid."

In a few moments, he was back on the streets driving towards Jamal's apartment. The next call he made was to the cell phone of his old partner from the night before. "Hey, Adrian, it's Sean," he said, once the detective had answered the phone. "I had to swing by Cook County and I thought I'd check on our boy. I was surprised he was released. Did you get any updates on this?"

"Hey, Sean," Adrian replied, his voice filled with concern. "What? He was released…"

The conversation stopped and Sean could hear a murmur of voices on the other end. Adrian spoke a moment later. "Give me a minute, okay?" he asked. "I need to go somewhere a little quieter."

Sean could hear Adrian moving and then he heard a door close. "Sorry, this is better," he said. "I'm going to put you on speaker phone."

Before Sean could protest, he could hear the phone being placed on a desk and the echoing audio of the speaker. "So, Sean," Adrian began, and Sean noticed that the tenor in Adrian's voice was slightly altered. "You were saying you went to see the boy this morning?"

Not knowing who might be in the room with Adrian, Sean decided to play it safe. "No, man, I had to go by on another case I'm working on," he replied easily. "I thought I'd swing in and see how the kid was doing and found out he was released. Just wanted to be sure you got all you needed."

"Yeah, I did," Adrian replied slowly. "But I thought you gave the hospital orders not to release the kid."

"Really?" Sean asked, knowing that he had, indeed, given the orders. "I thought that you did that. But, no harm no foul, sounds like the kid is doing fine."

He could hear muffled sounds, like a pencil being scratched against a pad of paper.

"Oh, yeah," Adrian finally said. "I was looking for your report this morning and I couldn't find it."

Scan recalled the unfinished report still sitting on his laptop and silently breathed a quick sigh of relief. Now that he had this new information, he was glad he hadn't uploaded his findings.

"I uploaded it early, like eight," Sean replied. "Check again, and if you can't find it, let me know. Sometimes the wireless in my building goes haywire."

Sean rolled his eyes when he heard even more scratching. *Do these people think I was born yesterday?*

"So, did the kid tell you anything interesting last night?" Adrian asked.

"No, not really," Sean lied. "He was scared shitless, that's for sure. Then he started out with these weird stories, but once I calmed him down, he admitted he'd been cowering in a corner pretty much the whole time it went down. He's not going to be able to ID any perp."

"You sure?" Adrian asked.

"Yeah, sorry, dude," Sean replied. "We're barking up the wrong tree with this one."

Adrian didn't speak for a moment, and Sean could swear someone pushed the mute button on the phone. "Hey, Sean, thanks for your help," Adrian said. "If I find out anything else, I'll call you."

"That's okay man," Sean said. "It looks like this one is just gang related, and I've got enough on my desk. I don't need to be looking into cases that are definitely your jurisdiction."

"Okay, then, well thanks for the help last night," Adrian said.

"No problem, call me anytime," Sean replied easily. "But, you know, try to avoid the middle of the night."

Adrian laughed, but Sean could hear a strain in his voice. "Yeah, I'll do that."

Chapter Fifteen

Adrian pressed the button on his cell phone and disconnected the conversation. "Sean's a great guy," he said to the man sitting at the desk in the private interrogation room.

"Do you believe him?" the man asked, leaning back in the chair and propping his Italian leather shoe-clad feet on the corner of the desk.

"Oh, yeah, I believe him," Adrian said, straddling the chair on the other side of the desk. "If there's anything wrong with the O'Reillys it's that they're too damn honest. Not a bad cop between them."

"And how about smart?" he asked, looking into the detective's eyes. "How smart is he?"

"Well, you know, he graduated college at the top of his class. He's moved up the food chain here at the department pretty quickly," he replied. "So, yeah, I'd say he's smart."

The man shook his head impatiently. "Not that kind of smart," he said, waving his hand dismissively. "The other kind...what do you call it...the internal smart."

"Oh, you mean like gut feelings? Intuition? Right?" Adrian asked.

"Yes, exactly," the man replied. "How are his guts?"

Adrian pondered the question for a moment. "You know, he's one of those guys who's kind of spooky," he admitted. "It's like he knows something's going to happen before it does. I don't know how he does that."

Slipping his feet off the table and standing up in one nimble movement, the man placed his fists on the edge of the table and leaned towards Adrian. "This does not bode well for us," he said. "We don't want someone like Sean O'Reilly getting wind of our plan."

"Right," Adrian replied, nodding his head. "Right. But Sean would understand. He's been out there. His own sister was shot by a gang member. He'd get what we're doing."

The man lifted one delicate eyebrow and stared at Adrian. "I hasten to remind you," he said angrily. "This is something *you* are doing. I really have no part in it at all. You do remember that, don't you?"

"Oh, yeah, I just forgot," he said. "This is me. This is all me."

"Good," the man replied, the tension leaving his voice. "Now, go ahead back to your desk. You have a few things to take care of before tonight's event. Did you destroy the notes from last night's event?"

"Yeah, I burned them," he said, "just as you instructed."

"Excellent," the man replied. "You may go."

Adrian immediately stood, picked up his phone and walked to the door. He grasped the door handle and was about to turn it when the man stopped him. "Oh, Adrian," the man said softly.

Adrian looked over his shoulder. "Yes?"

"You won't remember any of this. You won't remember speaking with Sean. You won't remember coming into this room. And you won't remember me."

Adrian nodded slowly, opened the door and returned to his desk. He tossed his phone on the paperwork piled up on the corner of his desk, sat down, and immediately began typing on his keyboard. A few minutes later he looked up, grabbed his phone and dialed Sean's number, but it went straight to voicemail.

"Damn," he muttered. "Where's your report, O'Reilly?"

Chapter Sixteen

Turning right on a street corner near Jamal's place, Sean placed another call to the District Office. "Hey, this is O'Reilly," he said when the station house operator answered. "I need to talk to Sarah Powers."

"Just a minute, Detective, I'll patch you upstairs."

Sean waited for a few moments listening to the public service announcements. The CPD had hired a big-name marketing company to produce them. He really hated the trite, candy-covered non-warnings that appeased both the Tourism Bureau and the Mayor's Office. If he were to produce radio warnings, instead of softball catch-phrases like "Be Aware" or "Don't Let Crime Ruin Your Day," he would use phrases that would catch the public's attention. "People Are Trying to Kill You. Don't Be an Idiot." or "They Don't Give a Shit about You. Protect Yourself." He nodded to himself, "Yeah, those would work."

Finally, he heard a click of a connection. "Hey, O'Reilly?"

"Yeah, I need to find out who released Jamal Gage from Cook County Hospital this morning," he said. "But I need to keep this between you and me."

"Okay, give me a second," she replied immediately, putting him back on hold.

Sarah Powers was a new recruit who was quickly working her way up to detective. She was smart, brave and feisty. Sean smiled. He especially appreciated the feisty. But, because she was the new recruit, she also got all the crap work—like checking back on phone records.

"I got nothing," she said. "No one from our office called it in."

"Are you sure?"

Sarah began to respond but paused, and Sean nearly smiled, knowing Sarah was counting to ten before she opened her mouth with a smart-ass retort. "Yes, Detective," she replied calmly. "I've checked the phone records twice, and I even went through all the phones in the department and checked their memories to see if someone called but didn't log it in."

"Thanks, Sarah," he said. "I should have known you'd be thorough."

"Yeah, you should have," she replied with a smile in her voice. "Is the kid going to be okay?"

"I hope so, Sarah," he said. "I really hope so."

Fifteen minutes later Sean pulled his unmarked car up to the front door of the projects.

He'd had enough experience to know that parking in the lot or on the street and walking to the door just made you a target for snipers.

He jogged to the front lobby and paused. There was a stillness in the building that he had never experienced before when coming to one of the projects in the middle of the day. The lobby was clear. The staircase was empty. And, he noted when he glanced through the bullet-proof glass to the parking lot, even the grounds were empty. People were scared.

He made his way up to the fourth floor and knocked on the apartment number the receptionist had given him.

"Don't you answer that door," a high-pitched and elderly voice called from inside the apartment. "You ain't gonna go with those no-good, trouble-making, worthless pieces of trash. So you can just halt in your tracks, young man."

Sean bit the inside of his cheek to keep from smiling. He knocked again. "Chicago Police Department," he said. "I'm Detective O'Reilly looking for Jamal Gage."

"What's taking you so long, boy?" Sean heard the same voice reply in an urgent tone. "You go answer that door. Don't leave no policeman waiting."

A few minutes later, sitting on a small, lumpy couch whose cushions sunk down several inches when he sat on them, Sean found himself in the uncomfortable position of having to look up at Jamal and his grandmother seated in tall wooden chairs.

"Are you here to arrest my grandson?" the older woman snapped, ready to do battle against whoever threatened one of her own.

"No, ma'am," Sean replied. "I'm actually here for two reasons, to ask him some more questions and to protect him."

He saw a moment of relief pass across the old woman's face, but then her features stiffened as she gazed down at him.

"Protect him?" she huffed. "Ain't no one thinking about protection when they sent him home on the bus through these neighborhoods. Boys get stabbed on buses every day around here."

Sean nodded. "Yes, ma'am," he said. "I agree with you, and I apologize on behalf of the department. There was some kind of miscommunication."

"That miscommunication could have cost my boy his life," she replied sternly.

"But it didn't, Grandma," Jamal inserted, feeling sorry for the poor detective who was facing off against his grandmother. He would hate to be in his shoes. "I'm fine."

She whipped her head over to look at him. "You ain't fine, Jamal Gage," she stated emphatically. "You left this house without my permission. You got yourself involved with that gang and nearly got yourself killed. You is so far from fine, you might not ever see fine in your lifetime."

Sean sent Jamal a quick, sympathetic look and cleared his throat to draw the grandmother's ire back to him. "From what Jamal reported yesterday, the only reason he agreed to participate in the gang activity is because they threatened to hurt you," Sean said. "Did you know that?"

She turned from Sean to Jamal and stared at him for a moment. "Is that true?" she asked.

He shrugged and nodded. "Yes, ma'am," he said. "Devonte stopped me when I was coming up the stairs. He told me if I didn't come to the throw down, something bad would happen to you."

He paused for a moment, searching her eyes for understanding. "I couldn't let them hurt you, Grandma," he whispered, his voice thick with emotion. "You're all I have in this world."

"I'd like to see them try and hurt me," she blustered, but Sean could see the old woman was afraid.

"Grandma, this ain't no game," Jamal said. "They don't care about no one but themselves. They would have hurt you. They would have hurt you bad."

She took a deep breath and turned to Sean. He could see that her frail hand clutching tightly to a handkerchief was trembling slightly. "So, what you gonna do about this?" she demanded. "How you gonna protect us?"

A thunderous pounding on the door interrupted the conversation. "Police," the word was shouted through the closed door. "Open up immediately."

Jamal and his grandmother looked at Sean in confusion. "What's this all about?" the old woman asked.

"I don't know. But I'm going to find out," Sean said, standing and walking to the door.

He started to open the door and was in the process of pulling out his badge when the door was kicked open the rest of the way, and four SWAT members ran into the room, their weapons drawn.

"Freeze!" one of the officers shouted.

Jamal wrapped his arms protectively around his grandmother and stood behind the wooden chairs. His grandmother's eyes were wide with fear.

"There's been a mistake," Sean said, holding his hands away from his body. "I'm Detective

O'Reilly, First Precinct, and I'm interrogating this witness. We haven't charged him with anything."

The lead officer turned to Sean. "You got ID?"

Sean slowly reached into his jacket pocket and pulled out his identification and badge and showed it to the officer. The officer reviewed it and nodded. "Okay, you're clear," he said. "But I've got to take your witness in."

He turned to Jamal. "Jamal Gage, you have been charged with multiple counts of murder in the gang-related deaths of over one hundred victims. You have the right to remain silent. Anything you say can and will be used against you in a court of law. You have the right to an attorney. If you cannot afford an attorney, one will be provided for you. Do you understand the rights I have just read to you?"

Dumbstruck, Jamal just nodded.

"My boy didn't kill no one," the grandmother wept. "My boy's a good boy. He didn't kill no one. You tell him, Detective, you tell him the truth."

"Wait," Sean said, stepping between the officers and Jamal. "There's been a mistake. This kid is just a witness. He didn't kill anyone. He didn't even make it all the way to the crime scene. He was across the street."

"We got a witness who will swear he saw the perp swinging some kind of machete-like weapon and causing the deaths of the gang members," the officer replied.

Sean was incredulous. "Are you freaking kidding me?" he asked. "Did you see the crime scene? What do you think, this kid is a ninja? Whoever you got as a witness is lying."

"Sorry, Detective, I gotta do what the warrant states," he said. "I've got to take him in."

"I get that," Sean said, coming up alongside the officer and lowering his voice. "But this is a good kid. He didn't do it. I'll stake my badge on it. So, do me a favor and keep an eye on him."

The officer met Sean's eyes and a quick connection of understanding passed between the two men. "Yeah, I can do that," he replied softly.

Pulling handcuffs from his tactical belt, the officer walked over to Jamal. "Okay, son, put your hands out in front of you," he said, his voice firm but gentle.

"Wait, you can't take my boy," the grandmother cried, clinging to Jamal. She looked up at Sean, tears streaming down her face. "If they take him in, something bad is gonna happen to him. The Whispers are warning me. Don't let them take him in."

Sean was too Irish not to understand the pit that was growing in the center of his stomach. Whatever those whispers were, Sean believed them, too.

"Officer Trudeau," Sean said, addressing the lead man. "How long can you keep an eye on him?"

The man shook his head regretfully. "I've got two more hours on my shift," he said. "After that, he gets turned over to someone else."

"You got kids?" Sean asked.

The man nodded. "Yeah, a son about his age," he replied softly. "And my gut tells me this kid's no killer."

"Where are you taking him?"

The officer took hold of Sean's arm and guided him to the far corner of the room. "For some reason, I was told that if there were other law enforcement personnel at the scene I was not to tell them that I am taking the perp to the Twelfth District," he said softly and then continued in a louder voice. "So, I'm sorry, Detective, I can't tell you where we are taking him."

Sean nodded and whispered, "How slow can you drive?"

"We'll take the scenic route," Officer Trudeau replied.

The officer turned away from Sean and clapped a hand on Jamal's shoulder. "We've got to go, son," he said.

"You take care of my grandma," Jamal pleaded with Sean. "If someone thinks I had something to do with those killings, she ain't safe."

"I'll take care of her," he said. "I promise."

The officer guided Jamal forward while his grandmother collapsed against the chair and wept. Sean pulled out his cell and pressed one button for speed dial. He waited a moment for someone to answer and said, "Pete O'Bryan, please. This is Sean O'Reilly calling."

He waited another moment and then, without taking any time for greetings, spoke urgently into the phone. "Hey Pete, I need you to drop everything and get down to the Twelfth District," he said. "You got about ten minutes to be there waiting, or this kid is going to get lost in the system. Yeah, this one seems more than a little suspicious. Kid's name is Jamal Gage. You need to habeas corpus his ass out of there. Yeah, thanks. Call me when you are both out of there, and I'll tell you where to meet me. Oh, and Pete, I'm doing you a big favor. You just got a great adventure tossed in your lap."

Chapter Seventeen

Attorney Peter J. O'Bryan had an Ivy League law degree, played quarterback at Notre Dame, was one of the most respected lawyers in the city of Chicago, and loved flashy sports cars. Although getting his wheelchair in and out of the backseat was a pain in the ass, the handling of the car was worth the grief. He pulled into the handicapped parking spot, opened his door, shifted in his seat and one-armed the wheelchair over the seat and onto the pavement next to him. Positioning it correctly, he swung his body from the car into the chair, flipped the car door closed and clicked the locking mechanism on his keychain.

Setting his tie straight and making sure his expensive, Italian-made suit was aligned, he touched the controls on his wheelchair and rolled up the ramp into the front lobby of the Twelfth Precinct.

"Can I help you?" the officer behind the tall, reception desk inquired, looking down at Pete.

Pete pressed a lever, and the seat of the chair rose so he could be eye to eye with the officer. "Yes, you can help me," Pete said, drawing a card from his coat pocket and sliding it under the partition between them. "My client, Jamal Gage, has just been picked up by some of your officers and is on his way here. I need to see him immediately, before any processing takes place."

"I don't know…" the officer began.

"My client is a juvenile," Pete said firmly. "The officers did not give his guardian the option of accompanying him here and did not give her the address of where he was going to be held, pursuant to Section 4-405, Illinois Statute 705 of the Juvenile Court Act of 1987. Now, Officer, I suggest you get on the radio and have those officers deliver my client to the front lobby before any other infringements of his rights occur."

Turning away from the lawyer, the officer picked up the phone and spoke quietly into it for a few moments, making furtive glances in Pete's direction. Pete pulled out his phone, looked at his texts and smiled. He watched the officer for another moment, biding his time, and then tapped on the glass. The officer stopped his conversation and came back to the window. "Is there something else?" he asked.

Pete nodded. "Why yes, as a matter of fact, there is," he said. "My associate has been following the police cars that have custody of my client. I just wanted to inform them that all of my associates' vehicles are equipped with a dash cam that is required to be running at all times. I'm afraid the officers may be inadvertently videotaped. Nothing

131

personal. They don't have a problem with that, do they?"

The officer quickly went back to the phone and relayed the information. He came back a few minutes later. "They don't have a problem with that, Mr. O'Bryan," he replied politely, although his jaw was clenched tightly. "And they will be arriving with your client directly."

Smiling, Pete rolled back a few inches from the counter. "Thank you for your help," he said. "I have lunch once a week with the police commissioner. I'll be glad to let him know how professional you and your colleagues have been in this matter."

"The police commissioner?" the officer repeated, his face turning a light shade of purple.

"Old family friend," Pete replied with a shrug. "No big deal. He was the best man at my father's wedding."

The officer pasted a smile on his face and nodded. Pete rolled farther away from the counter, noting the officer's dash to the phone and his frantic conversation.

As promised, Jamal was led into the precinct lobby in a matter of moments. Other than looking scared to death, Pete noted, he didn't look any worse for wear. Pete rolled forward. "Hey, Jamal, I'm Pete," he said. "I'm your lawyer."

"Yeah? For real?" Jamal asked.

"Yeah, for real," Pete replied. "Did you talk to these officers at all?"

Jamal shook his head. "No. Officer Trudeau, he told me to keep quiet and don't say nothing to nobody 'til I had a lawyer."

Pete looked over Jamal's head to the officer that was behind him. "Thank you, Officer Trudeau," he replied with a nod.

"You a friend of O'Reilly?" Trudeau asked.

"We played football together at Notre Dame," he replied. "I was taller back then."

The officer smiled. "You take care of this kid, okay?"

"Yeah, I will," Pete said, his respect for the officer growing. "Is there a place he and I can talk?"

"Yeah, follow me," Trudeau said, buzzing them through the security door and leading them to a small office with a couple of plastic chairs and a metal desk.

"We spare no expense for our attorney friends," he joked.

"Yeah, real homey," Pete replied. "Thanks."

Pete pulled out his phone and then turned to Jamal. "When was the last time you had something to eat?" he asked.

"Last night Detective O'Reilly got me some food at the hospital," he said. "But they let me out too early for me to eat any breakfast."

"Burgers or chicken?" the attorney asked.

"Burgers," Jamal said with a relieved smile.

"You want fries with that?" Pete teased.

"Yes, sir," Jamal replied. "That'd be great!"

Chapter Eighteen

Sean O'Reilly was getting nervous. He had already carried four large boxes down to his car, and Mrs. Gage was still packing what she called her "necessities." He had no idea how he was going to fit her and her stuff into his car.

"Mrs. Gage," he said, walking back into the apartment. "We need to hurry…"

The knife was fixed against her wrinkled neck, only fractions of an inch from her jugular vein. Sean's heart accelerated as he quickly considered the situation.

The attacker was about five feet six inches tall and fairly hefty. He was probably sixteen years old. His hair was long and braided into cornrows that reached nearly to his shoulders. He was wearing an oversized jersey with gang colors unlike the colors worn by the bodies in the park.

"You need to let the lady go," he said calmly, slowly reaching behind his back.

One arm was wrapped around Mrs. Gage's neck, pulling her body close to his, and his other hand clutched a knife angled against her throat. "She ain't going nowheres," he spat at Sean. "And you ain't going nowheres either."

Mrs. Gage's eyes were wide with fear, and her hands were clasped together like she was praying. And, Sean thought, it wouldn't be a bad idea if she was.

"Well, shit," Sean muttered, pulling out his gun and pointing it at the young man. "Just let her go and no one has to die. And by no one, I mean you."

"Makes no matter to me," he replied. "She gotta die 'cause of what her boy did at the throw down."

"What did he do?" Sean asked, trying to keep him talking while he worked out a plan.

"He killed them all," the boy replied. "He sliced 'em up."

"He didn't do that," Sean replied. "He just saw it go down. Do you really think one kid could do all that damage? And if you thought he could, why the hell would you come messing with his grandmother?"

"It's the law," he said. "We kill them before they kill us."

"What does this have to do with you anyway?" Sean asked. "It was other gangs, not yours that died. This doesn't have anything to do with you."

"That's not what we heard," he said, tightening his hold and causing the old woman to gasp. "We was told he did it, by hisself, and he was coming after us next. We was told by someone who knows."

"Well, whoever told you was yanking your chain, because Jamal was a street away from the park when it went down," he said.

"My man don't yank no chains," the boy replied.

Sean sighed. "Okay, then, if you're not going to listen to reason, how about this? I'm a detective. I'm trained with a gun, and I can shoot you dead," he said. "And it's just you against me."

The boy stared at Sean for a moment and then looked beyond him and smiled. "I guess you don't know as much as you think you do," he said.

"Shit," Sean murmured, without even looking behind him. He stepped sideways, his back towards the apartment wall and turned, his heart dropping at the sight of eight more armed gang members. Some held knives, but several had guns and they were currently pointed at him.

One of them stepped forward, and it was obvious to Sean that he was the leader of the group. Unfortunately, he had to demonstrate his authority. He was skinny and tall. His arms were covered with tattoos, and his eyes were cold and hard. He lifted his gun so it was level with Sean's forehead, sneered at him and nodded slowly. "We gonna lay you out,

137

pig," he said. "And then we gonna have a good time with grandma before we slice her."

He grabbed his crotch suggestively and turned his gaze towards the old woman. "You want some, don't you Grandma?"

Blood spurting, the thump of a gun hitting the floor and the sound of tearing material seemed to Sean to happen simultaneously. Then, suddenly, Em appeared out of nowhere and was standing between the gang member and Sean, the tip of her long sword hidden within the boy's saggy jeans and pointing at the spot the young man had grabbed just moments before.

"Bitch! What you doing?" he screamed, clutching his hand that was less a trigger finger now, beads of sweat now glistening on his forehead. "You better back off."

"I think I would be careful about giving orders, just now," she said, jabbing slightly with the sword. "One twist of my wrist could change your life forever."

He froze, looked down at the blade and looked up at her. "My boys could kill you and your friends."

"But not before I cut you," she replied evenly. "Cut it right off."

He stared at her, his eyes wide. "What you want?" he begged.

"First, your friend needs to back away from the older lady," she said firmly.

"Lee-Ron, you step away," he commanded.

"But, Marcus, you said we had to kill her," the other young man argued.

Em moved the sword slightly and Marcus winced. "You do what I say," he shouted, his voice strained. "You do it now."

Lowering his knife, Lee-Ron released his hold on Mrs. Gage, and then gave the elderly woman a hard shove. She stumbled, but Sean leapt forward and caught her in his arms. She leaned against him, her heart racing, and he guided her to a chair out of the line of fire.

"Are you okay?" he asked her softly.

Tears slid down her wrinkled cheeks and she nodded. "Thank you," she whispered.

"That was not well done," Em said to Lee-Ron, her eyes blazing with anger.

He backed up and raised his arms so they were extended out on either side of his body. "So, what you gonna do about it?" he asked, a sneering grin on his face.

139

Using her other hand, she raised it into the air and, as if grabbing something, twisted it quickly and pulled back. Immediately Lee-Ron gasped and clutched his throat. He opened his mouth, but couldn't breathe in. His eyes grew wide as he struggled, trying to move towards Em. Finally, he fell to his knees. His panic increasing, he ripped at his shirt collar, fighting for air.

"Em," Sean said urgently. "We can't just kill people. That's not how the law works in this country."

She quickly glanced at him and then at Lee-Ron. "He dishonored the old woman," she said, her eyes still blazing.

"Yes, he did," Sean said. "And he will answer for it, but this is not the way."

Exhaling impatiently, she turned back to Lee-Ron, now lying on the floor, and made an impatient wave motion with her hand. The young man inhaled with a shudder and continued to gasp for air. He glanced up at Em, saw the anger still visible in her face, and crawled into the corner of the apartment.

Em turned to Marcus. "This one," she said, nodding in the direction of Lee-Ron. "He is one of yours? He is under your command?"

He shook his head. "I ain't no leader," he cried. "We just heard Jamal was gonna come get us next. We needed to stop him."

140

"And by stop him, you mean to inflict pain on a helpless woman?" Em demanded, putting a little more pressure on the hilt of her sword.

"Ahhhhh," Marcus screamed. "Please don't cut me. Please don't cut me."

She glanced at Sean once again. "Is there a rule in this law of yours that prohibits me from castrating their leader?" she asked.

Sean scratched his head, actually enjoying the terror in the creep's eyes. "Wow, that's a good question," he said. "I'd really have to look through the book on that one. I don't know if I've ever been asked about castration."

"Hey, brutha, we all good," Marcus pleaded to Sean. "It's all a misunderstanding. You know, a mistake."

Sean looked at Marcus. "You know what she is?" he asked.

Marcus shook his head.

Well, damn, Sean thought, *neither do I.*

"She's like an alien," he replied. "You can't hurt her, but she can find you and hurt you. She just appears—like she did today—whenever and wherever she wants. And the next time she appears, I might not be here to tell her what the rules are. You get me?"

141

"Yeah, man, I get you," he replied, his voice shaking.

"She might show up when you're in bed, or in the shower, or with your lady," Sean said. "And she might just decide to finish off what she started here."

Marcus looked at Em and swallowed hard. "What you want from me?" he begged.

"Take your gang back to your own hood," Sean said, walking up to Marcus and sliding one of his cards into Marcus' shirt pocket. "And then you call me and let me know how I can find you when I need you."

Marcus nodded eagerly.

"And if you don't," Sean said. "Then I'll let my friend here find you for me."

"Yeah, I'll call you," he said. "You got my word."

Sean turned to Em and could actually see a flicker of humor in her green eyes. Then he walked over to the kitchen, picked up an empty laundry basket and put it in the middle of the room. "Have your homies put all of their weapons in the basket before they leave," Sean instructed.

Marcus looked at the men standing in the hallway and nodded his head in the direction of the basket. "You heard what the man said," he shouted. "Do it now."

They shuffled in, muttering under their breaths, but dropped knives and guns into the basket. Em studied them. "You, number four," she demanded. "You have a hidden weapon on your leg. Take it out."

Shocked, the man rolled up his overly large pant leg and pulled out the hidden pistol. He placed it on the pile and backed away, keeping his eyes on Em.

"They can go downstairs now," Sean said. "Then I want them all standing under this window, where I can see them."

"You heard him," Marcus said. "Go. And take Lee-Ron."

Sean shook his head. "Sorry, Lee-Ron is going to take a ride down to the police station," he said. "I promised the lady he would answer for his crimes."

"Yeah, that's good," Marcus said, looking at Em. "That's all good. The lady here, she's calling the shots."

Sean nodded and smiled. "Yes, it seems like she is."

Chapter Nineteen

Sean followed the police cruiser out of the parking lot of the housing project. He could see Lee-Ron's head in the backseat and wondered how long it would take for the young hoodlum to get out of jail.

"You should have let me kill him," Em said, following the direction of Sean's gaze.

"Although it would have been satisfying," he said softly, "it's not the way we do things here. If the good guys don't follow the law, how can we expect anyone else to do it?"

She sighed and then looked down at the sword that lay angled alongside the door from the top of her shoulder to the floor mat under her feet. "I'm going to have to clean this, you know," she said, motioning to the edge of her sword. "What does Gillian call it? Disinfect it. That's what I'm going to have to do."

"Yeah, that's a real good idea," Mrs. Gage said, with the first chuckle Sean had heard since he helped her into the back seat. "I wouldn't touch it until you get it good and disinfected. That boy was nasty."

Em turned in her seat to look at the elderly woman. "How are you faring, Mrs. Gage?" she asked. "Do you need to see a doctor?"

"Oh, no, I'm fine," she said. "More than fine now that you got me out of that place. Now if you can just drive us over to get Jamal, then I'll be as right as rain."

"Oh, I'm so sorry," Em said suddenly, turning to Sean. "That's why I came to see you. To tell you about Jamal."

"What about Jamal?" Sean asked.

"We received a call at the church from one of the members of the Order," Em explained. "He said that Jamal was being set up because he saw too much."

Turning to look at her for a moment, Sean studied her questioningly and then returned his attention to the traffic. "A call from one of the members?" he asked her quietly.

She leaned towards him. "Father Jack told you there were people in positions of power all around the world," she whispered. "The Chicago government is an important place for us to have eyes and ears."

"Can you trust the caller?" he asked.

"Only if it's in their best interest," she replied bluntly.

"So, how do you know who to trust?" he asked, glancing over to meet her eyes.

"Well for my part, I trust no one," she replied softly. "And I've never been disappointed."

"What are you two whispering about up there," Mrs. Gage asked. "Is something wrong with my boy?"

Sean shook his head and looked at her through his rearview mirror. "No, actually, Jamal is fine," he said. "I called a friend of mine, best lawyer in Chicago, and all around good guy. He's already at the station with Jamal. He didn't give anyone a chance to play games."

"Is your friend a warrior?" Em asked.

Sean smiled to himself and nodded. "Yeah, he is," he said. "And I think he'd be a good guy to have on our side."

Em smiled at him. "Our side is it?" she asked. "So, you've decided we aren't a bunch of lunatics after all."

Shrugging, Sean took a right turn, away from the police station, and headed towards the church. "I guess I'll have to wait and see about that," he said. "In the meantime, do you think Father Jack will have any problems keeping Jamal and his grandmother secure at the church?"

"We've sheltered others before," she said. "And it seems they have more reason than most to be granted asylum."

"I agree," Sean said. "And after I drop both of you off at the church, I'll head over to the Twelfth District to see if I can help expedite things with Jamal."

Em reached over and placed her hand on Sean's arm, which immediately drew his attention. "Do you trust this friend of yours? This lawyer?" she asked, her voice low.

"With my life," he responded immediately.

"Then unless he needs your help, do not go."

"Why not?"

"There are those in your police organization that try to obstruct the work of the Order," she replied. "If you show your loyalties, you too will be obstructed."

"But don't they already know I'm in?" he asked. "Those uniforms who picked up Lee-Ron, they'll…"

"That's been taken care of," she explained. "When we found out you were going to Jamal's home, we had some of our own patrol the area so they could take the call. Your name will be left off the report."

"You found out?" he asked, incredulous. "How the hell did you find out?"

Turning back towards the front of the vehicle, she simply shrugged. "Trust no one."

"Is there some trouble up there?" Mrs. Gage asked.

Taking a deep breath, Sean shook his head. "No, Em just surprised me, that's all," he said. "She just told me she has a crush on me."

Inhaling sharply, Em glared at Sean.

"Pretty girl like that, you'd be stupid to turn her away," Mrs. Gage said.

"I do not find this amusing at all," Em snapped quietly.

"You're right," Sean said to Mrs. Gage and then looked meaningfully into Em's eyes. "And my mother didn't raise a stupid son."

Chapter Twenty

Father Jack exited the CTA's elevated train on Wells Avenue and walked down the iron steps to the street level. The train tracks ran above Wells, creating a cave-like atmosphere with tall buildings on both sides and latticed steel and wooden construction overhead. He quickened his steps, hurried down Wells and turned onto Jackson Boulevard. Leaving the train tracks behind, the sky opened up, but the tall, stone buildings gave the impression of mountains on either side of a canyon. This was the area of the financial district in downtown Chicago that was actually known as the LaSalle Street Canyon because of the majestic edifices of stone, steel and glass. And none was as magnificent as The Chicago Board of Trade Building.

He stood just across the street from the structure and, once again, wondered about its beginnings. It was dedicated in 1930 and, at the time, was the tallest building in Chicago, exceeding over 600 feet. Covered in gray limestone, it was designed in an art-deco style, with carvings depicting the harvest etched around the circumference of the building, a copper pyramid roof and a 31 foot tall aluminum statue of the Roman goddess, Ceres.

He gazed up at Ceres. Was it truly the Roman goddess of the harvest depicted at the pinnacle of the building, or another goddess, one closer to the beliefs of the Tuatha Da Danann?

He'd often wondered if it were not, instead, Danu, the mother goddess of the Sidhe. According to his research, the branch of the Tuatha da Danann that had been in Chicago had come far before the 1930s and would have enjoyed the clever disguise of their favored goddess.

Crossing the street, he entered the revolving doors that led to the three-story, black and white marbled entrance of the building and made his way to the elevators on the far end of the lobby. Pressing the button for his desired floor, he waited, tapping his foot nervously. This was not a confrontation he was looking forward to, but he had no other choice.

The ride up was smooth and quick, the doors opening to a lobby that looked more like an atrium than a corporate headquarters. But, he thought, considering the occupants it was quite understandable. He inhaled deeply. The air always held the freshness of a recent lightning storm in the spring, and it was intoxicating. Perhaps that was part of their magic.

Moving past several large, potted trees, he walked up to the reception desk. The young woman behind it smiled at him, and for a moment, he forgot everything. She was luminescent, her skin glowing like mother-of-pearl, her hair shining like wheat under a Midwestern sun, and her eyes shimmering like deep blue pools of crystalline water. Then his gazed traveled to her ears. Although cosmetic surgery had removed most of the sharp point of the exterior, the interior rim still had a decided point inside, and Father Jack was brought back to reality. He searched inside his pocket to locate the iron cross he carried, and as soon as his fingers touched the cool metal, he could think clearly once again.

"I'm here to see Aengus and Caer," he said briskly.

"Would you care for something to drink?" the young woman asked.

But now, with his vision clear, he would see the deviltry in her eye and knew, upon partaking of anything offered, he would succumb to their wishes.

"No, thank you, kindly," he replied politely, not wishing to offend them.

The smile left her face and a pout replaced it. "I don't know if they are available," she snapped. "Do you have an appointment?"

Clutching the cross in his hand, he lifted his hand from his pocket and placed it on the surface of the reception desk. "Please tell them Father Jack is here," he said firmly.

Quickly pushing back her chair so it rolled to the opposite side of the reception area, she nearly hissed at him. "You stay back there," she said. "I'll announce you."

He watched her disappear down a hall that looked more like a path in a forest. One moment she was visible and the next hidden behind immense undergrowth. The foliage reached to the vaulted ceilings, and vines stretched from one wall to the other, covering any manmade materials. Sunlight, whether natural or artificial Father Jack couldn't tell, peeked through the leaves and glistened against the many water features scattered throughout the space.

A few minutes later he heard the rustling sound of someone coming back up the path to the lobby. He expected the receptionist, but instead it was Caer herself.

She had always reminded him of a dangerous jungle cat, a red-haired, green-eyed panther, he mused. She was tall, sleek, and moved with an angular grace that seemed fitted for a dark jungle or a high-fashioned runway. Her high cheekbones and arched features reminded him that she was indeed one of the fae. But the way she observed him, boldly and insolently, warned him she was part of the aristocracy that traded her own people's freedom for her own comfort. She was dressed in green skinny pants, a brown lace corset top with a silver-threaded embroidery, an autumn-colored open jacket and brown leather high heels. Her necklace and earrings were copper-colored oak leaves with amber stones.

He bowed his head respectfully. "Caer, you are looking lovely, as usual," he said.

She smiled, please at the compliment. "Father Jack, you honor us with your presence," she replied with the appropriate response. "Aengus is eager to see you. Will you please follow me?"

She turned, not waiting for his response and walked back down the path. Father Jack returned his hand into his jacket pocket, but kept the cross gripped tightly in his palm and followed her.

"And how is your health, Father Jack?" she asked over her shoulder.

"I'm well, thank you," he replied. "And how are you?"

Laughing melodically, she paused for a moment and turned, her long auburn hair flowing over one shoulder. "Perfect, as you can see," she replied with a smile.

He nodded. "Yes, it does appear so," he agreed.

She stepped close to him and lifted a slender hand to his chest. Immediately he was sheathed in her scent, a combination of wildflowers and musk.

"You have only to ask, Father Jack," she whispered. "And I would be pleased to show you how perfect I am."

153

He slowly stepped back and met her eyes. "As tempting as that is," he replied, wishing his voice was stronger. "I have made vows that forbid such an activity."

She slowly ran her tongue over her upper lip, moistening the already rosy skin. "My gods are much more fun than yours," she replied. "And they can offer you so much more."

Shaking his head, he met her eyes. "No thank you," he said resolutely.

Warm, inviting eyes quickly turned cold, and Caer turned away from him, striding up the path. "Then be quick about it," she called. "Aengus does not like to be kept waiting."

Aengus's private office had always reminded Father Jack of a throne room. The large leather chair and oversized mahogany desk sat on a raised dais at the end of the long, rectangular space. Behind the desk, the tall, art-deco windows looked out over Jackson Boulevard, as a king would look down over his domain. The décor in the room was also stately, with deeper shades of the forest present here: hunter green, mustard yellow, cobalt blue and Tyrian purple. On one wall hung an ancient tapestry depicting Midsummer's Night, the detailed artistry creating an image that looked more like a photograph than embroidered cloth.

Aengus sat, one leg lolled over the arm of his chair and the rest of his body in repose, and stared insolently at Father Jack as he neared the desk. He was tall and lean, with a shock of strawberry blond hair that lifted high off his forehead and fell softly to one side, feathering to just above his neckline. He wore an expensive three-piece suit in a soft fawn brown and, although Father Jack knew Aengus was centuries old, he looked like a young thirty-something in the prime of life.

Lifting a long, narrow hand, Aengus studied his fingernails and, without acknowledging the priest, asked, "I don't recall having any appointments today, Caer. Do you recall anyone calling and asking if I might be available to meet?"

Caer smiled wickedly. "No, Aengus. No one called and asked permission to meet with you," she replied.

"And am I not the leader of the Tuatha da Danann in this region?" he asked. "Would that not invoke a certain protocol out of respect for my station?"

"One would think so," she answered. "Although, not all of our acquaintances are so well-mannered."

He nodded, still looking at his nails. "So it would seem," he said with a dramatic sigh. "And have we not spent decades, nay, centuries, trying to educate these humans on the importance of decorum?"

"We've had an eye witness report of the Wild Hunt killing over a hundred people last night," Father Jack interrupted abruptly.

A set of expensive Italian leather shoes hit the ground behind the desk. Aengus leaned forward, his hands clasped to the edge of the desk before him. "Repeat yourself," he demanded.

"We have an eye witness who saw the Wild Hunt descend from the skies last night and mutilate over one hundred people in a park less than ten miles from here," he replied decisively. "A clear violation of the truce."

"Impossible," Aengus stated, sitting back in his chair.

"Nonetheless, it happened," Father Jack replied.

Aengus jumped up from his chair and cleared his desk with the swipe of one hand. "Are you calling me a liar?" he shouted.

His heart beating rapidly, the priest held his ground. "I am just informing you, as per the dictates of the truce, that someone has violated the agreement," he said slowly. "This is the second violation in the past few months. If you did not sanction either of these occurrences, then someone on your side seems to be usurping your authority."

Shoving his chair out of his way so it clattered down the dais, Aengus stepped down and walked over to the priest. "Who is the eyewitness?" he asked, his eyes sparkling with anger.

"A young boy, frightened out of his wits," the priest replied. "He had no idea what the creatures were, but he described them perfectly. The Elk King led the slaughter."

Aengus paced away from him, shaking his head. "The Hunt does not act on their own," he said, shaking his head. "They must be specifically directed."

"Whoever directed them knew exactly when a gang fight was going to take place in the park," the priest stated. "The Hunt arrived only minutes after the two groups had gathered on their field of battle."

"And the boy?" the faerie asked. "Why was he not killed?"

"I understand he was late to the battle," he explained. "He witnessed the arrival and the decimation from across the street."

Aengus walked to one of the windows and stared, unseeing, out across the city. "My subjects are loyal to me," he said, his voice softer than before. "They know the punishment for violating the truce."

He turned and faced Father Jack. "I want to see the boy."

The priest shook his head. "Someone on your side has already tried to get rid of the boy," he stated. "We've been warned to keep him safe."

"He would be safe with me. I would not harm the boy," he spat. "That is beyond insolence."

Gripping the cross tighter, Father Jack stepped up to Aengus. "It seems that you have lost control over at least a portion of your kingdom," he said tightly. "You cannot guarantee his safety or the welfare of the truce while there is a traitor in your midst. Do not make promises we both know you cannot keep."

"Men have died for saying less," Aengus snarled, his eyes blazing with anger.

"I believe that, old friend," the priest replied calmly. "But we both know that you and I are not adversaries in this cause. And killing me will not rid you of the conspirator in your ranks."

Aengus reached out and placed his hand on Father Jack's shoulder. "I did not order the Hunt, Jack," he said earnestly.

Father Jack nodded. "I will contact you if I discover any useful information."

"I will not let this go unanswered," Aengus vowed.

"See that you don't," Father Jack replied, turning and walking out of the room.

Chapter Twenty-one

Sean watched as Gillian took Mrs. Gage underwing, gently guiding her through the church and up to Father Jack's residence for a promised cup of tea. But as soon as they were both out of eyeshot, he turned to Em, the façade of congeniality gone. "Now you're going to tell me what the hell is going on here," he said, keeping his voice low.

Crossing her arms over her chest, Em leaned against the thick plaster wall. "You've been told, O'Reilly," she said. "Or do you have a problem with your memory?"

"I don't like people tracking me," he said.

She shrugged carelessly. "We've been watching you for a while," she replied.

Sean stepped away and paced quickly up the hall, trying to dissipate some of his anger before he spoke again. Finally, keeping himself several feet away from her he met her eyes. "You've been watching me?" he asked, his teeth gritted. "And just how the hell long has that been going on?"

Unfolding her arms, she stood up straight and walked over to him. "For a long time," she said softly. "A very long time."

"Like what? Three months? A year? Two years?" he demanded.

"Like ever since you became a cop," she answered.

Stunned, he backed away, shaking his head. "No. I would have known," he countered. "There is no way..."

"You and I were connected," she interrupted. "They knew it. They knew that you would be one of the few who would, who could, accept what we are and what we do because of that experience. We needed someone we could trust."

"Trust?" he spat, raking his hand through his hair. He stormed back down the hallway, his footsteps echoing on the wooden floor. Reaching the end of the hall, he paused and kicked a classroom door. The sound of the door crashing against the interior wall of the empty classroom resounded through the hall, and Em winced.

Sean turned back to her and strode back up the hallway, standing before her, his eyes blazing with anger. "You talk about trust?" he demanded, his voice an irate whisper. "You dare talk to me about trust? You and your organization have been spying on me since I became a cop. What? Did you influence my posts and transfers, too?"

Even knowing it would make him even more furious, Em couldn't lie to him. "If it suited our

161

needs, yes, we did," she said. "For the most part your career was your own. Every commendation, every promotion, were ones you earned, we did nothing to influence that. But the track you were taken down, the direction those promotions turned you towards. Yes, we did, at times, influence those."

"Special Crimes Unit?" he asked.

She nodded. "Yes, we needed you there," she admitted.

"I wanted Narcotics," he said.

"Yes, I know," she said. "But we felt—"

He slammed his fist against the wall beside him. "You felt?" he demanded. "You felt? This is my life. How about how I felt?"

She didn't flinch, but this time there was no sympathy in her voice when she spoke. "Stop your whining, O'Reilly," she said. "You have many more choices than I. You wanted to be a cop to make sure all was right with the world. Well, you've been given a chance. And a grand chance it is. This isn't narcotics or vice. This is a war, O'Reilly. A war against a race that is stronger, smarter, and has more tools than we can ever imagine. We have only ourselves and a few bits of magic and cunning to win this war. We look for soldiers who are brave, strong, and honest. If you feel we've offered you a slight when we put you in that category, that's just too bad. And if you feel manipulated or maneuvered, you've only yourself to blame. 'Twas you that walked into that forest when you were a lad. 'Twas you who came to answer the distress call of an unknown child. 'Twas you who fought so valiantly and nearly died."

Taking a deep breath and exhaling slowly, Sean felt the anger seep from his body. "You weren't part of this?" he asked.

She shook her head. "No more than you," she admitted. "But my birthright has more to do with my position than yours. My mother was seduced by a Sidhe and then wasted away in longing. The good nuns found me when I was five years old, near starving, dirty, and basically raising myself. My mother was in a near comatose state, crying once again for the faerie who'd taken her heart. She had no thought for me. I don't know if she even realized she had a child."

Em stepped away from Sean and looked down the long hallway, so similar to the ones in the orphanages where she spent her formative years. "The authorities claimed my mother was an addict, yet try as they might, they found no drug in her system," she said. "Which by court order, led to years of them giving me back to her for months at a time. The psychologists were sure that her maternal instincts would kick in sooner or later. I would beg them not to leave me with her. But you know, they believed in a mother's love."

"Surely she loved you," Sean said, thinking about his own mother and what she would do to protect her children.

"There is no such thing as love," Em snapped, and then she shook her head. "I learned the truth of that a long time ago."

"What finally happened?" Sean asked, deciding now was not the time to argue that particular point.

"It was winter. Our home was back on the Child Services check-up route," she said. "I understand I was blue with cold, my life nearly gone. I had snuggled up against the body of my mother, who been a corpse for nearly two weeks. I was seven years old."

She took a moment and neither of them spoke. "The nuns took me in," she said. "And when they realized what I was, they brought me to the Order and trained me. I was quite a handful, always sneaking out and chasing the fae on my own."

"That's when I met you?" Sean asked. "When you were on your own chasing the Sidhe?"

"Aye, that Sidhe, whoever he was, took my mother's life and nearly my own," she said. "I've a great appetite to even the score."

Sean studied the woman before him, and now understanding her story, his admiration for her grew.

164

He nodded and then held out his hand. "I'll help you," he said simply.

She hesitated. "I'm not looking for your pity," she said.

He shook his head. "No, the pity is for the little girl who lived through what she did when she should have been cared for," he said. "But the woman who she became needs no pity, only another partner in her war."

She nodded, smiled and took his hand. "Aye, I'll take it."

Chapter Twenty-two

The distinguished law offices of Peter O'Bryan, attorney-at-law, were usually encased in hushed tones and soft, classical music while junior partners and assistants worked on various contracts, lawsuits and other legal matters for their high-end clientele. Pete eschewed the modern glass and steel environment for a more traditional one of highly polished wood, overstuffed leather and a richly hued accent palette. But the Monet oil hanging in his private office next to the framed, vintage, sports photographs more fully exemplified his eclectic decorating tastes.

This afternoon, however, there were noises coming from the employee lounge that were generally saved for later in the day when the work was done, the doors were locked, and the people Pete enjoyed working with kicked back for a while waiting for the rush-hour traffic to dissipate. Today, Jamal's shouts of victory as he thoroughly trounced one of Pete's younger associates in a video game on the widescreen HD television could be heard throughout the office. And that sound, Pete decided, was a joyful noise.

Picking up the phone, he dialed Sean's cell and waited a moment for his friend to pick up.

"Hey, I've got him. He's safe here at the office giving Joey a run for his money at video games," he said.

He heard Sean's audible sigh of relief. "Thanks, I really owe you," Sean replied. "So, how far in do you want to be?"

Pete leaned back in his specially designed chair and smiled. "How far in do you think I should be?"

He tapped his fingers softly on the desk as he waited for Sean to reply, intrigued by the time it was taking his usually quick-witted friend to speak. "Okay, this is the thing," Sean finally said. "Remember that stuff I told you about when I went to Ireland as a kid?"

"Yeah, your scar, right?"

"That's right," Sean said. "And the thorns that were hallucinogenic?"

"Yeah, we spent four hours trying to find out what they were so we could get a legal high," Pete replied with a smile.

"And we couldn't find anything about them," Sean said, exhaling slowly. "Well, now I know the reason why."

"Okay, spill it."

"What I saw. What I thought I saw and everyone told me was a dream? Well, it wasn't."

Pete sat forward and placed his elbows on the desk top. "What the hell are you saying?"

"You know, it's probably a good idea if we don't talk about this over the phone," Sean said. "Remember our place?"

Nodding, Pete pictured the small tavern in his old neighborhood. A place where neither he nor Sean would be considered outsiders. "Yeah, I remember," he said. "Should I bring him with?"

"Yeah, that's a good idea," Sean replied. "But take the long way around."

The long way around, Pete thought, their code phrase for someone might be following you.

"Yeah, I got it," he said.

He hung up the phone and slipped his hand down to the controls on the chair. Lowering it slightly, he back up away from the desk and crossed the room to the heavy, oak door. With another touch of a button, the door opened, and he was able to roll through to the hallway.

Liza Pope, Pete's legal secretary, a statuesque black woman, twisted around in her chair, hands posed over her keyboard, and smiled at Pete. "Hey boss, what's up?"

"I'm heading out for the day," Pete replied. "Did you have a chance to get those things I needed?"

Reaching under her desk, she pulled out a large shopping bag with the logo of a trendy store for teenagers and handed it to him. "I went to my son's favorite store and bought him a new wardrobe. I brought two outfits with me," she said. "The rest are waiting for an address to be delivered."

"Outfits?" Pete asked. "Do guys really use the word outfits?"

She grinned. "I got him a couple of shirts, two pairs of jeans, a sweatshirt, some new shoes and the basics—socks, tees and underwear. Better?"

Nodding, he returned the smile. "Yeah, better," he said. "Now, what I need you to do is get him to change his clothes so he looks nothing like the kid we brought in here today, okay?"

"I get it," she said. "I'll make sure he looks like my son."

"Did you talk to Maria?" he asked and when she nodded added. "How angry is she?"

She paused for a moment, biting the inside of her mouth to control the laughter. "She says if height were a protected discrimination category, she would be thinking about suing you for all you've got."

"And?"

"And she will change into Jamal's clothes and be ready to leave with you as soon as you need her."

"Tell her I owe her," he replied, then he handed her an index card with an address on it. "Once Maria and I leave, wait about fifteen minutes and drive to this address with Jamal. Sean O'Reilly will be there. Only leave Jamal with him, no one else."

She nodded. "Got it," she said and then asked. "How much trouble is he in?"

"I don't know yet," he replied. "But if Sean O'Reilly is telling me to be careful, then we all need to watch our backs."

He started to roll past her desk and then stopped. "You know that security firm we contract with?" he asked.

"Yes."

"Give them a call," he said. "I want someone outside your house and Maria's house tonight. Just in case."

"How about your place?"

He chuckled. "I don't think anyone is getting into my place without my knowledge," he said. "And if they try it will be interesting meeting with them."

He continued down the hall towards the employee lounge, stopped his chair and waited for a few moments, watching the young boy's relaxed and happy face as he took another one of Joey's troops out. "Hey, Jamal, it looks like you've whipped Joey," he said.

Jamal grinned at him. "I beat him bad," he replied. "I totally thrashed him."

Joey put down his controller and shook his head. "The kid's a natural," he said. "I can't believe he's never played this game before today."

Pete glanced up at the scores on the screen, impressed by the numbers, and turned to Jamal. "You're kidding, right?" he asked. "You've played this before, haven't you?"

Jamal shook his head. "No, sir," he answered. "We ain't got a game system or a TV that would even hook up with a game system if we had one. My grandma, she ain't got no use for things like this. She says it's a waste of time."

"Your grandma is a smart woman," Pete said. "But sometimes these games can be more than just games." He paused for another moment, and then shook his head. "But that's for another day. Today, we got to get you out of here without anyone knowing it's you."

"How we gonna do that?"

171

Pete handed Jamal the bag of clothes. "You need to change your clothes and put on these new ones," he said. "Then I'm going to have someone else put on your clothes and pretend to be you. After we leave, Liza's going to pretend that you're one of her sons and she's going to take you to meet Detective O'Reilly."

"Detective O'Reilly?" Jamal asked. "He's got my grandma."

"Yeah, he brought her somewhere safe," Pete said. "And he wants to take you there, too, but he wants to be sure no one is following you."

Jamal nodded. "Yeah, I got that," he said.

"Okay, go change and be quick about it."

Jamal looked into the bag for the first time, and a shy smile flashed across his face. "Yes, sir," he replied enthusiastically.

Fifteen minutes later, Jamal was dressed in clothes that probably cost more than he and his grandma's month's living allowance, Maria Perez, a petite associate, was dressed in Jamal's old clothes, her long, black hair hidden beneath a cap and the hood of his sweatshirt.

"Wow, for a grownup, you're really short," Jamal said.

"I'm not short. I'm petite," Maria replied.

172

"So, Jamal, show her how you walk," Pete said, biting back a smile.

Jamal walked up and down the hallway, striding with a slightly rhythmic bounce.

"You really walk like that?" Maria asked. "Or are you just pulling my chain?"

He grinned. "I really walk like that," he said. "It's the bad way to walk."

Pete nodded. "Okay, Maria," he said. "Now it's your turn."

Maria's imitation of Jamal's saunter was stiff and a little exaggerated. Jamal and Pete glanced at each other and shook their heads simultaneously. "Well, the good news," Pete said, "is that it's a really short walk from the back of the office to my car."

Maria scowled at Pete. "Very funny, Mr. O'Bryan. Very funny."

Chapter Twenty-three

Pete put his car in reverse and pulled out of the private, underground parking lot beneath the firm's offices.

"Bingo," Maria said, watching in the side mirror. "We got a car following us."

Pete nodded. "So, what does it look like?" he said, concentrating on the traffic around him.

"Black, unmarked SUV," she replied, rolling her eyes. "Could they be any more obvious?"

Chuckling, Pete shifted gears and pulled onto Lake Shore Drive. "Beautiful afternoon for a drive," he said.

She settled back in the soft leather seat. "Yeah, I could get used to this," she commented. "So, where are you taking me?"

"I thought I'd drive you home," he said. "You still live in the Edgewater?"

She nodded. "Yeah, but how am I supposed to get my car for tomorrow?"

"I'll send a car for you," he said. "Besides, I'll feel safer."

"You think these guys are that bad?" she asked.

"No, I've seen your driving," he replied with a quick grin, glancing over at her. "This is purely a public service."

"Well, if you ever give up the attorney gig, you can still get a job as a stand-up comic," she retorted. "Oh, wait. I mean a roll-on comic."

Chuckling, he accelerated and passed a couple of cars and moved back into the right lane. "Oh, yeah, make fun of the crippled guy."

"Yeah, poke fun at the Mexican," she said. "You got any border-running jokes you want to try out?"

"Yeah, why did…"

"Okay, we got trouble coming hard and fast," she said, interrupting him as she stared into the mirror. "They've got a couple more cars joining them. We've got to get off."

They had nearly passed the exit, but Pete turned sharply to the right, bumped over a curve and slid onto the exit ramp at Lawrence. "Suggestions?" he asked.

"Yeah, turn left and take Lawrence to Sheridan, then make a right on Sheridan," she said.

Following her suggestions, he made a quick left onto Lawrence, swerving around an oncoming car and speeding down the street.

"Nice one," she said.

"And that's why you shouldn't drive," he replied, slipping through a yellow light on Marine Drive.

"Oh, was I supposed to be terrified?" she asked. "You'll have to do better than that."

"Do you think they'll put out an APB on us?" he mused.

She shook her head. "No, if there not supposed to draw attention to themselves, it would be kind of hard to justify tailing the top attorney in Chicago."

"Thank you," Pete said.

"I was talking about myself," Maria replied. "You're just my driver."

He turned onto Sheridan Road, skirted around a CTA bus, and continued to drive north. "Where's the next exit on Lake Shore Drive?" he asked.

"Foster," she replied. "But they are going to spend some time checking out the lakefront to see if we are hiding in the park."

"But we won't be hiding in the park," Pete said. "Because…"

"Because, you are going to be buying me a Starbucks," she said. "Turn right on Foster, then a left into the parking lot and take the ramp to the rooftop parking."

He followed her directions and pulled into a spot next to the street-side wall and put the vehicle into park. Maria pulled off the cap, letting her black hair fall tousled to her shoulders, and took off the oversized sweatshirt. The striped t-shirt hugged her feminine curves, and the loose jeans fell to her hips.

"You don't look like a thirteen year old boy anymore," Pete said.

Smiling at him, she nodded. "Yeah, that's the point," she said. "What do you want from Starbucks?"

"I thought I was buying," he said.

She pulled a credit card out of her pocket and grinned. "You are," she said. "Corporate card."

"I'll take a small, black coffee," he said.

"They don't have small," she corrected. "They have short."

"They're not short," he corrected. "They're petite."

Rolling her eyes, she slipped out of the car. "You are such a jerk," she said, bending over and looking into the car.

"Hey, Maria," he said, suddenly serious.

"Yeah?"

"Be careful, okay?"

She nodded and met his eyes, the amusement gone from hers, too. "Yeah, I will."

Jogging to the stairs, she hurried down to street level and casually walked along Foster to the coffee shop entrance. Pulling out her cellphone, she dialed Pete as she took her place in line, nonchalantly looking out the plate glass windows to the street beyond.

"Hey," Pete said, answering his phone.

"Okay, nothing but a long line," she began and then stopped suddenly. "Well, hello there…"

The line moved forward and Maria followed along. "Yeah, number one is stopped momentarily," she said. "Heading west."

While Maria had been heading down to Starbucks, Pete had pulled his wheelchair out of the back of the car and was now sitting next to the rooftop retaining wall. "Yeah, I see him," Pete said.

Turning, he looked farther east on Foster. "And if I'm not mistaken, one of his buddies is going to join him at the light."

Maria stepped up to the counter and placed her order. "When did Liza plan on going home tonight?" she asked matter-of-factly.

"About fifteen minutes after we left," he said, glancing down at his watch. "She should be home by now."

Popping a ten dollar tip in the jar, Maria picked up the cups and slipped outside. "Okay, well, I think we're good then," she said, watching the light change and two unmarked SUVs head east into the city.

"We're still missing number three," he replied.

"Yeah, well, if I were number three, I would have headed back the other way, just in case we got off and then turned around and got back on the other way," she said.

She jogged up the stairs and walked over to Pete, handing him the cup of coffee.

Taking a sip, he stared down the street. "Why don't you give Liza a call?" he said. "Just in case someone is tracing my line."

Nodding, she punched in the number. "Hey girl," she said. "How did your shopping go?"

She paused and smiled. "Yeah, I totally love my new outfit," she replied, grinning at Pete. "And it did what I wanted it to do. Swept that man off his feet."

She listened and nodded again. "Well, yeah, thanks. I'll let him know," she said. "See you tomorrow."

She hung up the phone and slid it into her pocket. "Your package was delivered safe and sound."

Exhaling slowly, Pete placed his cup in a carrier on his chair and rolled towards the car. "Thanks for your help," he said.

"No problem," she said, climbing in on the other side, knowing enough about her boss to know that he did not want her help getting into his car and stowing his wheelchair away.

He handed her his coffee, and she slipped it into the cup holder between the seats. Then he lifted his body up with his arms' strength and slowly lowered himself into the driver's seat.

"Remind me to never arm wrestle with you," she said.

With a quick grin, he nodded. "I'll do that."

He twisted back to his chair, flipped the releases that collapsed it and picked it up and placed it behind his seat. Turning back, he pulled his seatbelt across his body and started the car. "Ready to go home?" he asked.

She nodded. "More than ready."

He maneuvered the car down the ramp and onto the street, driving north on Sheridan towards Maria's condo. "Oh, by the way," he said when he pulled up to the front of her building. "Today, well, this was above and beyond the call of duty. So, I'd like to do something for you."

Surprised, Maria turned to him. "Really, that's not necessary…"

"No, I insist," he said, taking one of her hands in his and meeting her eyes. "Maria, you can keep the clothes."

Chapter Twenty-four

The quaint tavern sat on the corner of a quiet, Irish neighborhood. It didn't advertise in any papers, didn't run ads on any of the radio stations in the Chicago area and didn't have an obnoxious neon sign blazing over the door. But every night it was filled with people looking for a good meal, a quiet place to meet and the company of old friends.

About ten years earlier, because of a new city ordinance, the owners had put in a handicapped accessible ramp, a change that Pete was very grateful for as he rolled down the easy grade towards the big, oak door that had a simple wooden sign on it saying "Slainte," an old Irish toast meaning "to your health."

Pete pulled the door open and slipped inside. Quickly scanning the room, he found Sean and Jamal at a corner table. He looked over to the bar and saw the owner, Robby O'Sullivan, wiping down the ancient wooden bar with a white towel. Pete had known Robby since he was a boy in high school, when Robby's hair was still red, his inseam matched his waist size and his son had been one of Pete's best friends. Now, the hair Robby had left was silvery white and the belly hiding under his apron overlapped his belt by more than a few inches.

"Well, if it isn't the mighty attorney come to share a glass with us," Robby said as he tucked the towel into his back pocket. "I'm sorry, I am, that we don't have none of them girlie drinks you've become so fond of."

A rousing chuckle spread across the dimly lit room like a soft wave.

Pete paused near the bar and raised his chair, so he was eye to eye with O'Sullivan. "It's not the drinks I'm fond of, Robby, my boy. It's the girlies that come with them. They can't keep their hands off me."

"Isn't that the truth," Katherine Mary O'Sullivan, Robby's wife, called out as she came through the swinging kitchen door into the bar. With a tray filled with food in her hand, she quickly paused to give Pete a quick kiss on the lips. "If it wasn't for my Robby, they'd have competition."

"If it wasn't for Robby, there'd be no others to compete with," Pete called after her, laughing at the swish of her hips and the cheeky wink she tossed back at him.

"What will you have, Pete?" Robby asked with a grin.

"Could you build me a Guinness?" he asked. "And what's tonight's special?"

"Fish and chips with a side of house coleslaw," he replied.

"Sounds perfect," Pete said. "I'll be with O'Reilly."

He rolled across the room, shaking hands and being greeted by many of the regulars, and finally reached the corner table. Jamal sat in one chair with a large burger and steak fries in front of him. Sean sat next to him, his back against the wall and the door in plain sight, enjoying a Rueben sandwich.

"Took you long enough," Sean commented, scooping up a bit of ketchup with a steak fry. "I was worried I'd have to buy more food for Jamal."

Jamal smiled and took another large bite of his burger.

"This kid must have a hollow leg," Sean added.

"I don't have a hollow leg," he argued with a grin. "I'm just a growing kid."

"Yeah, and I just bet you want dessert, too," Sean said.

His mouth full of food, Jamal could only nod his head eagerly.

Pete snatched a fry from Sean's plate, dipped it in the ketchup and tasted it. "Well, we had a little company on the drive home," he said, lowering his voice and edging closer to the table. "But we lost them near Foster and Sheridan."

Nodding, Sean put his food down and leaned towards Pete. "Who were they?"

"Unmarked, black SUVs," Pete said. "They could have been anybody. But I'm guessing CPD."

Sean shook his head. "Yeah, I think you're right," he said. "And I'm not surprised."

"They didn't hurt that little lady from your office, did they?" Jamal asked, the smile gone from his face.

"No, Maria made it home safe and sound," Pete told him and then turned to Sean. "Are you going to tell me what this is all about?"

"Are you in?" Sean asked, picking up another fry and leaning back in his chair just before Katherine swept in with Pete's plate.

"Don't you both look like you're plotting something fearful," she said, placing the food down in front of Pete and putting her hands on her hips.

"Just saving the world again," Sean said.

Katherine stared at Sean for a moment and cocked her head slightly. "Why do I feel you're telling me the truth of it?" she asked slowly, searching Sean's eyes. "And why is my blood running cold?"

"Don't worry," Pete replied. "When O'Reilly and O'Bryan work together, even the devil himself runs away."

"And we're working together?" Sean asked.

Pete lifted his Guinness in Sean's direction and toasted him. "Slainte," he replied before taking a sip of the dark ale.

Sean picked up his glass of water and saluted his friend. "And to you," he replied.

Chapter Twenty-five

Pete rolled his chair across the scarred wooden floor of the tavern and stopped in front of the bar. He pushed the button on the arm rail, and the chair rose so once again he was eyelevel with Robby. Leaning forward, his forearm resting on the bar, Robby nodded. "What can I do for you?" he asked, his voice lowered.

Pete smiled. Robby and Katherine were in the very small circle of people Pete considered trusted friends. They had helped him with a number of his cases, digging out information he couldn't get because of both his handicap and his high profile. They were true blue and it had nothing to do with the fact that he had purchased this tavern for them when the owner was trying to close them down and sell the property to the city for a parking lot. They had been friends before and that's what friends did for each other.

Pete slid the keys to his car slowly across the bar surface, and Robby closed his hands over them. "I need to run an errand with Sean," he whispered. "Could you put her in the garage when it's a little quieter?"

If someone were to overhear the conversation, they would assume Pete was speaking about the busyness of the tavern. But Robby knew Pete wanted the car hidden when there was nobody, especially police officers, around to witness it.

Robby nodded. "I'll see it's done and I'll place the keys in the usual spot," he said.

"You're a good man, Robby O'Sullivan," Pete said.

"No better than the man I'm looking at," Robbie replied.

Lowering the chair, Pete rolled back, turned his chair and moved towards a small hall at the back of the taverns that housed the bathrooms and access to the storeroom. Katherine was waiting there, with Sean and Jamal, and a keychain in her hand. "I'm ready when you are," he said.

She pushed a key into the deadbolt to the storeroom and then shoved open the heavy door. The room was narrow and long, holding shelves with the accoutrements needed to run a thriving tavern. Katherine let them all in, then went behind, pushing the door closed and locking it behind them.

"This is so cool," Jamal whispered, looking at the shelves filled with large cans and jars.

"Aye, but not so cool as the freezer," Katherine said as she pulled on the latch of a metal door and revealed a large, walk-in freezer.

The space was narrow, with metal shelves filled with all kinds of meat, as well as frozen desserts. Katherine led the way, followed by Pete with Sean holding onto the chair handles and pushing his friend across the slippery, frozen floor, with Jamal taking up the rear.

"This is the only place we have a loading dock," she explained as they walked to the other end of the freezer space. "So, it's the safest place for you to exit the place."

Turning another lock, she pushed the door open and peered outside. "There's no one about," she said. "You'll be safe."

It was more of an order than a question and Pete nodded. "Yes, we'll be fine," he said. "We just want to keep our little friend here under the radar."

Turning to Jamal, she smiled. "Well, you're welcome back here any time, young man," she said.

"Thank you, ma'am," he replied. "You make some fine food here. My grandma would even like it."

She chuckled softly. "Well, that's high praise indeed," she said. "You be sure to bring your grandmother with you the next time you come."

"I will, ma'am," he said with an eager nod. "I sure will."

Sean crept around Pete and out the door to the loading dock. He'd already parked his cruiser in the back but quickly jogged down the ramp to move the car closer to the building. In a matter of moments, Pete was in the passenger seat, his chair stowed in the trunk. Jamal was in the back seat and Sean was ready to put the car in reverse and pull out of the small lot near the alley.

Sean glanced up and nodded to Katherine who waved and stepped back inside, pulling the door securely closed behind her. Then he turned to Jamal. "Okay, I need you to make yourself as short as possible back there," he said. "And if we are coming up to any cars, you hit the cushions, got it?"

Jamal nodded, a look of fear replacing the smile he'd just been wearing.

"Hey, kid, don't worry," Sean said with an easy smile. "No one is going to catch us. I'm just taking precautions. That's all."

Watching through the rearview, Sean saw Jamal's face ease up a little, but there was still concern etched across it. Smart kid, he thought.

He pulled down the narrow, side streets and headed west, towards the church. The neighborhood they'd been in, Canaryville, was on the southwest side of the city. It was a close-knit community that looked out for its own. Both Sean and Pete had known they'd be safe there. But moving beyond those borders, down Pershing Road past Halsted Street, they'd need to be on the alert for the people who had been following Pete earlier that evening.

The sky was the gray-lavender hue of twilight, and the street lights were beginning to glow. The traffic was light, most of the rush hour traffic having dissipated about an hour earlier. Sean and Pete didn't talk at first, each watching for a sign they were being pursued.

"They don't know you're involved," Pete finally said.

Sean shook his head. "No, and I'm trying to keep it that way."

"Smart move," Pete replied. "It'll give you more access to whatever we might need to solve this."

"Yeah, about that," Sean said. "This is not going to be one of those 'we got the bad guys and now we're done' kind of crimes."

"You telling me I thought I signed up for a date to the prom and we're actually married now?"

Sean grinned. "Pretty much."

"Shit."

Jamal giggled.

Pete turned and looked over at Jamal. "You probably shouldn't repeat words like that in front of your grandmother," he said.

Jamal nodded. "Yeah, I know. She'd tan my hide for sure."

Pete choked and Sean chuckled. "Jamal," Pete finally said, "I think I'm going to like your grandmother."

Suddenly, Jamal's eyes went wide and he inhaled sharply.

"What?" Pete asked.

Lifting a shaking arm, Jamal pointed up into the sky in the west and a little north of where they were driving. Pete and Sean looked over. "What are we looking for, Jamal?" Sean asked, taking his foot off the accelerator.

"That cloud, over there," Jamal said. "It's just like last night. Swirling and all. It's just like what brought those things to the park. It's happening again."

Sean turned his attention to the northwest. "Damn," he muttered, seeing the powerful, black vortex wrapping around itself. Switching on his siren, he accelerated down the street.

"Well, holy hell," Pete said. "I've never seen anything like it."

"Yeah, me either," Sean said, passing Ashland Avenue and heading towards Damen. "It looks like it's right over the park."

"What the hell is going on?" Pete asked.

"Well, don't look now, but I'm going to be showing you a wedding reception you're never going to forget."

Chapter Twenty-six

Sean's unmarked police car sailed past Damen Avenue and then slowed as it moved parallel to the large, city park. The park totaled about 70 acres and featured a large lagoon in the center. Trees on the outskirts of the property hid the center of the park from the street view, making it a popular place for gangs.

"Are you going to call in some backup?" Pete asked.

Shaking his head, Sean sent an apologetic glance to his friend. "Sorry, I can't," he said. "I don't know who the good guys are yet, and I can't risk Jamal's safety."

Pete glanced over his shoulder to see Jamal cowering in the back seat, his eyes transfixed on the cloud.

"Then maybe we ought to give up the chase and just take Jamal to wherever we started to go in the first place," Pete suggested, turning back to Sean.

"Yeah, that would seem to be the safest way to handle it," Sean said. "But I've got a feeling that the more people that witness what's going down, the safer Jamal is going to be."

Sean turned onto an access road leading into the park as the cloud dipped below the tree line. "I think it's dropping over by the baseball diamonds," he said, passing by the lagoon on the right and following the twisting path through a forested area. "I'll park behind the fieldhouse."

The parking lot was deserted, and Sean drove the car to the edge of the lot, pulling up onto the grass. The sky was now dark and opaque, and Sean flipped on his high beams to see into the baseball fields. Suddenly, debris started slamming up against the side of the car.

Pete looked up at the cloud lowering itself towards the ground. "Is this what Jamal was telling me about?" he asked. "Like something out of a slasher movie?"

"Yeah, exactly," he said. "And if we have a couple more witnesses…"

"It makes it harder to shut us up," Pete finished and then added, "Not impossible…"

Sean nodded, his face grim. "But harder."

Jamal whimpered and clapped his hands over his ears, sliding lower into the back seat. Sean looked out the window and his stomach twisted. Bodies, more than a hundred bodies, lay scattered in the grass less than fifty yards away, and even from this distance, Sean could see they had been brutally dismembered.

Sean felt a tug on his shirt and turned to see Pete pointing to a rise just beyond the bodies. Sean followed Pete's direction, and his heart stopped for a moment. He'd never seen anything like them. Tall, skeletal and fierce, they moved with long, gangly gaits, their arms like tree limbs scraping against the ground. Their backs were slightly rounded and their heads bowed as they followed their leader across the field, blood shimmering on their weapons. As the leader, mounted on a white horse, reached the top of the rise, he stopped and turned. The horse reared, its mighty hooves slashed the air, and its mane whipped in the wind, demonstrating its supremacy. But the actions of the horse did not affect the leader who had turned in his saddle and now stared back at Sean and Pete with blood-red glowing eyes.

"Holy shit," Pete whispered, his mouth dry. "What the hell have you gotten me into this time?"

Jamal sobbed. "It's them again," he cried. "They gonna kill everyone."

Sean ripped his seatbelt off and grabbed hold of the door, Pete's hand on his arm staying him for a moment. "Are you crazy?" Pete asked.

Sean shook his head. "I've got to go," he said. "It's my job."

He paused and lowered his voice. "You stay in here with Jamal," he said. "If I'm not back in five minutes, you take the radio and call for backup.

Then call my friend Ian and have him come and get you. His number is on my phone."

Pete nodded. "Don't be stupid, Sean," he said.

Sean took a deep breath. "Yeah, good advice."

The wind nearly threw him back against the car when he got out. It blew the door shut with a slam, and Sean was nearly doubled over as he pushed against the wind, his weapon drawn, and moved towards the murky mist before him. Up ahead, he could hear screams filled with horror and pain, and he rushed forward.

The gray, swirling cloud was right in front of him. Sean took a deep breath and then stepped inside, tiny bits of dirt hammering his face felt like a sandblaster against his skin. He lifted one arm, protecting himself from the larger pieces, batting his arm against the newspapers, soda cans, and bottles, and muscled his way forward. A few more steps and he stepped out of the wind into the dim twilight of the park. He could hear the screams again, but this time they were nearer. His stomach twisted as he watched the horror unfold before him.

Creatures. Monsters. He didn't know what to call them, but they were still at the other end of the field. They were huge, at least twelve to fourteen feet tall. They looked like...trees...but not trees. Their arms were like long branches and their bodies were moss covered. Their faces were long and fierce, their eyes devoid of humanity.

They welded long swords and swept them back in forth in a scything movement, decapitating and dismembering the horror-struck gang members before them. Sean pulled his gun from his waistband and ran forward.

"Stop!" he yelled. "Police!"

The creatures paid no attention, moving forward like harvesters reaping a field with giant, brutal swings.

Sean stopped, anchored himself and fired at the monster closest to him, fifteen yards away. It paused and turned, glaring at Sean with glowing red eyes. Sean swallowed. "Stop!" he forced himself to yell again. "Police!"

The creature turned and whipped its sword around, cutting off the screams of yet another human being.

Sean could smell the metallic tang of blood; he could taste it in his mouth. The creatures had cut a wide swath through the gangs and had left body parts strewn all around the baseball field in pools of the victims' own blood. Moving forward, Sean stepped around the bodies and the blood and pursued the creatures as they made their way forward, increasing the carnage on the field.

Why the hell weren't these kids running?

Then he realized it. They were so frightened, they were in shock.

"Run!" Sean yelled. "Run to the lagoon!"

The gang members, frozen in fear, finally started to move.

"Now!" Sean screamed. "Run like hell!"

There were only a few dozen left, but almost as one they started to run beyond the field and towards the lagoon. Sean watched as they pushed through the wall of wind, slapping at the dirt and debris, and disappeared from his sight. The sigh of relief caught in his throat when he turned back to see the creatures were now facing him.

"Shit."

He brought his gun forward and pointed it at them. For a brief, hysterical moment, he thought about telling them they were all under arrest, and then he took a deep breath, wondering what it felt like to die.

The wall of creatures parted in military precision, and the rider on the white horse appeared from the rear of the group and galloped towards him. He was like the other creatures, but he wore the skull and antlers of an elk on his head.

So this is what the Elk King looks like, Sean thought. At least I'll get taken down by royalty.

Sean fired a warning shot above its head. "Stop! Police!" he yelled, pleased with himself that he still could use his voice.

The Elk King came closer and lifted its long, sinewy arm, the silver blade of the sword glistening in the dim light. Everything seems to be happening in slow motion, Sean thought. He could hear the pounding of the horse's hooves on the sod, could actually see the dirt being ripped up from the ground and flying into the air. He could feel the ground trembling beneath him and smell the combination of primeval forest and death in the air. He widened his stance, held his arms out in front of him and emptied his gun into the oncoming creature. The bullets did nothing and his enemy continued forward.

The Elk King pulled his arm back, cocking it as you would a gun, ready for the release. For one moment, Sean pictured his family and hoped they would understand that he died doing his job. The sword started to move forward. Sean could almost hear the blade cutting the air before him. He didn't close his eyes. He had made that decision when he was twelve years old. He wasn't going to meet death with his eyes closed.

The sword arched and Sean took a deep breath.

Clang!

It took him a moment to realize that was not the sound he was supposed to hear. He turned to see Em, her sword before her, parrying her sword against the Elk King. Even though she was at a disadvantage because she was on her feet, she was engaging him stroke for stroke. But how long would she be able to do hold on?

Em had moved to the left, causing the Elk King to swing to his right, over the side of his horse. There was only one thing Sean could think of doing. He ran forward and punched the horse in the face with all his might. Faltering, the horse slipped sideways on the bloodied ground, and the Elk King lost concentration for a moment. But that was all Em needed. Swinging her sword, she brought it down on his wrist.

Sean heard a sound, like an ax cutting wood, and a moment later the hand and the sword of the Elk King lay on the ground.

The Elk King stared at Em for a moment, lifted his head and screamed. A long, blood-curdling wail echoed in the park. Urging his horse into action, he galloped back to his army, and in a moment, they were enveloped by the whirling cloud and disappeared into the sky.

Sean turned to Em. "Who the hell are you? Batman?" he asked.

"Who?" she responded.

Shaking his head, he stepped forward but tripped on something lying in the grass. Looking down, he recoiled when he saw a decapitated head, eyes staring up at him. He stumbled backwards, landing upright against a tree, and gagged.

"Sean, what's wrong?" Em asked, the darkness of the night covering the head.

He wanted to reply, wanted to say something pithy, but his body decided to finally react to the carnage all around him. He held up his hand, then turned around and lost all of his dinner on the roots of the tree.

Em lifted her sword and it started to glow, casting a soft light around them. She gasped softly when she realized what had happened. "This is what the boy saw?" Em asked.

Sean nodded. "Yes," he whispered, taking a deep breath. "Yeah, I think this is exactly what he saw."

"It was the Elk King and the Wild Hunt."

"I kind of thought it might be," he replied, turning and meeting her eyes. "I would have died..."

She shrugged. "You need to get a sword," she interrupted him and bent down to retrieve the sword the Elk King had left behind. "This is Chrysaor."

He shook his head. "I won't use that," he said.

"Chrysaor is the sword of the Knight of Justice," she replied, walking to him with the sword lying on her outstretched hands. "It is the right sword for you."

"No, it still has their blood on it," he replied.

"What better reminder of the lives you must avenge?" she asked, lifting her eyebrows in question. "What better reminder of the heartless creatures you fight against?"

Tentatively he reached forward and took the hilt in his hand. He could feel a jolt of power surge through him when he touched it. "I can feel it," he whispered.

She nodded. "Then you can control it," she said. "It will be a good partner for you."

He lifted the sword from her hands and held it against his side. "No, the only partner I want right now is you," he said, and then he hefted the sword, testing its weight and balance. "But this will be an excellent tool. Thank you again."

"It was my honor," she replied, "Partner."

Chapter Twenty-seven

"Pete and Jamal, I'd like you to meet Em," Sean said as he opened the back door and helped her slide inside, placing his sword on the floor in the back seat.

"She's a good guy," Sean added. "She's on our side."

Jamal slowly nodded his head, still too traumatized to speak.

Once Sean had settled into the driver's seat, Pete turned to him. "So, do you want to explain what happened?" Pete asked.

Sean shook his head. "Let's wait until we get back to the church," he said. "Then we can have a long conversation."

On a hunch, he flicked on his radio scanner and listened to the dispatcher's calls. At first they were regular calls, accident reports and a domestic violence call. But a few moments later, a call went out to all available cars and named their park.

"That's my signal to go," he said, putting the car into reverse and pulling out of the parking lot onto the street. He continued down Pershing Road in silence until his cell phone rang, startling all of them.

Sean picked it up and put it through the car's speaker system.

"O'Reilly."

"Hey, Sean, it's Adrian. I think we've got another call like last night," he said. "Do you want in?"

Closing his eyes for just a moment, Sean shook his head slowly. "Hey, thanks, but my case load is too heavy right now," Sean said, his voice feigning lightness. "Besides, I'm heading home to Tiny, and you know how he gets when dinner is late."

Adrian chuckled. "Yeah, your cat is worse than a wife," he replied.

"So, was anyone hurt this time?" Sean asked.

"No one that matters," Adrian said chuckling, "just a bunch of gang-bangers. This keeps up and we'll have Chicago cleaned up in no time."

"Yeah, but then they'll transfer you to Animal Control," Sean joked, though his stomach was twisting in his gut.

"Just one group of animals to another," Adrian replied. "Well, gotta go. Oh, wait, your report from last night never did come through."

Sean met Em's eyes through the rearview mirror. "I'll send it again once I get home," Sean said.

"Great, just trying to tie up all the loose ends," Adrian said. "Thanks."

The connection on the other end died. Sean picked up his phone and turned it off, just to be sure there was no way their conversation could be heard.

"The call just came through from dispatch," Pete said. "There's no way he could have known the incident tonight was like the one from last night."

"No way unless he knew what was going to happen before it happened," Sean said.

"Could a detective—" Pete began.

Sean shook his head, cutting him off. "No, he couldn't do this on his own, but who the hell he's working with is a good question."

"We don't know who they have," Em interjected. "We just know it's above district level."

"Someone from headquarters?" Pete asked.

"Or someone who has a hold over someone from headquarters," Sean surmised.

"Yes, exactly," Em said. "We just know that strings have been pulled in the past to stop our investigations from getting too close."

"So what is this all about?" Pete asked. "What does this mean?"

Sean pulled into the parking lot of the church and pulled around to the back, hiding the car behind a cinderblock wall. He turned off the car and turned to his friend. "I would like to say that all of your questions will be answered once we get inside," he said. "But I'm afraid that you're going to have even more questions once you get the first ones answered."

Chapter Twenty-eight

Before they got to the door, Gillian and Ian already had it opened and were waiting for them. Coming forward, Gillian hurried over to Jamal and smiled. "I bet you'd like to see your grandmother first thing," she said.

He nodded, his voice trembling. "Yes, ma'am, I would."

She looked up, met Em's eyes, nodded, and then placed her arm around Jamal's shoulders. "Well, why don't you let me show you the way," she said and then turned to Em. "And I'll meet up with the rest of you later."

Sean stood by the open door and watched Gillian lead Jamal down the hall and up the stairs. When he could no longer hear their footsteps, he staggered back into the parking lot and, grabbing hold of a garbage can, vomited again. Ian hurried to his side. "That bad, was it?" he asked softly.

"I pray I never see anything like it again," he said, his voice low. "The carnage. The savagery. The blood. And when I think that Jamal saw something just as bad..."

He bent over the garbage can, emptying out the last vestige of any food in his stomach and then took a shuddering breath. "We've got to stop this," he said.

"Aye and we will," Ian said. "Are you ready to talk about it?"

Sean nodded. "Yeah, I'm good now."

They all moved inside to reconvene in Father Jack's living area where the tea pot had already been put on the burner. Once Sean had introduced them all to Pete, he recounted his experience at the park.

"Dammit, Sean, you can't put yourself in that kind of situation again," Ian insisted. "You can't go in there unprotected."

"I'm not unprotected anymore," he said. "Em gave me a sword."

"And now you need to learn how to use it," Em said simply. "And you must carry it with you at all times."

"Sorry, a sword isn't standard issue," Sean replied. "And I don't know how the chief would feel about me carrying a sword around the streets of Chicago."

"Well, your chief wouldn't have to know," Em said. "I can make it invisible to all but you and those of us who can see through glamour."

"Aye, faery glamour," Ian said slowly. "I've been doing some research today. It seems to me that glamour could be a formidable weapon."

"What do you mean?" Sean asked.

"These creatures, the Wild Hunt, could be seen, not only today, but yesterday with Jamal," he replied. "You could all see all of them. They weren't using glamour."

"So?" Sean asked. "I mean, they were ugly sons-of-bitches, and I would have preferred not to see them."

"Sure a lot harder to fight things you can't see," Ian replied. "And, more to the point, if they ever decide to use their glamour, how do we see through it?"

Sean nodded. "I hadn't thought of that."

"He's got a good point," Em said. "We've never been at war before. We haven't thought things through from a defensive angle."

Father Jack nodded. "That's true," he said. "I've never worked with a group so large before, nor in a situation so treacherous."

"I know I'm the new kid on the block," Pete said. "But can you give me an overview of what's going on here?"

Sean nodded. "Sorry, I forgot to let you know that Pete signed on to the group."

"Signed on? Without knowing the particulars?" Em asked.

"Well, Sean told me it would be worth my time," Pete said. "So, I'm in."

Surprised, Em stared at Pete. "You trust him that completely?" Em asked.

Pete glanced at Sean and then back at Em. "With my life," he said.

The tea kettle whistled and Father Jack stood up, walked over to the small kitchenette and poured the water into a large tea pot. Placing the pot on a tray with cups, saucers, cream and sugar, he carried it across the room and set it on the coffee table in the center of the room. Em walked over to the pantry next to the kitchenette and retrieved a couple of packages of cookies and, without pretention, placed them on the table next to the tea.

"Em, you're supposed to put them on a serving plate," Father Jack said with a wry grin. "To make it look pretty."

Em pulled a gingersnap from the box and bit down. "Why? It just dirties a plate," she replied.

Pete looked over at Sean and grinned. "You two *are* made for each other," he teased.

211

Father Jack sent Pete a quick smile, poured himself a cup of tea and sat back in his chair. "So, Pete, let me tell you a story to try and help you understand what Sean has gotten you into," he said.

Chapter Twenty-nine

Before Father Jack began his story, Ian stood. "I'm going to find Gillian," he said. "Please excuse me."

He closed the apartment door softly behind him and walked slowly down the hallway, his mind racing with the events of the day. He'd seen the photos of yesterday's crime scene, had seen what condition those bodies had been in, and to think that Sean had nearly been another victim. How could he ever explain to Mary, Sean's sister and Ian's dear friend, what had happened? How could he tell the rest of Sean's family?

He knew that Sean was safe. He knew that his concerns were now unfounded. But he also knew that he needed to express those thoughts and fears, and he also knew there was only one person who would understand.

He spied Gillian backing out of a room ahead of him and waited until she had closed the door before he spoke. "Is everything fine in there?" he asked.

She jumped and turned. "Ian, you gave me a start," she replied, holding her hand to her chest, and then she saw his face. "Tell me."

For a moment his throat tightened with emotion and he just shook his head. "He nearly died," he said, his voice low. "He nearly became a victim, like the ones we saw in the crime scene photos. He nearly had his head…"

He couldn't go on. Couldn't say the words.

Gillian hurried to him and put her arms around his waist, pulling him close. He wrapped his arms around her and laid his cheek on her head, absorbing the comfort she was offering. She nestled closer and sighed. "Aye, Jamal told me he'd gone into the cloud to fight the creatures," she whispered. "Your Sean is a great, wondrous fool and a very brave man."

"He saved some of them," Ian said. "He yelled at them to run and they did. That's when the creatures turned on him."

She shuddered in his arms. "Why weren't they running on their own? Why did it take Sean to warn them?"

He stepped back, his hands sliding to her waist and shrugged, as he tried to make sense of it himself. "I don't know, perhaps it was because they were frightened by the sight of them," he said. "They saw their friends being hacked to bits, saw the creatures attacking, and froze." He paused and met her eyes. "It seems to me they could see them. But I had an awful thought as I was listening to Sean's account. What if it had been even worse? What if Sean hadn't been able to see the creatures?"

"Glamour," she replied with a nod. "It's been one of the weapons of choice of the fae for centuries."

"Aye, and it also means that we never know if we are being followed or spied upon," he said.

"Or walking into a trap," Gillian added.

"And if this truly is a war we're getting into," he said slowly, "we need some kind of faery radar."

"I like that idea," she said. "It would be helpful, especially if we are to give shelter to those the faery seek. Since the church is decommissioned, it does not offer the same protection it once would have."

Ian was silent for a moment, ruminating over their conversation. A few moments later he looked at her and Gillian could see by the intensity of his eyes, he was already into research mode.

"The laboratory you have downstairs; is it only for research on the Book of Kells?" he asked.

Gillian shook her head and smiled. "No, as a matter of fact, it's set up with a wide array of material we might need for the Order."

"And the Internet access, is it secure?"

She nodded. "Aye, it's safe."

He cradled her head in his hands, gave her a quick kiss on the lips and stepped back. "Well, then, let's go discover a way to view the fae," he said, grabbing her hand and leading her down the hallway.

"Well, let's just," she repeated as she jogged down the hall to keep up with him.

They stepped inside the pristine facility and Ian immediately headed to the computer. "Come along," he urged Gillian. "I need you to do a search."

"A search?" she asked, incredulous. "Do you really think all we need to do is search 'how to see faeries' and it will appear?"

He nodded. "It's worth a shot, isn't it? Sometimes in research you start with the most obvious before you tackle the obscure."

Rolling her eyes, she moved past him and sat down behind the monitor. After logging in, she accessed a search engine and typed in the question. More than two dozen responses appeared, although half of them seemed to have something to do with a video game.

"Go to the oldest ones first," Ian said, "The ones that deal with legends."

She clicked on a site that dealt with faerie lore from an encyclopedia about fairy folklore that was originally published in the late 1800s. "This is the oldest information I can find," she said.

"Excellent, now search for faerie sight," he instructed, leaning over her shoulder.

Using the search engine within the site, she searched and found several entries. "This one talks about those born with sight," she sighed. "Not what we need."

"Ah, but look at the next one," Ian said, reading the description. "A wash of marigold."

"Marigold?" Gillian asked.

"It's also known as calendula," Ian said. "It's been around since early Egypt."

"I've heard of calendula," Gillian said. "As a matter of fact, I've used it as an ointment."

Ian nodded. "It has healing properties and supposedly it increases physic properties," he said. "So it makes sense that it could be used to see the fae. I was actually going to do a study on herbal lore in the future and calendula was one that has always intrigued me."

Gillian swung her chair around, stood up and wrapped her arms around Ian's neck. "I don't know which I find sexier," she whispered, kissing him lightly on the lips, "your body or your mind."

He wrapped his arms around her waist and kissed her back deeply, leaving them both breathless. "And here I thought it was my delightful personality."

She smiled up at him and then exhaled slowly. "Sorry, I distracted us. What do we do next?" she asked.

"Well, unless you've got a storehouse of dried herbs somewhere in here," Ian replied, "we need to wait until tomorrow and visit an herbalist to get what we need."

He bent over and kissed her neck. "And, in the meantime," he said softly, his breath tickling her ear, "I suggest we continue to be distracted."

She sighed and melted against him. "I could allow myself to be distracted for a wee break," she said, ending her sentence on a soft moan as his kisses traveled up her neck to the lobe of her ear.

He was just starting to kiss his way back down her neck when he paused and looked past her to the wall where the replicas of the pages of the Book of Kells hung. "Gillian?" he asked, all passion gone from his voice.

Aye, it's his body, she thought, frustrated. *I'm a wee bit tired of his mind just now.*

"Yes, Ian?" she replied, trying to be patient.

"That picture, it's one from the book, right?" he asked, moving away from her and walking over to the wall.

She wrapped her arms around her chest, instantly feeling the cold, and nodded. "Yes, it's one of the reasons I came to Chicago," she replied. "I did it because…"

But he was no longer listening to her. Instead, he studied the facsimile for another moment. The illuminated drawing seemed to be abstract, with one third of the picture having a blue background that formed a long, elliptical shape that was then surrounded on the bottom and one side by a tan background. On top of the background were drawings and inked words scattered willy-nilly across the face of the page.

Ian turned away from the drawing and hurried back to the computer. He bent over the keyboard and quickly typed into the search engine, and then he pressed the button to send his find to the printer sitting across the room. Once the page had been ejected, he walked over to Gillian, placed his arm around her shoulders and guided her back to the reproduction hanging on the wall.

"You've got to see this," he said, excited about his finding.

"Aye, I see it," she said.

Then, without saying a word, he lifted up the page with a full-color map of the city of Chicago, with Lake Michigan's blue waters matching the blue from the reproduction. Looking from the printed page back to the wall, Gillian nodded and smiled. "Aye, it's Chicago," she replied calmly. "And that's why I'm here."

"Wait. You knew the Book of Kells had a drawing of the city of Chicago?" he asked. "Somehow a monk from 6 A.D. in Ireland painted a picture of the city of Chicago?"

She nodded, biting back a smile. "Aye, it really was quite obvious once you took a good look at it," she replied, and then she patted him on the shoulder. "But don't worry me darling, I still think you're brilliant."

Not amused, he stepped away from her and walked back to the enlarged photo. "Okay, since I'm obviously the student here," he replied with a wry smile, "what are all of these markings?"

She joined him and shook her head. "I'm still working on it," she said.

She pointed to circles on the map, some of them small pin dots and some slightly larger. "Could they be portals to Tír na nÓg? And, if they are, what's the difference between their sizes?" she mused.

Ian quietly studied it and, without saying a word, went back to the computer. Soon the printer was discharging another sheet of paper. He picked it up and brought it back to Gillian and, once again, lifted it up to compare it to their photo from the Book of Kells. The printout showed Chicago, but this time there were a series of long lines of different thicknesses drawn across the city, intersecting each other at the different markings on the map.

"What's this?" Gillian asked.

"A ley line map of the city," Ian replied. "Do you know ley lines?"

She nodded. "Like rivers of magic or energy," she replied. "They seem to run from one ancient structure to another throughout the world. I didn't realize Chicago had so many."

"Aye, Chicago seems to be a major intersection of ley lines," he said, pointing to one of the thicker ones. "And this one ought to be of great interest to you. It not only runs from Chicago to Stonehenge, but it also runs through Glendalough County in Wicklow, Ireland."

Gillian turned to him. "The monastery?" she asked.

He nodded. "The oldest monastery in Ireland," he replied. "From about 6 A.D., which is about when your Book of Kells appeared on the scene. It's interesting, isn't it, that a line directly from that place would end up in Chicago?"

Moving Ian's map closer to the illustrated photo, she followed the line until in intersected with the largest circle on the drawing. "Interesting, yes," she replied. "But hardly a coincidence, I'm thinking."

Chapter Thirty

"So, what do you think?" Sean asked Pete as he drove him back to get his car at the bar.

"I think this whole thing is crazy," Pete replied. "And if I hadn't seen those creatures with my own eyes, I would be writing up commitment papers for your own good."

Chuckling, Sean nodded. "Well, keep those papers handy," he suggested. "This whole thing might drive me crazy yet."

Pete studied his friend for a moment and then spoke. "So, what's next?"

Sean shook his head. "Just like every other crime I've investigated," he replied. "I gather facts and collect evidence. I figure out means, motive and opportunity."

"What about your friend, Adrian?" Pete asked.

"Yeah, seems like he's caught up in it," Sean replied. "But he was a good cop, so that one is a little confusing."

"Not really," Pete said. "Think about what he said this evening. No one that matters got killed, just a bunch of gang-bangers. He could be convinced that he's doing a public service by allowing the Wild Hunt to kill them."

"But cops aren't supposed to think that way," Sean said. "We're not the judicial part of the system. We enforce the laws; we bring people to justice and then let the courts decide."

Pete shrugged. "Well, I've been in enough courtrooms to see that justice doesn't always happen," he said. "If they've got a good lawyer, if the police mess up on procedure, if they can intimidate the witness, they walk free. I can see a frustrated cop start to take things into his own hands."

Nodding slowly, Sean looked over at Pete. "Especially if you have some high-powered, faery friends who can magically take care of things for you," he agreed.

"And we can't rule out that he might be doing this against his will," Pete added. "It seems like the fae are known for manipulating situations for their benefit."

"Yeah," Sean said readily. "That makes a lot more sense than Adrian going bad."

"Wait a minute, Sean. I know you like the guy," Pete said. "But don't give him the benefit of the doubt too quickly. He seemed pretty happy to report on those deaths."

Sean pulled up next to the garage behind the bar and turned to Pete. "Are you sure you want to drive home tonight?" he asked. "We don't know who might be waiting for you."

"I can handle it," Pete replied. "I've had plenty of people after me in my line of business. It's just another case."

"Yeah, well, this time the folks after you have supernatural powers," Sean reminded him. "Watch your back."

Pete nodded. "I will," he said. "And if I run into any problems, I'll call you."

Sean grinned. "Make sure you do," he said.

Sean pulled Pete's wheelchair out of the trunk and set it next to the passenger door. Pete grabbed hold of the arms, lifted himself into it and rolled over to the garage. A small lockbox with punch keys was attached to the frame of the garage. Pete punched in a series of numbers and the box opened. Pulling out his keys and a garage door opener, Pete pressed the opener, then put it back in the box and locked it up.

He rolled into the garage, unlocked the car and was soon sitting behind the driver's seat.

"Be safe," Sean called, standing next to his car.

Pete nodded. "Yeah, and if I call, remember to bring your new sword," he replied with a laugh.

Sean looked down at the sword laying on the floor of his car and nodded. "You've got it," he said.

Waiting until Pete had pulled out of the garage, Sean walked over, pressed the button on the garage and waited for the large door to close. Then he climbed back into his car and drove down the alley towards Pershing Avenue. Once he was on Pershing and headed home, he saw a sign for an all-night donut shop and remembered his nightly appointment.

"Well, damn, I almost forgot," he muttered, turning into the drive-through lane.

"I need a large tea with extra cream and honey," he ordered. "And two blueberry muffins."

A few minutes later he was back on the road headed to Lower Wacker Drive and his nightly rendezvous with Hettie.

Chapter Thirty-one

Pete circled the block a couple of times, just to be sure he wasn't being followed and then finally drove into the secured parking garage adjacent to his high-rise. He pushed the security card into the reader, and the barrier to the garage opened smoothly, allowing him to drive through, and then closed quickly behind him. His parking spot was located in a bright area right next to the entrance to the lobby, so he wasn't worried about thugs waiting for him there.

Rolling into the lobby, he greeted the night watchman. "How's school going, Jeff?" he asked the young man who was a law student by day and a security guard by night.

"Great, Mr. O'Bryan," he replied with a wide smile. "Are you working late on a case?"

Pete nodded. "Yeah, I am," he said, pausing before the guard desk. "And it's one of those cases where a little extra caution isn't a bad idea."

Jeff's eyes widened. "Do you think you're in danger?" he asked.

Biting back a smile at the young man's enthusiasm, Pete shook his head. "Not if we're both alert," Pete replied. "Can I count on you?"

"Oh, yes, sir," Jeff said. "If I hear anything, I'll call the police."

Pete stopped on his way towards the elevator and looked over his shoulder. "Do you still have the phone number for Detective Sean O'Reilly?" he asked. "I gave it to you a couple of months ago."

Accessing his computer, Jeff looked up and nodded. "Yes, it's right here," he said.

"If anything happens, call Sean," Pete said. "I'm not sure who the bad guys and who the good guys are on this case. I know Sean's a good guy."

"Got it," Jeff said. "I'll call him."

"Thanks, Jeff," Pete said. "Have a good night."

The elevator opened, and Pete pushed the button for the Penthouse Suite. Then he inserted his passkey into the elevator controls to allow the elevator access to the top floor. In a few short moments, the doors opened into his suite. Pete pulled out his key and rolled out, then sent the elevator back down to the first floor.

His alarm system controls were next to the door. Scanning the readout for any irregularities, Pete felt a modicum of relief that nothing was out of the ordinary. He punched in his alarm code and deactivated it before rolling into his apartment.

The large picture windows in the front of his apartment looked out over the bright skyline of downtown Chicago and the dark depths of Lake Michigan. He placed his briefcase on the table behind the couch and rolled into the kitchen to pull a sparkling water out of the refrigerator. All he wanted to do right now was take a hot shower, change into sweats and relax.

He took a swig of the water, placed it in the cup holder in his wheelchair and rolled to his bedroom. The view from the bedroom was just as impressive as the one from the front room, the lights from the city sparkling in the distance. French doors in the middle of the wall led to a small balcony that he rarely used, and large picture windows stood on either side. He pressed a button on a control panel near the door, and vertical blinds began to automatically move across the window. He pressed another switch that flooded the room with soft light.

He was instantly on alert when he felt a rush of wind in the room. *Who the hell opened the French doors?*

He started forward when he caught sight of a movement in his bed.

"Hello, Pete."

He automatically reached for the gun he carried in an inner pocket of his wheelchair and pulled it out. "Who the hell are you?" he growled.

229

She sat up in his bed, her red hair flowing nearly to her waist and his silk sheet barely covering her naked body. She ran her tongue over her upper lip and smiled. "I'm your fantasy," she whispered. "I can make all of your dreams come true."

He laughed harshly while he secretly pressed the speed dial for Sean's phone. "Lady, I don't think so," he said. "Now, why don't you tell me why you are really here?"

"Pete," she purred, running a hand along the bed. "As you can see, I'm totally unarmed. Why don't you climb up here and we can get better acquainted."

"Thanks, but I don't really like aggressive women who show up in my apartment unannounced," he said. "It takes away a lot of the mystery."

She dropped the sheet and let it fall to her waist. "Some men don't like mystery."

He had to admit, she was very attractive. Inhumanly so. And he was surprised to find himself intrigued and even tempted.

"So, what are you? A faery whore?" he asked.

The comment hit home as her green eyes narrowed and her smile disappeared.

"You would do well to show some respect," she spat.

"I don't have a lot of respect for women who use their bodies to manipulate men."

She lay back against the pillows, the sheet dropping even further and she raised her arms over her head. "Tell me you aren't tempted," she whispered.

He shrugged, trying to maintain an outwardly calm façade while he mentally fought with his own desires. "So, how old would you be now?" he asked with a grimace. "I mean, would this be like making love with my great-great-great-grandmother or something like that?"

She hissed at him and leapt out of the bed in one graceful move. "Does your great-grandmother look like this?" she screamed.

Damn, he thought, clenching his jaw so it didn't drop open at the sight of her naked body in front of him. *She was beyond beautiful, she was flawless. Every curve, every inch of alabaster skin was begging to be touched and enjoyed.*

Her eyes widened as though she could read his mind. "Pete," she coaxed. "I could give you everything. I could make you walk again."

He felt a tingle in the muscles of his legs and looked down in shock. "How?"

231

"I have powers beyond that of your human doctors," she breathed as she came closer, stroking a hand down his chest. "You could sweep me up in your arms and carry me away to lavender fields where we could make love all day long. You could run again."

She slipped her hand lower, to his abdomen. "You could be a whole man again."

He looked up at her and seemed to forget why he was afraid, why he had been cautious. She was only a beautiful woman, a woman who wanted him, and he wanted her.

She smiled at him, stepped back and held out her arms. "Stand up, Pete," she said. "Stand up and take what's yours."

He looked down at his legs and saw in amazement that he could actually flex his feet. The shrapnel from the IED had severed his spinal cord, but somehow, he could feel his feet again. Bracing his hands on the arms of his wheelchair, he slipped his feet from the footplates onto the wood floor.

He nearly cried in astonishment as he felt the pressure from the floor against his feet. He could feel them. He could feel the pain of the atrophied muscles coming back to life. He could feel the blood moving through his calves, making them burn with pain. But it was an amazing pain!

He straightened up and stood. For the first time in nearly ten years, he was standing on his own.

She moved up to him, sliding her arms up around his neck, pressing her body against his own. She smelled like summertime and sex. He felt the hunger and the heat. He felt his heart race and his passions stir. He wanted her. No, he needed her. Just as he needed the air to breathe, he needed to make her his own. He needed—

"What the hell?" Sean yelled from the bedroom doorway.

Like a dousing of cold water, Pete was pulled back to reality. The room seemed to be spinning, and he reached out. But there was no one there. He looked around, gasping for air.\

He wasn't standing, he realized, he was sitting on the floor, his useless legs flailed out in front of him and his wheelchair collapsed on the ground.

"What?" he cried. "What happened?"

Sean stepped between Pete and the faerie –, his sword glowing with fire. "I think it's time you left," he said to the faerie, pulling a small, cork-topped bottle from his pocket. "Does holy water really scar the faces of faeries, or is that just a fable?"

"It's just a fable, mortal," she replied, stepping away from him. "You put that away or I will curse you."

Shrugging, Sean stepped closer to her. "I don't believe you," he said. He lifted the bottle to his mouth, pulled out the cork with his teeth and spit the cork across the room. "I guess there's only one way to find out," he said.

Screaming, she jumped out onto the patio and threw herself over the balcony into the night sky.

Sean laid the sword and bottle down then turned and knelt next to his friend who was stone-faced and staring at his fallen wheelchair. "She made me believe I could stand," Pete whispered hoarsely. "She made me think I could be a whole man again."

Sean had never known how much hate he could have for any creature until that moment. She had preyed upon his friend, used his deepest desires and manipulated them to destroy him.

Placing his hand on his friend's shoulder, Sean took a deep breath. "Who the hell told you that you aren't a whole man?" Sean asked.

"Listen, asshole, I can't stand up," Pete yelled.

"Yeah, I noticed," Sean yelled back. "That doesn't make you any less of a man. I see bastards out there every day who can walk on both legs who will never measure up to the man you are. Don't let some faery whore get into your head, man."

Pete chuckled. "She wasn't real happy when I called her that."

"Yeah, I floored the accelerator after that comment. I thought for sure you were going to be toast," Sean agreed with a grin. "And then the making love to your great-great-great-grandmother. Charming."

"I know how to flatter the ladies," Pete replied, and then he exhaled loudly and turned to Sean. "Thanks for saving me from the crypt keeper."

"Hey, no problem," he replied, reaching over and pulling Pete's chair next to him.

"Good thing you were carrying holy water," Pete said as he maneuvered himself back into his chair.

"Father Jack gave it to me this afternoon," Sean replied. "I'm sorry I didn't think to get some for you. But now we need to faery-proof your apartment."

"Do you think she'll be back?" Pete asked.

Sean met his friend's eyes. "I think this war has just begun."

Chapter Thirty-two

Sean slowed down the car as he traveled down Lower Wacker searching for Hettie. He'd received Pete's call before he'd had a chance to drop off her tea and muffins, and now that Pete's apartment was secure, he wanted to check on her before he went home.

A little worried that she wasn't in her usual spot, he was about to turn the car around and check the area again when he spotted her on the corner, pacing back and forth. He pulled up to the curb, grabbed the bag and the cup and climbed out of the car. She was still pacing and seemed distracted. She didn't even notice his approach. "Hettie, you had me worried for you," he said as he got closer.

She quickly turned in his direction, and he could see that her wizened eyes were wrought with worry. "I should say the same about you, Sean O'Reilly," she scolded. "There are things about this night that hold more harm than good."

Sean had read that people with mental illness often were more sensitive to paranormal phenomena, and he wondered if this was the case with Hettie. He handed her the tea and nodded. "Yes, it's been a night filled with strange goings-on," he admitted. "But I was able to hold my own."

She sipped her tea and studied him over the top of the cup. "Tell me," she commanded.

Shaking his head, he chuckled ruefully. "Hettie, you wouldn't believe me if I told you," he replied.

She snaked her bony hand into the bag and pulled out a muffin. Taking a large bite, she met his eyes. "Tell me," she said through a mouth full of food.

Leaning back against the street post, he nodded. "Okay, I will," he said. "But only if you promise me that if you see anything like a big cloud or a tornado approaching you will get away quickly."

She stuffed another portion into her mouth. "A cloud?" she asked, nodding as if she already understood.

"Yeah, a cloud," he repeated, making sure she comprehended the seriousness of the situation. "Don't worry about your cart. I'll replace everything, I promise. You just have to promise to get out of harm's way."

She smiled at him, and for a moment, the insanity was gone from her eyes. "You are a good man, Sean O'Reilly," she said softly. "And I am honored to be your friend. Now tell me."

He watched her eyes change back to the furtive nervousness he'd come to expect, and he wondered once again what tragedy had caused her to become who she was. "Okay, Hettie," he said, stifling a yawn. "I've promised you a story and a story you'll have."

He recounted the story of the Wild Hunt, and she listened with avid attention, devouring her food and drink while she listened. Wiping a grimy sleeve across her face and releasing a burp that would have made a man twice her size proud, she nodded to him. "You did fine, Sean, just fine," she said. "A braver man wouldn't have done what you did this night." She paused for a moment and sent him a devilish grin. "Nor would a smarter man."

Chuckling, he nodded. "Yeah, it was a little stupid, I agree," he replied. "But it was the only thing I could think of at the time."

"And the magic sword?" she asked. "Did you keep it?"

He nodded. "Yes, and actually it came in handy this evening when I had to chase a faerie from my friend's bedroom."

"I'm thinking he was not too pleased with that," she said, with a sly wink.

"Actually, once I broke in on their little tête-à-tête he seemed much more himself," Sean said.

"Ah, yes, they spin their glamour around mortals so most don't know which way is up," Hettie acknowledged.

Sean was taken aback for a moment by Hettie's familiarity with faery tricks. "How do you know about glamour?" he asked.

She paused for a moment and seemed to consider her words. *Or maybe*, Sean thought, *she is just trying to remember when in her life she first heard that term.*

"My family is from the old country," she replied, squinting her eyes and glancing up at him. "I know a bit of the traditions of the Sidhe."

"My family used to talk about the faery folk, too," Sean said. "My grandmother was the most superstitious."

"Aye, well is it superstition or knowledge?" Hettie asked with a rising of her eyebrows.

"Good point," Sean said. "I would now gladly bow to Grandma's far greater knowledge. Especially after the encounter in Pete's bedroom."

"And did the slut run away at the sight of the sword?" Hettie asked.

Sean grinned at Hettie's word choice, deciding the faerie wouldn't have been too happy with that designation either. "Well, she didn't run away at first, but when I threatened her with holy water, she was out the window in a flash, her long, red hair trailing behind her," he said.

Hettie's eyes sharpened. "Red hair?" she asked.

"Yeah," Sean nodded. "Clear down to her—"

He paused for a moment and Hettie cackled. "Her arse?" she asked.

Chuckling, Sean nodded. "Exactly."

"Well, that's surely interesting," she said, thoughtfully fingering her chin. "There are certainly curious things happening in Chicago."

"And I have a feeling that it's going to get curiouser and curiouser," Sean replied.

Hettie placed her frail, claw-like hand on Sean's arm and held it tightly. "You watch yourself, Sean O'Reilly," she said. "Do not trust the fae. They are a tricky and ungrateful race. They have no loyalties or allegiances. They care for themselves, first and only. Do you understand?"

Her tone was solemn and her face, grim. He nodded. "Thank you, Hettie," he said. "I understand."

She loosened her grip on his arm and stepped back, shaking a little. "Good," she said. "Now light my kindling and be off with you. You've wasted enough of my time this night."

Grinning, he knelt down and lit the small pile of sticks and paper until the flame was steady. "There you are, my lady," he said, offering her a slight bow.

She smiled at him. "If you have need of my help, you've only to ask."

"Thank you, Hettie," he replied, his heart warmed at her generous if not absurd offer. "I'll remember that."

Chapter Thirty-three

Em stood in the shadows near the northeast corner of Pete's high-rise and waited, ready to spring to action at a moment's notice. She didn't totally understand this bond she had with Sean, but since she'd been in closer proximity to him, she knew instinctively whenever he was in danger. The pit of her stomach would twist, and all of her senses would go on alert. Now, however, her feelings were calm, and she felt no apprehension. Whatever was happening in Pete's apartment seemed to be under control.

She stayed in the shadows, making sure that if Sean happened to step out on the balcony and glance down, he wouldn't see her. He didn't know she had been following him and, she admitted to herself, he wouldn't be happy if he found out about it. But twice she'd been able to pull him out of a dangerous situation and he seemed grateful. *Batman?* She shook her head. *Do I remind him of a man or a creature of the night?* She puzzled over it for a moment more. *But he said it in such a complimentary way... Besides,* she thought shaking her head decisively. *I really don't care what he thinks of me.*

She paused in her thoughts, looked up to the penthouse apartment, and sighed. She had never hidden from the truth; even as a child she had preferred truth over compassion. And now, she had to admit the truth, there was something about Sean O'Reilly that attracted her unlike any man she'd ever met. And perhaps that was the problem. Once she had bonded with Sean as a child, there had been no other men. He was in her dreams, in her thoughts, and now, in her life.

A movement on the balcony brought her springing forward, her sword in hand. Her use of glamour allowed her to move among most humans without being detected, but she didn't need to use it now because the street in front of the building was entirely deserted. Looking up, she saw the faerie jump through the patio door, onto the balcony, and then dive from the balcony, landing on the rooftop of the much shorter building across the street.

Em dashed forward, sheathing her sword as she ran across the street. She looked around the brownstone and ran to the back alleyway. Finding a fire escape platform attached to the back of the building about ten feet above the ground, she jumped up, caught the metal bar on the side and swung herself up to the first landing. Flattening herself against the side of the building, she waited for only a moment to ensure she hadn't been seen, and then she dashed up the metal steps to the roof. Quickly looking around, Em could see that the faerie was half a block away, leaping from rooftop to rooftop with little effort.

"Oh no, you are not getting away so easily," Em said, dashing across the gravel-topped roof and leaping to the next one, following in the faerie's path.

At the end of the block, the faerie climbed down a fire escape similar to the one Em had used to get to the rooftop, jumped down, and disappeared down a gangway between two apartment buildings. Em followed, stealthily stalking the faerie, more interested in following than apprehending. Em kept herself to the shadows and the ledges of the apartment buildings and, when forced to come out to the open, stayed low behind parked cars.

There was little traffic on the streets of the Lincoln Park neighborhood, a neighborhood made up of high-rises and brownstones with an occasional single-family home built between them. The shops on the main streets were a mixture of eclectic restaurants, exclusive day spas and high-end boutiques catering to the tastes of the residents. The strains of blues drifted out of the door of a corner pub but were quickly muffled by the metallic clanging of the elevated train only a block away.

The faerie turned left onto Oakdale Avenue, a residential street, and a block later dashed across Clark Street, a main, four-lane artery. Em wondered where she was leading her. Most of the fae were drawn to parks or other places where nature was prominent, but instead of heading towards the lake or Lincoln Park, she was going in the opposite direction into the residential area.

244

Em decided to get closer, just in case they had some kind of hideout in a home or apartment building. Jogging lightly, she was soon only a half-block from the faerie. The faerie reached the underpass of the elevated train, and Em smiled. Surrounded by iron pilings, she was sure the faerie was incredibly uncomfortable. If she was interested in interrogating the creature, this would be the perfect opportunity, when she was weakened by the metal.

Dashing forward, ready to apprehend the faerie, she suddenly realized the faerie had disappeared. Stopping in the middle of the gravel lot under the train tracks, she slowly turned around, studying the area. There was no place she could have gone. A train rushed by overhead, its sound nearly deafening, and Em looked up at it, wondering if the faerie had jumped up and hitched a ride.

She searched the area for another fifteen minutes and finally decided the faerie had given her the slip. With a sigh of disgust, she climbed the steps to the train station to ride back to the church on the other side of town.

As she climbed the steps she didn't notice the ground below shifting slightly. Two shadowed shapes emerged from below the earth and watched her, their green eyes luminous in the night sky. One whispered to the other, an inhuman chatter that was more like cicadas in the night. The other nodded and laughed softly.

245

Em paused at the top of the stairs, peered over the rail to the darkness and rubbed her hand over the back of her neck. *That's odd*, she thought, seeing nothing but the empty lot below. *I could have sworn I heard something.*

Chapter Thirty-four

Sean entered the station house at 7:30 am and hurried to the elevator. He had sent a revised version of his report to Adrian the night before, and now he needed to act like nothing out of the ordinary had happened.

"Hey, O'Reilly," Sarah Powers called out as he stepped out of the elevator on the second floor.

"Yeah, Powers, what do you need?" he asked.

"Aren't you supposed to be the donut guy this morning?" she asked.

Sean slapped his forehead with the palm of his hand. "Really, today's my turn?" he asked.

Shaking her head, she walked away in disgust. "My whole day is ruined," she muttered. "Thanks a lot."

Sean sat down at his desk, picked up the phone and punched in a couple numbers. The phone rang at a desk across the room, and Sarah hurried across the room to answer it. "Powers," she said into the phone.

Grinning, Sean leaned back in his chair and propped his feet on the top of his desk. "Is this the new recruit for the station?" he asked.

"No, I can't believe—" she began.

"This is Detective O'Reilly," he said. "And did you notice how I just used my title to emphasize that I outrank you?"

Sighing, she nodded. "Yes, I noticed."

"So, Sarah, I seem to have forgotten a major responsibility," he explained, biting back laughter. "And it seems that I might have even ruined someone's day because of my negligence."

"So, you're going to make it worse, right?" she replied.

"I'll pay," he said. "I just need you to pick out and pick up."

"O'Reilly," she growled.

"Think of it this way," he inserted. "You'll get the first pick."

She sighed. "Fine, I'll go," she said ungraciously. "But only because I've been dreaming about a Bavarian Cream-filled Long John all morning long."

"Yeah, get at least two of those," Sean said. "And Sarah?"

"What?" she muttered.

"Thank you," he said.

Standing, he walked across the room and handed her a ten and a twenty dollar bill. "Will that be enough?" he asked.

She grinned and shook her head. "Nope, I think I'll need at least forty more," she said, holding out her hand.

"Yeah, make it do," he replied. "And I'll be looking for—"

"O'Reilly," Captain Douglas called from his office doorway. "You got a minute?"

"Yeah, sure Captain," he replied, and then he turned to Sarah. "Thanks again, really."

She shrugged. "No problem," she said, lowering her voice. "And good luck with..." she motioned with her head in the Captain's direction, "whatever that ends up being."

"Yeah, thanks," he replied. "I might need it."

He tapped on the captain's door before entering.

"Come in," the captain called.

Sean entered, closed the door and, observing protocol, remained standing.

"Have a seat, O'Reilly."

"Thank you, sir," Sean said, slipping into a chair on the other side of the captain's desk.

The captain studied him for a few moments in silence. Sean wondered if he had heard anything about Jamal, and then an idea flashed into his mind. Could his captain be one of those working with Adrian? He'd really hate to discover that. He'd always admired and respected his captain.

"So, what are you working on, O'Reilly?" he asked.

Shrugging, Sean tried to look at ease even though his stomach was turning. "Just some follow-up on routine cases," he said.

The captain nodded and paused again. "I understand you got pulled into the incident the other night," he said. "The gang fight in the park. A young man was taken into Cook County, and you interviewed him?"

Sean nodded slowly and pasted a casual smile on his face. "Oh, yeah, that," he said offhandedly. "Adrian Williams called me in as a favor. He thought I could get the kid to talk about what happened."

"And did you?" the captain asked. "Get the kid to talk?"

Sean had never lied to his commanding officer. He understood the importance of the chain of command, and he also understood loyalty. He took a deep breath and nodded. "Yes, sir," he said. "He did talk to me."

The captain sat back in his chair, his fingers steepled in front of his mouth, and once again studied Sean. "Would you like to share what he told you?" he asked.

"Actually, sir, no I would rather not share that information," he replied.

A shadow of a smile appeared and then, just as quickly, disappeared on the captain's face. "You wouldn't," he repeated.

Sean shook his head. "No, sir. With all due respect, I wouldn't."

"And what would your father say about your response?" the captain asked.

Taking a deep breath, Sean thought about his response for a moment. "He would expect me to obey my oath to serve and protect the citizens of this community."

"And you believe that by not telling me what this young man said, it would both serve and protect the citizens of the community?" the captain asked.

"Yes, sir, I do."

"And what if I demanded that you share that information with me?" the captain asked, pushing his chair back away from his desk and standing.

"I'd tell you that I submitted a report with my findings last night and you'd be able to get that information from there," Sean said, keeping his eyes on the captain.

"And would the report have a full accounting of the interview?" the captain asked.

Sean paused only for a moment. "To the best of my recollection, sir," he said. "It was late and Williams called me in the middle of the night."

The captain walked around his desk and perched on the front of his desk in front of Sean. He pulled a small box out of the pocket of his suit jacket and opened it. "Stand up, O'Reilly," he said. Sean stood. Reaching into the box, the captain pulled out a small, gold lapel pin, stood up and pinned it on Sean's lapel. "I don't know anyone I'd rather pin this on than you," the captain said.

Sean tried to look down and see what had been pinned to his chest. "Excuse me, sir, but what is it?" Sean asked.

"It's an old Celtic symbol called St. Brigid's Cross," the captain replied softly. "It's worn by those who have sworn allegiance to an Order by the same name."

Exhaling softly with a great deal of relief, Sean nodded and met his captain's eyes. "Do you have one of these, too?" he asked.

The captain opened his jacket, and Sean saw the gold pin on the inside of his lapel. "I have found," the captain admitted, "that it's probably wiser to wear it in a less conspicuous place."

Sean unpinned it and pinned it to the inside of his jacket. "That's a good idea," he agreed.

"Why don't you take a few days off on paid leave to work on that special project I just assigned you?" the captain suggested.

Sean nodded. "Yeah, that would be very helpful," he agreed, then paused. "What would you like me to do about updates?"

"I believe in matters like these, the less said and written, the better," the captain replied meaningfully.

"That makes perfect sense to me," Sean agreed. "Thank you, sir."

The captain offered Sean his hand. "It's good working with you, Sean," he said.

"Thank you, sir," Sean said. "I feel the same way."

Chapter Thirty-five

The gymnasium on the third floor was Em's favorite place in the entire church. The tall ceilings, polished wood floor and bright skylights gave her the sensation of space, a feeling she rarely got in the city. A series of old, cotton gym mats were laid end to end on one side of the room for Em to practice self-defense moves and yoga for concentration. Rings, ropes and bars hanging from the ceiling created an above-ground obstacle course for elevated parkour training. And the old gymnastic equipment of parallel bars, balance beams, horizontal bars and a pommel horse substituted for her days of roaming the woods and fields near her birthplace in Ireland.

This morning she had searched through the old supply closets to locate some old fencing gear including face masks, padded jackets and a couple of jousting sabers in fairly good shape. She sniffed the jackets and then held them out at arm's length. They could certainly use a good airing and perhaps some sachets of lavender to hide their current aroma of old sweat and mold.

She held up the mask and wondered if Sean would even fit into one obviously designed for high school students. *He certainly was not built like a teenager*, she thought with a smile, remembering the view she received after his shower.

Even when wet, the golden highlights shone in his brown hair as he carelessly had toweled it dry, his toned biceps and pecs flexing easily with the movement. He had stepped away from the bathroom mirror and glanced out of the room. His eyes, a dark hazel green, had been distant, and she'd been sure he was contemplating her disappearance. A smile had tugged on her lips as she had watched him gaze around the hall once again, his white teeth worrying his full, lower lip for a moment. Then with a brisk shake of his head and a sexy scowl, he had tossed the towel he'd been using to dry his hair over the shower rod and turned towards her.

She remembered her quick intake of breath when he had nearly walked into her, and she had been barely able to move out of his way, so caught up in enjoying the view.

He had walked past her towards his bedroom, a towel slung low on his hips, and she'd had to bite back a sigh of pure admiration. He was built like one of the statues she'd seen in Europe, all smooth muscles and hard lines. The light dusting of hair on his chest and legs only enhanced his masculinity. He had moved with effortless ease and grace, a natural athlete, and Em's only regret was that she had stood behind him when he yanked off the towel, tossed it to the bed and pulled on a pair of briefs. However, she had to admit, the view from the back had been more than pleasing.

Remembering the back view, she grinned and shook her head. *No, definitely not a teenager.*

The faerie watched her from the doorway. Em was so distracted with her thoughts that he needed very little glamour to hide himself. Studying her, he saw her grin and was a little surprised. *So, the little warrior has been wounded by cupid's arrow*, he thought with a smile of his own. *Now this is an interesting development. But which one is it that holds the key to her heart?*

He turned his concentration to her thoughts. He couldn't dig very deep, but those thoughts on the upmost part of her consciousness were easy to access.

Em placed the mask back on the shelf and picked up a saber, holding it in her hand for balance. It would be far better for Sean to learn some basic fencing skills with something this light than swinging the broadsword around. The memory of Sean as a young man swinging the tree limb around, pounding the head of the Heldeofol, came rushing back to her mind, and she shook her head with an ironic smile on her lips. *Perhaps he was ready for a broadsword.*

The sound of the gym door opening brought her back to the present, and she turned quickly, her hand reaching for her own sword. But when she saw Sean standing next to the door, a hesitant look on his face, her heart melted a little bit more.

"Am I bothering you?" he asked.

Shaking her head, she walked forward to meet him. "No, you are welcome here," she said.

He looked around the room slowly. "Is this your sanctuary?" he asked, stepping forward to meet her.

She nodded. "It's where I keep my skills sharp. It's where I practice."

Stopping just in front of her, he lifted his hand to her cheek and stroked it lightly. "From where I stand," he whispered tenderly, "you have no need of practice when it comes to warfare. But what of other skills?"

Em stood, transfixed by his touch. The world seemed to have tilted just a bit below her feet, and she was taken off guard, a feeling she didn't really care for. The air around her seemed stifling instead of open as it had only a few moments earlier. And Sean's scent was unusual, like dark woods and musk. She had a hard time concentrating on his words. "I...I don't understand," she stammered. "What skills?"

Bending his head, he touched his lips to the underside of her jaw bone, and she felt a tingle of electricity race through her body. "These kinds of skills," he breathed, continuing his path from her jawbone up the side of her face to catch her earlobe between his teeth. "The skills between a man and a woman."

257

"No!" she stammered, trying to step away but coming to the horrifying realization that she couldn't move. "I don't want this. I don't believe in love."

He slowly moved his other hand up her arm, caressing her skin with his fingers. "So soft," he sighed. "So inviting. So ripe."

Her breath caught and her body trembled at the power of his touch.

"How does this make you feel?" he asked softly as he continued caressing her.

She moaned softly as he pulled her body against his and slipped his hand into her hair, grabbed a handful, and immobilized her so she couldn't turn away. He lifted his head and held it just inches from hers. She could feel her body pulsating with need. Her breath was escaping in small gasps and she was feeling light-headed.

He smiled triumphantly as he looked down at her flushed face and widened eyes. "How does this make you feel?" he demanded.

"Frightened," she confessed, wondering if this heart-pounding panic was really what humans desired in their relationships. "Please, I don't—"

"You don't want to disappoint me," he interrupted. "How sweet."

She was at war with her own body, caught under some kind of spell. She didn't want to desire him, didn't want to feel out of control. But she couldn't seem to help herself.

"I'm not ready," she pleaded as the fog of desire clouded her reason.

His lips curved in a vicious smile. "Good."

He crushed his lips against hers with an aggression that bruised her lips and ground her delicate inner mouth against her teeth. She tried to pull away, but he clenched her hair in his fist and yanked her head back, forcing her mouth open. He then plundered it mercilessly. He pushed against her, tripping her backwards until she was against the wall, pinned against his hard body. She felt his free hand gliding underneath her shirt and moving from her waist down her side, slipping into the waistband of her yoga pants and pushing them down.

No! her mind screamed through the fog. *I am not my mother. I will not end up like my mother.*

She struggled against him, trying to stop his hand, trying to get some space between them, trying to stop the onslaught against her body. Finally, she grasped his upper arms and pushed with all her might, forcing him to release his hold on her.

He stood only inches away, his eyes glittering with dominance and satisfaction.

She lifted her hand to her swollen lips and stared at him in shock. "I don't understand," she sobbed.

He took a quick, shuddering breath and smiled coolly. "No you wouldn't," he said with a contemptuous manner. "Although I have to admit, I am both surprised and disappointed." He straightened his jacket and shrugged. "I thought since your mother was a whore, you know, you might have inherited some of her passionate tendencies. But no such luck."

Reeling back as if he had struck her, Em shook her head. "No," she breathed. "What are you saying?"

Sean shrugged and walked towards the door. "I'm just saying you should stick to fighting," he replied with a smirk. "Unless, of course, you want to bore a man to death."

He walked out, closing the door sharply behind him. Em stared at the door, slowly sinking down against the wall until she was seated on the floor. She gasped for breath as the pain of his words sunk in, and she felt as if her heart had been ripped out of her chest. She stared at the door, her vision clouded by her tears, and screamed, "I hate you, Sean O'Reilly, you bloody bastard! I hate you!" Then she buried her head in her hands and wept.

Chapter Thirty-six

Sean parked his car back behind the church and texted Ian that he'd arrived. He opened the back door of the car and picked up a camo-colored canvas shotgun case that now housed the broadsword. *It doesn't look great,* he decided, *but for now it's better than carrying the exposed sword everywhere.* He slung the case over his shoulder and walked towards the back door.

Ever since he'd left the station, he'd had a nagging feeling about Em, and he'd feel a lot more comfortable when he could see for himself that she was safe. Ian opened the door before Sean reached it and greeted him with a cheery welcome. "You going to do some duck hunting today?" Ian asked.

"Yeah, right," Sean replied, following Ian into the church and securely closing the door. "As soon as I finish up with my faerie hunting. I had a wild time last night at Pete's place."

Gillian joined them in the hall. "What happened?"

"Some femme fatale faerie decided to try her luck with Pete," he said. "I had to convince her that the party was over with my sword and some holy water."

"They're not going to be too happy with you," Gillian said. "You'll need to watch yourself."

Sean shrugged. "I'm not too worried," he said.

"How's Pete?" Ian asked.

"He was fine when I left him last night, once we faery-proofed his house," Sean replied. "I called this morning, but he was already in meetings."

"Well, do you have a moment?" Ian asked. "Gillian and I have some things we'd like to show you."

Sean nodded. "Yeah, sure," he said, and then he looked around. "Where's Em? I thought she'd be down here with you."

Gillian smiled. "Well, I think she's up on the third floor in the gym," she said. "Em mentioned that she wanted to look at the old fencing gear so she could teach you how to use your new weapon."

Sean unzipped the gun case and pulled out the sword. "Yeah, I'm all about learning the ins and outs of this baby before I slice a foot off," he agreed. "Would you mind if I went up first?"

"No problem. Go and find Em," Ian suggested. "Then bring her down and we can show you both what we found."

Nodding, Sean hefted the sword over his shoulder and hurried down the hall towards the stairs. "Great, we'll be down soon," he said.

When he reached the third floor, he saw the double doors with the words "Gymnasium" painted over them in black, block letters. It brought back memories of his days in high school. He hurried over to the door and pushed it open. Em was standing on the other side of the gym, her own sword in her hands, performing a series of moves that looked like something out of a martial arts movie.

"Hey, good moves," he called out, eager to see her smiling face again.

She froze in her steps, but didn't turn his way.

"Em?" he called, slowly walking towards her. "I'm sorry; I didn't mean to startle you. I thought we could go a few rounds, you know, just for practice."

She stood still, listening to his footsteps echo on the gym floor. He dare approach her? What did he think? They'd go another round just so he could assault her and leave her once again?

Just minutes earlier she had pulled herself off the floor and turned her pain into anger. How dare he treat her in such a way? How dare he touch her without her consent? How dare he taunt her with insults about her own mother? The rage she felt inside was just beginning a slow simmer, but she was more than fine with turning up the heat.

Her sword clasped in both hands, Em turned and, with a wild war cry, charged Sean.

"Whoa!" Sean cried out, backing up quickly. "Hey, give me a chance. I'm new at this."

But she wasn't retreating, and if the look in her eye was any gauge to her mind set, he was going to get his ass kicked big time. He lifted his sword in front of his body and shifted his weight so he was resting on the balls of his feet for more agility. "Okay, let's have it," he said.

She lifted her sword and set it crashing down against his. He felt the hit all the way to his shoulders, but he was able to knock her sword to the side and pivot sideways, bringing his sword up against hers in a cross blow. She spun around and then swept her weapon around at shoulder height, causing Sean to jump back in astonishment.

"Hey!" he yelled. "You almost took my head off."

"That might be an improvement of your looks," she spat back.

Puzzled, he shook his head. "Um, Em, is there something we should talk about?" he asked.

"No," she said, lifting her sword again. "The time for talking is gone—now it's time to defend yourself."

She rushed him, but in her anger, she overstepped her abilities. Rattled by the earlier incident, she knew she was thinking clearly or strategically. Although she was more agile than Sean, he was a few inches taller and quite a bit stronger. She should have calculated that strength and height into her attack, but instead, she wanted to punish him and scare him away. Instead of retreating, however, he stepped up and met her parry for parry, pushing her slowly backwards. She fought hard, swiping and lunging, but his counters were every bit as solid and she started to feel her muscles tire.

"Do you want to stop?" Sean asked, seeing her fatigue.

"Why? Do you think I can't take it?" she demanded. She lifted both arms over her head, the sword clasped in both hands, and ran towards him with a cry of anger.

A little surprised at her advance, Sean knew she thought he'd retreat, giving her more room to maneuver. So instead, he grabbed both the hilt and the blade of the sword in his hands and charged her, using his broadsword like a quarterstaff and catching the blade of her sword against the flat of his own.

He continued to charge forward, forcing her back until finally she was against the wall, her arms and sword captive by his. She looked up at him, his face only inches away, his eyes filled with triumph, and suddenly she was frightened. She turned her face away, her cheek pressed against the cool brick of the wall. "Please don't hurt me again," she pleaded.

"What?" he exclaimed.

She dared a glance at him. He seemed truly puzzled. What game was he trying to play?

She could feel his heat, she could see his exhaustion, she could smell... She stopped and inhaled slowly. His scent was different. It wasn't dark woods and musk. It was more...

She thought back to his apartment, to the scent that wafted from the steamy bathroom into the hall. It was more masculine, less...less fae!

Her eyes widened and she looked up at him. "How long have you been here?" she asked, a horrible realization coming over her.

"Here, like at the church?" he asked.

She nodded.

"I don't know," he said. "I spoke with Ian and Gillian for a few moments downstairs, and then I came up here to work on sword handling."

"You've only been up here once today?" she asked.

He looked down at her as if she was losing her mind, and, God help her, maybe she was. He lowered his arms and his sword, but didn't step away

266

from her. "I've only been up here once," he said. "When I walked through that door a few minutes ago, it was the first time I'd been in this room."

She lowered her sword to her side, closed her eyes and shook her head. "I've a great deal to apologize for," she sighed. "I'm ashamed of myself, twice over. Once for believing them and once for doubting you."

"Would you like to repeat that?" Sean asked. "In English?"

"We've been compromised," she said, her voice firm. "And we have to warn the others."

Chapter Thirty-seven

Ian and Gillian looked up from the computer screen when they heard footsteps running down the hall. Keeping Gillian behind him, Ian dashed to the doorway to see Sean and Em running in their direction.

"What?" Ian asked, seeing the concern in their faces.

"We've been infiltrated," Sean said. "A faery took my shape and attacked Em."

Gillian moved around Ian and hurried to Em's side. "Oh, Em. Are you all right?" she asked.

Em nodded quickly. "He might still be in the church," she replied, all business. "We need to check—"

"Jamal," Gillian interrupted, pushing past them and running towards the staircase. "He's probably after him."

They all hurried up the stairs to the second floor and ran down the west wing towards the rooms that housed Jamal and his grandmother. The hall was empty and there was no noise coming from the small apartment. Gillian pounded on the door. "Jamal! Mrs. Gage!" she called. "Are you in there?"

The sound of shuffling feet could be heard through the door, and moments later it was opened a crack when Mrs. Gage peered out. "What's the problem?" she asked, her voice shaking with fear. "Have the police come again?"

Gillian breathed a sigh of relief and shook her head. "No," she said. "I'm sorry for frightening you, but there was an...an intruder in the church. We just wanted to be sure you and Jamal were unharmed."

Shaking her head slowly, she looked at the others in the hall. "Do you want to come in and see for yourselves?" she asked.

"If you don't mind, Mrs. Gage," Sean replied. "That way we will know you haven't been coerced."

Mrs. Gage snorted. "As if someone else was gonna tell me what to do," she said, opening the door and letting them in.

Jamal sat at a desk in the corner of the room working on school work. He looked up and started to speak but was cut off by his grandmother. "You can talk to them after you finish your school work," she said.

Em looked from the boy to his grandmother and stepped forward. "I beg your pardon," she said. "But the creature we are searching for has the ability to assume other shapes. I would like to hear from Jamal that he is safe."

"Assume other shapes?" Mrs. Gage repeated, looking at the group gathered around her. "But then how do I know that you all aren't demons yourselves?"

"Well, of course we aren't demons," Ian said. "Why in the world would we come to your door and tell you about ourselves if we were trying to trick you?"

"To gain her confidence," Em said. "That's how the fae work. They trick you and manipulate you." She turned to Mrs. Gage. "They cannot touch iron. It burns their skin. So, if you doubt one of us, all you have to do is ask us to touch iron."

Glancing around, Mrs. Gage spied a cast iron kettle lying next to the stove and picked it up. "Will this do?" she asked Em.

Em nodded. "Aye, it will," she said. She stepped forward and stood before Mrs. Gage. "Now, you need to know that because I am half-fae, the iron will burn my skin slightly. If I was the one we are seeking, I would not be able to stand the pain."

She lifted her hand to touch the kettle when Sean jumped forward and grabbed her hand before she could lay it on the pot.

"No," he said, holding it back. "There is no reason for you to harm yourself to prove the point." He turned to Mrs. Gage. "If I prove that I'm not fae and I vouch for Em, will you be satisfied?"

270

"Of course," she said. "If you're not the demon, then you'll tell me the truth. I trust you and I trust Em."

"Thank you," Em replied, touched at the trust the old woman would offer her.

Sean placed his hand down on the kettle and held it there. "I am not the demon, er faerie," he said. "And Em was the one who discovered that we'd been infiltrated and I will vouch for her."

Ian and Gillian hurried forward and placed their hands on the kettle with the same results.

Mrs. Gage nodded and then turned to her grandson. "Jamal, you come over here right now and touch this kettle, hear?"

Jamal stood, smiled at the group and nodded. "Sure, grandma, no problem," he said.

He walked away from the desk and, at the last moment, dashed past them across the room to the door, flung it open and ran out.

Chapter Thirty-eight

"Jamal!" Mrs. Gage screamed. "They've taken my Jamal."

Sean was out the door and after the faerie immediately.

"Ian and Gillian, you check on Father Jack," Em commanded, standing in the doorway for a moment. "And then check the rest of the church for Jamal. Mrs. Gage, stay here and wait for us. And keep hold of that pot."

Running out the door, Em saw Sean turn the corner and dash down the stairs. She followed, quickly gaining on him and running alongside of him as they chased the creature through the hallway of the church.

"Do you think he's playing with us?" Em asked, as they ran after him. "Trying to lead us into a trap?"

Sean shook his head. "He looks more scared than calculated," he replied. "Besides, it's not a trap if we know where we're going, right?"

She smiled and nodded. "Right."

They chased him through the first floor and nearly had him cornered near the chapel, but at the last moment, he feinted to one side and charged past them. Sean tried to tackle him but missed him by inches. Em charged after him, her sword held above her head, ready and eager to take him out. The faerie looked over his shoulder at Em, and his eyes widened as he increased his pace.

The faerie, still disguised as Jamal, stopped at the top of the stairs that led down to the basement, looked around frantically and then dashed down the stairs. Sean stopped Em at the top of the stairs. "Wait just a second," he said. "The doors to the basement are all boarded shut, right?"

She nodded. "Yes, we boarded them from the inside and the outside, as well as the windows and any other openings," she said. "And we used iron nails to be sure the fae couldn't sneak up on us."

Nodding, he looked down the stairwell and smiled slightly. "Okay, I admit I don't know a whole lot about faeries, but my da is passionate about old churches," he said. "And this church was one of my da's favorites, so I got to hear about the architecture a lot. I happen to know this church was built with Cream City brick, from Milwaukee."

Em shook her head impatiently. "Yes?" she encouraged, hoping he would hurry with his explanation so she could follow the faerie down the stairs. "And I need to know that now because?"

"It's red clay," he said. "High iron oxide content."

She stared at him. "There's iron in the walls of the basement?"

He nodded. "Yeah, so I don't think he's leading us into a trap," he explained. "I think we've got a fairly uncomfortable faerie down there."

A slow smile spread over Em's lips. "That's the best news I've heard all day," she said.

They continued down the stairs and found the faerie standing in the middle of the basement, twisting and turning, trying to find a way out. Sean had to get his head around the fact that this thing was not Jamal, the kid who had been frightened to death in the hospital bed and could eat food like he had a hollow leg. But it was hard when your eyes said one thing and your mind was supposed to realize another. But Em had no problem discerning the truth of the situation.

Em pulled out her sword and held it up. "You have one chance to speak," she said, holding the edge of her sword to his neck. "Or refuse and I will kill you."

"I will not talk, mongrel," he spat at her.

"Your choice," she replied, pulling her sword back in order to swing it forward. But before she could swing, Sean placed his hand on her arm and

274

held her back. "I'm sorry, Em," he said softly so the faerie could not hear them. "I know this is not the way you do things, but since I'm involved, I have to follow the rules."

"There are no rules when it comes to these creatures," she whispered fiercely. "You cannot use your human laws."

He shrugged. "Those are the only ones I've got," he said and stepped towards the faerie. He looked at the face of the creature; it held Jamal's features except for the eyes. That's how Em did it, Sean decided. If you looked in its eyes, you could see they were not the wide, innocent eyes of a thirteen year-old kid. They were ancient and filled with contempt and malevolence. And Sean wondered how those eyes looked when it tried to seduce her.

Sean stood in front of the fake Jamal and looked down at him. "I just have one question. Your answer will not be used against you in a court of law, but I want to ask you before I read you your rights."

"I have no answers for your questions, human," the faerie spat, his voice changing from Jamal's to an older one with a slight Irish accent.

"Just one," Sean said, as if the faerie hadn't replied. "Were you the one with Em this morning, or is there another faerie in the church?"

Chuckling, the faerie immediately transformed into Sean's likeness and stood eye to eye with the man who had been questioning him. He smiled slowly and nodded, using Sean's own voice. "I nearly bedded her," he taunted. "And she was eager, just like her mother."

Em gasped and tightened her hold on her sword. Sean glanced at her and shook his head. "No, Em, we have to do this the right way," he said, and then he turned back to the faerie, his double. "You have the right to remain silent. Anything you say can and will be used against you in a court of law. You have the right to an attorney. If you cannot afford an attorney, one will be provided for you. Do you understand the rights I have just repeated to you?"

The faerie stared at him for a moment. "Are you mad?" he asked. "You don't read rights to a faerie because you, human, are not able to capture a faerie."

"Do you understand the rights I have just repeated to you?" Sean asked as he moved next to the faerie.

"Are you now deaf as well as crazy?" the faerie asked.

"Yes or no?" Sean said.

"Yes. I understand what you have said," he replied sarcastically.

"Good," Sean replied, slipping behind him, pulling handcuffs from his back waistband and slapping them on the faerie's wrists, "because now you are arrested."

The faerie screamed and jumped around the room, changing from looking like Sean to his own, natural shape, a slender and blonde young man. He waved his arms frantically behind his back. "Get them off!" he screamed. "Get them off!"

"What's wrong?" Em asked, looking over at Sean. "What's happening?"

"Oh, did I forget to mention that handcuffs are made with stainless steel?" Sean asked, with a nonchalant shrug. "And stainless steel has iron in it."

He grabbed the faerie's arm and pulled up towards the stairs. "Let's just see how tough you really are," he said, "when you're not taking advantage of women."

Chapter Thirty-nine

The door to Father Jack's apartment was ajar, and Ian and Gillian approached it cautiously. Wordlessly, Ian placed his hands on Gillian's upper arms and moved her against the wall in the hallway, motioning for her to stay put. She shook her head angrily, but he motioned to her again and moved on his own towards the door.

Creeping quietly, he peered around the door frame and gasped silently. The room had been tossed. Furniture was overturned, pictures hung haphazardly on the walls, and bits and pieces of what remained of dishes were scattered on the floor. Ian hugged the wall as he moved from the front room, through the small kitchen, into what he assumed was the Father's bedroom.

Father Jack lay on the floor, an angry red gash on his forehead. "Gillian," Ian called, running towards Father Jack. "He's in the bedroom."

Ian knelt next to the older man, felt for a pulse and breathed a sigh of relief. His heart was still beating. He looked up as Gillian ran into the room. "He's breathing," he reported. "I'll get some ice and give Sean a call to let him know we didn't find Jamal."

Nodding, Gillian knelt down next to the priest. "Aye, and after this is over, we'll have words about your actions in the hallway," she replied with an arched look in her eye. Then she looked turned her attention to Father Jack. "Father Jack. Can you hear me?"

He moaned softly and blinked open his eyes. "What…what happened?" he croaked.

"It looks like you might have had a run-in with a faerie," she said.

His eyes widened. "Jamal," he exclaimed, trying to sit up. "The faerie has him."

Gillian held him down. "Ian is calling Sean right now," she said. "And you need to stay put until we make sure you aren't hurt."

"Ian," she called out. "Father Jack is conscious. He says the faerie has Jamal."

"The other faerie has Jamal?" Sean called out as he and Em entered the priest's apartment, pulling their faerie along with them. Sean threw the faerie against the wall. "Where did your friend take Jamal?" he demanded, clutching the clothing around the faerie's neck in his grip.

The faerie shook his head. "You'll not hear it from me," he choked.

"Em, lend me your sword," Sean said, holding his hand out, keeping his focus on the creature in front of him.

"Sean, where's your sword?" Em asked.

Shrugging, Sean shook his head. "Up in the gym, where I left it," he replied.

"You left it?" she cried. "Don't you understand?"

Sean turned to her. "What?" he asked.

"It's got magic," she said. "Powerful magic that the fae would love to get into their hands."

Sean closed his eyes for a moment. "Damn it," he swore.

He pulled the faerie away from the wall and tossed him to the ground at Ian's feet. "Watch him for me, will you?" he asked. "I think I know where the other faerie might be heading."

Sean and Em ran out of the apartment and ran to the staircase to the third floor.

"He's probably taken the sword and Jamal and escaped," Gillian said.

"He would have had to pass by at least one of us on the way out," Sean argued.

They reached the third floor in record time and dashed towards the gymnasium.

"Wait," Em whispered. "If we go in through the front door, Jamal could be hurt."

"What's our choice?" Sean asked.

"There's a balcony above the gym," she said, pointing to a narrow set of stairs.

"Okay, you stay here and guard the door," Sean said. "I'll go up."

"But you can't fight a faerie," she said. "You need more experience."

He winked at her. "Nothing like on the job training," he said, and then he quietly dashed up the stairs.

Em slid to the door and peeked into the room through the glass window. Jamal was in one corner of the room bound with rope. He was unhurt and conscious, but he also seemed scared to death. She wondered what in the world the fae would want with Jamal. By now, other humans had seen the Wild Hunt, so he really wasn't a threat to them. She was considering that when a movement on the other side of the room caught her eyes.

He was older than the faerie they caught in the basement. His red hair was longer and the lines around his face more severe. He was slowly walking

281

the parameter of the gym, pausing every few steps and sweeping the area with his own sword. Em sighed with relief as she realized the glamour spell she'd placed on the sword for Sean the night before had worked. The faerie could feel the power of the magic but hadn't been able to find the sword.

Once upstairs, Sean slipped through the open door that led to the narrow balcony directly above the door Em had been peeking through. The balcony was filled with old gym equipment: extra mats piled on top of each other, a dozen or so deflated basketballs and volleyballs, an old volleyball net that was stained orange with rust and a couple aluminum baseball bats. The iron railings at the edge of the balcony were also used to tie the ends of some of the climbing ropes that were suspended from the ceiling of the gym. The thick ropes brought back memories of grade school gym class and hands and legs raw with rope burns from frantic relay races up to the top and down again.

Crouching low, he used the floor of the balcony as a blind and slid to the edge to peer down. Jamal was lying on a thin, cotton mat on one side of the gym, his legs and arms tied together. Turning his head, Sean saw the faerie on the other side of the gym waving a sword around and moving closer to Sean's sword.

Some kind of weird faery dance? he wondered. *Why the hell doesn't he just pick it up?*

Gauging the distance between the faerie and Jamal, Sean knew he'd only have a few moments to get down to the gym floor and stop the faerie before it could reach the boy. He glanced over the side. *Crap!* It was higher than he had anticipated. If he wanted to jump, he'd have to slide through the railings, hang from the side and then drop down to the gym floor.

Yeah, that's not going to work.

He needed to act quickly and before the faerie left the other side of the gym.

Looking back to the old equipment, he smiled slightly. Maybe there was another option. Sliding along the tiled floor, Sean untied one of the lengths of rope from the railing and gave it a quick pull to be sure it was still sound. He tied a secure loop at the end and put his foot inside, pushing against it to make sure it would hold. Then he picked up one of the aluminum bats and stuck it securely underneath his arm.

Climbing onto the ledge, keeping his eyes on the faerie who was turned away from him, he placed his foot into the loop at the end of the rope and jumped.

He actually expected some kind of graceful swing—like in all of the pirate movies he'd seen. But instead, he just dropped towards the floor, nearly breaking his teeth at the sudden, jaw-jarring, jerking stop. Spinning around in a tight circle, he was relieved to discover that the rope descent had at least been quiet and the faerie was still dancing with his sword. He glanced over at Jamal as he spun around and saw that the boy's eyes were widened in hope. When he spun past the gymnasium door however, he saw that Em's eyes were filled with mirth.

Sliding a foot to the ground, he dismounted as ungracefully as he had descended and quietly stumbled onto the polished, gymnasium floor. Dashing towards the faerie, he set the bat in a line-drive stance over his right shoulder. As luck would have it, at the last moment the faerie turned, and Sean aimed the bat at the faerie's face, swinging with all his might.

The bat connected, and the faerie fell back and slid several feet, blood spurting from his nose. Sean ran to the corner of the gym to retrieve his sword. He grabbed it and turned just in time to block the faerie's parry, sword clanging against sword. Twisting to the side, Sean disengaged and attacked, using both arms and the same swing that gave him his stellar reputation in Chicago-style, 16-inch softball. He whipped his sword forward, using more power than technique. The faerie stumbled back, unprepared for such a physical attack. Sean continued knocking his opponent's sword to the side with each parry, forcing the faerie back to the corner of the gym.

Finally, his back against the wall, the faerie dropped his sword and raised his hands over his head. "This is the sign, no?" the faerie gasped. "When someone in your culture admits defeat?"

Sean stared at the creature, his eyes hardened. "I wouldn't know," he growled, holding the sword to the neck of the creature.

He could feel the power from the sword coursing through his veins, could feel the bloodlust pounding with every heartbeat. *It would be so simple,* he thought, *to just finish the job. One flick of my wrist and the creature would be destroyed at my hand. I would be like a god authorizing life or death.*

What the hell? Sean shook his head. *Where did that come from?*

He looked up and saw the smile on the faerie's face. "What? I'd forfeit my soul if I killed you?" Sean asked.

The faerie's smile grew broader. "No, you would have more power," the faerie whispered enticingly. "Think of it, human. You could rule the faery world. You could make us all do as you wished. You could have the mongrel."

Sean shook his head, trying to clear fog from his brain. *This could be a good thing,* his inner voice whispered, *ruling the faery world. Clearing up all this lawlessness. Protecting the people of the city. It's just one death. And it's not like he's human.*

285

"I would take the mongrel, if given the chance," the faerie taunted, malice twinkling in his bright green eyes. "I would take her as my brother took her mother. I would use her, over and over and over again. And she would cry out my name, begging for more."

Rage replaced reason. A vivid picture of Em writhing in passion below the faerie burned in his mind. Jealousy consumed him as he pulled back the sword, readying it for the mortal blow.

Chapter Forty

As soon as Sean appeared before her, swinging by a rope with a look of surprise on his face, Em didn't know if she should be impressed or incredulous. *What the hell was he thinking?* Shaking her head, she realized it was just like the little boy back in Ireland who came running to help with no thought of his own safety. He wasn't thinking.

"Sean to the rescue," she muttered, allowing the humor of the situation to rest a moment in her eyes. But when she realized he was going to fight armed with only an aluminum baseball bat, the mirth left her eyes.

"Damn!" she whispered, knowing she couldn't open the door for fear it would alert the faerie.

She heard the crack of the bat and jumped to action. Pulling the door open, she began to run in the direction of the fight but stopped in her tracks as she watched Sean outmaneuver and overpower his opponent. She stood, transfixed by the pure, male beauty of his movement. He was fighting like a warrior, all his power and concentration fixed upon the faerie who could do nothing but retreat. Em felt a strange mix of emotions—pride, exhilaration, fascination and desire. He was crushing one of her mortal enemies, and for the first time in her life, she felt she had a true champion and partner.

It took her a few moments to remember that Jamal was still tied up in the corner of the room. She dashed over to him and cut through the ropes that held him. Then she untied the gag over his mouth. "Are you okay?" she asked. "Did they hurt you?"

"No, I'm good," Jamal replied, rubbing his arms and legs to get the circulation back. "But I was sure glad to see Sean jump down from the balcony." He stretched to look around her to Sean. "I didn't know he could fight like that."

Em shook her head. "He can't," she replied automatically. Then she paused and looked over her shoulder at Sean. He couldn't fight like that! She was just fighting with him, and although he was strong, he wasn't very skilled. That ancient faerie should have been a much greater opponent. It was almost as if—

Em looked back at Jamal. "Stay here," she commanded, and then she lifted her sword and dashed across the room.

She couldn't call out Sean's name, didn't want to distract him and give the faerie any chance to harm him. But she could tell by the malevolent gleam in the faerie's eye that it was planning some kind of trick. Em had fought faeries long enough to understand their strength came more from their ability to manipulate their enemies minds than just from sheer fighting prowess.

She was only a few feet away when she heard the faerie threaten her. She saw the muscles in Sean's hand tense and watched his hand pull back, his sword ready to take the faerie's life, and she suddenly understood the plan. Jumping forward, she pushed Sean back with one hand and thrust her sword with the other, impaling the faerie through its heart. Immediately, the faerie burst into a thousand, tiny pieces of ash.

Furious, Sean stormed at her, his sword raised. "What the hell did you do?" he asked. "That was my kill."

"Your kill, is it?" she countered, moving up and facing him. "And what happened to following the rules? Or does that only apply when I'm the angry one with the sword?"

"No," Sean said, shaking his head and wondering why he felt so confused. "He was…I was…he deserved…" He looked up at Em, his face a study in confusion. "What the hell just happened?"

"The sword you now carry is Chrysaor," she explained. "It was the sword of the Knight of Justice."

Sean hefted the sword in his hand and then looked up at Em. "Yeah, you told me," he said. "So?"

She took a deep breath. "So, it was testing you," she said. "To see which you would choose. The faerie understood it and tried to get you to choose evil."

"The sword was testing me?" he asked, more than a little skeptical. "Em, it's a piece of metal. It takes orders from the hand that holds it."

"Aye, that would be the case if it were," she raised an eyebrow and purposely imitated his tone, "Only a piece of metal. But Chrysaor has magic forged into it, and that magic serves the master of the sword. It was testing you to see if you chose white or dark magic."

"White or dark?" Sean asked. "This is a sword, not a turkey."

She sighed audibly and rolled her eyes. "I didn't realize you were so dense," she complained. "And so, let me explain it to you as I would a wee bairn."

"Oh, thank you," he replied sarcastically. "And make sure you speak slowly, too."

She grinned. "Magic is very much like electricity," she explained. "It travels in waves, often using predetermined paths that you humans call ley lines."

"Ian has mentioned them to me," he said.

"Aye, he's one of the intelligent ones," she teased. "So, your electricity has two kinds of currents, alternating or direct. The magic waves can be light, or a power used for good, or they can be dark, a power used for destruction. And magic tools, like swords, can access their power from one of those two sources."

"But the Elk King had this sword last," Sean questioned. "Doesn't that mean it's wired for dark power?"

She shook her head. "As the sword takes on a new owner, it gives the owner the chance to choose the source," she said.

"The test," Sean added.

"Exactly," she said. "And the faerie could feel that you and the sword had not yet connected. He was trying to have you use the sword in anger against a foe who had already surrendered to you."

"And if I had succumbed?" he asked.

"Well, the sword and you are partners now," she said. "And you would have had dark power at your disposal; it's a temptation that few have been able to resist."

"It would have turned me dark, you're saying."

"It would have tried," she replied. "And if you continued to resist, it might have driven you mad."

Sean exhaled slowly and ran his hand through his hair. "Well, there's a lot about this magic I still need to learn," he said and then he stopped. "Wait. Why didn't it do the same for you? You killed him. Are you at risk?"

She shook her head. "No, my sword and I have been together for a long time," she said. "It knows my heart and motivation. Besides, I wasn't killing in anger, I was killing to protect—" She paused for only a moment. "My friend. I was killing to protect my friend."

A smile spread across his face, although his heart was not quite satisfied. "Thank you, Em," he said. "It's an honor to be considered a friend."

"I should have told you about the sword and the test sooner," she replied, angry at herself for not thinking of it sooner. "And for that, I apologize."

He smiled at her and put his hand on her shoulder. "Well, it has been a busy couple of days," he teased gently. "Thank you for stepping in as you did."

Nodding, she smiled back. "You're welcome."

He looked past her to Jamal. "You okay?" he asked.

Jamal stood up and nodded slowly, looking around as if he were waiting for something else to appear. "I didn't know the world was so weird."

Sean smiled. "Yeah, neither did I."

Em and Sean walked across the gym to Jamal. "So, what happened?" Sean asked.

Jamal shook his head. "I don't really know," he replied. "I was doing my schoolwork, and grandma said she was going to lay down for a little bit. A few minutes later I hear her calling for me, needing my help. I get out of the chair and start heading towards her bedroom, but then I realize her voice is coming from out in the hall. I pull the door open and she's lying on the floor in the hall."

"Was she hurt?" Sean asked.

Jamal shook his head. "I don't know. Last thing I remember I was running down the hall towards her and then I'm here, tied up," he said.

"Well, your grandmother is fine," Em said. "We just left her a few minutes ago."

"She's not hurt?" he asked.

"No, it probably wasn't even her that you saw in the hallway," Sean said. "These faeries can shape shift and make us think they are someone they're not." He turned and smiled at Em. "Right Em?"

"So we need to be smarter than they are," she agreed.

"We should have a code word," Jamal said. "Something that only we know and we could use to each other to know we're really who we say we are."

"That's a brilliant idea, kid," Sean said, placing his arm around Jamal's shoulder. "Let's get downstairs and tell everyone else about your idea."

He guided Jamal to the door, then stopped and turned to Em. "We don't know if there are any more of them in the church," he stated. "Do you want to take lead or should I?"

She moved in front of the two of them, her sword in front of her. "I'll take lead," she said. "But don't forget to watch your back."

They traveled down the corridor to the staircase, Sean with one arm still around Jamal's shoulders and the other hand clenching his sword. Em was a few steps ahead of them, prepared for an attack. They reached the staircase, and once again, Em started ahead of them, peering over the railing to make sure they were alone.

Jamal looked up at Sean. "I don't get it," he whispered. "Why do they want me so bad? Other folks have seen those monsters, not just me."

"That's a good question," Sean replied. "And one that we need to figure out soon, to keep you safe."

Chapter Forty-one

When Ian stepped up into the stairwell, all Em saw was a shadow, and she immediately sprang into action. With one hand on the banister and the other grasping her sword, she pushed herself up and over the banister to the stairs on the other side. Landing with ease, she leapt the few remaining stairs to engage the threat.

All Ian saw was a darkened figure, sword in hand, jumping at him. Feinting to the side, he pushed off the wall of the stairwell, came in low and grabbed his attacker's arm, slapping it back against the brick wall.

"Why you…." Em shouted, struggling to get out of his grip.

"Em?" Ian asked.

She froze. "Ian?" she said and looked down at the man who captured her arm. "What the hell are you doing? Sneaking up on us like that? I could have killed you."

"I was just coming up to help," he said, releasing her arm. "And didn't think it was very strategic to announce myself before coming up the stairs."

"Is everyone okay?" Sean asked, running down the stairs, his sword in one hand and his gun in the other with Jamal following close behind.

Sighing, Em nodded. "Yes, Sean, it's Ian coming up to help," she said, and then she turned to Ian. "And we were coming down, thinking the same thing." She rubbed her forearm, still stinging from his hold. "That's quite a move. Where did you learn it?"

"It's called aikido," Ian said. "It's a defensive martial art. I'll show you some of the moves."

"I'd like that," she replied, following him down the stairs. "How's Father Jack?"

"He's angry," Ian said. "Mostly at the faeries, but there's a little reserved for himself. He seems to think he should have known they would have come here to the church."

"And why should he have known?" Em asked as they all walked back down the hall together. "They've never come to the church before."

"Never?" Sean asked, stopping in his tracks. "You've never had an attack like this before?"

She looked at him. "No. Why? Should that concern us?"

He looked up and down the hall slowly. "Let's just wait on the rest of this conversation until I can be sure we aren't being heard," he said.

As soon as they entered Father Jack's apartment, Jamal was enfolded in his grandmother's arms. "I was so scared for you," she sobbed, and then she stood back and shook him gently. "Don't you never do something like this again."

Jamal grinned at her and hugged her again. "Yes, ma'am, I won't," he said.

Sean walked over to the kitchen where the faerie sat, tied to a chair, the handcuffs no longer on his wrists. He looked over at Father Jack, who sat on the other side of the table, and raised a questioning eyebrow.

"Well, I couldn't bear to hear him suffer," Father Jack said, not needing Sean to express his question vocally.

"And how can you be sure he won't escape?" Sean asked.

Father Jack held up a high-end squirt gun and pointed it at the faerie. "Holy water," he replied. "This thing can shoot over twenty feet."

Biting back a smile, Sean nodded and then pulled up a chair and placed it close to the faerie. "I have a few questions for you," he said. "And if you don't answer them quickly enough, I'm going to have my friend Em encourage you to talk. She's a little pissed at you already, so if I were you, I'd talk."

The faerie looked over at Em who'd entered the kitchen and was leaning against the wall, cleaning the edge of her sword with a towel. "I'm just now wiping off the remains of your friend," she said. "If you'd do me the favor of not speaking with Sean, I can save myself an additional clean-up."

His eyes widening, the faerie sat back in his chair. "You killed Tup?" he asked.

"Aye, I did," she replied easily. "And I have no qualms about killing another faerie before the day is through."

The faerie turned to Sean. "What is it you want from me?" he asked.

"Why were you sent here?" Sean asked.

"I was supposed to distract the mongrel," he replied. "While Tup got the boy."

"Are there more of you?" Sean asked.

Shaking his head, the faerie looked very nervous. "No, just the two of us," he stammered. "That's all they thought it would take."

"They? Who are they?" Em asked, stepping closer to the table.

"I don't know," he stammered, his voice shaking. "Tup got the orders. I followed Tup. He told me where to find you, told me to read your thoughts and when I found that—"

Em slammed her sword on the table, desperate to stop the faerie's babbling before he admitted to all in the room that her thoughts had been about Sean and his body. "Enough," she commanded. "Why only me? Why not the others?"

The faerie shrugged. "None of the rest were considered a threat," he replied evenly.

"Well, I have to say I'm more than slightly offended," Ian remarked. "And so Tup came for the boy. Why is Jamal so important to you?"

"I don't know," the faerie pleaded. "Truly. I only know that we were supposed to take him from here and deliver him to the Elk King."

Jamal gasped. "The Elk King?"

"Why does the Elk King need the boy?" Sean asked.

"The Elk King would not need Jamal," Gillian inserted. "The Elk King is an assassin; his only focus is the hunt. He is guided by others, more powerful than he. He would not have asked for Jamal."

"But if he got him…" Ian left the end of the sentence hanging, and Gillian quickly nodded.

"Were you sent by Aengus?" Father Jack asked.

"No, Tup hates Aengus and all the aristocracy who think they are better than the faeries they betrayed," the faerie spat. "He wanted to see Aengus buried deep in the depths of Tir Na Nog."

Father Jack nodded. "Well, unfortunately for you, Aengus is the only representative of the Sidhe we have an agreement with," he said. "So, we will be returning you to him."

"But he'll kill me," the faerie cried.

"Like you would have killed Jamal?" Sean asked, feeling no sympathy for the creature. "Somehow I can't bring myself to feel any pity for you."

"We will encourage Aengus to spare your life," Father Jack said, "if you continue to cooperate with us."

The faerie eagerly nodded his head. "Oh, aye, I'll cooperate in any way you wish," he said.

"Well, we'll just see about that," Father Jack replied skeptically.

Chapter Forty-two

The corridor that led from the chapel on the first floor to the parking lot door was quiet except for the constant ticking of the clock positioned next to the door to the lab. Sean leaned against the brick wall and waited, watching the monitor on the wall that displayed the view from the hidden camera in the parking lot.

"Any sign of them?" Ian asked, coming out of the lab.

Sean shook his head. "No, nothing," he said. "I've also asked Pete to join us. It never hurts to have a genius attorney on your side."

Ian nodded. "I agree," he said, leaning on the wall across from Sean. "And he has a little more in the game now."

"Yes, he does," Sean agreed grimly.

"Seems like you have a little more in the game, too," Ian observed casually.

Sean turned his eyes from the monitor to Ian. "Are you going all psychologist on me now?" he asked, one eyebrow lifted.

Smiling slightly, Ian nodded, acknowledging the hit. "Aye, well, that does tend to be my default mode," he confessed. "If it's not scientist mode."

"I guess we can't help but be who we are," Sean acknowledged. "So, doc, what do you want to know?"

"What happened to Em?" Ian asked.

Shrugging, Sean turned his gaze away from Ian back to the monitor. "She won't tell me," he said, and Ian could hear the hurt in Sean's voice.

"Why not?" Ian asked.

Meeting Ian's eyes again, Sean tried not to let his emotions show. "I don't know, doc," he replied tersely. "I thought explaining her actions was your job."

Ian grinned. "It is, yes," he said. "But I wanted to hear what you thought."

"I think she doesn't trust me," Sean said. "No, I know she doesn't trust me." He stood up and began to pace. "If you could have seen the hate and the anger. Really, Ian, she wanted to hurt me when I walked into that gym this morning."

"Well, we know that the faerie disguised himself as you," Ian said slowly as he dissected the situation. "So, what could you do that would hurt Em enough that she would be angry enough to attack you?"

Shaking his head, Sean stopped pacing for a moment. "What?"

"Em's vulnerable areas," Ian said. "What are they? For example, if you beat her in a sword fight would she be upset?"

"No, she would be pleased," Sean said. "She doesn't seem to have that kind of an ego." He smiled slightly. "Granted, she'd go at you harder next time, but you ought to consider that a compliment."

"So, the faerie didn't fence with her," Ian said. "We can rule that out. What would leave Em most vulnerable?"

Frustrated, Sean continued to pace. "She's just not vulnerable," he said. "She's powerful and confident and damn near a superhero. Except for her total distrust of men…"

Ian stood up. He and Sean stared at each other for a moment. "He seduced her," Sean said. "He came on to her."

Ian nodded. "And she trusted him, because she thought it was you," he said, nodding in agreement.

Sean exhaled slowly. "When I backed her against the wall and trapped her sword, she actually pleaded with me not to hurt her again," he said softly. "I didn't even think about it then. But that's the only thing that would really hurt her."

"She's afraid of becoming her mother," Ian said. "She doesn't want to be attracted to anyone."

"So what do we do?" Sean asked. "Just ignore it, like she wants us to?"

"Well, if she was your partner on the force, and you had a problem between the two of you, what would you do?" Ian asked.

"We'd have to talk it out," Sean replied immediately. "Partners need to trust each other."

"Yeah, that's what I thought, too," Ian said easily. "You need to talk to her."

Sean's attention was drawn to the monitor as a car pulled into the parking lot. He recognized it as Pete's and started towards the door. Ian reached out and caught Sean's arm. "I know it's different," he said pointedly, "but that only makes it more important to take care of it."

"But, damn it, I didn't do anything wrong," Sean stated angrily.

"Yeah, and neither did she," Ian replied. "But it seems the faeries are able to discern our weaknesses and use them against us. You are her greatest weakness. What does that tell you about her feelings for you?"

Sean closed his eyes for a moment and sighed. "Yeah, I get it," he said. "I was one of the few humans she actually trusted. I've got to help her trust again."

Sean moved past Ian and walked out the door to the parking lot to greet Pete. Ian watched his clueless friend walk away and shook his head. "You dunderhead," he whispered.

Chapter Forty-three

Sean walked across the lot towards Pete's car. The day was bright and crisp with no clouds in the bright blue sky, and pieces of gravel on the ground actually sparkled in the sunshine. Sean stopped and stared at them for a moment. *Natural phenomenon or magic*, he wondered. *Crap, I'm losing my mind.*

Pete opened his car door, reached over and pulled his wheelchair out, setting it up next to the car. "Morning," Pete called as he hefted himself from the driver seat to the chair. "Anything interesting going on in your life today?"

Sean shrugged casually as he walked up to Pete. "No, man, pretty ordinary day," Sean replied as he listed things off. "I fought two fairies, was impersonated by one of them, sword fought with Em because the guy that impersonated me was not nice to her, jumped down from a gym balcony and found out that pirate movies lie…" He thought for a moment. "Oh, yeah, my captain put me on permanent Order of Brigid's Cross assignment. So, how are you doing?"

Pete actually chuckled and shook his head. "Boy, you live a boring life," he replied as he moved the wheelchair towards the door. "Okay, after an evening of nearly being seduced by a naked faerie, I had a night of fairly bizarre dreams."

"Understandable," Sean inserted, walking alongside him.

"And when I got into the office, I discovered that several of my employees had been followed home last night and needed the assistance of the security personnel I had requested," he said.

"Was anyone hurt?" Sean asked, stopping in his tracks, the smile dropping from his face.

Ian stepped forward from the door, overhearing Sean and Pete. "Is everything all right?" he asked.

Pete stopped the wheelchair and turned to Sean and Ian. "No one was hurt, but I spent a lot of time thinking about this whole situation," he said slowly. "I don't think we have all the information about Jamal yet."

"You think Jamal is holding out on us?" Sean asked skeptically.

"No. No, that's not it at all," he said. "I think Jamal is in the dark as much as we are. But things just don't seem to add up."

"I agree," Ian added, studying the outside of the church building and the statues of the saints staring down at him. "I feel we're walking into the middle of a puzzle, and I'm not quite sure who I trust yet."

Sean recalled Em's comment about trust. *Well for my part, I trust no one,* she had told him. *And I've never been disappointed.*

"Maybe trusting no one is the wisest course for the time being," Sean said aloud.

Pete nodded. "I agree," he said. "Trust no one and keep your eyes open."

They entered the church and walked towards the elevator. "So, who are we meeting?" Pete asked as they waited for the elevator to appear.

"Two of the aristocracy of the faery realm," Sean said. "Aengus and Caer, the lord and lady of Chicagoland. Must be my peasant background, but I've never trusted aristocracy."

"Excuse me?" Ian countered.

Sean grinned. "Present company excepted, of course."

Ian nodded. "That's more like it," he replied with a smile. "So, in our cast of characters, who should we each be watching as this drama unfolds?"

"Well, I think it takes one to know one," Sean replied. "So you, Sir Ian, get Aengus and Caer."

Pete nodded. "That works for me," he said. "I'll keep an eye on Jamal's grandmother. I have a feeling Mrs. Gage might not have told us everything she could have."

"Okay," Sean agreed. "And I'll watch everyone else."

Ian chuckled. "Well, if you need to trim that down a bit, I'd say the most interesting person to watch would be the good Father," he suggested. "He's a man who's used to living with a secret, at least one, and I don't find him as forthcoming as I'd like."

The elevator door opened, and the three stepped inside. "Off to another adventure," Sean murmured.

"Why the hell can't we just play pool like the other guys?" Pete asked with a smile.

"Trust me, you'd be bored in ten minutes," Sean replied.

The door opened, and they moved down the hall to Father Jack's residence. Seeing that the door was not closed, they entered without knocking, and Sean glanced around the room at the occupants. Father Jack was in the kitchen pouring hot water into a tea pot. Gillian was sitting in a chair, facing the couch. Two people sat with their backs to Sean, and he assumed they were Aengus and Caer. But Em, Jamal and Mrs. Gage were nowhere to be seen.

"Ah, you're here," Father Jack said, looking across the room. "Good, now we can get things started."

310

The two occupants on the couch turned, and immediately Pete gasped in surprise while Sean pulled his gun out of his holster and pointed it at the woman.

"You want to slowly stand with your hands in the air?" he commanded her.

Chapter Forty-four

"I beg your pardon?" Aengus demanded, turning in his chair and then standing to face Sean, Ian and Pete. "Do you know who she is?"

"Sean, put your gun down," Father Jack pleaded. "This is Aengus and Caer. They are the diplomats of faery."

"All I know is that she broke into my friend's apartment last night, was waiting for him in his bed, and tried to seduce him," Sean replied. "Then she escaped capture by jumping from his balcony."

Aengus turned to Caer, one eyebrow lifted. "You seduced a human last night?"

Slowly, the beautiful, red-headed faerie stood, her face calm and slightly amused. She studied Pete for a moment, slowly licked her lips and then sighed with exaggerated disappointment. "No, I didn't seduce him," she said, looping her arm around her husband's. "But I can certainly see why one would try."

"Do you have a twin?" Pete asked. "If not, you were certainly in my bedroom last night, and you were definitely without clothing."

Shrugging lightly, she met his eyes. "I do not have a twin," she replied. "And I was not in your room last night, human."

"I don't believe you," Pete replied.

The echo of Gillian's sharp gasp was the only sound heard as the room slowly filled with silence. "I will have you killed," Aengus roared, his eyes growing luminous with anger.

"You'll have to go through me first," Sean said, stepping between his friend and the faerie. "And it won't be that easy."

"Pete, faeries can't lie," Gillian said, standing and hurrying across the room. "They can trick you and manipulate things, but they can't out and out lie."

"I recorded you on my phone," Pete said, pulling out the phone and offering it. "I didn't realize it until this morning. But when I put the call into Sean, I must have hit the video record. It's not a good angle, but enough to see who was in my room. Tell me that's not your wife."

Gillian took the proffered phone and handed it to Aengus. He watched it for a moment, his eyes widening, and then rewound it and watched it again. Without making a comment, he handed it to his wife. The amusement in her face changed to outrage as she watched the video. "Who would dare do this?" she asked, lifting her hand in an attempt to smash the offending device.

313

"Wait! Phone!" Pete called, stretching his hands out. "Don't damage the phone!"

Tossing him a defiant look, she hurled it against the wooden floor. Pete winced as he heard the delicate, electronic device crack upon impact.

Shaking his head slowly, Aengus stood and picked up the pieces. "My darling, we can't take our temper out on inanimate objects that had nothing to do with the betrayal," he said easily, cupping the phone inside both of his hands. "We need to save that anger up, let it simmer and use it on those who deserve our wrath."

He turned to Pete and bowed slightly. "Your phone," he said, surprising Pete by sliding an unbroken phone into his hands. "I do apologize for my wife's display of anger. We generally don't appreciate someone duplicating our likeness for their own use."

Pete returned the nod. "I fully understand that feeling," he said. Then he shifted his gaze to Caer. "And I apologize for doubting your word. I did not understand your culture."

Caer stared at Pete for a moment and then shook her head. "The uncertainty was understandable, given the circumstance," she replied as she sat back down on the couch. "We will not have you killed."

Sean shook his head in amazement. "Okay, now that we're all buddy-buddy like, can someone please tell me what the hell is going on?" he asked.

Chapter Forty-five

Aengus cleared his throat lightly and looked across the room. "Well, Father Jack, you are much more acquainted with the realms of both hell and heaven," he said sardonically. "Perhaps you might be the more appropriate person to lead this conversation."

Father Jack sat back in his chair and templed his hands for a moment before he spoke. Finally, after taking a deep breath, he turned to Sean. "As you know, from the very beginning of our existence in the human race there has been a need for opposition in all things," he said.

"Father, with all due respect," Sean interrupted, "can we have the condensed version of the story?"

A slight smile appeared on Aengus' lips. "Ah, it seems he has already begun to understand you, Jack."

Father Jack nodded. "Yes, it appears he has," he said. "The short version, Detective O'Reilly, is that when there is an organization for good, there generally is an opposing organization for bad. Such is the case in this instance."

"You mean there are people out there who want to let the jailed up fairies go free?" Sean asked. "Doesn't seem like such a bad idea to me. I'm all about emancipation."

"Are you?" Aengus interrupted, turning to Sean. "Would you let the animals in the zoo go free?"

"Well, not in the middle of the city," Sean replied with a shrug. "But, back in the wilds where they came from, hell yeah."

"You are not alone in your thinking," Aengus said, standing and pacing across the room. "We had some earlier members of the Order who felt the same way. Not only did they feel the Unseelies should have been freed, but they thought they would have been a superior weapon when we were fighting against the unspeakable atrocities of World War II."

Sean nodded. "Yeah, I can see that," he said. "An army of immortal, magical guys on your side. I can't see a downside."

Aengus turned towards him quickly. "You cannot?" he asked. "What if those who control them decided they didn't feel democracy was the correct way to organize a nation? What if they felt they had advanced intelligence and, for the betterment of the entire world, forced their way of thinking on all? All, of course, in the name of improving humanity. What if they, like Hitler, decided there ought to be a super race, and they were the ones who decided which characteristics, beliefs, or cultures were superior?"

Sean considered Aengus' response, images of creatures like those he'd seen in the past few months escaping from an underground lair flashing through his mind. But then, other images, more poignant and real took their place: images of emaciated prisoners standing near the fences of the concentration camps, hollowed out trenches for mass graves, and long, stockade buildings that held gas chambers. He shook his head. Which set of monsters were worse?

"Okay. Okay, I can see a downside," he said. "But, by freeing those Unseelies, what if you could have prevented some of the carnage that occurred. Did you think of that?"

Aengus shook his head. "When we made our decision, we didn't understand all that was occurring in the enemy camp. And had we known of the horrors we would find in the following months, perhaps we would have changed our minds," he said with a tightening of his jaw. "But we, as a council, agreed the risk of releasing them was far too great, and we denied the request."

"So, you guys nixed the plan to open the gates and let out the Unseelies," Sean said. "Where does this other group, the bad guys, come in?"

"They were those in the Order who did not agree with that decision," Aengus replied. "They thought we were wrong. They thought they would be able to control the fae, and they wanted the power that would come with it."

"Okay, crazy, egotistical, angry guys," Sean said, nodding his head. "And they're what, about a hundred years old now? Are they coming after us in their walkers?"

"Not all of them were human," Aengus explained.

Sean studied the tall faerie for a moment and then nodded slowly. "So some of your kind jumped ship on you," he said.

"Yes," Aengus replied shortly, "Some of my kind and some others. And those who were human and had a shorter lifespan passed their hate and their legacy on to their family members."

"So, this is a family business," Sean said. "And I'm guessing they are big, rich, important families."

"Exactly," Father Jack said. "Rich, important, wealthy and ruthless. They do not play by the same rules we play by, and they don't care who they step on to get there."

"Are they as widespread as members of the Order?" Sean asked.

"Yes," Aengus replied. "They are all over the world."

"What kind of advantage do they have over us?" Sean asked.

"They know who we are," Father Jack answered. "But we are not sure who all of their members are."

"And they have no problem manipulating humans to do their bidding," Aengus added. "Which often leads our inquiries into a dead end."

"Manipulating?" Sean repeated.

"Yes, the fae have the ability to use humans to do their work for them and then, if necessary, they have them forget," Aengus said.

"So what happened to the fae can't lie rule?" Sean asked.

"Generally, the relationship starts with a desire hidden in the subconscious of the human," Aengus explained. "The fae merely gives the human access to that desire. But, if it's more convenient for them to encourage the human to forget they were involved, they can suggest the humans have a lapse in memory."

"Like hypnosis," Ian inserted, "Power of suggestion."

320

Aengus nodded. "Exactly," he said, "With an emphasis on power."

Chapter Forty-six

There was silence in the room for a long moment as everyone considered what had just been spoken. Sean rubbed the back of his neck, wondering when it was that the whole world turned upside down and brought him with it. He let his gaze wander around the room, mentally sorting between the people he could trust and those he wouldn't turn his back on. The room was about evenly divided at this point.

"And these guys want Chicago?" he finally asked.

Aengus shrugged. "Chicago. New York. Los Angeles," he said. "They want control, and Chicago is the first step."

"Why here?" Sean asked.

"It's the ley lines, isn't it?" Ian inserted. "They have more power here."

Aengus nodded, a look of surprise on his face. "Yes. Exactly," he admitted. "Chicago has more energy than the other places."

"And the ley lines are linked back to where all this started," Ian added. "The monastery in Ireland."

Aengus' eyes widened. "Yes, they are," he said, studying Ian for a moment longer and then added with an arched eyebrow. "Is there anything else you'd like to add?"

Ian bit back a smile when he heard Sean's soft chuckle but never lost eye contact with Aengus. "Actually, yes, but first I have a question," he replied. "This all seemed to escalate suddenly when we got involved with Jamal. Why is he so important?"

"Jamal?" Aengus asked, confused.

"The boy who witnessed the Wild Hunt," Father Jack interjected.

Aengus nodded slowly. "Ah, yes, the survivor," he said. "It would seem the answer would be obvious."

"It would be obvious, except we now have at least a dozen more survivors from last night," Sean added. "So, why the attack this morning?"

"There were no survivors from last night," Aengus replied coolly. "At least according to my sources."

"But, I..." Sean began, but Pete's hand on his arm stopped him. Sean turned to see a warning in Pete's eyes and a barely noticeable shake of his head. Sean swallowed his words and took a slow breath.

"You were going to say?" Aengus asked.

"If you don't mind, I'd prefer to hear what your sources told you," Pete said. "As it specifically pertains to the well-being of my client."

Aengus shrugged. "Very well," he said. "There were a large number of casualties who were obviously victims of the hunt. But there were also a smaller number, perhaps a few dozen, who had been shot."

"Shot?" Sean choked. "But the Hunt doesn't use guns."

"No. They don't," Aengus replied. "One must assume that the gang war had started before the Hunt appeared, and those deaths occurred first."

Before Sean could speak, Pete tightened his hold on Sean's arm and then turned his attention to Aengus. "Well, that makes sense," Pete said calmly. "So, there are no survivors except for Jamal."

Aengus nodded. "I would like to meet your client," he said. "I'm curious to see why the Hunt would pass him by and let him live."

"Come again?" Sean asked.

"If the Hunt's direction was to kill all of the humans, why didn't they start with Jamal?" Aengus asked.

"Because the whispers were protecting him," Mrs. Gage said, her voice firm with faith as she stepped into the room from Father's Jack study on the other side of the room.

"The whispers," Caer chuckled. "Really?"

"Those too stupid to comprehend often mock," Em inserted as she followed Mrs. Gage into the room. Then she turned to Father Jack. "I apologize; she slipped out before I could stop her."

Caer stood up and glared at Em, then turned to Father Jack. "What is *she* doing here?" she demanded. "She is not fit to be in my presence."

"You can leave," Sean said, directing his comment at Caer with a casual shrug.

Caer turned and looked at Sean with astonishment. "What did you say?" she asked, incredulous.

Sean stepped sideways and opened the door. "I said, you can leave," Sean replied evenly. "Em is a valuable member of this team, and I won't have her insulted in any way."

"You know what she is, don't you?" Caer asked with contempt.

Sean nodded, his eyes never leaving Caer's. "Yes, I do," he said. "She's the best damn warrior I've ever met."

Aengus took hold of his wife's arm and guided her firmly back into her chair. "Sit down,

Caer," he said quietly, with a tone that brooked no argument. "We have far too much at stake here to let petty annoyances distract us."

Caer hissed softly, pulled her arm out of Aengus' grasp and sat down with a huff.

Sean decided that it was best to continue as if nothing had happened. "Mrs. Gage," he said, "I don't know if it's a good idea for you to be here."

"If you are talking about my Jamal, then this is the only place I ought to be," she replied firmly. "He's my responsibility and has been since he was a baby."

"His mother?" Aengus inquired.

"She was killed," Mrs. Gage replied softly. "The whispers, they told her to stay home, but she didn't listen. She thought she would be protected. Thought she knew better. But she was wrong and I'm not going to let that happen to my Jamal."

Aengus studied her for a moment. "And what do you think of his story?" he asked her. "The creatures he's claimed to have seen."

"My Jamal don't lie to me," she said. "And if he said he saw those things, then he saw them. The Good Book tells us about demons and creatures. I ain't got no reason to disbelieve my boy."

326

"Well, I would like to help protect your boy," Aengus said. "I would ask you, as his guardian, to turn over his protection to me."

Mrs. Gage looked slowly around the room at the faces of each person engaged in the conversation, unknowingly mirroring Sean's actions of just a few minutes prior. Then she met Aengus's eyes. "No thank you, kindly," she replied. "I have faith in the people in this room who have protected us so far. I don't know you and, no offense meant, but I don't know why I should trust you."

With a deferential nod in her direction, Aengus put his hand out towards Caer. "It seems, my dear, that we are no longer needed here," he said, helping her from her chair. He paused for a moment and then turned back to Mrs. Gage. "Madame, I abide by your decision, but should you ever need my help, you need only ask."

"Can you stop them?" she asked. "Stop them demons who killed those children?"

"I'm afraid I cannot," he replied. "They can only be stopped by the one who summoned them or by his champion, and I am neither."

"That's the only way to stop them?" Sean asked.

Aengus turned to Sean. "I'm afraid so," he said. "I fear that many more are going to die before this is over."

Chapter Forty-seven

The sound of the door latch clicking in place after Aengus and Caer left echoed in the quiet room. "So, these other guys, the bad guys," Sean said, breaking the silence. "They were there waiting for the kids on the other side of the park with guns."

Pete nodded. "Yeah, to make sure there were no other loose ends to tie up," he said, the disgust showing on his face. "Mowed them down in cold blood."

"Why didn't we hear them? Why didn't we know?" Sean asked, slapping his palm against the wall. "Damn it, they were frightened kids."

"They probably used silencers," Ian said. "And, with all the noise from the windstorm the Hunt created, it probably would have been hard to even hear unsilenced guns."

"We've got to stop them," Sean said, his face set.

"How?" Gillian asked. "We don't know who summoned them."

"Yeah, well we know someone who's pretty damn close to the situation," Sean replied, moving towards the door. "I'm going to have a little chat with Detective Adrian Williams."

Pete rolled his wheelchair forward, effectively blocking Sean from the door. "I'm going with you," he said.

"What?" Sean asked, anger and frustration on the edge of his voice. "You don't think I can handle him?"

Pete shook his head. "No, I'm going there to protect Adrian," he replied calmly. "You're not thinking straight right now."

Sean turned on his friend. "Thinking straight? Thinking straight?" he yelled. "How the hell am I supposed to think? Adrian was part of the group that allowed this in my city. No one gets away with that!"

Pete took a moment and met Sean's eyes. "You're supposed to remember that Adrian was probably under the power of something he doesn't understand," he explained. "You're supposed to remember the Adrian you trained, not the one who is under the influence of the fae."

Sean exhaled slowly and closed his eyes for a moment. "Okay, dammit, you're right," he admitted.

"When have I ever been wrong, O'Reilly?" Pete asked.

The light jest did what it was intended to do, and Sean felt the tightness easing in his chest.

"Do you still want to go?" Sean asked.

Pete smiled at his friend. "Are you kidding?" he asked. "I wouldn't miss this for the world."

A movement behind Em caught Sean's attention as Jamal stuck his head out from Father Jack's study. "Can I come out now?" Jamal asked.

Sean nodded. "Yeah, the coast is clear," he said. "How are you doing?"

The young boy shrugged, but Sean could see the apprehension in his eyes. "What did you hear?" Sean asked.

Jamal looked down at the floor, trying to ignore the question. Sean moved across the room and knelt down in front of him. "Hey, we're all on the same side," he said. "We're a team. You can't hold back from your team."

Lifting his head, he met Sean's eyes. "I heard those other kids, from last night, got shot," Jamal replied. "The ones you saved, they died anyway." Taking a deep breath, he summoned his courage to ask the next question. "Am I going to die, too?"

"No," Sean replied resolutely. "You are not going to die. We are going to keep you safe, and we are going to end the Wild Hunt."

"You are?" Jamal asked, his eyes widening in admiration.

"Yes, we are," Sean said. "Pete and I are going out to meet with someone who knows about them. We're going to find a way to take them down."

Jamal studied Sean for a moment, meeting his eyes and reading the confidence in them. His chest didn't feel nearly as tight as it had a moment ago, and he let out a breath he hadn't realized he'd been holding in.

"You okay?" Sean asked.

Jamal's mouth curved into a small smile. "You gonna jump from any more balconies?" he asked.

"Oh, funny kid, real funny," Sean replied, smiling back at the boy. "You keep this up and I'm cutting off your supply of burgers and fries."

"Now that would be a tragedy," Em replied, walking over and standing next to Jamal. "We might actually have to feed him something nourishing, like vegetables."

Sean and Jamal made identical faces of disgust. Then Sean looked up and met Em's gaze. "Can you watch over Jamal and Mrs. Gage while Pete and I meet with Adrian?" he asked.

She nodded. "Yes, they won't leave my side," she said.

"How do you feel about homemade chocolate chip cookies?" Mrs. Gage asked, taking a deep breath and smiling at Em. "Maybe you, me and Jamal could mix them up and have them waiting for everyone when they get back."

"Well, I feel good about eating them," she replied. "But I'm more handy with a sword than I am with a mixing bowl."

"That's okay," Jamal inserted. "I can help mix and you can taste test."

Em put her arm around the boy's shoulders. "Now that sounds like an ideal plan to me."

"Thanks," Sean said, sending Em a grateful nod. "We'll keep in touch and let you know how things are going."

"If it's okay with everyone else, I've a project in mind that might help us," Ian inserted. "I'd like to spend a little more time in the lab with Gillian, if that's fine with you."

"Yeah, we need any advantage we can get," Sean said.

"And while everyone else is occupied, I'm going to see about faery-proofing the church," Father Jack said. "I never thought we'd need it, but it's obvious that we're vulnerable here."

"Okay, it looks like everyone has a plan," Sean said taking a deep breath. "Now let's put them in action."

Chapter Forty-eight

"So, how are you going to persuade Adrian to meet with us without making him suspicious?" Pete asked, sitting next to Sean in the cruiser.

His eyes focused on the road ahead of him, Sean didn't answer.

"Don't have a clue, do you?" Pete asked.

"Yeah. I got nothing," Sean said.

"Well, good," Pete replied, nodding. "At least we know what our weaknesses are."

Sean grinned. "Yeah, that's a good way to look at it," he said.

An incoming call on Sean's cell phone halted their conversation as he reached forward and pressed the hands-free button on the cruiser to have the call go through the radio. "O'Reilly here," he said.

"Hey, Irish, it's Adrian." Adrian's voice slipped through the car's speaker.

Pete lifted his eyebrows in surprise and shook his head.

"Hey, Skinny, how's it going?" Sean asked.

"Good. It's going good," he replied. "Hey, you remember that case earlier in the week?"

"The one with the kid at the hospital?" Sean asked.

"Yeah, that one," Adrian answered.

"Yeah, what's up?"

"Well, I got some information that a friend of yours is helping the kid out," Adrian said. "Pete O'Bryan is representing him."

"Why does he need representation?" Sean asked, trying to get more information from Adrian. "He was just a witness, right?"

There was a long pause and a heavy sigh. "Yeah, well, it looks like he might have had more to do with the crime than we initially thought."

"You're pulling my leg, right?" Sean asked. "That kid isn't a gang-banger, much less a murderer. What the hell is going on, Adrian?"

"Can we meet?" Adrian asked, lowering his voice to a whisper. "I gotta talk to you."

"Yeah, we can meet," Sean replied. "When and where?"

There was a pause. Then Adrian's lowered voice came over the speaker again. "I can be at Slainte in twenty," he said. "Can you be there?"

"Yeah, I can," Sean answered. "There's a backroom where we can meet privately. Robby will bring you there, and I'll come in the back so no one will see us together."

"Yeah, that'd be good," he replied. "Thanks, Sean."

"No problem," Sean said. "I'll see you there."

Sean disconnected the phone and turned to Pete. "See, I had a plan all along," he said.

"I'd say it was the luck of the Irish," Pete replied, sitting back as Sean accelerated with sirens blasting towards Slainte, "but I'm Irish, too, and I never have the kind of luck you do."

"Well, let's see how long this O'Reilly luck holds out when we meet with Adrian," Sean said.

Sean cut the sirens a couple blocks away from the restaurant in order to avoid drawing attention. He turned into an alley a block away from the restaurant and glided past garbage cans and garages until he reached his destination. Pulling into the back of the restaurant, he parked the cruiser discreetly behind some dumpsters.

"It's not going to work," Pete said as Sean put the car into park.

"What?" Sean asked.

"Even the smell of the dumpsters isn't going to help the inside of your car," he replied, reaching over and picking up an old styrofoam drink container from between the seats. "Do you ever clean this thing out?"

"Nope, it adds to the ambiance of the vehicle," Sean replied with a grin. "Besides, no one ever asks to borrow my cruiser, so it's an added bonus."

He slid out of the car, grabbed Pete's wheelchair and walked over to the passenger side. Pete pushed the door open and studied the area before he maneuvered himself into the chair. "Do you think we're good?" his voice softer and more intense.

"Hell, Pete," Sean whispered back, also scanning the back lot. "I have no idea what we're fighting. So, keep your weapon close and ready."

Pete patted his pocket and nodded. "Good idea. But I think I would still feel better if I had something like holy water at my disposal."

Sean reached in his jacket, pulled out a small capped vial and handed it to Pete.

"You're kidding me, right?" Pete asked, staring at the small bottle.

"Nope," Sean said, shaking his head definitively. "And I've got garlic in my other pocket, just in case."

Pete shook his head and pushed his wheelchair forward. "What? Just in case they want Alfredo?" he asked.

"I'm more of a garlic bread kind of guy," Sean replied, matching his pace to Pete's chair. "Hey, I did want to say thanks."

Pete stopped and looked up at Sean. "For what?"

Sean shrugged. "You know, for getting into this crazy thing with me," he replied. "I mean, this is a lot more dangerous than what I initially thought when I called you. And, quite frankly, this is batshit crazy."

Pete continued pushing his chair forward. "No more crazy than running back into the line of fire in the Shahi-Kot Valley to rescue a friend who was hit by RPG shrapnel. I should have died that day."

Placing a hand on Pete's shoulder, Sean smiled. "No big deal. You would have done the same for me."

Pete looked up over his shoulder. "I have realized, in the past few days, that you tend to run towards danger," he replied with his own smile. "Didn't anyone ever teach you to run away?"

Shaking his head, Sean chuckled. "You know, I never did learn that lesson, did I?"

"And that's why I stay around," Pete replied. "To try and keep your butt out of trouble."

Sean sighed. "Well," he said as they traveled up the ramp to the loading dock at the back of Slainte. "You need to work harder."

Chapter Forty-nine

Adrian shook his head when he entered the small back room and saw Pete sitting next to Sean at the table. "Yeah, I shoulda known," he said with a wry shake of his head. "I thought we were friends. I thought I could trust you."

"Sit down," Sean said, his voice sharp. "And we'll talk about trust."

Adrian sat on a wooden chair, his bulking mass almost too much for the piece of furniture. "Yeah, go on," he taunted. "You tell me about trust."

"Do you even know who you're dealing with?" Sean asked. "Have you even seen those things you are setting loose on those kids? Adrian, what's happened to you? You used to be all about saving the kids in the gangs, not slaughtering them."

Shaking his head, Adrian leaned forward. "What are you talking about?" he asked. "I didn't slaughter any kids. That criminal you've been hiding is responsible for those deaths."

Sean searched Adrian's eyes and was more than a little disturbed to see that Adrian was serious about his accusations. "Okay, do me a favor, for old time's sake," he said. "Deal?"

Adrian nodded his head curtly. "Fine."

"Okay, think back to the night at the hospital, the night you called me," Sean said. "And think like a cop. What do you remember about that night?"

Adrian leaned back in the chair and took a deep breath, lifting his eyes to the ceiling for a moment as he searched his memory. "Okay, I got called in because there had been a gang fight," he started.

"Who made the call?" Pete asked.

Adrian shrugged. "It was dispatch."

Pete shook his head. "No, it wasn't," he said. "Dispatch didn't call you that night. I checked. You went to the hospital on your own."

Leaning forward, Adrian shook his head. "What?" he asked. "Then why in the hell would I go to the hospital in the middle of the night?"

"That's a good question," Sean inserted. "And why did you know about the second fight and what was happening on the ground before any squad cars got there?"

Adrian looked from Pete to Sean. "I didn't—"

"Yeah, you did," Sean interrupted. "Because I was there at the park when it went down. And you called me before any other cars reached the park."

Burying his head in his hands for a moment, Adrian was silent. "Sean, you're wrong. You've got to be messing with me."

"Adrian, you worked with me for two years," Sean replied, his voice gentle. "Have I ever lied to you?"

Looking up and meeting Sean's eyes, Adrian slowly shook his head. "No. No, you haven't," he said.

"And that's why you called him the first night," Pete said. "There was something inside you, deep inside you, that wanted the truth to be out there. That's why you called the only man you knew you could trust."

Staring at Sean again, Adrian shook his head. "Damn, I don't even remember calling you," he said.

"Yeah, I'm not surprised," Sean replied. "So, now, think back to that night. What do you actually remember?"

He leaned back again, linking his hands together and resting his head in the palms as he gazed up to the ceiling. "Okay, okay, I remember watching the clock at my apartment," he said slowly. "It was like I had an appointment. Then, at ten o'clock, I got up, got into my car and drove to the park." He looked at Sean with confusion in his eyes. "I didn't get a call. How the hell did I know to go to the park?"

"Yeah, we'll get there in a minute," Sean said. "But you need to keep remembering."

"I drove down the street and saw the kid," he continued. "Jamal. He was huddled in a doorway across the street from the park. His hands were cut real bad, and he looked pretty beat up. He was scared to death, babbling about monsters."

"Yeah, sounds like a real killer to me," Pete inserted.

Oblivious to Pete's comment, Adrian continued. "I helped him into my car. I knew he needed to be at the hospital."

"Why didn't you wait for an ambulance?" Pete asked.

"'Cause I knew no ambulances were going to be dispatched," he answered automatically.

"And how would you know that," Sean asked, "if if dispatch never called you about the incident?"?" Sean asked quickly, not giving Adrian a chance to think.

"'Cause there wasn't supposed to be survivors," Adrian said, his eyes widening as the words slipped from his mouth. "What the hell is wrong with me?"

"Have you noticed that you're forgetting things lately?" Pete asked. "Like you can't remember why you were standing up next to your desk or why you are suddenly in the break room?"

Adrian paused for a moment and then slowly shook his head. "Yeah. Yeah, that seems to be happening a lot lately," he admitted. "I thought it was just work stress."

"How about having the feeling that you're losing time?" Sean inserted. "Like you look up at the clock and wonder where the time went."

"Yeah, that's been happening a lot too," Adrian said. "But I don't dwell on it. I mean, that's normal, right?"

"Was it normal a couple of months ago?" Pete asked.

"No," Adrian said softly, his jaw tensing. "No it wasn't." He looked over and met Sean's eyes. "Irish, I don't like this. I don't like this at all. What's going on? What's happening to me?"

"You're being played," Sean replied. "Someone's messing with your mind."

"Like Manchurian candidate or sleeper agent stuff?" Adrian asked.

Sean nodded. "Yeah, something like that," he said. "But from what I understand, these guys are real good at what they do."

"How do I get this to stop?" Adrian asked.

"I'm not the guy who can help you, but I know one who can. Do you trust me?" Sean asked.

Adrian shrugged. "Yeah, well, it seems like you're the only one I really trust," he said.

"Yeah, so leave your cruiser here, and let's take a ride, okay?" Sean asked.

"Yeah, okay," he said, pulling out his cell phone. "Can I make a call first?"

"No!" shouted Pete and Sean at the same time.

Adrian looked at the phone in his hand and dropped it on the table as if it had suddenly stung him. Then he looked up at Sean and Pete. "Why doesn't one of you take my phone," he said, "just so I don't do anything stupid."

Pete reached across the picked it up. "I'd like to make a list of incoming and outgoing calls if you don't mind," he said.

Adrian shook his head. "No, I don't mind," he replied. "I think it'd be good for all of us to figure this out."

Chapter Fifty

Gillian looked up from the microscope in front of her on the stainless steel table in the large laboratory located on the first floor of the old church. She sighed softly and absently pushed her long, auburn hair away from her face. She knew she needed to focus on the project in front of her, but she had too many thoughts rushing through her mind to concentrate. She turned her head slightly, secretly watching Ian working at the next table, and another soft sigh escaped her lips. He was such a paradox: the mind of a genius in the body of an athlete and all that wrapped around a person who genuinely cared about others. No wonder she was madly, hopelessly in love with him.

Rolling her chair soundlessly back, she stood and quietly stole across the room to stand behind him. Slipping her arms around his waist, she leaned against him, breathing in his unique, male scent.

"Well, hello there," Ian murmured, his face still pressed close to the microscope. "I'll be with you in just a moment."

She watched him adjust the setting on the microscope, his long, masculine fingers slowly stroking the metal dials until he was satisfied, and she felt a corresponding shiver in her body.

"Cold?" he asked, still concentrating on the specimen under the glass.

She grinned and shook her head against his back. "No, not at all," she replied.

Finally, he lifted his head and turned around in her embrace, pulling her even closer. "And to what do I owe this wonderful distraction?" he asked, looking down at her upturned face.

She inhaled deeply and then smiled at him. "Nothing, except I love you," she said.

Watching her face, examining every nuance, like the researcher he was, she was not surprised to see the doubt in his eyes. But the initial doubt was replaced by a soft smile and a smoldering heat in his eyes. "Oh, and I love you is nothing, is it?" he whispered as he slowly lowered his head towards her. "Perhaps I need to remind you how something it really is."

His lips brushed against hers gently at first, teasing and tasting her. She quivered in his arms, and her lips parted slightly. He slipped his hands up to cradle her head and angled his head to take full advantage of her mouth, pouring his feelings into the passion of the kiss. Her world tilted, and her heart raced as her body responded to him. As a scientific researcher she realized that her body was reacting normally to sexual stimulus, but as a woman she realized that it was only one man, this man, who could cause her to have this kind of reaction.

The kiss gentled, and his embraced loosened as he rained light kisses around her face. "Ah, Gillian, darling," he whispered. "You are my life."

He rested his forehead on hers and held her for a moment. "My heart would stop beating without you," he said.

She slipped her hand up and rested it against his chest. "Aye, I know how you feel," she replied softly.

"So, why do I see fear in your eyes?" he questioned gently.

She looked up, surprised, and then smiled wryly. "And do you read minds as well, Professor?"

He smiled down at her and placed a kiss on the tip of her nose. "Only on rare occasions," he teased, and then his face sobered. "Tell me."

"This," she said, waving her arms for emphasis. "All of this. I had no idea things would be so dangerous when I brought you into this. I thought it would be interesting research. I thought we'd be studying another aspect of paranormal activity. I thought... I thought." Her voice broke, and her eyes shimmered with unshed tears. "If something were to happen to you because I invited..."

He placed a finger over her lips and shook his head. "Nothing is going to happen to me," he said. "And you didn't invite me in. I invited myself."

"But you had no idea what you'd be facing," she said. "When I chose this path in Ireland I set things in motion."

"No, darling, 'twas fate, that's all," he replied. "Sean and Em set this path a long time ago, a path they've been traveling together for years whether they knew it or not. And we've been pulled down the path with them because this is where we're supposed to be. It's no coincidence that I accepted the fellowship with the University of Chicago and you were hired by Trinity."

Laying her head against his chest, finding comfort in the solid beat of his heart, she thought about his words for a few moments. "We're supposed to be here?" she finally whispered.

"Aye," he replied, kissing the top of her head. "And perhaps this course was decided before we were even born. We are part of this darling, and that should give you comfort. We are in the right place at the right time. We are meant to win."

She looked up at him, wanting to believe his words. "I'm afraid," she finally admitted.

"And you'd be foolish not to be," he replied. "But we've so much going for us, we have to win."

"You mean our love?" she asked.

"Well, actually I was referring to my brains and boyish good looks," he teased, placing a quick kiss on her forehead. "But, aye, love's a good thing, too."

She slapped her hand against his chest, and he laughed. "You are such an eejit," she laughed softly. "But you're right. Love's a good thing, too."

"Aye," he said, his eyes turning from teasing to smoldering once again. "And perhaps we need to get a little more of that good thing."

He started to lower his head again when the door to the lab opened.

"Ah, um, well, excuse me," Father Jack said, coughing into his hand and turning to face away from the embracing couple. "I apologize for interrupting."

Ian and Gillian stepped away from each other. "Ah, no problem Father," Ian said. "What can I do for you?"

"Well, actually, I was hoping Gillian could assist me with some of the protection ideas I have for the front of the church," he said. "But I don't want to interrupt your…" he paused for an uncomfortable moment, "work."

Ian chuckled. "Actually, your timing is nearly perfect," he said, sending Gillian a quick wink. "I think we've created an application that is going to help us discern glamour. I just have to test it out, and I'll probably need Em for that."

"You've figured it out?" Gillian asked, surprised.

He smiled at her. "Aye, and I would have mentioned it," he said, "but we got a little distracted. It needs but a few tweaks and I'll be ready to test it."

Blushing, Gillian turned from Ian and towards Father Jack. "I would be happy to help you, Father," she said. "It seems I have become a distraction."

"A delightful one," Ian added.

Father Jack laughed and nodded. "Well, then, let me take you away from here, and we'll let Ian continue his work."

Gillian turned back to Ian for a moment. "I love you," she mouthed.

Ian placed his hand over his heart and nodded, watching her until she left the room. "You are my heart," he whispered softly to the empty room. "And I vow with my life that I won't let anything hurt you."

Chapter Fifty-one

"Oh good. Sean. Gillian's up with Father Jack securing the front of the building," Ian said as Sean entered the laboratory. "I have something I want..." He stopped when he saw Adrian follow Sean into the room with Pete close behind. "Well," he continued, "I didn't know we were having company."

"Ian, perfect, just the guy I was looking for," Sean said. "I need your help. This is my friend Adrian."

Ian folded his arms across his chest, nodded mutely and waited for more information. He recognized the name as the fellow who'd been setting Sean up and putting Jamal in danger. He already didn't like the man, and he was certain he didn't trust him.

"We think someone's been messing with his mind," Sean continued, "and I'd like you to take a peek."

Cocking his head to one side, Ian studied Adrian for another moment. "And why would you be thinking someone's messing with your mind?" Ian asked skeptically.

"I don't know that someone has," Adrian replied defensively. "It was Sean's idea."

Ian's eyes narrowed. "Aye, and was it Sean's idea to meet with you or was it yours?" he asked.

"It was Adrian's," Sean replied. "Why?"

"And if I were trying to see how involved Sean was in the Order of Brigid's Cross what better way than to appeal to his sense of loyalty and friendship," Ian said. "And get yourself into the church as a friend, although you're naught but a spy."

Pete rolled forward. "Wait. Wait just a minute here," he said. "Adrian actually seems to be confused about what has been happening, and he called Sean to talk about me. I don't think it's a set up."

Ian shook his head, still not convinced. "And how hard would it be for those against us to know that you and Sean were here together this morning?" Ian asked. "If they've been watching your apartment and been following you?"

Eyes widening, Pete glanced at Sean. "You know, I hadn't even thought of that," he replied. "Sean what do you think?"

Sean looked at his former partner. "I've got to know, Adrian," he asked, his tone sober. "Were you asked to meet with me so you could get into the church and learn more about what we are doing?"

Adrian's quick shifting of his eyes downward caused Sean to curse softly and shake his head. "Dude, I trusted you," he said.

353

Adrian met Sean's eyes. "You don't get it," he said. "You don't understand the plan here, Sean. We are going to be able to get rid of the gangs. We are going to eliminate the drive-by shootings. We're going to be able to stop the drug wars. We're going to let people live in neighborhoods where they can sit on their front porches and visit with each other without fear. This is a good thing."

Closing his eyes in weariness for a moment, Sean slowly shook his head. "No, Adrian, you don't understand," he said. "That's not how we do things. We are not the judge and jury. We only enforce the laws. When we forget that, we're screwed." He grabbed Adrian's shoulders. "Don't you get it? You're an accomplice to murder! You murdered those kids in cold blood."

Brushing Sean's arms away, Adrian shook his head and stepped back. "No! No! You don't understand," he argued. "The Hunt, they only kill people who are corrupt. People who have already killed. People who have evil in their hearts. So, it's all good, Sean. It's all good."

"Adrian," Pete interrupted softly. "They tried to kill Sean."

Adrian stopped. "What?" He shook his head. "No. They can't do that. They can't kill someone who's good."

"Someone's been feeding you a line," Sean said. "And you bought it, hook, line and sinker."

"No, it's worse than that," Ian said, moving forward towards Adrian and studying his eyes. "You had the right of it. He's under the influence of another."

"What?" Sean said, shifting his gaze from Adrian to Ian. "I thought you said he was a spy?" Then he looked back at Adrian. "And he admitted he was a spy."

Nodding, Ian didn't reply to Sean but continued to study Adrian. "So, Adrian, would you like me to take you to the place we keep all of our secrets?" he asked.

Adrian smiled and nodded. "Yeah, that would be nice."

"Aye, and if you'd just walk in here, into the lab area, I'll show it to you," he said, taking Adrian's arm, leading him further into the room and guiding him to a chair. "Now, you just relax for a moment and I'll clear everything with Sean."

He left Adrian in the chair and returned to Sean and Pete.

"Okay, this is more than weird," Sean said. "I feel like I just walked into another episode of the Twilight Zone. What the hell is going on with Adrian?"

"It's just a suspicion I have," Ian said. "And I'll need your help." He started to walk back into the lab and then turned back to the men following him. "Oh, and just play along with anything I say."

Sean watched Ian walk back into the lab and then turned to Pete. "Here we go again."

They followed Ian to a supply closet in the corner of the lab. When they got close, Ian handed Sean three stainless steel trays. "Are we making cookies?" Sean asked, looking at the trays that resembled cookie sheets.

"No. We're not," Ian replied, grabbing a couple more for himself. "We're testing a theory."

Sean and Pete followed Ian back to Adrian. Ian placed the sheets on the stainless steel table next to them and then turned to speak with Adrian. "Are you ready?" he asked.

Adrian nodded. "Yes, I'd like to see the secrets."

"Fine," Ian said. "But first we need to make things a little more discreet in here." He looked over to Pete and Sean. "If you two wouldn't mind holding up the sheets to form a box of sorts around Adrian's head."

Shrugging, Pete adjusted his chair so it rose up, then took two of the sheets Sean handed him and angled them to form a ninety degree angle. Sean followed Pete's lead, but placed one sheet against the two Pete held and then one on top, leaving the front open.

"Adrian, what is it you'd like to know?" Ian asked.

Adrian stared at Ian and shook his head several times, as if to clear his thoughts. "What did you say?" he asked.

"What is it you'd like to know?" Ian asked.

"I'd like to know who the hell you are and where the hell I am," he answered, his voice filled with apprehension.

"Aye, I thought you might feel that way," Ian said. "Give me a moment and I'll be able to answer a few more of your questions."

He walked away from Adrian back towards the closet.

"You want to fill us in on what's happening?" Sean asked.

"Sean is that you?" Adrian asked.

"Yeah, I'm the guy behind the metal curtain," Sean replied. "Don't worry, buddy, I've got your back."

Ian went back into the closet and came out with the headpiece from a suit of armor in his hands.

357

"What the hell?" Sean asked. "Doing a little interior decorating to make it feel like home?"

Ian grinned. "Actually, Gillian found this at an antique store and purchased it for me," he explained. "Who knew I'd need it for something like this?"

"Like what?" Pete asked.

"Just a moment," Ian said, moving back in front of Adrian and lowering the helmet onto his head. Adrian raised his eyes towards the helmet in confusion.

"What the hell?" he asked.

"It will all be clearer in a moment," Ian replied. Then he fit the helmet securely to Adrain's head. "And now we can talk." He stepped back and leaned against the table. "Sean and Pete, you can lower the trays."

Adrian looked around and met Sean's eyes. "How the hell did I get here?" he asked.

Sean sighed. "Skinny, I think that's the least of your problems."

Chapter Fifty-two

Ian walked across the room and closed the door to the lab, locking it securely. "I don't anticipate any problems," he said as he clicked the bolt into its moorings. "But I would rather prefer to be safe than sorry."

Turning, he met Adrian's wary and confused eyes. "Tell me, Adrian," he started. "Do you mind if I call you Adrian?" he interrupted himself. At Adrian's acquiescent nod, Ian continued. "What is the last thing you remember?"

Adrian thought for a few moments. "I was at my house after work and I got a phone call," he said. "They wanted to meet me and talk about the gang problems in Chicago."

"Who?" Sean asked.

Shaking his head, Adrian clamped his eyelids together in concentration. Finally, with a sigh he opened them and looked at Sean. "I can't remember."

"That's okay," Ian said. "It's not important right now. What's today's date?"

"I don't know," he said with a shrug and then he named a date.

"Dude, you've lost two weeks," Sean said and then he turned to Ian. "What's going on?"

Ian scratched his head thoughtfully and finally replied. "Well, as near as I can guess, he's been under faery control for the past few weeks," he replied.

"Okay, yeah, we already said he was hypnotized," Sean inserted.

Shaking his head, Ian leaned back against the table. "No, not hypnotism," he said. "More like mind control."

"Like the Manchurian candidate?" Pete asked.

"Well, yes and no," Ian answered. "I'm guessing with faery it's more of a collective thought process, connecting the lower level faeries' minds with the higher level faeries', so they are controlled."

"Like the Borg?" Sean asked.

Ian smiled. "Aye, in a way," he answered. "But I don't think there is just one main computer system controlling them all; I believe that the Seelie court dominates the UnSeelies."

"Okay Professor, back up and come again," Sean said. "I'm not sure I'm following you here."

Ian stood up and walked across the room to a large whiteboard. He picked up a black marker and drew a head. "So here we have a brain," he said.

360

"Looks more like a mushroom," Sean commented.

"You're not helping," Ian replied, shaking his head and turning back to the drawing and drawing a spinal cord. "The brain controls the rest of the body using electrical impulses that run through the nervous system. Got it?"

The three men observing nodded and Ian smiled. "Good."

Then he drew a long arch from the head across to the other side of the board. "But what happens if the electrical impulses you're receiving don't come from your brain, but somewhere else. What happens if your impulses are superseded by something else?"

"Can that happen?" Pete asked.

"Aye, there was a recent study at the University of Washington where they could send one person's thoughts through a computer to the mind of a second person and have the second person react to the thoughts of the person," Ian replied. "And they were a half mile away from each other."

"But Skinny doesn't have a computer hooked up to his brain," Sean inserted.

"No, you're right," Ian said. "But I think the fae are far more advanced than we are in this kind of thing, and they don't need computers, just a willing

361

mind. Which is how they are able to use glamour on us. It's mini mind control. Their minds tell our minds what they want us to see and we see it."

"Well damn," Pete said. "That makes a lot of sense."

"So, they controlled Adrian's mind and got him to do the stuff he did," Sean said. "So, now he's not under their spell anymore."

Ian shook his head. "Right now, because of the iron in the helmet, I've blocked their access," he said. "But I think that once the connection is made, it's not easily broken."

"Does that mean I'm going to be under their spell for the rest of my life?" Adrian asked.

Ian shrugged. "I don't know the answer to that," he said. "The stories that have been passed down tend to insinuate that once a mortal is under the influence of fae, they never quite get over it."

Sean thought about Em's mother and the power one faerie had over her until she died of longing. "So, we're just going to have to figure out how to break the connection," he said with determination. "That's all."

Then he walked over to his friend and tapped on the helmet. "Or you're going to have really bad helmet hair for the rest of your life."

"Funny, Irish, real funny," Adrian replied. "But, really, what do I do now?"

"Well, before you do anything else," Ian said, "I want to hypnotize you."

"Wait. What?" Sean asked. "I thought you said this wasn't hypnotism."

"It's not," Ian said. "But right now your friend has information in his mind that he might not be able to get to because he's not under their influence. Information that might help us find out where the next attack is going to occur."

Adrian turned to face Sean. "What the hell did I do when I was under their control?" he asked. "What the hell is going on?"

Placing his hand on his friend's shoulder, Sean patted it gently. "Yeah, once Ian gets his information, we'll have a long conversation," he said. "I promise. Are you okay with us taking a peek under the lid?"

A slight smile appeared on Adrian's lips. "Yeah, go ahead," he said, leaning back in the chair. "Just don't go probing where you don't belong."

"Oh, you mean that crush you've had on me since you first saw me?" Sean teased. "Don't worry, that's perfectly normal. I'm damn near irresistible."

Chapter Fifty-three

"Irresistible!" Em moaned softly, her eyes closed in pure ecstasy. She lifted the teaspoon to her mouth and licked off the remaining cookie dough. "I have never tasted anything so delicious."

"Yeah, Grandma makes sick cookies," Jamal added.

"Sick?" Mrs. Gage asked, her face tightened in disapproval. "Boy, my cookies never made no one sick."

Jamal grinned. "No, Grandma, sick don't mean that anymore," he explained. "Sick means good. Real good."

"Then why didn't you say good?" Mrs. Gage asked, shaking her wooden spoon in Jamal's direction. "Don't make no sense to change the meaning of a word what's been around for hundreds of years." Shaking her head, she turned back to her mixing bowl. "Don't know what's wrong with people today."

Em winked at Jamal and moved closer to Mrs. Gage, peeking over her shoulder into the bowl. Mrs. Gage looked back at Em and lifted her eyebrows. "Something you looking for?" she asked.

Em nodded. "Yes, I wanted to see if you put any magic in there," she teased.

Mrs. Gage's jaw dropped for a moment and her eyes widened in surprise, but Em had already turned to smile at Jamal and didn't see the shock in the older woman's face. Mrs. Gage took a quick recovery breath and pasted a smile on her face while she held her trembling hands together to steady them. "I don't need any magic for my cookies," she replied with a slightly shaky voice. "I've got skills."

Jamal chuckled. "Yeah, that's right," he said. "Grandma got skills."

Em studied Mrs. Gage for a moment and placed her hand on the woman's shoulder. "Mrs. Gage, you look a little tired," she said. "Do you need to sit down?"

Shaking her head, Mrs. Gage turned back to the cookie dough. "Oh, no, dear, but thank you for your concern," she said. "I just want to get these on cookie sheets and into the oven."

"Jamal and I can do that," Em said, glancing over to Jamal and noting his agreement. "You've been through an awful lot today with everything that's gone on. It's amazing that you are still standing on your feet."

Wrapping her arm around Mrs. Gage's shoulders, Em gently urged her away from the counter and back towards the living area. She guided her to a small, overstuffed chair and helped her sit down. "You sit down and I'll make you a cup of tea," she said. "And just rest for a little bit."

Once seated, Mrs. Gage was surprised at how tired she actually felt. "Are you sure you can handle baking the cookies?" she asked.

"Of course I can," she said with more confidence than she felt. "And Jamal can show me how to put cookies on a sheet."

It was Mrs. Gage's turn to be suspicious. "You do know what a cookie sheet is, don't you?" she asked.

Em smiled and nodded nervously. "Of course I know what a sheet is," she replied. "I sleep on a bed, don't I?"

Jamal laughed out loud, but when his grandmother shot him a warning look, he covered his mouth with his hand and tried to muffle his mirth.

"What?" Em asked, looking from grandson to grandmother.

"Cookie sheets are thin, flat, baking pans," Mrs. Gage said. "Didn't your mother ever teach you to cook, child?"

"My mother died when I was a child," Em replied softly.

Mrs. Gage grabbed the arms of the chair and started to stand up but found her strength was spent. She slowly lowered herself back into the chair and stretched out her hands towards Em. "Come here, honey," she insisted.

"I'm fine," Em insisted, shaking her head and stepping back. "It was a long time ago."

"Don't matter how long ago it was," Mrs. Gage insisted. "When you lose a member of your family, the pain never totally goes away."

Shrugging, Em tried to brush it off and was surprised to discover a tear sliding down her cheek. She quickly whisked it away with her hand, but Mrs. Gage met her eyes and shook her head. "Child, you come over to me right now or I promise you I will chase you across this apartment."

Hesitantly, Em moved towards her and allowed her hands to be enfolded into a pair of fragile, soft ones. "I'm so sorry," Mrs. Gage said, her eyes filled with sympathy and understanding. "I know what it's like to lose someone you loved."

Em took a deep, shaky breath. "I didn't love her," she insisted, wiping away another tear. "She never loved me. She didn't even realize I was alive."

Mrs. Gage shook her head. "I don't know what happened when you were a child," she said, "but I do know you wanted your mother's love. It's only human."

367

"But you see, that's where you have it wrong," Em said, gently pulling her hands away from the elderly woman. "I am anything but human."

Chapter Fifty-four

Ian, Sean and Pete surrounded the chair where Adrian was breathing deeply and in a deep hypnotic trance.

"Well, he's under," Ian whispered to Sean and Pete. "Is there anything specific you want me to find out?"

"Who the hell did this to him," Sean said, the teasing tone gone from his voice, "and where he lives."

Ian nodded. "I'll see what I can do," he said.

"And more importantly," Pete added, "what the next steps are in their plan."

"Aye, I think that's where I'm going to go first," he said.

He turned to Adrian. "Adrian, I want you to think back to your first meeting about two weeks ago with the person who wanted to help you with the gangs in Chicago," Ian said. "Can you remember that night?"

Adrian nodded slowly.

"Good," Ian said. "Do you know that person? Have you met him before?"

Adrian nodded again.

"Good," Ian replied. "Who is it?"

"Captain Douglas," Adrian said softly. "It's Captain Douglas."

"What the...," Sean whispered harshly. "It can't be Douglas, he's one of us. He's one of the good guys."

Pete put his hand on Sean's arm. "Remember about glamour," he reminded Sean. "They could have used Captain Douglas's face in order to influence Adrian."

Sean nodded. "Yeah man, you're right," he said with a deep breath. "Sorry, Ian."

"No problem, Sean," he replied. "And I think Pete has the right of it. What better person to use than a trusted superior?"

Ian turned back to Adrian. "What did Captain Douglas say to you?" he asked.

"He told me that he had a new weapon in the war against drugs," Adrian replied. "That it was an army of warriors that could tell good folk from evil folk. That it could stop the bad guys and no one else would get hurt."

"And what did you think?"

"Well, at first, you know, I thought it was crazy because we can't let people get hurt, even if they've done bad things," Adrian said. "But the captain said he'd cleared it with a judge and the mayor. They were all for it. He said it would save lives, hundreds of lives. And all I had to do was work with the group."

"What's the name of the group?" Ian asked.

"The Hunt," Adrian answered. "He gave me this connection, like this mind thing, and I could call on them to be at gang wars to stop them. To save kids from being killed."

"What dates did you give them?" Ian asked.

Adrian repeated the dates of the last two attacks and then added one more.

"That's two days from now," Sean said, moving up and putting his hand on Ian's shoulder. "Find out when and where."

"And where were the Hunt supposed to show up?" Ian asked.

Adrian supplied the parks that had hosted the last two attacks and then he paused.

"Adrian, the next one," Ian said. "The one that's scheduled in the future. Where is that going to be held?"

Adrian shook his head. "That's a special one," he said. "It's supposed to be a big surprise. The captain said he didn't want me to tell anyone about it."

"But you already told the Hunt about it?" Ian asked.

"Yes, sir," Adrian replied. "I'm their Summoner. I'm the only one they listen to."

"Well, then, you can tell me," Ian said, "because I'm your trusted friend."

"Are you?" Adrian asked, cocking his head to the side.

"Aye," Ian said. "I am."

Adrian shook his head. "No, I can't trust you," he said. "The captain told me not to trust anyone. This one is too special. This one will show everyone how much power we have."

Sean stepped up and glanced at Ian, silently asking permission to try. With a quick nod of his head, Ian stepped back and gave Sean access.

"Hey, Skinny," Sean said.

A smile grew on Adrian's face. "Hey, Irish," he replied.

"Hey, I got a problem, and I'm hoping you can help me," Sean said. "I know the captain is working on something big and he's put you in charge."

"Yeah, Sean," Adrian replied, his voice enthused. "He said he trusted me to do it."

"Well, I know he couldn't have picked a better man for the job," Sean said.

"Hey, thanks man, that really means a lot coming from you," Adrian said.

"Okay, here's the deal," Sean said. "You're the Summoner and everything, but I'm supposed to be, um, I'm supposed to be your…"

"Champion," Ian whispered. "That's a trusted friend."

"Yeah, right, your champion," Sean said. "Did the cap mention that to you?"

Adrian shook his head. "No, he didn't."

"Well, damn," Sean said. "'Cause I kind of forgot where I was supposed to be for this big deal event, and the cap is not going to be too happy about this."

"You know about Grant Park?" Adrian asked.

Sean's eyes widened when Adrian mentioned the most popular park in the city's downtown district. "Yeah, of course I know," he lied. "Like I said, the cap asked me to be your champion. You're the guy in charge, and I get the coffee and donuts."

Adrian chuckled. "I'm surprised you're not getting the beer and pretzels, Irish."

Sean nodded and tried to lighten his voice. "Well, yeah, those are for the victory celebration afterwards."

"Yeah, it's going to be so cool," Adrian replied. "All those kids watching, seeing justice and honor before them. It's going to make a lasting impression."

"Yeah, I know it will," Sean agreed. "Especially for those kids. Do you remember how many kids?"

"Yeah, the cap told me over a thousand grammar school kids are going to be there," Adrian replied. "Didn't he tell you?"

"He told me that you'd give me the details, because you were lead on this one," Sean said.

Pete rolled up next to Sean and handed him his tablet. "This is not good," he whispered.

Sean looked down at the screen, and his heart dropped. In two days' time, in Grant Park, a Children's Music Festival was being held. Children's choirs from all over the city would be participating at the Grant Park band shell.

Taking a deep, unsteady breath before he spoke again, Sean tried to make his voice light. "So, do you want me to meet you at the band shell?" he asked.

Adrian shook his head. "No, that's too close to the action," he replied. "The cap said it would be better to just let the Hunt do their work and then appear after they're done, like the other times."

Sean felt physically ill, picturing what the Hunt would do to all of those children. "Why did the cap say we were doing this one?" he asked. "These kids aren't gang members."

"Oh, he told me this was to help the mayor understand the strength of our new program," Adrian replied. "He said this will be like nothing Chicago's ever seen."

"So, what happens if it rains?" Sean asked. "Can we cancel the demonstration?"

Adrian shook his head. "No. Once the Hunt has been called, they can't be stopped."

Chapter Fifty-five

"We've got to call off this event," Sean said. "We've got to alert the mayor's office and call the whole damn thing off."

"Yeah, that will work," Pete said. "You'll be thrown into a looney bin."

"How about if we say there's a terrorist threat?" Adrian suggested.

Pete shook his head. "They'll just call in more security," he said.

"More people to get killed," Sean said. "We've just got to stop this."

Adrian dropped his head into his hands. "Oh, man, Sean, I am so sorry," he said. "It's all my fault."

Sean put his hand on his friend's arm. "No, it's not your fault," he said. "They used and manipulated you. You are as much a victim as anyone else."

"Yeah, but how do I keep from falling into their trap again?" he asked. "I really believed I saw the captain."

Ian walked over to the table and picked up a small, plastic, spray bottle. "Actually, I was going to talk to Sean about this when he came in. It's an herbal mixture that's sprayed into your eyes to reveal the truth behind any faery glamour."

"Does it work?" Sean asked.

"Well, in theory," Ian said. "We haven't tested it yet."

"I'll try it," Adrian offered. "I'd like to be able to figure out who I'm really talking to."

"How long does it last?" Pete asked.

Ian shook his head. "I'm not sure about that either," he said. "The old recipe I took it from suggested that travelers spray it in their eyes before a journey so they wouldn't be deceived."

Sean shrugged. "Well, it's probably good for at least a couple of hours," he said. "You should give it a shot."

Ian walked over to them and sprayed the bottle. A fine mist of spray filled the area.

"Hey," Sean exclaimed, wiping the excess moisture off his face. "I didn't volunteer to try this stuff."

"Sorry, the sprayer was more powerful than I thought," he said. "But, it's only herbs, so it won't hurt you."

"In the meantime," Pete interrupted, "we've got to figure out how to either stop the Hunt or how to fight them."

Ian nodded. "Aye, we'll need to call a meeting and put together a battle plan."

Sean nodded. "Yeah, but before we do that," he said, "we better get Adrian back to work so no one gets suspicious. So, Ian, he can't walk around with a helmet on his head. What's he supposed to do?"

Ian picked up a small stainless steel bowl and a roll of gauze. "I'm afraid, Adrian, that you had a bit of a run-in with your head and a heavy object," he said. "And the doctor told you to keep it bandaged for several days to avoid infection."

Ian removed the helmet, quickly placed the bowl on Adrian's head and started covering it with gauze.

"As soon as you're done," Sean said, "I'll get him back to Slainte to pick up his car. Then I have to run one quick errand and I'll be back for the meeting. Give me an hour, okay?"

Ian nodded as he tucked the last strand of gauze underneath the others and applied some medical tape. "I'll get everyone together," he said. "And Adrian, you need to act like nothing's wrong. If someone you don't recognize starts up a conversation, remember to play along."

"Yeah, I can do that," he said. "Do you need me at this meeting?"

Sean shook his head. "No, because I really don't know who I can trust yet," he said. "And I don't want to risk your safety."

"Dude, I caused this," Adrian said. "My safety ain't worth shit."

"I already told you," Sean said. "This wasn't you, it was them. You're nothing but a victim, too."

"Yeah, well I sure wish I felt that way," Adrian said.

"Start thinking that way," Sean replied. "That's an order."

Chapter Fifty-six

After dropping Adrian off at Slainte, Sean drove through a coffee shop for a tea and a couple of scones and headed for lower Wacker Drive. It was early, but he was sure he'd find Hettie in her usual place. He wanted to be sure he had a chance to see her before he got pulled into the meetings with the Order.

The downtown rush hour traffic had thinned and Lower Wacker was already a ghost town with late sunbeams filtering between the mazes of downtown skyscrapers and creating a haze of sunlight and dust in the subterranean community. Sean felt like he was driving into a post-apocalyptic faery tale.

He spotted Hettie's familiar dress at the end of the block and guided the cruiser to the curb nearby. She was turned away from him, sorting through her shopping cart, and he paused to look at her as he pulled the drink and bag from the car.

Okay, this day has been way too long, he thought. *How can Hettie look taller?*

He stared for another moment and then shrugged. *Maybe she found a pair of high heels.*

"Delivery is a little early today," he called as he walked up behind her. His jaw and the bag of scones both dropped when she turned to face him. This wasn't Hettie. The young, breathtakingly beautiful woman inside the green ball gown filled out the dress in a way that made Sean's body react in an entirely unprofessional manner.

"Ah, Sean, you remembered me," she replied.

Shaking his head, Sean now knew he was going crazy. Hettie's voice was coming out of the woman's mouth.

"Who the hell are you and what have you done with Hettie?" he demanded.

Cocking her head slightly to the side, she stared back at him. "What do you mean, Sean?" she asked, confusion evident on her face. "It's just me, as always."

"Yeah, you might have the voice down, but that body doesn't belong to Hettie," he replied firmly, moving closer to the imposter.

Eyes widening in understanding, she looked down at herself and then back at Sean. "Have you been playing with magic then, Sean O'Reilly?" she asked, a smile flitting across her face. "Have you done something to chase the glamour from your eyes?"

He stumbled back and stared. "What the hell do you know about glamour?" he whispered.

Her beautiful smile widened. "Oh, aye, my secret's been revealed hasn't it?" she replied. "You see me for myself, don't you?"

"You are going to have to explain yourself to me," he replied. "Are you Hettie?"

"Oh, aye, I am and I'm not," she said, a twinkle of mischief in her eyes. "For those not clever enough to see through my glamour, I'm Hettie the elderly hag, and to those whose eyes have been opened, I'm Mab."

"Mab?" Sean asked.

"Aye, Mab, the Queen of the Unseelies," she said. "Part of the aristocracy, but, as you humans so aptly put it, born on the wrong side of the tracks. So even though I'm not forced to live underground, I am forced to live without my subjects and my protectors. I am a queen without a court and have been alone for hundreds of years."

Sean looked at the vibrant faerie with her golden hair, her glowing green eyes and her youthful appearance. She hadn't been a helpless, homeless woman, and he'd been a gullible fool. She must have enjoyed laughing at him.

Placing the cup of tea on the sidewalk, Sean stepped back. "Well, your majesty, I'm glad I

381

provided you some amusement," he said, his voice tight with anger. "Now, if you'll excuse me, I have some important things to deal with."

The smile left her face and she stepped forward, her arm raised towards him. "Oh, no, Sean O'Reilly," she said. "'Twas not amusement I felt when you took the time to care for an elderly woman. 'Twas friendship and gratitude. You showed me that the human race could be noble and not just self-serving and silly. You taught me a great lesson, and I owe you for that."

Taking a deep breath, trying to release some of the anger, he nodded and smiled tightly. "Well, thank you for that," he said. "And now, really, I do have to get back."

He started to turn and she stopped him again. "I want to help you," she said. "Ask me for a favor, and I'll grant it."

He studied her for another moment. "Are you like a faery godmother then?" he asked.

Her smiled widened. "Oh, aye, and would you be wanting a fancy dress and a pumpkin carriage, Sean O'Reilly?"

"No, I want to stop the Wild Hunt," he replied seriously.

Sighing, she shook her head. "I can't stop them," she said. "Once they've been summoned they can't be turned back. Unless…"

"Unless?" Sean asked.

"Unless the Summoner or his champion challenge the Elk King to a battle in lieu of a hunt," she said.

"I'm the Champion," Sean replied. "How do I challenge the Elk King?"

"Please don't ask me to do this for you, Sean," she begged. "You don't understand the consequences."

"It doesn't matter," Sean replied. "I have no choice."

She looked into his eyes and sighed. "Aye, that's the problem with the noble," she said sadly. "They die too young."

Shrugging, he smiled at her. "Well, maybe you're not giving me enough credit," he said. "I beat the Elk King's horse. I bet I could do enough damage to get him to cry uncle."

"Aye, but whether you win or lose, you have to pay the forfeit," she said.

"The forfeit?" he asked.

She nodded slowly. "The Hunt has to bring back a prize," she said. "If you defeat the Elk King, you will still be bound to go with them back to faery."

"Underground?" he asked. "Forever?"

The sadness in her eyes made his stomach clench. "Aye, unless you escape," she said. "And that's a rare event."

"But, if I win, they don't come back, right?" he asked.

"Aye, they must return to faery," she said. "Your world would be safe."

Taking a deep breath, he paused for only a moment. "Set it up," he said. "For tomorrow night. I'll let you know where."

"Are you sure, Sean O'Reilly?" she asked. "Because once a challenge has been issued, it cannot be revoked."

He nodded. "Yeah, I'm sure," he replied. "Thank you."

"No, Sean O'Reilly, do not thank me for this thing I am doing for you," she replied sadly. "For I am doing naught but helping you end your own life."

Chapter Fifty-seven

Sean pulled the cruiser over once he had driven away from Lower Wacker, pulled into an empty parking lot, put the cruiser into park and laid his head in his hands.

What the hell have I just done?

He rubbed his hands over his face and took a deep breath. "Well, there's no use crying over spilt milk. What's done is done," he said to his reflection in the rearview mirror. "Now all I have to figure out is a venue and how to escape from the faery world afterwards. No problem."

He pulled out his wallet and found the small piece of paper that held the phone number of Marcus, the leader of the gang Em had nearly castrated with her sword. "Hey, Marcus, this is Detective O'Reilly," he said when there was an answer on the other end of the line. "Do you remember who I am?"

"Yeah. Yeah, I remember you and that lady," Marcus replied. Noting the nervous tremor in his voice, Sean had to smile slightly.

"I need your help," Sean continued.

"Sure. Anything you need, man," Marcus said.

"I need a place. A private place where I can have a throw down," Sean said.

"You gonna have a throw down?" Marcus asked. "Why the hell you doing that? You're the cops?"

"Yeah, well, it's kind of a private throw down between me and the leader of the gang that took your friends down," Sean explained. "I just want it to be held somewhere isolated, so no one innocent gets hurt."

"Yeah, I get that," Marcus said. He was quiet for a moment. "When do you need it?"

"Tomorrow night," Sean replied.

"Okay, I can get you Soldier Field," Marcus said.

"Soldier Field?" Sean asked incredulously, picturing the historic football field that was the home of the Chicago Bears. "Are you messing with me?"

"No, man, I know some people," Marcus said. "That work for you?"

"Yeah," Sean replied slowly. "That would be great."

"What time?" Marcus asked.

"How about nine o'clock?" Sean suggested.

"Works for me," Marcus replied. "And me and some of my homies will show up for security. We got your back."

"Thanks, Marcus," Sean said, thinking the backup wouldn't be a bad idea. "I appreciate it."

"We on the same team, you and me," Marcus replied. "See you then."

"Yeah, see you," Sean said and then he hung up the phone.

He put the cruiser in drive and pulled to the edge of the driveway, clicking his turn signal to show a right turn but, at the last moment, flicked it over to the other side and drove back to Lower Wacker.

A few minutes later he pulled up to the curb next to Hettie, or Mab he corrected mentally. He got out of the car and walked over to the faery queen who was sitting quietly on a tattered lawn chair drinking her tea. "Not the throne I would have expected for a queen," he said.

She looked up at him and shrugged. "Aye, things have gone downhill for me," she said.

"Downhill enough that you would like the treaty to be broken?" he asked.

"Are you now thinking that I'm an accomplice to murder?" she asked.

Sean placed his hands on his hips and shook his head. "I don't know what I think," he answered honestly. "I feel like my world has been turned upside down in the past few days. The things I thought I knew to be true are now lies."

She stood with the grace and dignity of a queen and folded her arms across her chest. "Not lies, Sean O'Reilly. You just didn't have the whole picture in front of you," she said. "The greatest power of faery is the ability to only present what we want to present, give you a portion of the truth, or a part of the picture, so you proceed in a fog. The fog is lifted for you; you have to decide how to deal with it."

Studying her for a moment, Sean rocked back on his heels thoughtfully. "We have a place for the contest. It will be at Soldier Field tomorrow night at nine. How do I win against the Elk King?" he asked.

She smiled. "Good for you, a direct question," she replied, nodding her head in approval. "The Elk King is a hunter, not a warrior. He is used to pursuing unarmed and often surprised prey. You will be both armed and prepared, so you will have that advantage. He will be on horseback, so he will have speed but not maneuverability. You must be both nimble and quick in order to avoid his sword."

"Does he have a weak spot?" Sean asked.

Her smile broadened. "Another excellent question," she said. "Yes, the skull of the elk protects his vulnerable area. If you were able to thrust your sword into the darkness where his face should be, you will destroy him."

"Does that mean I won't have to forfeit my life?" Sean asked.

Her smile disappeared. "No, sadly it does not," she replied. "He is an immortal creature. You will have destroyed him on this playing field, but he will live yet again. And once the tournament is over, the rest of the Hunt will seize you and bring you down to faery."

Sean nodded. "Thank you, Hettie...or Mab...or Your Highness," he stammered, closing his eyes in frustration. Finally, he opened them again and met hers. "Thank you for helping me. Thank you for truly being a friend. I apologize for doubting you."

Her smile was sad as she stepped forward and placed a gentle hand on his cheek. "Oh, you must always doubt a faerie," she said softly. "We are forever engaged in mischief."

He smiled at her and nodded.

"And where will you go now?" she asked.

He took a quick, shuddering breath and looked over her shoulder for a moment. "I need to meet with my friends and tell them as much about tomorrow night as I can," he said. "And then I need to visit my parents and tell them goodbye."

389

Chapter Fifty-eight

The back door of the church was opened before Sean reached it, and Em stood in the doorway waiting for him. "The others are in Father Jack's apartment waiting for us," she said. "But I wanted a few moments alone with you before you met with them."

He nodded silently, entered the church and leaned back against the wall in the hallway. "What can I do for you?" he asked.

She studied him for a long moment and then finally spoke. "What have you done?" she asked.

"What do you mean?" he asked, surprised.

"You and I are linked," she replied, moving closer to him. "I get…" She paused, searching for the words. "Feelings. I get feelings about you, and there is something wrong. There is something different."

He shrugged. "Probably nerves," he admitted. "I set up a duel with the Elk King for tomorrow night."

"You did what?" she exclaimed. "What the hell were you thinking?"

He had to admit, it felt good to have Em react that way. She cared. Not that it would do either of them much good. But it was a nice feeling.

"Hey, no big deal," he said with a casual shrug. "I'm going to fight him tomorrow night. I've beat him once. I can do it again."

Em stepped even closer so that they were only inches apart, her eyes blazing with anger. "I beat him," she reminded him. "You punched his horse in the nose. You are no match for the Elk King. You should have let me fight him."

He shook his head. "I couldn't do that, Em," he said softly, hoping she'd understand. "I'm the guy with the special sword. It's my job to take on the bad guys."

He pushed away from the wall, placed his hand on her shoulder, and leaned forward so their foreheads were touching. "I know you're a better warrior than me," he said softly. "I'm hoping you'll give me some pointers before tomorrow night."

She sighed softly. "There's so much for you to learn," she explained, trying to keep the frustration out of her voice. "You have to call this off. There has to be another way."

"I can't," he said simply. "People will die. Children will die. This is the only way."

He lifted his hand and caressed her cheek. She lifted her head and their eyes met. "Em," he whispered as he slid his hand around to the back of her neck to pull her closer.

"Ah, there you are," Ian called from down the hall. "I've assembled the team, as you requested."

"We'll be there in a moment," Sean called back.

He dropped his hand from Em's neck and stepped back slowly, his eyes still on hers. "I'm sorry about what happened to you today, in the gym," he said softly. "I'm sorry he used my face. I'm sorry he hurt you. I would have never hurt you like that."

She nodded mutely.

"Do you believe me?" he asked.

"Aye," she said. "And I should have known that it would not be like you to force yourself on a woman. I'm sorry I didn't trust you more."

He shook his head. "You've nothing to apologize for," he insisted. "You just always have to remember…" He stopped himself and inhaled sharply.

"What?" she insisted.

He shrugged and sent her a crooked smile. "I guess I forgot."

Her eyes narrowed. "Sean O'Reilly," she threatened. "You will tell me what you were going to say."

He nodded. "I will," he said, stepping further away. "But not today. Come on, there's a meeting waiting for us."

Chapter Fifty-nine

The faces in the room were grim when Sean and Em entered. Sean closed the door behind them and stayed standing, waiting until Em took a seat, before he addressed them. "I suppose Ian and Pete told you what we learned about the next target of The Hunt," he said.

"We have to stop them," Gillian said.

"I've called my contacts at city hall," Father Jack said. "And their hands are tied. They can't cancel the event on a rumor of danger."

Pete studied Sean, saw the set of his jaw and the steady resolve in his eyes. "What have you done?" he asked quietly.

"Do you remember Hettie?" he asked Pete.

Pete nodded. "The old, homeless woman under Lower Wacker," he replied.

"Yeah," Sean said, smiling dryly. "Except it turns out she's not homeless, she's not old, and she's not a woman."

"She's a young, wealthy, cross-dresser?" Pete asked.

Sean actually chuckled, and it felt good to laugh. "No, she's actually Mab," he said. "The Queen of the Unseelie Court. I guess I got enough of Ian's spray in my eyes to see past her glamour. It was a surprise to both of us."

"I imagine it was," Ian said. "But if she's Unseelie, she's not on our side of this war."

Sean shrugged. "Well, actually, she is," he said. "She is the queen, but she's been cast out of her kingdom by the treaty and really doesn't have a whole lot to do with them. And, because of the tea and scones I bring her, she feels that she owes me."

"What did she promise you?" Em asked, her suspicion evident.

"She told me how to stop the Hunt," he replied.

"And just how do you do that?" Ian asked. "Adrian said that once the Hunt was called, it could not be stopped."

"Unless you challenge the Elk King to a duel," Sean inserted.

"But who would be foolish enough to..." Gillian's stopped halfway through her sentence and shook her head. "Oh, no, Sean, you didn't."

"Of course he did," Pete said, his anger evident. "Because he's an ass who thinks he's the only one who can save the day."

Sean turned to Gillian. "Yes, I did," he replied, and then he turned to Pete. "Partially because I'm an ass and partially because I couldn't see another way around it."

"Please explain," Father Jack insisted.

"When Ian hypnotized Adrian, we gave him the suggestion that I was his champion," Sean explained. "The only people allowed to challenge the Elk King are either the Summoner or the Champion. So, it's not like I didn't want your help, it's just that I kind of fell into the job."

"And where is this duel supposed to take place?" Ian asked.

"Soldier Field. Tomorrow night at nine," Sean replied. "Marcus, the gang leader we met at the Gages' apartment, set things up for me."

"But you can't trust him," Mrs. Gage cried. "He's a criminal."

Sean nodded. "Yes, but he's a criminal who is terrified of Em," he said. "So he was very obliging. He even said he and his boys would run security for us."

"Well, that's comforting," Pete said. "Is there anything else you want to tell us about the duel?"

Sean turned and met his friend's eyes. "No," he said. "Nothing else. But Hettie, or should I say Mab, gave me some pointers on how to fight him. She told me that he was not very agile and that his weak spot was underneath the elk skull."

"Well, then, that should be easy," Ian quipped. "All you have to do is outrun a magical horse and outfight an opponent with an arm span three times the length of your own. Piece of cake."

Sean grinned. "See, that's the attitude we need to have," he said.

"And what happens if you lose?" Em asked.

"I don't lose," Sean replied. "That's not an option."

"Well, if it's not an option, I think we all have some work to do tonight." Father Jack said, pushing himself out of his chair. "I think there's a shirt of chainmail that was blessed by the Pope himself somewhere here in the church. I'll take a look."

"I'll start researching the Elk King, there might be something out there that can give you an advantage," Ian said, getting up and walking across the room.

"I'll help," Gillian offered, joining him.

Pete shook his head and rolled forward. "You are not just an idiot, you are a damn idiot," he said, placing his hand on his friend's arm. "But I know some guys that work the pyrotechnics at Soldier Field for the concerts. I'm thinking a couple of well-placed explosions or flares might distract the creature long enough for you to take advantage of him."

"Thanks, Pete," Sean said. "I'd appreciate that."

Mrs. Gage stood and walked over to Sean, taking both of his hands in hers. "We are going to pray for you," she said. "I know it might not seem like much…"

He shook his head, stopping her. "No, I know the power of prayer," he said. "And I would appreciate it very much."

She leaned up and placed a kiss on his cheek. "God Bless You, Sean O'Reilly," she whispered, a tear sliding down her wrinkled cheek. She brushed it away and then turned to Jamal. "Come on, boy, we've got some heavy praying to do."

Finally, only Em and Sean were left in the room. "We should get up to the gym and practice your swordplay," she said.

He nodded. "Yeah, we should," he agreed. "But there's one more stop I need to make before I practice."

"It's more important than improving your skills?" she asked, incredulous.

He nodded. "Yes. Yes it is."

Chapter Sixty

"Meow."

The soft, plaintive cry came from the carrier Sean had in his arms as he walked up the sidewalk to his parents' yellow, brick bungalow on the city's far northwest side.

"Shhhhh, Tiny," Sean coaxed. "Don't be such a baby. You love coming here. Mom always gives you chicken livers. Besides, I don't know when I'll be coming home."

"Meow," was the response.

"Yeah, well, me too," Sean said. "But we can't always get what we want."

He opened the front door and walked inside, breathing in the enticing aroma from the kitchen. His mother's family-famous spaghetti sauce must be on the stovetop and garlic bread must be in the oven. That was one of their family jokes. The best Italian food they ever had was made by their completely Irish mother.

"I'm here," he called, closing the door behind him. "And I brought company."

Margaret O'Reilly called to him from the kitchen. "Your father is not home yet, but I'm expecting him anytime." Coming around the corner, wiping her hands on an apron, she hurried into the room. "Ah, well, so you've brought Tiny," she exclaimed, shaking her head. "And here I was thinking you might have brought a lady friend to meet us."

Helping Tiny out of his cage, Sean covered Tiny's ears with his hand and shook his head. "Shhhh, Ma," he teased. "Tiny will think he's not welcome."

Margaret O'Reilly grinned and took the giant cat from Sean's arms into her own, scratching the cat lovingly behind the ears. "Tiny knows he's always welcome here," she said as the cat purred its approval of her actions. "And I seem to remember some chicken livers I might have saved in the fridge for just an occasion."

Tiny looked up and met Sean's eyes. "Yeah, what did I tell you?" Sean replied to the cat.

"So, I'm on this case that might keep me away from home for a while," Sean said, following his mother into the kitchen. "And I was wondering if Tiny could spend some time with you."

"Of course," she said, placing Tiny on the floor in the kitchen and opening the fridge to find the small container of chicken livers. "What are you working on?"

Sean slipped onto a tall stool next to the kitchen counter and grabbed a piece of garlic bread. "Well, it's kind of weird, Ma," he said, breaking off a piece of bread and popping it into his mouth. "Do you remember that scar I got when we were in Ireland back when I was a kid?"

She instantly turned and met his eyes. "Yes," she said, her face a little tense.

He studied her for a moment and shook his head. "You knew," he said, his eyes widening in amazement. "You knew it wasn't a thorn bush all along."

She took a deep breath and nodded. "Aye, I knew," she admitted.

"Why didn't you tell me the truth?" he asked. "Why didn't you let me know that those creatures were real and they lived among us?"

She pulled a stool over to the other side of the counter and sat across from him. "Well, I'll tell you that I was more concerned about my son than I was about any legends, be they real or not," she said.

"What do you mean?" he asked.

"What would have happened, do you think, when you came back to Chicago and told your friends about the scary beastie in the forest in Ireland?" she asked.

He thought about it for a moment. He thought about the grief his sister Mary received because she could see ghosts, and she didn't get that gift until she was an adult. And beyond the grief from his friends, how would it have been if he, as a twelve year-old boy, had come back with the knowledge that the creature he saw in the woods was real and not a hallucination?

"It would have changed me," he admitted. "I think I would have been more fearful."

She nodded slowly and then cocked her head to the side and studied him. "And did you ever really believe that we told you the truth?" she asked.

He smiled back at her. "Well, truth be told, I always had my doubts," he said.

"And that doubt, did it make you ready for the truth when it presented itself again?" she asked.

He nodded. "Yeah, actually, it did." He realized the truth in the words as he said them. "It really did. Why? Why did you choose to handle it that way?"

She took a piece of garlic bread from the basket and toyed with it for a moment. "Do you remember the first time you asked about where babies came from?" she asked, looking up from the bread and meeting his eyes.

He grinned. "What was I? Five?"

403

She nodded. "Aye. You'd come off the bus from your kindergarten class and marched into the kitchen demanding to know where babies came from."

He nodded. "It's funny that I can remember that far back," he said.

"And do you remember how I answered?"

His smile widened. "Yeah, I remember you asked me what I thought."

"And you told me that you thought babies came from the hospital," she said with a chuckle. "And I told you that you were 100 percent correct. Do you know why I answered your question like that?"

He shook his head.

"Because I knew when you were ready for it, the truth would be waiting for you," she explained.

He reached across the counter, took her hands in his and then lifted them to his lips and kissed them. "Thank you," he said, "for the right answers at the right time all through my life."

Her hands tightened their grip on his as she met his eyes. "Sean, what kind of special case are you working on?" she asked, fear in her voice.

He lifted her hands to his lips one more time and met her eyes. "What kind of case do you think it is, Ma?"

Tears slipped from her eyes and trailed down her cheeks. "The kind of case where you walk away safe and sound," she whispered, her voice cracking with emotion. "The kind of case where you come back to me, Sean O'Reilly."

He nodded slowly. "Yes, Ma, that's exactly the kind of case it is."

Chapter Sixty-one

Sean placed the key into the ignition of his car and turned it on. He looked over his shoulder to see his parents standing on the front porch waving at him, a tradition they'd always had. He knew they wouldn't go inside until he turned right at the end of the corner. He smiled at them, waved, and put the cruiser into drive. Taking a deep breath, he pulled out of the parking spot and drove down the street, trying not to remember the look of sadness in his mother's eyes.

By some unspoken communication, they had both decided not to share the information about Sean's case with his father. Instead, the dinner conversation had been filled with talk about family, memories and laughter. It was exactly what Sean had needed. And when he hugged his father goodbye and felt those bear-like arms around him, he knew he'd done the right thing.

Having a family of police officers, it was understood that each day at work could be your last. They'd never allowed that idea to overwhelm or depress them, but they had understood that love needed to be shared, anger needed to be brief and life needed to be lived. This was just another one of those nights. Tomorrow would bring what it would bring, but for tonight, he and his family were safe and secure in their love for each other.

As Sean turned the corner, he looked around at the neighborhood he'd grown up in. The baseball diamond where he'd learned to play softball. The small playground where he'd stolen his first kiss. The corner store where he and his siblings had agonizingly decided how to spend the money they'd had on penny candy. He smiled to himself. He'd had a great life.

He turned onto Cicero Avenue and headed into the city. The small, family-owned stores were closed for the night, and the glow of light from apartments and homes lit the sidewalks. The low rumble from the Eden's Expressway just to the left of him could be heard through the closed window, and somewhere in the distance he could hear the siren on a squad car responding to an emergency.

He sighed and thought about his siblings. He knew Mary was happy and safe. Bradley Alden was a good man, and he adored his new wife. It was a little ironic that the youngest of the O'Reilly clan had been the first to get married. Tom and Art had each other, and although he knew they'd miss him, the special bond twins shared would get them through their grief. He thought about calling them, just to speak one last time. But he knew they would figure out something was wrong and they'd worry. None of them had the luxury of allowing themselves to be distracted in

407

their line of work. It was better that they find out the news afterwards.

Pulling into the church parking lot, he sat in his car for a moment longer. The first stars of the evening had appeared in the night sky. The birds had quieted, and moths danced around the glow of the streetlights. The old church stood silhouetted against the glow of the downtown lights. He wanted to put the car in reverse and pull away. He wanted to drive back to his parents' house. He wanted to go back and not answer the phone call that had changed his life earlier that week.

A movement caught his eye at the other end of the parking lot. Two children ran down the street towards their home followed by parents who cautiously warned them to stay close in order to be safe. Safe. Sean bent his head, laid it against the steering wheel for a moment and took a deep breath. Sometimes you just didn't have a choice.

He unlatched his seatbelt, pulled his sword from the back seat, got out of the car and walked over to the door of the church. Before he could access the security panel, the door was opened and Ian stood in the doorway. "I've done a bit of research and I found out about the forfeit," he said, his tone tense. "You have a bit of explaining to do."

"I have to practice with Em," Sean said, trying to move past Ian into the hallway.

"The hell you do," Ian said, grabbing Sean's arm and stopping him. "You had no right to put yourself in this kind of situation."

"No right?" Sean yelled back at him. "No right? Do you think for one moment that this was actually my choice? Do you think I enjoyed saying goodbye to my parents? Do you think that I want to live the rest of my life locked away in some kind of faery prison?"

"What did you say?" Em asked, standing at the end of the hall, her eyes wide with fear.

Sean shook his head. "Dammit. This is not what I wanted."

"What is it you wanted?" Ian asked. "For us to sit back and let them take you down to faery?"

Em rushed down the hall and faced Sean. "They are taking you to faery?" she asked. "You're letting them take you?"

"I don't have a choice," Sean explained, his voice tired. "There has to be a forfeit. Those are the rules."

"There has to be another way," Ian said. "This is totally unacceptable."

Sean nearly laughed. "Yeah, I agree," he said, his voice calm. "And if you can figure out a way to rescue me, I'm all for it. But in the meantime, I need to practice to make sure there's something left of me to rescue."

Ian shook his head in resignation. "Fine. Go. Practice," he said. "I'll figure this out."

Sean took Em's arm and started to guide her back down the hall when he stopped and turned back to Ian. "While you're at it," he said, "why don't you look into how someone escapes from faery?"

Chapter Sixty-two

Sean and Em took the stairs to the gym, and once inside, Em turned on him. "And when where you going to share your information with me?" she asked.

"This evening, before we started practicing," he replied evenly.

She froze and stared at him. "What?"

He sighed and ran his hand through his hair. "I figured that our…" He paused for a moment searching for the right word. "Connection. Our connection would probably be the only link I'd have with the real world. If it could still be maintained between earth and faery," he explained. "So you needed to know what happened. And besides…"

"Besides?" she prompted.

He let a small smile play on his lips. "The rest of the group would be upset and might even feel sorry for me," he said. "But when you found out I knew beforehand, I figured you'd get really mad."

"Aye, I would have been," she admitted with a quick nod.

He reached his hand out and placed it on her arm. "And I didn't want you to think I'd abandoned you."

She tried to shake it off, but he held it there firmly. "I'm not a child to be coddled," she said.

"No, you're not," he agreed firmly. "But you are my partner, and partners share information."

"Then share," she said. "How do you think you're going to defeat the Elk King?"

Closing his eyes for a moment, he took a deep breath, involuntarily tightening the grip he had on her shoulder. When he opened his eyes, they were bleak with uncertainty. "I really have no idea," he said. "All I know is that I don't have a choice."

Em sighed slowly and nodded. "Well, at least you're not trying to fight him off with a dammed stick."

Sean smiled for a moment, but then, as another idea came to him, his smile disappeared. "No matter what, you can't come to the rescue this time," he insisted, his voice low. "If you step in to help me, it will give the rest of the Hunt the sign to become involved. Everyone in the stadium and for God knows how many miles around would be destroyed. I have to do this one on my own."

"I can't stand back and watch you die," she whispered back vehemently.

"My choice, Em," he replied. "You need to let me honor my choice."

She looked like she was going to argue for a moment, but finally shook her head, stepped back and held her sword up. "Then we better practice," she said. "Because you're going to need all the help you can get."

Three hours later, Sean placed his sword down and picked up a towel to wipe the sweat off of his forehead. He leaned back against the gym wall and looked at Em with amazement. "You don't even look winded," he said.

"I just don't show it as much as you," she replied, leaning back against the wall next to him, her breathing slightly quickened. "But you gave me as good a fight as I've had in a long time. You'll do, Sean O'Reilly, you'll do."

He turned and looked over at her. "Thank you," he said. "I finally feel like I might have a chance tomorrow." He stopped and looked down at his watch. "I mean today."

Pushing himself away from the wall, he bent over, picked up his sword and nodded to Em. "I have one more stop, and then I'm going to get some sleep."

"I'll see you in the morning," she replied.

He nodded. "See you then."

Letting himself out of the gym, he closed the door behind him and jogged down the stairs to the first floor. He paused as he passed the lab at the end of the hall and saw Ian bent over his computer. "Get some sleep," he called into the room. "I'm going to need you tomorrow."

Ian turned around and met his eyes. "Getting you out of faery is not going to be an easy task," he said. "But it's not impossible either. So, tomorrow your main goal is to not die."

Sean grinned and nodded. "That's been my main goal for most of my life," he replied.

"Good," Ian said, turning back to his computer. "Keep up the good work."

Chapter Sixty-three

Maria Perez tapped her foot impatiently as she waited for the elevator to take her to Pete's penthouse apartment. She'd worked with Pete long enough to have seen his reaction to almost every kind of situation. But tonight, when he had called, his voice held a totally different tone. Pete O'Bryan sounded frightened.

The door finally slid open, and she stepped into his apartment. "Hey, Pete, I'm here," Maria called.

"Back here, in the office," Pete called back.

She hurried down the hall and waited in the doorway while Pete finished a call. "Yes, General, thank you very much," Pete said. "Of course, I will personally be responsible for its safety. Yes, I will have my associate, Maria Perez, at your office by 0700 tomorrow morning. Once again, thank you, sir."

He jotted a few notes down, hung up the phone and turned his chair to face Maria.

"So, am I taking a trip?" she asked.

He nodded. "Yeah, sorry, I would have asked—"

She shook her head. "No, I'm good," she interrupted. "Besides, I can tell by your expression that this is important."

"Life or death," he replied. "Sean O'Reilly."

"The guy that saved your life?" she asked.

He nodded.

"Where am I going?"

Exhaling slowly, he nodded at her with a slight smile. "Thank you, I really appreciate this," he said, and then he turned his chair back to his table and picked up a notepad. "Okay, my jet is waiting for you at Midway. It should be gassed up and have a flight plan scheduled by now. You'll fly into Dulles, and then I'll have a car waiting for you."

"And where will I be going?" she asked, trying to be patient.

"Oh, yeah, sorry," he said. "You'll be going to the Pentagon to meet with four-star General Abernathy. He'll have a package for you."

"A package?" she asked.

"Yeah, and you're going to need help to get it into the car and then back on the plane," he said. "It will probably weigh over 100 pounds."

She looked down at her petite body and then looked back at Pete. "And you choose me for this assignment because?"

"Because I trust you," he said simply. "And I know that no matter what, you'll get the job done."

"Thank you, Pete," she replied. "Where do you want it delivered once I get back in town?"

"It's got to be at Soldier Field by seven o'clock tomorrow night," he said. "I'm really hoping that you're back here by midday, but even if the pilot has to land on Lake Shore Drive, I need that package at Soldier Field."

She nodded. "You got it," she said. "Anything else?"

"No, but thank you," he said. "I owe you one."

Smiling, she nodded. "And I'll remember you said that."

Chapter Sixty-four

Sean pulled his cruiser up to the curb on Lower Wacker Drive and put the vehicle in park. Hettie was standing behind her filled shopping cart. The gorgeous Mab was nowhere to be seen. When she saw him, she pushed the cart towards the curb to meet him.

He got out of the car, went around to the passenger side and leaned against the hood, his long legs extended in front of him, his arms crossed over his chest. "I just wanted to be sure everything was set for tomorrow," he said emotionlessly.

"Oh, Sean O'Reilly, are you mad at Hettie now?" she asked, her eyes wide with sorrow.

He sighed and shook his head. "No, I'm just tired of games," he said. "So, is everything set up?"

She nodded. "Aye, it's all set up for tomorrow at nine o'clock at the Soldier Field," she answered, her head bowed.

"And once the fight is over, they go away and never come back again, right?" he asked.

"Aye, once you win, your city is safe," she said. "But if you lose…"

"I won't lose," he said, stopping her.

She shot a sideways glance at him, and her eyes twinkled with curiosity. "And what did you do with your last day on this earth? Did you find a hospitable tavern and a welcoming wench or two and celebrate your upcoming battle?"

"No, I didn't," he said. "I had dinner with my parents and, in my own way, said goodbye."

Lifting her head, she placed her claw-like hands on her narrow hips and glared at him. "Do you not know what adventures are ahead of you, Sean?" she asked. "The faery world is all you could wish for: fine food and drink, wonderful landscapes, hunting, dancing, celebrating and womanizing. Sean, it's like going to heaven. You'll have everything you've ever wanted."

"No, Hettie," he said. "It's everything you ever wanted, not me."

"Then tell me, Sean me lad, what do you want?" she argued.

He looked up at the concrete ceiling above him for a moment, and then finally brought his eyes back to the wizened, old woman before him. "I want my family and friends," he said. "I want to laugh with them, argue with them and share their joys and their sorrows. I want to work hard and be proud of the things I've done, and, I suppose, I want my parents to be proud of me. I want to find love." He stopped when it looked like she would interrupt and shook his head. "Not lust, love. I want to find the right person who wants to be with me forever and loves me in spite of my weaknesses."

Hettie shook her head. "I don't understand you," she replied. "You can have wealth, power, immortality, and fulfill all your desires, yet you act as if leaving this place will cause you sorrow."

"Leaving this place will break my heart, Hettie," he admitted. "And I know it will break the hearts of those who love me. I can't find any joy in the treasures you offer. They're just hollow imitations of the real things I'll be leaving behind."

"Then why are you doing this?" she asked, clearly confused. "Why would you risk so much?"

"Because it has to be done and I'm the one who has to do it," he said. "I can't stand back and watch innocents die."

"But you're an innocent," she argued. "Why sacrifice yourself for people you don't even know?"

"Because I'm an officer of the law, Hettie," he said slowly. "And that's what I took an oath to do."

"I'd give anything to go back and see my homeland," Hettie said with wistfulness in her voice. "I'd give anything to dance in the grand ballrooms and feast in the great dining halls. The air is so sparkling it's like breathing champagne. The colors

420

around you are so vivid they hurt your eyes, and the music, ah, Sean, the music is so sweet it would likely break your heart."

"Well, Hettie, I wish you could take my place," he said with a sad smile as he stood up and took her hand. He placed a light kiss on the wrinkled, age-spotted skin and then smiled at her. "Thank you for helping me," he said. "It was an honor to know you."

She stared at him, confusion in her eyes. "You are such an odd man, Sean O'Reilly," she replied.

He nodded. "I've been told that before," he said, walking around to the other side of the car. He started to open the door, then paused and looked at her over the roof of the cruiser. "I have a good friend. His name is Peter O'Boyle, and he's a good man. He'll be coming by and bringing you your tea after tonight."

"I thank you, Sean O'Reilly," she replied. "It seems that I owe you another boon."

"No, you owe me nothing," he said. "Be safe, Hettie."

He climbed into the car and drove away. Hettie watched him until he turned off the street. "Aye, Sean O'Reilly, it seems that I still owe you a boon."

Chapter Sixty-five

"Dammit Pete. Not even the Bears show up three hours before a game," Sean complained as they pulled up in front of Soldier Field the next evening.

"Yeah, well they don't need the kind of last minute practice you do," Pete replied, grabbing his chair and pulling it out of the back of his car. "Now stop complaining and help me break into the stadium."

"Break in?" Sean asked. "I thought you knew a guy."

"I thought *you* knew a guy," Pete replied as he lifted himself from the driver's seat into his chair.

Sean looked over the roof of the car towards the stadium and saw Marcus coming towards them from the shadows of the entranceway. "I do know a guy," Sean said. "And I'm sure he's got the keys to let us in."

Sean pulled his sword out of the back seat, came around the car and walked alongside Pete as they approached Marcus.

"Hey, dude, is this for real?" Marcus asked. "This ain't no sting or nothing like that?"

Sean shook his head. "No, this is for real," he replied. "We've got some pretty bad characters coming to the stadium tonight, and I don't want anyone to get close and get hurt."

"Me and my homies, we got you," he said, and then he paused for a moment. "But, like, if it's down with you, we'd like to watch."

"So, you've never seen a real, live ass-whooping before?" Pete asked.

Marcus smiled. "Whose ass is gonna be whipped?"

"I'm hoping it's the other guy," Sean replied, adjusting the sword's case over his shoulder. "But if it looks like it's me, I want you and your homies to get out of the stadium as quickly as possible."

"Yeah, man, okay," Marcus said. "So do you want me to bring you where the girl is?"

"Girl? What girl?" Sean asked.

"She's a real looker. She's a nice piece of…"

"She's my associate Maria," Pete interrupted. "And she's one of the toughest and smartest lawyers in Chicago. So I wouldn't mess with her if I were you."

Marcus shrugged. "Hey, no problem," he said. "It's just, you know, if she was interested."

Pete nodded. "I'll let you know."

Soldier Field looked like an ancient Greek stadium standing on the shores of Lake Michigan. Giant, Doric columns rose above the entrance, creating an imposing façade that Sean hoped would intimidate the creatures of the Hunt. They weren't in the forests of faery anymore; they were in a stadium where Bears devoured lesser creatures.

Marcus led them to a maintenance entrance at the ground level. After three discreet knocks, the door was opened, and the three of them slipped into the stadium. "The girl, Maria, she told me you wanted to set up at the north end zone," Marcus said.

Pete grinned. "Yeah, that's the Bears' end zone," he said. "We're defending our turf, too. That's perfect."

They walked down the underground passageway, came up through the locker rooms, and finally climbed the ramp that led onto the field.

"This was my ultimate dream," Pete said softly so only Sean could hear him as he rolled up the ramp in his chair. "Quarterback for the Chicago Bears. Running up the ramp, having the fans screaming for me."

"You were good enough," Sean said. "I'd have screamed for you."

424

Pete chuckled. "Thanks," he said. "And tonight I'll be sure to scream for you."

"Yeah, well hopefully I won't be screaming myself," Sean said.

They reached the top of the ramp and saw that Maria was standing at the edge of the field with a large case next to her. "I got you a present," Pete said.

"And I didn't get you anything," Sean replied as they got closer to Maria.

"That's okay," Pete said. "You can owe me."

Before Sean could answer, Maria walked over to them. "Hey, boss, I got your package, and the General said to say hi."

"The General?" Sean asked.

Pete rolled over to the case, flipped open the locks and pushed open the top of the case to expose a mechanical device.

"What the hell is this?" Sean asked, coming over and looking into the case.

"An exoskeleton," Pete said. "I did a little patent work for the company that created this for the military, so I've been following its design for a couple of years. It's created to fit around a soldier's body in order to enhance their strength."

Sean leaned over and pulled the device from the case. It was made of metal that was surprisingly light and was shaped to match the major joints and bends in a human body.

"You need to step back into it," Pete said. "It lies against your back and the back of your arms and legs."

Maria came over and helped Sean strap into the device. Then she turned on the power. "At this point, the battery doesn't last very long," she explained. "You have about thirty minutes of power."

Sean lifted up his arm, and with a responding whir of gears, the mechanical skeleton followed his actions. He stepped forward, and the skeleton mirrored his movements. "Okay, other than making me look really cool, what is this thing going to do for me?" he asked.

"It amplifies your strength about ten times," Pete said. "So when you punch the Elk King, he's really going to feel it."

Sean tried a couple of boxing moves and nodded approvingly. "Yeah, this is nice," he said. "This is real nice."

Chapter Sixty-six

"This is crazy," Em said as she watched Sean walk across the field with the exoskeleton on. Pete and Ian were next to him, shouting encouragement and testing his moves. "He can't use his sword, and that machine will slow him down."

"It's to give him strength, Em," Gillian said, standing next to Em near the edge of the field. "Ian thinks it's a great idea."

"He's a man, and it's a toy," Em muttered with contempt. "Of course he thinks it's great. But he hasn't practiced with Sean, and I have. He'll do better if he trusts his instincts and works with his sword."

Sean punched the four by four piece of wood that Ian and Pete held between them. The wood shattered and broke into two pieces. "This is awesome," Sean said. "It's like breaking a piece of styrofoam, it's so easy."

"Aye, the only disadvantage is that you're not as agile as you would be without it," Ian remarked.

"What? I can run in this thing, faster and longer than I ever had," Sean argued.

"Right, but it takes a while to get up to speed. It's not a device for sprinting or making quick, defensive moves," Ian replied. "You're not going to sneak up on anyone using it or dash quickly out of reach."

Sean nodded as he flexed his arms and the machine responded. "You're right," he admitted. "And I don't know which to be more concerned about, the Elk King's strength or his speed."

"Both," Pete said. "And when you feel the usefulness of the skeleton is done, just press the release button to step out of it. It's a tool, nothing more."

"Right," Sean said, taking a deep breath. "So, how much time do I have?"

Ian pulled his phone out of his pocket. "You've only five minutes," he said. "Shall we get back to the others?"

Sean looked across the large, empty stadium, the butterflies in his stomach feeling like raptors, and then nodded slowly. "Yeah, let's go back."

The wind started to pick up, and Em and Gillian both turned to look up at the swirling cloud that suddenly appeared above the stadium. "It's them," Em whispered, her heart in her throat.

Gillian put her hand on her friend's shoulder. "It'll be fine, Em," she said. "Father Jack, Mrs. Gage and Jamal are all back at the church praying for him.

And with the new device Pete got for him, he'll be fine."

Em turned to her. "You haven't seen them," she whispered harshly. "You haven't seen what he's up against. This is no faery creature from a storybook; this is a demon from your worst nightmare."

Sean, Ian and Pete arrived at the north end of the stadium. "Looks like it's show time," Sean said, turning to Em. "Wish me luck."

She took a deep breath and met his eyes. "You don't need luck," she said. "You have skill. You just have to trust it."

He nodded. "Thank you," he said. "That's what I needed to hear."

She pulled his sword from the padded gun and handed it to him. He grabbed the hilt and felt the surge of power. "I don't get it," Sean said. "I don't get the tinglies when I use my sword during practice."

"Chrysaor understands when you are in a real battle," she explained, "and when its power will be useful."

"Well, tonight I can use all the help I can get," he replied.

Maria came up behind him and swapped the battery pack on the back of the skeleton. "Okay, you're fully charged," she said. "You've got about thirty minutes of super power, so get out there and kick some Elk King ass."

He smiled at her and nodded. "I'm going to do my best," he said.

"My friend, the pyrotechnic guy, is watching from the control both," Pete said. "He laid some charges out on the field and said he'd watch you to see how he can help."

He handed Sean a small receiver. "Clip it over your ear, and you'll be able to hear when he's going to set things off."

"Tell him thanks for me," Sean said, adjusting it over his ear.

"Hey, you can tell him yourself," Pete said. "Once you take this guy down."

Sean smiled thinly and nodded at his friend, his heart sinking. "Yeah, that's right," he said with a nod. "I forgot."

The cloud lowered to the stadium floor, and a cloud of debris swirled around the field. Trash containers toppled, pieces of trash flew through the sky, and the banners attached to the upper decks nearly came loose from their moorings. The thick dust blinded all of the occupants for a moment.

Finally, when it cleared, Sean looked to the center of the field and saw the Elk King mounted on his cadaverous horse, its ribs clearly visible under its thinly stretched, grey hide. Its metallic hooves tore up the grass in the middle of the field as it reared on hind legs and pawed the air. The Elk King raised his new sword and screamed a high, piercing, battle cry that echoed throughout the stadium.

The rest of the Hunt stood at the south end of the field holding back the snarling, wolf-like creatures that foamed at the mouth and yanked against the thick chains that bound them to their masters. Their glowing yellow eyes hungrily assessed the group standing across the field.

Gillian grasped Em's hand tightly. "Oh, Em," she cried. "I had no idea. How can he…"

Em turned quickly to her with a look that cut her off mid-sentence. "He will be fine," she whispered, her eyes glistening with determination. "He will win. He has to win."

Chapter Sixty-seven

"Damn," Pete whispered to Sean. "If you want to back out of this right now, I wouldn't blame you."

Sean shook his head. "Thanks, but I'm good," he replied, taking a deep breath. "It's time to play RoboCop."

He was afraid that he wouldn't be able to move, wouldn't be able to take those few steps towards the creature before him, but his body obeyed, moving with strong, sure steps that were enhanced by the machine.

He studied the creature in front of him. It was tall, well over eight feet tall, Sean guessed as he moved closer. Its body was a jumble of tree limb and vines, intertwined to give the impression and shape of the muscles and sinews of a human body. Tattered burlap covered its loins and formed a cross over its chest. Its arms were as long as the length of its body, with long, thin, razor-sharp claws that took the place of fingers. Sean knew he would need to stay away from those if he wanted to survive.

Then he looked up to the place Hettie said was the only weak spot on the beast. The giant, parched, white elk skull that lay above the shoulders was shrouded with a burlap hood that circled around its shoulders. Inside the skull, there was depth of darkness that was more than just lack of light. It was a vast, bleak oblivion that seemed like a portal, occupying more space than just the boundary of the skull. The only signs of life were the glowing red eyes that followed Sean's every movement.

Sean stopped a few yards away from his opponent. The Elk King stared down at him as its horse pawed impatiently at the ground before it.

"Okay, I'm going to give you one chance before we get this thing started," Sean shouted at the creature. "You and your group can leave now and no one gets hurt."

The Elk King responded by screaming once again and kicking sides of his horse so it lunged forward towards Sean. With its sword raised above its head, the Elk King bore down on Sean and slashed powerfully in his direction. Sean pivoted in the metal skeleton and instinctively raised his arm in defense. The blade from the Elk King's sword ricocheted off the metal of the skeleton, and a spark exploded into the air.

Sean felt the force reverberate through his body. He stumbled back, the suit keeping him on his feet. Heart-pounding, he turned just in time to see the Elk King charging him from the other direction. He pivoted just in time to miss the thrust of the sword, swinging his sword afterwards and missing entirely.

The Elk King galloped his horse around the circumference of the field, spewing turf and dirt in its wake. He circled twice, screaming into the air.

"Oh, we got a little psyching out going on," Sean said. "Yeah, well two can play at that game."

He started with a jog and then increased his speed, easing the suit up to its full potential. He ran after the Elk King and then passed him by, zipping past the rest of the Hunt and finally heading back to the middle of the field and slowly jogging in place. "Yeah, I got this too," he said.

The Elk King turned his horse and galloped back to the forty yard line and faced Sean. Sean bent forward, like the linebacker he had been in college and stared back at his opponent. "You want me," he growled. "You come and get me."

As if they'd heard the threat, both horse and rider responding immediately and charged Sean with astonishing speed. Moving backwards, Sean tried to get out of the way, but the suit was slow in reacting. The horse barreled into him, sending him flying across the fields and smashing into the sideline walls. Sean groaned softly. Most of the final impact had been absorbed by the suit, but the initial impact had been his alone.

He pulled himself up and jogged slowly back to the field. "Fourth down," he gasped, sweat pouring down his forehead. "We're going for it."

Instead of his football stance, Sean planted his feet like he was standing in the batter's box, bringing his arms up as if he were holding a bat instead of a sword. "You just need to know when to change the rules," he said, looking up to see horse hurtling across the field towards him.

He could feel the ground beneath him shake as the Elk King came charging closer. When he could smell the sulfur scent and could feel the hot breath of the gaunt steed, Sean ducked, the sword barely missing him, and then swung in an upward motion, pushing all of his weight and power against the side of the horse.

The impact was strong, and the horse stumbled sideways screaming into the night, nearly unseating the Elk King. With a scream of anger, the Elk King yanked the reins around and whipped the horse forward, charging Sean once again.

"First and ten," Sean yelled, turning around to face them.

This time the attack was full on. He wouldn't have time to pivot to the side; the movement would make him too vulnerable. He stood on the balls of his feet, balancing his weight, and played a game of chicken with the beast. Closer and closer it came, grass and dirt churning up from all around it, its sword held forward like a spear in a jousting tournament. "Come on ugly, just a little closer," he whispered, his heart pumping with adrenalin. "Let's see if you guys can fly."

Sean waited another few endless seconds, his heart thundering in his chest as the wild-eyed horse and creature thundered toward him, and when it was nearly too late, he fell onto his back and lifted his legs, kicking them out against the horse's chest. He felt the contact and the power from the exoskeleton and saw the animal lift off the ground and fly over him.

The momentum of the kick rolled Sean over into a somersault. Once he was back on his feet, he turned in time to see his opponents land and roll, the horse finally coming to rest several feet away from the faery creature, the Elk King's sword embedded in its flesh.

"Okay, now you're on my level," Sean cried, pressing the release button and stepping out of the skeleton. He picked up his sword and ran across the field, ready to impart the finishing blow to his opponent. He could feel Chrysaor humming in his hand and felt renewed power.

The creature moved, shifting its arms to raise its skull. It looked at its horse lying lifeless on the stadium ground, and then it turned and looked at Sean. Red eyes glowed with hate, and the creature let out another blood curdling scream. Whipping out its arm, it grabbed hold of the sword and pulled it out of the horse's side, a green ooze dripping from the blade.

Sean tightened his grip on his sword and moved forward. The Elk King stood slowly, its limbs long and gangly, and countered Sean's move.

"Okay, mano a mano," Sean said, his jaw tight with fury. "It's just you and me."

Moving to a foot beyond the creature's arm length, Sean slowly circled around. The creature countered, turning slowly and watching Sean, its red glowing eyes floating in an endless pit of black. The Elk King lunged forward, but Sean twisted and countered, meeting sword with sword.

Twisting around, the Elk King swung his sword in the other direction, aiming for Sean's chest, but Sean parried and fought back the attack. Then Sean turned, whipped his sword around, and felt purchase as a portion of the creature's arm fell away. But the wound did nothing to stop the Elk King from turning and bringing his sword down from above Sean, towards his head. Sean dove to the side, and the sword hit the dirt only inches from his head, embedding the blade several inches into the turf.

"Okay, that was close," Sean said, wiping the dripping sweat from his brow.

He lifted Chrysaor up and engaged again, meeting the creature's pounding attack over and over again, each time blocking and countering as they moved over the field.

"Get him to the fifty yard line," said a voice in Sean's ear.

"Sure, piece of cake," Sean replied. He looked over and saw that he was halfway between the thirty and forty yard line. "Sure, only fifteen yards," he breathed heavily. "I can do that."

The Elk King strode towards Sean, it's long, sinewy arms extended fully, each fingernail a razor-sharp machete. Sean slowly back up to the thirty yard line and the creature followed.

"Okay, time for a quarterback sneak," he said to himself.

He stepped forward, with his sword in both hands, as if he were going to attack. The creature responded, bringing its arms together to parry his assault. Then, instead of attacking, Sean ran to the left and past the creature. It screamed, turned and ran after Sean.

"Forty-two, forty-four, forty-six," Sean wheezed as he ran. "Forty-eight. Fifty!"

He turned and brought his sword up, deflecting the creature's attack.

"Charge igniting in five, four, three, two, one," said the voice in Sean's ear.

Suddenly, to the right of the creature a flare exploded from the ground, and a volley of lights filled the night sky. The Elk King turned towards the explosion. Sean ran forward, his sword raised for battle.

The Elk King turned back, but it was too late. Sean twisted and dug his sword once again into his enemy's arm. He heard the sound of wood splintering, but this time he felt his sword catch. He yanked it back, but it was stuck fast. The Elk King looked down at him. His eyes seemed to be smiling as Sean struggled to regain his weapon.

Breathing heavily, Sean pulled again and it came loose, but the Elk King had taken that time to recover. The Elk King's sword whipped around. Sean ducked, but the edge of the sword caught his left arm. Sean screamed as the burning blade pierced his arm, and he heard the crack of his bone.

The smell of blood seemed to excite the Elk King. Its eyes glowed stronger, and its high pitched scream sounded more like a victory cry. Sean stumbled back out of its reach, but he knew the blow to his arm could be his death knell.

"Disney in five, four, three, two, one," the voice in his ear said.

"Disney?" Sean wondered, in a pain-filled mist.

Suddenly, the ground around the Elk King came to life with flares and fireworks exploding all around him. The stadium was filled with the sounds of a Fourth of July exhibition coming from all directions. The Elk King screamed and turned to face each threat, jumping one way and then the other, whipping his sword at the invisible enemy.

Sean realized that this was his only chance. He lifted his sword with his good arm and held it over his head. Then, with a scream of determination, he charged across the field. The Elk King turned towards him, his sword raised in defense when another charge exploded, just to his left. The Elk King glanced towards it for the smallest second, but it was enough; Sean leapt forward and plunged his sword into the blackness of the Elk King's Skull.

For a moment, there was complete, shocked silence, and then the Elk King screamed as he collapsed into a heap of broken limbs and shattered bones. Stumbling backwards, Sean dropped his sword and grabbed his upper arm, trying to stem the flow of blood from his wound. He glanced across the field and watched as the rest of the Hunt came to life and moved down the field towards him.

"I won," he whispered to himself as he struggled for consciousness. He looked to the north side of the stadium, rewarding himself with one final glance of his friends as he fell to his knees. "I won."

Suddenly, the earth below him shattered as another explosion ripped through the stadium. Sean felt his body being lifted and thrown. And then there was darkness.

Chapter Sixty-eight

"He won!" Gillian screamed, throwing herself into Ian's arms. "He won."

"Aye, he did," Ian said, his eyes shining with unshed tears as he watched his friend on the field.

"What?" Gillian asked, looking from Ian back to Sean. "What?"

"He has to go with them," Ian said. "Even if he wins, he has to go back with them."

"What?" Pete roared, rolling his chair out towards the middle of the field. "There is no way they're taking him while I've got a breath left in my body."

"I'll join you," Em called, her sword in her hands.

The explosion nearly knocked Em off her feet, and Pete's chair rolled back several feet. Once the smoke cleared, Sean was no longer where he had been standing.

"Where is he?" Em called out, placing her hand over her eyes to stare out into the dusty field. "Where is he?"

They all moved forward, scanning the field, searching for Sean.

The Hunt, on the other end of the field, had also moved forward, their snarling dogs leading the way.

"We have to find him before they do," Pete said, accelerating to a speed that made Em jog to keep up.

"There he is," Gillian shouted and pointed across the field at about the thirty yard mark on the other side.

"Sean," Pete called. "Sean, just stay put, we're coming for you."

Sean turned and looked at his friends for a moment, but then, with a shake of his head, jogged in the other direction towards the Hunt.

"No," Em screamed, breaking into a run. "No!"

But before she could even reach the fifty-yard line, the Hunt had swirled around him, and the cloud they created lifted from the ground.

"No!" Em cried, tears running down her cheeks as she still continued sprinting across the field towards the cloud. "No, give him back."

Like a funnel cloud, the Hunt spun around the stadium picking up the remains of the Elk King and his horse, and lifted off into the sky, finally disappearing from view.

Em dropped to her knees and buried her face in her hands, her body wracked with sobs. A moment later, she heard Pete's chair roll up next to her. He placed his hand on her shoulder and laid his head on top of hers. Eventually Ian, Gillian and Maria joined them, wordlessly looking up into the night sky.

"He knew he had to do it," Ian finally said. "That was the only way."

"The hell it was," Pete said, his voice hoarse with unshed tears. "There's always another way."

Em took a deep, shuddering breath and was about to speak when she froze and looked at Pete. "Something's wrong."

Chapter Sixty-nine

All Sean knew was that his arm hurt like hell. He sat up, looked around and could only see darkness. *What the hell happened to vibrant colors and air that smelled like champagne? This place smells like a...*

He paused, a thrill of hope coursing through his body. *A locker room. This place smells like an amazing locker room.*

He tried to stand up, grabbing onto the wooden bench next to him and pulling himself up. His head hurt like hell, too. Standing, he looked around and saw a dim light before him. Using the rest of his strength, he stumbled forward slowly, trying to get to the light.

This might be a trick, he thought. *I might be entering some faery torture chamber.*

He paused for a moment, shook his head and then moaned. *Damn it, that was dumb. I don't care if it's a torture chamber. I just don't want to sit in the dark anymore.*

He felt a waft of fresh air against his face, and suddenly the terrain seemed to go uphill. *Uphill can't be a bad thing if you've been taken underground*, he reasoned. *Maybe I'm escaping.*

Holding on to the wall next to him, he slowly pulled himself up the hill, his head throbbing and his vision slightly blurred. When he reached the top of the hill, he realized he was above ground. He was breathing fresh air.

He looked around and saw shadows moving in the distance. He tried to focus and realized that a group of people were coming towards him. Were they fae? Were they coming to take him back underground? He looked around for his sword, but he couldn't remember where he'd left it.

He tried to run, but he didn't have enough energy to even stumble forward anymore. He started to sink to the ground when he heard the voice.

"Look it's him! It's Sean!"

Em? he wondered.

"Em?" he called out.

"Sean!" she screamed, running towards him. "Sean."

She wrapped her arms around him, and he just held on, feeling her warmth and her strength. Then he realized what her presence meant and pushed her back. "I told you not to follow me," he rasped. "I told you not to come."

"Guess again, Sean, my friend," Pete said. "Somehow you got lost on your way to faery."

446

"What?" he asked. "What?"

"You're still here," Em said, her voice thick with tears. "At Soldier Field."

"How the hell did that happen?" Sean asked, and then, without waiting for an answer, he promptly passed out.

Chapter Seventy

A light was glaring down on him when Sean woke up. He tried to move, but strong hands held him down. "Just a few more minutes, Sean me boyo," a familiar voice said. "We aren't quite done with you."

"Ian," Sean croaked.

"Aye, it's me," he said.

"Where am I?"

"We're still at Soldier Field in the infirmary," Ian explained. "Pete has a doctor friend who does house calls, and he's seeing to your arm."

"My arm?" Sean asked groggily.

"Aye, the one the Elk King tried to remove from your person."

"The Elk King!" Sean struggled to sit up as several pairs of hands held him down. "I've got to go. I've got to see Hettie. I didn't go with them. They might come back."

"We'll go," Em said. "I promise we'll find her. But just give the doctor enough time to stitch you up."

Sean nodded and relaxed back against the table. "How bad am I Doc?" he asked.

The older man smiled down at Sean and shook his head. "It's Ben. Dr. Ben Cronin. Well, you have a mid-shaft fractured humerus," he explained. "But it feels like the bone wasn't broken all the way through, so you don't have to worry about any damage to your radial or median nerve." He took a moment to tie a knot in the final stitch and then cut off the thread before he continued. "I'm just putting a splint on it tonight because I want to be able to make sure the cut doesn't become infected, and I want to wait until the swelling goes down before we put it in a cast. But I want you in my office for an official x-ray in the next day or so."

"Thanks, Ben," Sean said. "I'll be sure to get there."

Ben secured a splint on Sean's upper arm with tape and gauze and reached into his medical bag. "Here's some pain medication," he said. "Take two of these before you go to bed, and don't try driving while you're medicating."

Sean nodded. "I won't," he said.

"He won't," Pete inserted. "I'm going to play chauffer until we're sure he doesn't have any other repercussions from tonight's adventure."

Sean slid off the table and rested against it for a moment while his head cleared.

"You okay?" Ian asked.

"Yeah, just a little light-headed," he replied.

"That's to be expected," Ben inserted. "You lost quite a bit of blood. You should be drinking a lot of fluids and resting. And no alcohol."

"Well, I guess the celebration is going to have to wait until after you've recovered," Pete replied.

"Everything has to wait until I've seen Hettie," Sean said. "Can I go now?"

Ben shook his head. "Yes, you're free to go."

"Thanks, Ben," Pete said. "I owe you."

Ben shook his head. "Yeah, well count it against all the ones I owe you," he said.

Ian helped Sean out the door where Marcus and several of his gang members were waiting. Marcus's eyes widened when he saw Sean walking out of the infirmary.

"Dude, I can't believe you are still breathing! Dude, that thing was the ugliest mother I've ever seen in my life," Marcus exclaimed. "Is that what killed all those other gangs?"

Sean nodded. "Yeah, that was it," he said. "That's what Jamal saw."

"Dude, that crazy," Marcus said. "And it ain't coming back, right?"

"That's what I'm going to find out right now," Sean said.

Marcus nodded. "Well, if it comes back, it better watch out, cause you'll kick its ass again," he said. "It better not show up with my bro O'Reilly here."

Sean smiled. "Thanks, Marcus. I appreciate your confidence."

"Hey, no problem," Marcus replied. "And if you ever need any back up, you call me. We got your back from now until eternity, man."

"Thanks again," Sean said. "I'd trust you with my back, Marcus."

Marcus got quiet for a moment. "Thanks, man," he finally said. "Thanks a lot."

A few minutes later, a convoy of several cars made its way to Lower Wacker Drive because no member of the group wanted to take their eyes off Sean. Pete's car pulled up first, and Sean pulled himself out of the passenger's side and looked around. Hettie was nowhere to be seen. He stumbled forward, and suddenly Em was at his side, her arm around his waist.

"Remember," she said, trying for a light tone. "I'm the bat guy."

Rolling his eyes, Sean smiled at her. "That's Batman, sweetheart," he replied. "And sometime soon we've got to sit down and watch those movies so you'll get the reference."

"I'd like that," she replied. "Now what do you want to do?"

"I want to walk around the corner, just to see if Hettie's there," he said.

She helped him walk away from the curb and downhill towards an abandoned, concrete, loading dock that stuck out about ten feet. "Around here," Sean said, guiding Em around the side. "When the weather is bad, she stays here for shelter."

They turned the corner, and Sean saw Hettie's beloved shopping cart parked in the corner. He slipped from Em's embrace and, using the dock for support, walked the rest of the way down to the cart. Examining it closely, Sean could tell the cart looked the same. No one had stolen any of Hettie's so-called treasures from it, and he felt a faint flicker of relief. The only thing out of place was a linen envelope resting on the top of the pile. He picked it up and shook his head when he saw it was addressed to him. Breaking the seal, he pulled out the notecard, which had been written in delicate handwriting.

My dear Sean,

I don't know if you owe me a boon or if, once again, I'm in your debt. I thought about what you said last night and realized faery was not the place for a noble soul like yours. You would soon grow bored of our foolishness. So, I decided to play a wee trick on the Hunt. If you are reading this, I must assume my little trick worked and I was whisked away to faery and you were sent to someplace safe near the Soldier Field. You have no need to worry about your city. The Hunt will not return. The forfeit was paid.

I will miss your visits and our friendship. I will always treasure what you taught me about the human race. I cannot promise that I will not darken your doorstep again. I might miss your nightly visits and your tea and scones.

Be well, Sean O'Reilly.

Mab

Chapter Seventy-one

"Hey, Mom," Sean said into his cell phone as Pete drove them to the church. "I just wanted to let you know the case went better than expected."

"Oh, well, that's wonderful," she replied, and he could hear the unshed tears in her voice. "I'm so happy to hear it."

"Yeah, me too," Sean said. "Ma, I've got a couple of things to tie up still, and I was wondering if Tiny could stay for another day or two."

"Ah, well, I suppose I'll have to go to the market in the morning for more chicken livers," she teased, "as your cat has eaten us out of house and home. But for you, darling, of course he can."

"Thanks, Ma," he said. "Give Tiny a hug from me."

"Aye, I will," she said. "God bless you, Sean."

"He already did, Ma," he replied. "He already did."

Pete pulled into the church parking lot as Sean hung up with his mom. "Good, you're off before we have to go in," Pete said.

Sean turned to look at his friend. "Yes?"

"Don't you 'yes' me, Sean," Pete said, his voice laced with anger. "Why didn't you tell me about the forfeit?"

"Because I knew you'd do some dumb-ass thing like roll your wheelchair out to the middle of the field and try to take on the entire Hunt for me," he said, his voice mild.

"Well, of course I would," he said. "That's what friends do."

"But, I needed you to be here," Sean explained. "I needed you to help the Order, take care of my parents and figure out how to get me the hell out of faery. I needed you to do what you do best."

"You could have told me," Pete grumbled.

Sean sighed. "Okay, the next time I have to battle a supernatural creature on the fifty yard line at Soldier Field with a sword, I'll be sure to let you know about any forfeit I may or may not be required to make."

"You are a smart ass," Pete complained.

Sean shrugged. "Yeah, but you love me anyway."

Pete turned back to his friend and met his eyes. "Yeah, I do," he said seriously. "You are the only brother I've ever had. And don't you forget that."

Nodding Sean smiled. "I won't."

They got out of the car, and Sean was immediately embraced and nearly knocked down by an excited Jamal. "You did it!" he cried. "You did it. You thrashed them."

"Jamal, you step away from Sean," Mrs. Gage called. "Can't you see that man can barely stand on his own two feet?"

Sean slipped his arm around Jamal's shoulders and smiled down at him. "Yeah, I thrashed him," he said. "And we won't have to worry about them anymore."

Jamal wrapped his arm around Sean's waist and helped him into the church. When they walked inside, Sean took a sniff in the air and smiled. "It smells like someone ordered food," he said hopefully.

"I took the liberty of getting some pizzas delivered," Father Jack said. "I don't know if it counts for a victory feast, but I thought you might be hungry."

"Famished," Sean replied. "And pizza sounds great right now."

In a few minutes, they were all gathered in Father Jack's apartment eating pizza and sharing stories about the night's events. Finally, Jamal leaned back in his chair and smiled. "And I get to go back to school," he said.

Mrs. Gage's smile froze on her face and her slice of pizza slipped from her hands onto her plate. Her eyes glassed over, and she slowly turned to Sean. "He's not safe," she said, although it wasn't her voice coming from her mouth, but a deeper and more ominous one. "There are those who are still looking for the boy, who would use him to harm the Order. You must keep him safe."

The room went silent as everyone stared at Mrs. Gage in astonishment. After a moment, she blinked and shook her head, as if waking from a dream, and then picked up her pizza. "How funny," she remarked, smiling at everyone in the room. "I don't remember dropping my pizza. This surely is a night for surprises."

Sean nodded slowly. "Yes it is," he said. "And it looks like there are more to come."

Chapter Seventy-two

Sean stood at the front window of his apartment building gazing out across the Chicago skyline and sighed with satisfaction. His city was safe for another night. With a towel slung low around his waist and the dripping garbage bags positioned about his body, he thought about going into his bedroom to dress, but he just couldn't seem to tear himself away from the view.

The hot shower he'd just taken had felt amazing, but the maneuvering to keep water away from his cast and other bandages had been more than a little tricky. He'd taped a large, lawn-leaf garbage bag around his arm to keep the cast and stitches dry, then he'd tied a few smaller grocery store plastic bags around various other parts of his body that had been stitched or stapled by the good doctor. Finally, with the water pouring out of the shower head, he'd luxuriated with a bar of manly smelling soap that his mother had purchased for him and the hottest water he could stand and washed the dirt and grass stains from Soldier Field off his body.

On the way from the bathroom to his bedroom, the window had caught his eye. Knowing he was safe from Peeping Toms because he was on the third floor, he walked over to gaze upon the city he loved. The city he almost had to leave. He moved closer to the window, saw his reflection and chuckled. He looked like a superhero from planet Recycle.

"Hi," he said to his reflection, lowering his voice an octave for drama. "I'm bagman."

"And here I thought you'd been referring to a bat?"

Sean spun around; gripping the towel tightly in both hands to be sure it didn't slip and faced Em. "Don't you ever knock?"

"I thought you might be sleeping after the night you had and I didn't want to wake you," she replied, the corner of her mouth turned up in a smile. "I had no idea that you were playing dress up."

"I'm not playing dress-up," he replied indignantly. "I'm protecting my wounds."

She cocked her head slightly. "The doctor gave you those?" she asked.

"No, he didn't. He just told me not to get my stitches wet and this was the only thing I could think of."

She nodded slowly. "Aye, oh well, when you put it that way it makes much more sense," she said, biting her lip to stifle her laughter.

"You're laughing at me," he accused.

"Oh, no," she said, lifting her hands in surrender. "I promise, I'm doing my very best not to laugh at you."

"I'm going to change," he huffed, moving past her.

"Don't do it on my account," she said, watching him as he strode down the hall.

The door slammed behind him and a wide smile appeared on her face. "Aye, he's a fine strapping lad," she whispered.

A few minutes later he was back, dressed in worn blue jeans and a dark t-shirt that showed wet spots from where he'd pulled it over his still damp body. He'd combed his wet hair back off his face with his fingers and the stubbled on his face was dark and pronounced. In Em's estimation he looked far more tempting than any of the faery she'd ever encountered.

"Okay," he huffed impatiently, marching barefoot back into the room. "What did you need?"

She stuck her hand into her purse and pulled out a small prescription bottle. "You left these in Father Jack's kitchen," she said, handing him the pain pills. "I thought you might be needing them tonight and I didn't want you to go without."

Sighing, he shook his head. "I'm sorry, Em," he said. "I was already beginning to feel the pain return. Thank you for bringing them."

She stepped up and placed them in his hand. He opened the bottle, poured three of them into his hand, popped them into his mouth and picked up a bottle of water on the kitchen counter to wash them down. "Thank you again," he said after he swallowed. "Sorry for being an ass."

"Ah, well, you are allowed to be an ass on the evening you vanquished the Elk King and you are almost..." she paused and her voice broke. Inhaling quickly, she tried to turn away, but Sean caught her shoulders and kept her in place.

"Em?" he asked softly. "Are you okay?"

She sniffled and wiped her face impatiently. "No, I'm not okay, you big, blundering dolt," she said angrily.

"I already said I was sorry," he said, confused.

"Said you were sorry?" she exclaimed. "Said you were sorry!?!"

She marched up to him, wrapped her arms around his neck and pulled his head down for a passionate kiss. The power of the kiss punched him with nearly as much force as the Elk King's sword and he almost staggered backwards, but instead wrapped his arms around her and kissed her back. She moaned softly and he deepened the kiss, exploring her mouth, the sweetness that tasted of wild heather and honey.

"Em," he whispered, sliding his mouth from her lips and tasting the delicate skin along her jawline.

"Aye," she breathed back, her eyes closed, her head thrown back to allow his more access.

"I like this more than fencing with you," he said, nibbling on the edge of her earlobe.

She shivered delicately and laughed softly. "I do too," she agreed. "But it's much more dangerous, Sean O'Reilly."

"Em," he said, but this time his voice held more confusion than passion.

She leaned back and looked at him. His eyes were wide and out of focus. "Sean?" she asked.

"Em," he repeated, his voice slightly slurred. "I think I might…"

She caught him as he passed out and gently dragged him back down the hall to his bedroom. Sliding up close to the bed, she angled him over and finally laid him across the bed, his legs dangling off the side. "I'm sorry," she said to the sleeping man. "I'm afraid to pull you for fear I'll pop your stitches."

She pulled the extra blanket from the bottom of the bed and covered him with it, then turned and switched off the bedside lamp. Leaning over, she placed a kiss on his forehead. "Good night, Sean," she whispered.

He smiled in his sleep and her heart fluttered.

"Good night, Ma," he replied, and then he rolled over on his side and began to snore.

Chuckling, she shook her head and smiled down at him. "You're nothing but a big, blundering dolt," she said tenderly. "Sweet dreams, Sean O'Reilly."

Chapter Seventy-three

The well-dressed man burst into the private interrogation room at the Chicago Police Department's Twelfth District office. "What the hell did you do?" he screamed at the detective sitting on the other side of the table.

"What do you mean?" Adrian Williams asked, leaning back in his chair.

"You know good and well what I mean," the man continued. "The Hunt was supposed to show up at Grant Park this afternoon, and nothing happened."

Adrian shook his head. "I'm sure I don't know what you're talking about," he replied.

The man slapped his hands on the other side of the table and stared down at Adrian. "Don't you play games with me, Detective," he said. "I own you. I tell you what to do. And I tell you how to do it. You were under strict orders from me to order the Hunt to Grant Park in time for the Children's Concert, and you screwed it up."

"Is that enough?" Adrian asked.

"Enough?" the man bellowed. "What the hell do you mean is that enough?"

Adrian stood up, placed his hands on his side of the table and leaned towards the man, the detective's large frame looming over the irate man. "I wasn't talking to you," he said.

"What?"

The door opened behind the man, and Sean, Father Jack and Aengus stepped inside the room. "It was enough for me," Sean said. "How about you two?"

Aengus stepped forward and grabbed the man by his collar, lifting him off the floor and shoving him into the wall. "Lugh. You are a traitor."

The faerie did not squirm but met Aengus's gaze with an equally vitriolic one of his own. "Who is the traitor here?" he spat. "The one who sits back in luxury while his brethren are trapped in the underworld or the one who fights for their freedom?"

"And how does killing innocents aid your cause in any way?" Aengus countered.

"There are no innocents in this war," he said. "If they are not the Unseelie, then they are our enemy."

"Children?" Sean asked. "Children are your enemy?"

"They will grow up," Lugh replied. "They will grow up and follow the beliefs of their parents.

465

The only way we will ever be truly free is if they are destroyed and we have rule over the entire world."

Aengus tightened his grip, and Lugh's face turned red as he fought for breath.

"Aengus, he will be of little use to us dead," Father Jack said softly. "He is not the head of this organization. He is only a hot-headed messenger boy and eminently expendable."

"I am not a messenger boy," Lugh growled.

"Then why were you not told that the Hunt was defeated last night and sent down to faery?" Father Jack asked, his eyebrow lifted in curiosity. "Surely, those above you would know the happenings in faery. Surely, if they valued you, they would not have allowed you to walk into this set-up. Obviously, they were willing to sacrifice you."

He shook his head. "No," he argued. "No, they would not do that."

Jack pulled a pair of old handcuffs out of his pocket and grabbed Lugh's arm, clicking the cuffs around his wrist. Lugh screamed in pain.

"Sorry, these old handcuffs are made of cast iron," Jack explained. "They are the only ones that seem to work when I'm dealing with the fae."

Aengus released his hold on Lugh's collar, and the faerie fell to the ground. Jack grabbed his other arm, pulled it behind him and slipped the other handcuff on. "Now, Aengus, I believe we would both like the opportunity to question Lugh," he said. "And I will be happy to remove these handcuffs for you, once he's answered my questions."

"Fine," Aengus replied, looking down at Lugh in disgust. "But once we are done questioning him, I will see to his…" He paused and smiled serenely at Jack. "Disposal."

"That's according to the rules of the treaty," Father Jack agreed. "And I won't argue that."

"Wait," Adrian said. "I don't think we can let you do that."

He turned to Sean. "Can we let them take our prisoner like that?"

Sean leaned back against the wall, his arms folded over his chest, and met Adrian's eyes. "What would you charge him with?" he asked.

Adrian opened his mouth several times and finally shook his head. "Yeah, you're right," he agreed. "I got nothing."

"I do have a request," Sean said, turning to Aengus.

Aengus nodded.

"Your buddy, Lugh here, messed up my friend's mind," Sean said. "I want you to take care of it so he's no longer getting updates from the bad guys."

Aengus strolled across the room and placed his hand on Adrian's head. He started to close his eyes, but then they popped open in surprise. "What the…"

"Oh, sorry," Adrian said then pulled his baseball cap off his head and removed the small stainless steel bowl beneath it. "Insurance."

"Indeed," Aengus remarked, his high eyebrows reaching even higher.

Once again, he placed his hands on Adrian's head, closed his eyes and whispered to himself. After a few moments, he stepped away.

"How do you feel?" Sean asked Adrian.

Adrian stood silent for a moment and then nodded his head. "Yeah, I feel better," he said. "There's no more ringing in the back of my head."

"You are welcome," Aengus said sardonically.

"Such a sweet guy," Sean said. "And if you took better care of your own subjects, we wouldn't have been in this mess, would we?"

Aengus glared at Sean. "You should learn some respect."

"My parents taught me to show respect," he said. "But first you have to earn it. So far, I haven't seen anything but a spoiled, rich brat with a bad sense of fashion. Grow up and start taking some responsibility for your people, and then I'll show you some respect."

Grabbing Lugh by the back of the collar, Aengus slammed open the door, stormed out of the room and down the hall.

Father Jack inhaled deeply and walked slowly to the door.

"Father," Sean said, stopping him in the doorway.

Jack turned back to Sean. "Yes?"

"I'm sorry," Sean said. "That was probably out of line."

Jack met Sean's eyes and smiled. "No, actually, it was perfect," he said. "And I wish I had had the courage to do that a long time ago." He chuckled softly and started walking out the door. Then he stopped and stuck his head back inside. "I'm glad you're on the team, Sean. You're going to make things a lot more interesting."

The End

About the author: Terri Reid lives near Freeport, the home of the Mary O'Reilly Mystery Series, and loves a good ghost story. She lives in a hundred year-old farmhouse complete with its own ghost. She loves hearing from her readers at author@terrireid.com

Other Books by Terri Reid:

Mary O'Reilly Paranormal Mystery Series:

Loose Ends (Book One)

Good Tidings (Book Two)

Never Forgotten (Book Three)

Final Call (Book Four)

Darkness Exposed (Book Five)

Natural Reaction (Book Six)

Secret Hollows (Book Seven)

Broken Promises (Book Eight)

Twisted Paths (Book Nine)

Veiled Passages (Book Ten)

Bumpy Roads (Book Eleven)

Treasured Legacies (Book Twelve)

Buried Innocence (Book Thirteen)

Stolen Dreams (Book Fourteen)

Mary O'Reilly Short Stories

Irish Mists – Sean's Story

The Three Wise Guides

Tales Around the Jack O'Lantern

PRCD Case Files:

The Ghosts Of New Orleans - A Paranormal Research and Containment Division Case File

Eochaidh:

Legend of the Horseman (Book One)

Romance:

Bearly in Love

Made in the USA
San Bernardino, CA
11 October 2015